ALREADY FAMOUS

Famous Series Book 4

By Heather C. Leigh

No one will hit you harder than life itself. It doesn't matter how you hit back. It's about how much you can take, and keep fighting, how much you can suffer and keep moving forward. That's how you win.

-Anderson Silva

When life knocks you down, calmly get back up, smile, and say, "You hit like a bitch".

-Miguel Torres

In the course of battle you could find a hundred different reasons to give up, but you got to find that one reason to stay in there, to stay in the fire.

-Chael Sonnen

Sometimes you need to be alone, in order to find out who you really are and what you really want out of life.

-Unknown

CHAPTER 1

The fist comes at my head so fast, I barely have time to lean back and dodge it. The wind that brushes by registers for a split second, and then I move in with a hook that catches my opponent's chin and his head snaps back violently.

Shit. He looks pissed.

He lands a lightening quick roundhouse kick to my ribs. It fucking hurts like hell, but I'm able to grab his foot and shove, knocking him off balance, sending him crashing to the ground.

My adversary pops back up off of the mat before I can get on top of him and lock him down.

I throw an uppercut, catching him again on the chin. He shakes his head and glares at me, a twisted smile on his face. I'm about to kick in his smug expression when I hear someone call out his name.

"Damien!"

We both stop fighting and turn to look across the rundown gym. Bruce, my driver, is near the entrance with a woman. No, not just a woman. That would mean she's average, one of thousands just like her. She's not. She might possibly be the most attractive woman I've ever seen and I've seen a lot.

Damien, my sparring partner and trainer, doesn't hesitate. He throws off his pads and gloves, exits the cage and crosses the room. I follow after him, not sure what I'm thinking as I head over to where

Bruce is standing. Maybe I'm not thinking, because being recognized in my gym would suck. Groupies and fans don't know that I train here and I like it that way. For all I know this girl will Tweet my location the second she leaves. That's one of the definite downsides of being a very recognizable actor.

Even though I know I should keep my distance, I find myself putting one bare foot in front of the other, getting closer to the stunning red-head with each step.

"Can you grab the first aid kit? She fell on some ice," Bruce says to Damien.

My gaze, which had been fixed on her perfect face and brilliant blue eyes, flicks down to see her cradling her arm. Her sleeve is ripped up and blood is steadily dripping onto the floor.

Shit, she's really hurt. How did I not notice that?

I'm shocked at how upset I get when I see the angry gash on her pale skin. She looks so fragile, breakable, like she might crumple to the ground from the slightest injury. I look back up at her face and see that she's flushed a deep red.

"Sorry to interrupt your workout," the gorgeous girl stammers.

Great, she knows me. The nervousness in her voice is as obvious as if she were carrying an Andrew Forrester fan club sign. Beautiful or not, I don't want to lose my sanctuary here. I need this place to let out my frustrations, the ones that come when I feel out of control. This is the only place I can go that no one has managed to find out about. The other guys that train here are all up and coming

UFC fighters. They have no interest in treating me differently or discussing my presence here.

I stand in front of her with my guard up, just waiting for her to start freaking out when she recognizes me. Then, something odd happens. Instead of gushing all over me like I expect her to, the girl deliberately avoids eye contact with me and stares down at a random spot on the ground. She keeps shifting uncomfortably, allowing another huge drop of blood to fall from her arm.

What a douche I am, letting her bleed everywhere while I worry about my ego and my petty selfishness. I know I can be a cold bastard most of the time, but I can't let an injured woman stand there helplessly.

"Here." I hand her my towel. "So you won't drip everywhere."

Wow Forrester, real smooth.

Her small hand brushes against mine as she takes the towel. *Holy shit!* It's as if a spark of electricity passes between us, jolting me right in the dick.

Nice asshole, I scold myself. She's injured and I'm thinking about sex.

"Thanks," she says as she wraps the towel around her arm. "I'm Sydney."

She shifts awkwardly again, as if she wants nothing more than to run out of here and never look back. Now she's clearly waiting for me to introduce myself. Does she really not know me? Since she's looking at me expectantly, waiting for me to tell her my name, I'm thinking she might not. That's not possible, is it?

"I'm Drew," I say hesitantly. "So, you fell?"

I want to punch myself right in the head for stating the obvious. This girl has me confused. I'm not used to having normal conversations with a female. Usually, there's just a lot of screaming, flattery, or attempts to get in my pants. Not Sydney, she doesn't act like she wants to fuck me, she acts like she wants to get the fuck *away* from me.

Interesting.

"Uhhh, yeah. It's no big deal, really. Nice to meet you, Drew."

Nice to meet me? I shoot a puzzled look at Bruce and he gives me a baffled one in return. I've been in two of the three highest grossing movies of the last four years. She has to know who I am. I decide to push the issue, testing to see if she's just pretending to not recognize me.

"Have we met before?" I ask.

Now Sydney is the one who looks bewildered. I can tell that she's racking her brain to see if she knows me from somewhere. Then, instead of a look of recognition or admiration crossing that stunning face, a look of horror appears.

"No, I don't think so," she says quickly.

I am so freaking confused right now. This girl not only doesn't know me, but she's so ill at ease in my presence that she wants to get as far away from me as she can. All I can do to make her feel more comfortable is stand there like an idiot with my mouth gaping open.

Damien brings the first aid kit over. "Got it."

He moves to open it and I snatch it from him. If anyone's going to spend more time with the stunning girl who has never heard of Andrew Forrester, it's going to be me.

"I'll do it," I snap, watching Sydney's eyes widen in surprise. "Bruce, thanks for bringing her in, I'll be out in a few minutes." I don't need Bruce hovering over me as I take care of Sydney. He nods and leaves the gym.

"You sure?" Damien asks, trying to give me a *'what the fuck is up with you?'* look without Sydney noticing. Pissed that he won't just leave, I stare back. I'll be damned if he's going to touch her instead of me. "Okay man, I'll see you later?"

"Yeah, I'll be here," I say distractedly. My gaze is already back on Sydney's deep blue eyes.

Damien takes off and I'm finally alone with her.

"Here, sit down," I point to a bench and she sits immediately. *Hmmm, compliant. Very sexy.*

I have to force myself to focus, she's in pain and I'm starting to get a fucking hard on like a horny thirteen year-old kid. I kneel down next to her and open up the first aid kit.

"Let's see what you did." I look to her for permission to touch her arm. She says nothing, so I take her delicate wrist and wrap my hand around it.

I inhale sharply at the contact with her skin as I feel the same pulse of energy flow between us. Twice that's happened now. I suddenly loathe the sports wrap that's wound around my hands, acting as a barrier from keeping more of our skin from touching. Slowly, I remove the towel and tear my eyes from hers to look down at her arm.

Thank god. I feel a rush of relief when I see that it's not as bad as I thought it would be with all that blood. What the hell is my problem? Why do I give two shits about her arm?

"It isn't that bad. It's big, but not deep, so it shouldn't leave a scar or anything." I look back up at Sydney and smile, "Wouldn't want to ruin that perfect skin."

What the fuck is wrong with me? Jesus, she's going to think I'm a fucking lunatic.

Or maybe not. Sydney is staring back at me, her gaze flicking back and forth between my mouth and my eyes. Her pupils dilate slightly when our eyes meet. Is it possible that she felt the same thing I did when we touched? The magnetic pull, the undeniable chemistry that exists?

Okay, totally not helping with the hard on.

"Take off that jacket while I get what I need," I bark at her.

Too late, I realize my tone is abrupt because I'm all worked up and frustrated and I don't want her to notice. She removes her jacket quickly, without hesitation.

Controlling my desire to throw her down and fuck her right here takes every bit of restraint that I can summon. Gorgeous, compliant, and doesn't recognize me? Not a common combination. I shove back the sexual thoughts that Sydney arouses in me and focus on finding what I need in the kit, roughly shoving shit out of the way until I see what I want.

"Here, this may sting, I'm sorry Sydney." I hate that I have to hurt her, but that cut is nasty and full of dirt. I pour some antiseptic onto a pad and gently wipe her arm with it as she flinches back in pain. "I'm sorry," I say again, feeling like a total ass.

Shit, I'm such a bastard. This girl is so delicate looking, with her almost translucent skin and tiny bone structure. I could probably wrap both of her wrists up in one of my hands and still have extra room. I should be protecting her, not inflicting more pain.

Where did that thought come from? I don't do feelings with women.

"It's okay," she says quietly.

Her soft, sweet voice does something to me. It reaches deep inside and ignites something that's been dormant for a long time. Maybe she's not as fragile as she seems on the outside. She's trying to make *me* feel better for hurting her, when she's the one who's in pain.

Snapping out of my bizarre thoughts, I grab a bandage and place it on the wound, quickly wrapping gauze around it to keep it in place.

"Looks like you've done this before," she says.

Only a million times. "Yeah, a few times…." I look up at her and lose my train of thought. I thought she was gorgeous, I was wrong. Sydney is now smiling at me, and she's fucking stunning. Like the sun lighting up the dark place in my heart, the place that's been cold and detached since I found out how fucked up Hollywood can be.

God, I have to stop acting like a total pussy.

I finish wrapping her arm and notice a jagged scar. A large, old one, running along the underside of her forearm and up past her elbow. Did someone fucking hurt her? I feel an overwhelming rage start to course through my veins, bubbling up in my gut like I was just kicked. I despise feeling out of control. It doesn't happen often, and even then, I only get upset if it involves protecting my family from the shit that follows me. It all stems from that one fucking night in L.A. so long ago that fucked with my head.

So why do I feel this way about a girl I don't even know?

"What happened?" I stay as calm as I can while I trace the scar with my finger, using it as an excuse to touch her again.

Sydney suddenly yanks her arm away, surprising the hell out of me so that I nearly fall back on my ass.

"Nothing, I'm fine," she snaps, jumping up and wrapping her arms around her tiny waist, as if she can protect herself from whatever shit put that scar there. "Thank you for fixing me up, I really appreciate it." Her tone is short, detached.

Then she ducks her head and runs for the door.

Holy hell, what just happened?

"Wait!"

I can't let her leave like this, upset, because of something I said. Thankfully, she stops before getting to the door, but she refuses to look at me, once again staring at the ground.

Shit, asshole! I curse myself for hurting her, again.

"Your jacket," I hand it to her, my pathetic attempt to keep her with me longer. "It's pretty much ruined though."

"Thanks," she murmurs. "Yeah, it is."

I look at her and realize that without her jacket, she's only wearing a thin T-shirt. It's fucking forty degrees out, she'll freeze to death! I can't let her walk home like that, injured and poorly dressed.

"Is that all you have to wear? It's freezing outside."

Sydney just shrugs.

Hell no. There's no way she's walking out of here like that. "Wait here," I tell her.

I have to put a shirt on and get my hat so I can walk outside with her. Not only am I half naked and barefoot, but I don't want anyone to recognize me and intrude on my very limited time left with Sydney. I grab my clothes and stuff my feet into my shoes and run back to her.

"Come on." Before she can protest, I take her small hand in mine and lead her outside.

Thank god for Bruce. He's still right out front, waiting to take me home. He's been driving me for years and I trust him implicitly. If I didn't, I'd never let Sydney get in the car with him.

I open the back door for her, "Get in."

Sydney stares at me like I'm insane, an untrusting look on her face. Good, she doesn't just jump into a strange car without thinking about it first. That pleases me for some unknown reason.

"Sydney, I'm going to have Bruce bring you home. It's too cold for you to walk like that." As much as I want to go with her, to spend more time in her presence, I know she'll never get in the car if I'm going. She doesn't think Bruce is a threat but I'm big and intimidating, so I could be dangerous for all she knows. I lean in and speak to my driver. "Bruce, take her home and then come back here. I'll be ready to go then."

I look back at Sydney. She's anxious, not sure what to do. She is already shivering in this cold, her thin shirt and tiny arms wrapped around her are no match for the icy New York weather.

"Please," I say to her, placing my hands on her shoulders. "I couldn't sleep knowing I sent you out on the street to freeze."

I'm not sure if it's the freezing cold wind, the fact that she's tired and hurt, or if she actually trusts me a little bit, but the skeptical look on her face disappears. "Okay. Thank you for everything," she says as she climbs into the warm car.

God I want to kiss her right now, claim her as mine, protect her from whatever shit is eating at her. But that's not me. I'm a heartless asshole who fucks women, nothing more. I don't take care of them.

Fighting my instincts, I lean into the car, as close as I can without freaking her out. "Take care Sydney." Standing up, I shut the door and watch the car pull away, wondering if I just let something great slip through my fingers.

"What the hell is wrong with you? Calm the fuck down," my best friend says.

I glare at Damien, and continue pacing back and forth in front of the cage, not responding to his words.

"Dude, you are so fucked," Damien laughs.

The tone of voice he uses gets my attention. I turn my head in his direction and see a giant smirk on his stupid face. He's making me want to get back in the ring and pound his ass again.

"What?" I bark at him.

"You," he laughs again. "You like that chick."

I scowl. "Shut up. I don't even know her,"

That asshole just keeps smiling at me. "You do like her. I don't blame you, she's fucking hot as hell. Even all banged up and bleeding. I'd do her."

I jump toward him and get in his face. "You fuckin' stay away from her!" I snarl at my him.

That makes Damien laugh even harder. Now I'm pissed off. I just proved him right. I do like Sydney, what little I know about her. Which, granted, isn't much. This isn't like me, I don't obsess over a woman. Ever.

"See? You totally have a thing for the redhead."

I turn away from Damien, pacing again. There has to be a way to see Sydney again. I curse myself again for not getting her phone number before she left. She was pretty freaked out though. She probably wouldn't have given it to me if I had asked. The thought makes my shoulders shake with laugher.

"What? So you finally realize that it's funny?" Damien asks.

"No, I just realized that the first girl in a long ass time that I've been interested in for more than just a fuck couldn't wait to get the hell away from me."

"More than just a fuck?" Damien asks, stunned. "You really do have it bad for her. Is it the whole damsel in distress thing?"

Lucky for Damien, I see the Town Car pull up in front of the gym, saving me from discussing this any further or punching him right on his loud mouth.

I grab my bag and shove the door open, leaving Damien behind. "See you tomorrow," I bark out, not bothering to wait for his reply.

"Did she get home okay?" I ask Bruce as soon as I shut the car door.

"Yes," Bruce answers calmly.

I pinch the bridge of my nose and breathe out heavily as I stare out the window. He's going to make me work for this and it's embarrassing enough without dragging out every bit of information from him.

"Don't fuck around with me, was she upset or anything?"

I catch Bruce glancing at me in the rearview mirror. "I don't think so. She didn't say a word until she got out of the car."

"And?"

"And all she said was thank you."

That's it? She didn't mention me or say a word? Somehow, I thought maybe she really did recognize me and just didn't want to let on in the gym. I guess not, or else she would have gushed about it to Bruce or wheedled him for information about me.

"Oh." I feel stupid, at a loss for words. Then a thought crosses my mind. "You took her to her place, right?"

"Yes, straight there."

"So, you know where she lives?"

Bruce pauses before answering. Great, he thinks I'm a stalker. Maybe I'm turning into one. I certainly don't feel like myself today. I've been completely fucked in the head by spending a measley fifteen minutes with Sydney.

"Yes. I do."

I sit back and think about this for a while, processing the information. I could hang out in front of her building all day like a psycho, but Sydney is way too suspicious for that. Something tells me she wouldn't like it at all. I could send flowers or some shit to her, but I don't know her last name, plus that's a total cliché.

Shit. I have no idea how to see her again without her thinking I'm a crazy, stalking, lunatic. Normal girls would probably love being pursued like that, but Sydney is different. Reserved, guarded somehow. Untrusting.

I think of the scar on her arm and feel the fury from earlier eclipse everything else. Did a man do that to her? Is that why she was uncomfortable around me? Why she ran away? The thought of anyone hurting her makes me so enraged that I see red.

"She did give me something you may find interesting," Bruce says, pulling me back to the present.

"What's that?"

Bruce holds his hand up over the front seat and I take a small, square napkin from him.

"A napkin? What am I supposed to do with this?" I growl. Now I'm confused on top of the irritation I was already feeling.

"Maybe that's where she gets her coffee every day. It's only two blocks from her building."

Bruce is a fucking genius. Sydney wouldn't think it was creepy if she bumped into me at her favorite coffee shop. I grin and read the name on the napkin.

Village Coffee Bar

"Thanks man, I owe you."

Especially if this works and I get to see her again.

CHAPTER 2

I think my toes are freezing solid.

I'm not sure why I decided it was a good idea to walk back from my radio interview this morning, but for some reason that's exactly what I'm doing. It's probably because all I've thought about since last week is Sydney. I can't get her out of my head and it's driving me nuts. An icy cold walk is exactly what I need to clear my mind before I get to the little coffee shop that the napkin came from.

I've grown out my facial hair over the past few days and I put my Trevor Caldwell 2004 World Series hat on when I left the radio station. It's important that no one recognizes me when I run into Sydney. If she doesn't know that I'm a famous actor, I don't want her to find out. I haven't met someone who sees me for me in a long fucking time.

My phone rings and I pull it out, sighing when I see the screen. It's Quentin, my agent.

"What?" I bark into the phone. I'm not happy with him after that interview this morning. I need some space away from all of that shit, the fake adoration and ass-kissing like I was subjected to today. Hell, that I'm subjected to everyday. People act like they know me, but they know the shell. The Andrew Forrester, *'Sexiest Man Alive'* machine that is created to sell my movies.

God I hate that bullshit title.

"Well good morning to you too Sunshine," he replies. "I wanted to see how the interview went."

"You know I hate doing in-person shit, Quentin. It sucked. That's how it went." I can picture him smirking at me, loving how uncomfortable it makes me to do live interviews.

I really am an asshole.

Sometimes, no most of the time, I just want to be a regular guy walking home from work like everyone else in New York. No one asking for anything or propositioning anything or pretending to be someone else to get to me. It's so exhausting dealing with all that crap every day. I love what I do but I despise what comes with it.

"You know the fans love it, Drew. Gotta give them a piece of you once and a while to keep it feeling real," he jokes. Only, he's not joking. He gets off sending me on these live interviews because he knows it pisses me off. Plus he says it makes me more likeable to the fans. I can feel the tension in my shoulders knot up as he speaks.

"Well, it went like it always does, Quentin. Lots of ass-kissing and completely awkward. Is there a point to this call? I'm busy."

"Just keeping in touch with my favorite client. Talk to you later. And hey, check your email. I sent you a contract for that script you were talking about producing."

"Yeah. I will." I shove my phone in my pocket and realize I'm already there, the Village Coffee Bar. It took every ounce of willpower I have to wait almost a week before turning up here to find Sydney. As much as I wanted to come here the very next day, I didn't want to freak her out and send her fleeing, plus I had to grow out this stupid scruff to cover my very recognizable face.

So instead of rushing down here and staking the place out, I spent a week jerking off in the shower while I thought about her. I've officially reverted back into a desperate, horny teenager.

I tug my hat down lower on my brow to cover my eyes and zip my coat up over my chin. There, that will have to do, I want to act like a regular guy but I'm not stupid enough to think I can just walk around in public without my 'costume' on, as I call it. I have one of the most identifiable faces in the world and it's easier to hide it when I'm not working and don't want to be bothered.

I step inside the café and am hit with a wave of warm cinnamon and coffee scented air. It smells really good in here. There's a display case full of different flavors of fluffy croissants. I shouldn't eat such fattening food, but I order an orange croissant anyway, along with a large coffee. The stressed out guy serving me doesn't even look twice.

Nice, my costume is serving me well already.

A quick glance around shows that the place has a cool vibe and isn't overly crowded, so I grab a table in the back and face the corner so no one will recognize me. I can still see the door in my peripheral vision to watch out for Sydney.

As if I have a chance in hell of bumping into her here. Maybe this was a stupid idea.

My phone buzzes in my pocket, interrupting my stalking. Groaning, I pull it out and take a look. Jane, my assistant, is emailing me my schedule for the next week. Not a whole lot, but a few commitments that I can't blow off. A magazine interview tomorrow morning, by phone. I can just call that one in. I text Jane that tomorrow morning's interview is fine. Also, I need her to make arrangements for my flights to and from the shoot in Los Angeles in a couple of weeks. Chad has been bugging me non-stop that I haven't given him my definite arrival date for our next project.

God, I hate L.A. That's why I've always lived here in New York City. If there were a bigger film industry back home, I'd have stayed in Boston where I grew up. New York is as far west as I'm willing to live.

L.A. is so fake and full of bullshit. Too many paparazzi, too many backstabbers, too many people pretending to give a crap. New York is more real, the people are real. For the most part, I get left alone when I'm here. Every once in a while there'll be a pic in some tabloid of me doing something completely stupid, like buying fruit.

Who the hell gives a shit that I buy fruit?

I answer a few more work related emails on my phone. I have one that says the premiere for *A Soldier's Burden* has been scheduled for March, so I'll have to go back to L.A. for that, then three more cities: Miami, New York and Chicago. I sigh, four red carpets.

Almost ten years I've been single, minus those annoying contractual relationships to promote a movie, and the reporters still speculate about my love life and ask who I'm dating even though I never bring a date. Every. Fucking. Time. Like I would tell them anything about my private life. Screw that. They'd ruin it in a heartbeat.

I don't do relationships anyway. I fuck. No attachments. Fans are too irritating to date, and actresses love themselves more than anything else. I usually hook up with a hot crew member during a shoot and cut ties at the end. She gets me for six weeks and I get laid. Easy.

So why am I here?

I sip my steaming black coffee and lift my head to look around. *Shit.* It's packed in here all of a sudden. What the hell is going on? There are *tons* of women lingering around the coffee shop, not eating or drinking, just hanging out. They didn't spot me did they?

No one is looking my way, so I'm not sure. To be safe, I duck my head and face the back corner again. And between the warm air and the hot coffee, I'm starting to burn up in my coat, but I can't take the chance by removing it and exposing my face.

Thump! A huge purse lands on my table. Damn, they found me. With my hat and my three day old beard, I'm surprised that anyone recognizes me. I glance up and am stunned see the object of my recent fantasies sitting down at my table.

Sydney.

My brain fails me and I'm unable to make words form. I must have missed her come in when I was checking my email. I can't believe she's actually here. My stalking worked.

Speechless, me. Who would have thought?

Sydney starts speaking without looking up as she sits, "I'm sorry to intrude, you don't have to talk to me if you want privacy, there's just nowhere else to sit."

Sydney cleans up well. She's so gorgeous that my brain has shut down and stopped functioning. She has a tall and athletic body, pale, perfect skin, long wavy dark red hair, and a big smile on her face. Just then, she looks up and realizes who I am. Her smile freezes on her face.

Her luscious pink mouth falls open and an adorable blush fills her cheeks.

"Sydney, what are you doing here?" I say smoothly. I have to play it cool so she doesn't know I was stalking her, but she's so cute I can hardly keep the smile off of my face.

She turns an even darker shade of red and drops her gaze to the table.

"Ummmm, my best friend owns this café. I can give you a proper introduction later, it's not usually this crowded in here."

Sydney looks back up at me and time seems to stop. I take in every detail of her face; the tiny freckles that dot her nose and cheeks, the long lashes that frame her vibrant blue eyes, the slightly too-full lips that I can't wait to taste.

I'm still committing every part of her to memory when she speaks, "What's with the repellant outfit?"

I'm taken aback by her words and playful tone. This is a different girl than the shy, withdrawn one I met last week. I hold in a smile. "Repellant? Interesting description, but accurate in a way." I wink at her and she laughs. She has no idea how funny it is. Women don't call me repellant. Ever. And I love that she just did.

"Obviously not repellant enough since I'm sitting here with you," she says with a smirk on her face. I was not expecting this snarky, playful girl.

I think I might love her. Fuck! Did I just think that?

"Yes, but you're only sitting here because there were no other tables free and from the looks of it…" I glance down at her sexy high-heeled boots and struggle to keep the lust off of my face as I imagine those heels around my waist, "your shoes are probably uncomfortable. I'm apparently just shy of being repellant enough to make you suffer blisters; I must be losing my touch. I'll have to step up my game and find a more offensive outfit next time."

I sit back and take another sip of my coffee, impatient to hear what she says next. A customer is getting too close to our table so I duck my head down to hide my face. Shit, I really want to be able to look at Sydney, but I can't be recognized in front of her.

"True, the comfort of my feet will always trump avoiding repellant men in coffee shops. Plus, you did save me from freezing to death the other day, so that counts for something." She fires right back at me, giggling the entire time.

Wow. Stunning, a sense of humor, and she's not intimidated by me. She just needs to be single. I think I would marry her tomorrow. Would it scare her away if I said that to her right now? I flinch internally at the thought.

What the fuck is wrong with me?

I shake my head to try to hide my smile and fail. She's completely charming and doesn't even know it. I'm still laughing when I notice that Sydney has stopped smiling and is staring at me, looking from my mouth to my eyes with a look I recognize. Interesting, Sydney finds me attractive.

It's mutual, believe me.

"Sorry, Syd. It's just nuts in here today." The little blond from behind the counter puts a croissant and a coffee in front of Sydney. I duck my head instinctively so she won't see my face. I'm having so much fun with Sydney, I don't want her friend to ruin it. "Well, I gotta get back behind the counter. These ladies are eating Ben alive!" The blond quickly hustles back to the register.

Desperate for something to do with my hands, I pick at my napkin to distract me from thinking about taking Sydney back to my place, making her tell me everything about herself then fucking her senseless. My awkward silence must get to her, because she speaks to me again.

"That's my friend Leah, who I told you owns this place. Like I said, it's never this crowded in here," she pauses. "So, you're new here, like a lot of these people. What brings you here this lovely morning?"

I'm still shocked that she doesn't recognize me. I figure for now, I'll just be myself, Drew Forrester. It seems to be working for me so far. "I had time to kill, wanted a cup of coffee, and walked past this place. It looked good, so I popped in. It wasn't this crowded when I got here."

I take a chance and look up at her again. "I didn't slip on the ice out front and come in bleeding if that's what you're wondering," I tease. She's staring right back at me, trapping me in her the depths of her intensely blue eyes. My gaze drops to her full pink lips. God, she's unbelievably gorgeous. I'm getting hard just from looking at her.

I really am a fifteen year-old with a permanent hard-on around her. Get it together, Forrester.

"Well, I'm glad you popped in." Her honest admission surprises me. She was pretty walled off the first time we met.

"I'm glad too. Maybe I'm not so repellant after all, huh?" My honest admission surprises me as well. I need to ask her out before she leaves. I can't let her get away without finding out who she is. For some reason my mind is telling me that she's better than the quick fuck my dick is trying to convince me that I need.

"No, I don't think you are. So …" she stops talking when her friend Leah throws an enormous magazine down on the table and it makes a loud *smack!* Are you kidding me? I want to know what Sydney was going to say next. Now, Sydney is cringing, obviously uncomfortable with the interruption. She's back to being the scared girl that I met in my gym.

"Leah, what are you doing?" I look down at the table again so her friend can't make out who I am. "You know I don't read magazines like that."

What kind of magazine? I peek over and see a *GQ* on the table. I hate not being able to see her face and take in her reactions. I've always been very good at reading people's facial expressions, especially hers. She reads like an open book.

I hear a chair being pulled over to the table and out of the corner of my eye I see Leah sitting down. I duck my head and pull at my napkin again. If I act weird enough, maybe she won't talk to me.

"I know Syd, I'm sorry for interrupting but I wanted to show you something and the counter is a little slower right now, so Ben can handle it alone…. Hi, I'm Leah."

She's talking to me. I can't be rude in front of Sydney. She'll think I'm a lunatic. Keeping my hat low, I respond, "Drew. Nice to meet you."

Fuck, this one definitely knows who I am. It's written all over her face when I glance up. *Please don't say anything to your friend.* If she only knew how hard it is for me to meet real people with no expectations, let alone someone as fascinating and beautiful as Sydney, she might take pity on me.

"Yes, well, like I said, I'm … I'm sorry to intrude but I've, uh, I've been waiting for Sydney to get here to uh … show her this." She looks from me to Sydney, then back again, but doesn't say anything.

She pushes the magazine towards Sydney who looks absolutely terrified of a *GQ*, like it's going to jump off the table and attack her. "Leah!" Yep, not happy.

Leah placates her but continues to force the magazine in front of her. "I know, I know. But you have to see this, it's why we're so busy today, and I thought it was time you knew something. Trust me, please."

Leah shifts her eyes over to me again, clearly knowing who I am, then back at Sydney to see her response to the *GQ*. Sydney looks to me for help. I just pull down my hat and shrug. I have no idea what's going on here.

"What? I don't … What the …? I'm not sure I … What the hell, Leah! Adam?" That gets my attention. I take another look at the magazine and see that fucking prick Adam Reynolds on the cover.

My blood feels like acid in my veins. I despise that douchebag. He fucked me over a long time ago. More recently, we got into it at a mutual friend's house because he was mad that I got the cover of *People* magazine's Sexiest Man issue instead of him.

Like I get a vote in that shit!

I don't want the attention. He can have it, but don't be such a fucking baby about it dude! He said something to me, I told him to fuck off. It wasn't my best moment. He was acting like a giant cocksucker at the gathering. When his girlfriend was cast opposite me in an upcoming movie, it really pissed him off. She was hanging all over me at the party, even I was uncomfortable with her forwardness. Serves him the fuck right though, asshole. He's lucky I didn't pulverize his face.

But this situation is strange. This beautiful, funny, interesting girl knows Adam Reynolds, as in 'on a first name basis' knows him. Now I really hate him. An icy cold sensation creeps down my spine, causing me to clutch my hands into fists under the table. What if he fucked Sydney? I'd have to break his neck, not that I wouldn't have before, but if he touched her. *Fuck!*

Struggling to contain my anger at the knowledge that this jerk knows this intriguing woman, I can't help but ask, "You know him?" I stab my finger at his stupid picture.

She seems bewildered, an almost sickened look on her face. "Yes. No. Kind of. I don't know. I don't understand. He comes in here a lot. We sit together when we're here at the same time, maybe a dozen times over the last few months. I only know him from the Coffee Bar. I've never seen him outside of here. And I guess I never asked enough personal questions for me to know that he would appear on the cover of freaking *GQ* magazine!"

Good. I let out the breath I had been holding. So she doesn't really know him. She's seen him in here though. And interestingly, she didn't know he was a celebrity either. This girl must literally live under a rock. There's no way she doesn't know who Adam Reynolds is.

"You had no idea that the man you have been chatting with for several months was Adam Reynolds? Grammy winning lead singer of *Sphere of Irony*, Adam Reynolds? That's crazy? Everyone knows who he is." Okay, now I sound like the cold bastard that I usually am around women. It's that damn Reynolds, I can't stand him!

"Look, Sydney doesn't own a TV. She doesn't read gossip rags, or follow celebrity bullshit, okay?" Shocked, I look over at Sydney's tiny blonde friend. She sounds angry, but she's actually assuring me that Sydney really has no idea who Adam is, and letting me know that Sydney doesn't know who I am either. "She doesn't care about that crap, so trust me, no, she had no clue who he was." I think I owe this girl a thank you. She's trying to explain Sydney to me and help me score with her friend.

"Leah!" Embarrassed, Sydney turns and looks at me after admonishing her friend. "I just don't care for that whole scene, you know? I'm not interested in famous people's lives, and everything on TV sucks so I just don't bother with it."

I study Sydney intently. Wanting to know what she's thinking more than I've ever wanted to know anything before. Doesn't like celebrity gossip, go to the movies, or watch TV? Who is this girl? I smile, she can't be real.

"Ok, I believe you. I've just never met anyone who wasn't at least familiar with most famous faces, let alone held multiple conversations with one on a first name basis and still didn't recognize them. I think it's great. People do spend too much time obsessing over celebrities and in front of the TV. It's nice to know that not everyone is like that."

She's too good to be true. I drink more coffee to keep from blurting out that I might be in love with her.

Leah's mouth falls open after my hypocritical, anti-celebrity speech. She must think I'm crazy, but it's true. I love acting, but all the famous shit is exactly that, *shit*.

She draws her eyebrows together in bewilderment and then relaxes her features to turn back to Sydney. "I wanted to show you his interview, Syd." She flips open the magazine to a folded page and points something out to Sydney. "Right here, see what Adam says?"

Sydney, clearly irritated, bats Leah's hand out of her way and reads from the article out loud.

GQ: So you've been in New York City for the last 3 months recording your new solo album, do you have any favorite haunts in the city?

AR: Well, I've been right busy, and the studio hours are really early, but Galaxy, a nightclub in SoHo is brilliant. And there's a neat little café, the Village Coffee Bar, in the West Village that makes the best specialty croissants you've ever had.

GQ: Who knew you were a croissant lover?

AR: I know, (laughing, he smacks his abs with his hand) I can't eat too many, it's too painful to sweat off later in the gym. I'm hoping to make it back to New York soon, because a friend of mine is redesigning Verve, the nightclub at the Warren Hotel, I've seen some of her work and she's quite the talent. I'm keen on checking it out.

GQ: I'm sure the Warren will send you an invite to the opening.

AR: Hopefully. (Crosses fingers and laughs)

Sydney's voice wavers as she reaches the last few sentences. Okay, so he mentions the coffee shop, Sydney already said that she met him here before. That explains why all these women are flocking into the café and standing around doing nothing. Each one of them is hoping to catch a glimpse of the magnificent asshat, Adam Reynolds. I know he's in New York recording an album because, lucky me, I saw him at that New Year's Eve Party last week.

"Shit."

I look up when Sydney curses and see that she appears ill. Her coloring is pale and she's shaking.

What the hell is going on?

"I know, Syd. I know." Leah's face crumples as she looks at her friend. "But think of all the publicity the Warren is getting. If they didn't already love you, they really love you now. This is why it's so busy in here today. I know Adam just thought he was helping you and me out. He doesn't know about you, Syd."

Adam doesn't know what? What is in the *GQ* article that helps Sydney out? I had already heard that the Warren Hotel is redesigning their nightclub. Adam even references that in the magazine. Does Sydney know something about the new nightclub? Can she get him into the opening? That's low even for Reynolds, using a magazine to ask a chick out. And what about Kiera? He'll just fuck both of them?

Jesus Forrester, control it. I can feel the anger clawing its way up from my gut. I have no idea why I'm feeling this way, I hardly know her.

Before I can ask any of the million or so questions that are overwhelming my mind, Sydney throws the magazine across the table and stands up, wrapping her arms around her waist as if she's physically holding herself together. "I can't talk about this now. Call me later."

What? She can't just leave again! I'm not done talking to her.

Leah snatches up the *GQ* and stares at me one last time, her intelligent eyes narrowing as if trying to figure out my motives with her friend. "Nice to meet you, *Drew*," she says and stalks off to the serving counter, her blonde ponytail bouncing around behind her.

While I'm sitting here worrying about Leah's reaction to me, I notice that Sydney is swiping all of her stuff into her giant purse and throwing away her trash. She's running away from me for the second time in a week! She can't just leave without giving me a way to contact her. I leap up out of my seat to follow Sydney out. "Are you leaving?"

Fuck, now I'm panting after this chick like a dog.

She's stuffing her arms into her coat like the place is on fire. "Yes, I need to get out of here." She finds out a guy she chats with occasionally is famous, so she freaks out and runs away? This makes no sense.

Sydney is clearly distraught. I can't let her walk home like this, what if someone takes advantage of her? "I'm going with you, you're upset. I can walk you home if you like."

Then maybe I'll get her to give me her number. God, I sound like a stalker. A famous, movie star, lunatic, Adam Reynolds-hating stalker.

"Drew, you're being very nice considering I just acted like a total psycho. Just because you saved me once doesn't mean that you have an obligation to walk me home." She looks in my eyes and I see it there, behind the fear. She doesn't want to end our conversation either, but for whatever reason, she needs to be somewhere else right now. I feel hope rising up in me.

Be honest with her Forrester.

I reach out and touch her arm to stop her from bolting out of the café. Just like the last time, a spark of electricity shoots straight to my dick. *Jesus, calm down.* I can't let her see a damn tent in my pants.

"First of all, you're not a psycho, well, maybe a little for sitting with a strange pseudo-repellant man who gives really good first aid and rides home to bleeding women. Second, I know I'm not obligated to walk you home, but I don't think you should be alone when you're upset. Plus, I just like talking to you and was hoping we could talk more."

She nods at me, a little stunned. Maybe when I touched her she felt it too. I grab the brim of my cap and pull it down to hide from the Adam Reynolds' fan club in the café and follow her outside.

Shit, this is my chance. Go big or go home, right?

CHAPTER 3

We're out on the freezing cold sidewalk and Sydney is just standing there twitching, her eyes wide with panic. Did she change her mind about me?

"So which way is your place? I'll walk you home and we can talk if you want." I'm praying that she doesn't tell me to get the hell away from her. Playful, fun Sydney is gone and the nervous and scared Sydney from the other day is back.

She turns her unfocused eyes to me and seems to snap out of her daze. "Okay. That sounds great." Sydney rattles off her street and building number. Her address is just a few blocks from mine, but then, Bruce already told me that.

God, I really am a stalker.

I feel the overwhelming need to hurry up and find out more about her in case she doesn't let me spend more time with her after this. Her place is close, so I may only get fifteen minutes at the most.

"So, how long have you lived in Manhattan, Sydney?"

Her face pales at my question. Damn, this girl is beyond private. She answers me reluctantly, "Twelve years, you?"

Good, actual back and forth conversation. That's much easier than trying to wheedle information out of her like a creepy lurker. "I've been here for ten years. Funny how the island is only thirty-three square miles but we can both live here for a decade and never meet and then run into each other twice in a week," I ramble, trying to fill the silence and encourage her to open up.

It's like fate, don't you think?

I decide not to ask the last part. She'd run away for sure, especially since it's not fate that I found her, I'm a goddamn fucking stalker. I smile at the ridiculousness of this situation, of what I've become since meeting her. A love sick puppy with a creepy stalking habit and a perpetual hard-on.

"That's what I love about New York. You can be invisible if you want to." She actually cringes after she tells me this. Who fucked this girl up so much? There has to be a reason that she's so afraid of discussing herself. I want to beat the ever loving shit out of whoever did this to her.

I stop, and grasp her small arm gently. I don't want to freak her out but I can't let her talk so badly about herself or watch her cower on the sidewalk like I'm going to kick her. "Sydney, you could never be invisible."

She came out of nowhere and fell into my isolated world, making me feel things I haven't felt in a long time and she can't see how amazing she is. It's so frustrating to finally find someone real and interesting, only to realize that they think they're worthless.

I let go of her arm and keep walking toward her place. I don't want her to see how upset I am, if she sees my horrific temper this early on, she'll never want to talk to me again.

We reach her building and stop out front. I'm relieved to see that it's a nice place. Safe, with a doorman and a concierge. I relax knowing she lives here and not in some dump. Her doorman greets her and steps aside to let her enter. "Miss Allen, welcome home." *Sydney Allen*, now I have a last name to go with her first.

The mysterious Sydney Allen speaks to me, her cheeks and nose slashed with pink from the cold. "Ummmm, do you want to come in and continue talking? I mean, well …"

Thank god, I had been holding my breath, anticipating her blowing me off and having to think of a way to stretch out this encounter. Grinning, I gladly accept her invitation to go upstairs.

Okay, so Sydney Allen has money. A lot of money. I wonder what she does. She's not in show business, that's for damn sure, and she's too young to have earned it on Wall Street. She can't be older than her early twenties.

"This place is great," I tell her as I look around. Her loft is big, maybe four or five thousand square feet if I had to guess. There are only two doors in the hallway, so I'm assuming she has half of the floor. Pre-war, five-thousand square foot, updated loft in the West Village with a doorman? Big money for sure.

She stops in the foyer and holds out a slender hand. "Thanks. Let me take your coat and, uhhh, hat." She looks disgusted by my choice of headwear.

My hat. I forgot I have my lucky Red Sox hat on. She probably wouldn't care that catcher Trevor Caldwell wore this for the entire 2004 World Series-winning season. He gave it to me when I met him and practically bowed at his feet.

I hand her my coat but keep the hat, removing it and tossing it onto the nearby coffee table. I can't wear it in the house, it's impolite, and besides she looks grossed out by it. "That's pretty old and sweaty; I wouldn't want you to have to touch it."

I try to hold in my laughter as she wrinkles her nose at my hat. It is fairly disgusting if you didn't realize that it was kept unwashed on purpose for an entire season of baseball in order to win with World Series. Well, maybe it's disgusting even if you do know that.

I wander into the living area and she turns toward the kitchen. "Would you like a drink? I know it's not even five o'clock, but I have no shame in indulging in a beer this early"

"A beer would be great. Thanks, Sydney," I call out to her.

While she's making noise in the kitchen, I take a closer look around the room, trying to gather any little bit of information about this girl from her possessions. She's not super forthcoming about herself so I'll take what I can get. A quick peek around and a few photos of her in Europe are the only personal items I can find. Even her home reveals nothing.

Sydney comes back and hands me an amber bottle of beer. "You've been to a lot of places." I motion toward the photos and look down at the drink in my hand. She gave me a Sam Adams, my hometown's best brew, *and* she drinks it straight from the bottle.

Seriously, is there nothing about this girl that I'm not already in love with?

She stands just out of my reach, eyeing me speculatively. "Yes, I've traveled a bit. How about you? Ever been to Europe?"

I don't want to talk about me, Miss Allen.

"Yes, I've been to most of Europe." I answer and take a seat on the couch, my eyes not leaving her. She sits on the other end of the couch and downs a huge portion of her beer, probably out of nervousness, but it's still sexy watching those lips wrapped around the bottle.

I need to know more about her. "I noticed that you really don't own a TV, unless you've hidden it somewhere. So, why don't you like the entertainment industry, Sydney?" I could be skating on thin ice with this question. She might recognize me and tell me to get the hell out.

Sydney's eyebrows shoot up in alarm and her shoulders hunch forward just a bit, like she's trying to protect herself again. "I … I really don't feel like answering that right now, if that's okay with you?"

Fuck, I upset her. Her eyes dart away and she drinks another huge gulp, leaving only a little beer left in her bottle. I'm making her uneasy, I need to fix this. I shift a little closer to her, so I can see her expressive eyes. "Sydney, I don't want to make you uncomfortable. You don't have to tell me anything you don't want to. Maybe someday you'll feel like you can trust me enough to tell me. I'm patient."

I shouldn't lie to her. I'm far from patient. Patience isn't even on my radar. I want her and I want her now, but for her I'll wait.

Her eyes open wide in surprise and her mouth falls open. I have no idea what she's thinking, and I'm usually very good at reading people. "Even though I barely know you I do feel like I can trust you, Drew, but that's a part of me that I don't like talking about. I'm just not able to go there. Not yet."

She gives me a tiny smile and I let out a huge breath. She trusts me, which is strange, because she's barely told me a thing about herself and knows next to nothing about me. I can only imagine how she treats people she doesn't trust. She pounds the rest of her beer and gets up, grabs the empty bottle from me that I don't remember drinking, and heads for her kitchen.

No way am I letting her get in there alone and give her time to decide to kick me out. I hop up and follow her. I'm going to go all in and see if she's as attracted to me as I am to her. Like I always say, go big or go home.

When I enter the kitchen, she's placing the bottles in the sink with her back to me. I walk right up behind her and get as close as I can without touching. She turns around and I'm inches from her gorgeous pink lips. *Shit*, it's so hard not to just throw her on the table and take what I want, what I'm used to getting without even trying. I know I could probably have her like that, but she's different. I'm interested in her, I want *more* from her.

I breathe deep and lean my hands on the countertop, trapping her between my body and the sink. She smells like oranges and flowers and I can feel the heat coming off of her delectable body. This girl is destroying my willpower. I can barely speak above a whisper, her closeness is making me crazy. "Are you hungry? We could order in, hang out. What do you think?"

Sydney meets my eyes with a dark look that makes my dick twitch. "Sure. Why don't you start a fire? Everything you need is in the wood box next to the fireplace. I'll just order the food, is sushi okay?" Her voice is raspy and her breathing is heavy. She's attracted to me all right.

No, I just want *you*, thank you very much. I smile at the thought of her naked and writhing beneath me. I need to leave the room before I do something stupid. "Sure thing, Sydney. Sushi sounds great."

Fire, living room, stop thinking about sex, dumbass.

I head out of the kitchen to try and tame the erection growing in my pants. I haven't had to work this hard to get a girl in almost ten years, and this moment makes it totally worth it. Women agreeing with everything I say, sucking up, trying to take their clothes off five minutes after meeting me… I think I prefer the building tension that's happening between me and the secretive girl in the other room.

Sydney's fireplace is wood burning, but it has a gas starter. Thank god. I won't have to look like an idiot if I can't get it started with just matches. It only takes a few minutes to get a good fire going. Working with the fireplace proves to be a good way to calm my dick down enough to keep her from seeing a giant bulge in my pants.

Sydney strides purposefully through the living room into what I assume is a bedroom and comes back with a huge quilt. She spreads it out on the floor in front of the fire and shrugs saying only, "Picnic-style," and produces a bottle of wine and two glasses.

We end up drinking wine and eating sushi on the floor. She ordered a bunch of different types for us to share and her concierge brought them to her door. She lets me feed her from my chopsticks, and watching her open that luscious mouth is enough to make my pants uncomfortable again for another twenty minutes.

We laugh and talk about random things. I stick to safe topics, nothing personal about her or me. I still want to know about that asshat Adam Reynolds and the Warren Hotel, but I'll have to wait, even though thinking about him makes me want to punch his face repeatedly.

My need to take her here on the quilt in front of the fire is another story altogether. I can't stay here much longer and not try to get her into bed. When she gathers up her dishes and brings them to the kitchen I decide it's time to leave, but not without a promise that she'll see me again tomorrow.

We place our things by the sink and head back toward the living room. It goes against every instinct I have to get my coat out of the closet by the door and put it on. She stops and looks at me, pressing her lips together tightly. "I'd better be going, Sydney. It's pretty late." I can see the disappointment in her eyes, she wants me to stay and fuck her. I can practically smell it coming off of her.

Without thinking, I step towards her and she instinctively backs up into the door. So fucking hot. When she lets out a little pant at my proximity, I reach out and stroke her soft, lightly freckled skin from her cheek down to her collarbone and lean forward to breathe in her scent. Everything about her draws me right in, I can't help myself.

Struggling to contain the lust coursing through my body, I force my brain to win out, refusing to let her get away. I will get what I want and I want her, *all* of her. "Can I see you again?" She closes her eyes and parts her lips, waiting for me to take her against the door.

No, not until you answer me, Miss Allen.

After a few seconds, Sydney blinks open those big blue eyes. "What? Am I wrong to expect a kiss goodbye?" she asks, somewhat confused and upset. I think she's disappointed that I won't make a move.

You're going to get kissed Sydney, as soon as you give me what I want.

I lean in just a little more so I can inhale the scent of her soft hair again, already addicted to it. "I'll kiss you. As soon as you say that you'll see me again." I pull back so I can see her face, once again resisting the overwhelming craving I have to rip off her clothes and sink into her wet heat.

She tilts a tiny bit toward me and whispers, "Yes, I'll see you again Drew. Now please, kiss me."

Fuck. I snap. My control evaporates when she says that to me. One step forward is all it takes to press into that soft, hot body. My mouth crashes over hers and I run my tongue over her luscious lips to see if they taste as good as they look. When Sydney moans and opens her mouth, my dick takes the driver's seat. I grab her tight ass and pull her against my hard cock in an attempt to get some badly needed friction. Our mouths clash together and I get even harder.

Trying to calm down, I run my teeth down her neck and put some space between us. I can't take her to bed tonight. Sydney is definitely not like any of the other women I've had and I'm not going to treat her like a groupie. I'm going to get her number. "Give me your phone, Sydney." She stands there with a blank look, her lips swollen and wet from our kisses. "Your phone. Please."

Her eyebrows pinch together in confusion as she reaches for her purse, pulls out her phone, and drops it into my hand. Good, now I'll have her phone number. I hastily send a text message from her phone to mine and hand it back to her.

Beep

Smiling, I pull my phone out of my pocket and wave it in front of her. "Well, well. You texted me and asked me to dinner tomorrow night." I type out a response and her phone beeps almost immediately in her hand. I slide mine back into my pocket and look right at her. "I said yes." I reach up and hold her face, giving her a quick kiss, any more than that and I won't stop. "I should go, Sydney. It was great seeing you again. I'll see you tomorrow?"

She nods and steps aside so I can leave. "Yes. Tomorrow." Sydney is adorably disheveled. She's as dazed as I am.

I grin at the thought of her wanting me. "I can't wait." Kissing her cheek, I force myself to walk out of the loft.

Thank god the elevator is slow. By the time I reach the lobby I'm able to walk without a tent in the front of my pants, but not without the huge, stupid smile on my face. I met a girl, and not just any girl. A gorgeous, interesting, secretive, sexy girl who's been living two blocks from me for six years and has never heard of Andrew Forrester. She likes Sam Adams and coffee, hates movies and television and Adam Reynolds interviews.

I think I'm in love.

CHAPTER 4

"OhmyGODyou'reAndrewForrester!"

I hear the squeal from two girls that are rushing towards me as I walk home from Sydney's place. I automatically reach up to pull my hat over my face. *Shit*, I left my hat at Sydney's.

I try not to cringe as they rush up to me and one of them grabs my arm. *Whoa!* I smoothly remove myself from her grasp. I try not to be an asshole about it, but don't fucking touch me. Ten years of strangers trying to grab your package and your ass makes you rethink letting people put their hands on you.

"Good evening ladies," I say, turning up the charm so I can keep walking and hopefully they won't realize they're being blown off.

"You're so hot!" the one who grabbed my arm screeches. What in the hell do they feed young girls that makes their voices so irritating?

"Could we get a picture with you, please?" the other one asks politely. At least one of them was raised with manners.

I stop, sighing before turning around to face them on the sidewalk. "Sure," I say with my best fake Andrew Forrester grin. The girls squeeze in next to me and the courteous one snaps a selfie with her cellphone. I need to keep moving before more people notice me. It's dark and it's late, but even the indifferent citizens of New York City can turn batshit crazy if they spot me.

"Have a nice evening, ladies." I quickly spin on my heel and take off, walking as quickly as I can without flat out running.

I reach my brownstone and duck inside, having lost the fans a few blocks back. My street is pretty quiet, it's strictly residential so there's not a lot of foot traffic on a normal day. Definitely not at eleven o'clock at night on a Thursday so I'm able to get home without anyone else seeing me.

I get inside and go straight up to my office on the third floor. Throwing my coat on the leather couch, I collapse into the chair at my desk and think about tomorrow night, twisting the chair back and forth slowly. How in the hell am I going to take Sydney on a date? I can't go out with her in public. Those girls are just the tip of the giant screeching iceberg that makes up the Andrew Forrester fan club.

I groan and run my hands through my hair. This is one of those times that I wish I could be a normal guy. Damien was right, I haven't met a woman that I've been interested in for more than a quick fuck for longer than I can remember.

The last semi-serious relationship I was in ended very badly when I found her passed out in a bed with Adam fucking Reynolds. She came to visit me in L.A. while I was filming my first big movie, got drunk at a party and disappeared. When I finally found her, it was in a bedroom and that douche was zipping up his pants. I failed to keep her safe at that party and let her wander off drunk. That hurt more than anything else, the guilt, the feeling that it was my fault.

My fame shot off the charts shortly after that, and I had Reynolds blacklisted from the film industry. He fucked my almost unconscious girlfriend with me right downstairs. That asshole got exactly what he deserved and I learned not to get close to anyone after that, that way I couldn't let them down and they couldn't let me down.

After a few painful early experiences, I learned not to trust actresses either and that fans are just too irritating to date, stealing your shit for trophies to show their friends. That leaves very few options for me when it comes to women. Hooking up with a crew member works best. You get a few weeks together, then they go back to their lives when we wrap and I go back to mine. No gossip, no problems.

Until now.

Sydney Allen. Everything about her is perfect for me. What could she be hiding? Why would someone be so scared of finding out an acquaintance is a celebrity? Did she used to date someone famous and get dumped? Maybe her last boyfriend was in the business and he used to smack her around. My hands are hurting and I realize that I'm gripping the armrests of my chair so severely that my fingers are gouging the wood.

The thought of someone hurting Sydney makes me so angry that I can barely think. *Calm down, Forrester, you're being irrational.* I don't even know this girl, how can she cause such a profound response in me? I shake it off and focus.

Okay, date, tomorrow night, with Sydney. Where can I take her? Looking out the window of my office, I have only one idea. I whip out my cellphone and dial up Jane, my assistant. Jane's been with me for a long time. She pretty much runs my life. I can't even imagine doing what I do without her. She makes sure everything goes smoothly, in my professional and personal life.

It's only eight thirty in L.A. where Jane is spending the weekend visiting her daughter. Since I'm between films and promotion for *A Soldier's Burden* hasn't really ramped up yet, I gave her a long weekend out of town. But she knows that I'll still bug her once in a while.

"Drew, I just left yesterday. You can't live without me, can you?" she says when she answers her phone.

I laugh. She's like my sister and my mother rolled into one. "You know it, Janey. I need your help."

"When do you not need my help? I'm the best and you know it."

"Yes, I do know it. I worship at your feet, my dear." I love playing around with her. She doesn't take my crap and doesn't act like a fan. I'd probably do anything to keep her happy. She's family as far as I'm concerned. "Listen, I have a date tomorrow night and I need to take her somewhere private. Where no one will recognize me or treat me weird. Do you have any ideas?"

There's dead silence on the other end.

"Jane? Did I lose you?" I check the screen, it's still connected. "Jane?"

"I'm sorry Drew. Did you say you have a date? Like a real date?"

I've rendered Jane speechless. Not an easy feat, and now I'm embarrassed. I'm not good with talking about shit like feelings. I drag my free hand through my hair nervously. "Yes, a real date. And I don't want to screw this up. I really like this girl and she doesn't know who I am. I'd like to keep it that way. So where can I take her? You know all the good places in this city." Jane was born and raised in midtown, so she knows everyone and everything.

"What? Did you say she doesn't know who you are?" Jane's tone indicates that she's not sure if she believes me.

"I know," I chuckle. "I thought she was full of it too." I explain to Jane what happened at the café with Sydney and the *GQ* article and how Leah recognized me but didn't say anything to Sydney.

"Adam Reynolds? Seriously? That guy is going to haunt you until you die," Jane says sarcastically. "Okay, Drew, I have an idea. They're still open so I should be able to get someone on the line. I'll call you right back."

"Thanks Jane." I disconnect and toss the phone onto the desk. I look around my office. It's huge for a home office. Because I don't live in L.A., it's the home base for the monster that is Andrew Forrester. I keep all of my important awards in here, two People's Choice, a SAG, and a Golden Globe, plus a bunch of other random shit.

Lining the wall behind the couch are photos of me with different celebrities and politicians. Of course, my favorite is the one of me taken with the Sox after they whipped the Yankees in the

ALCS. My New York buddies hate that picture. That makes it even sweeter.

The ringing of my phone snaps me out of my daydream. "Hey Jane, give me good news."

"You owe me Drew," she pouts. I can tell she's just pretending to be upset so I laugh at her. "Tomorrow night, 9pm at the Sunset House. I got you one of their private dining rooms. They're very discreet. I told them you don't want the staff to say anything in reference to who you are and they understand. They get celebrities all the time, so you should be fine."

"I don't want *'should be fine'* Jane. I want perfect. I don't want them fucking this up by asking for an autograph or some shit!" I bark into the phone.

"Listen here, Drew Forrester, don't you dare swear at me!" Crap, Jane can't stand cursing. It makes it really hard to be around her sometimes since my first word as a baby may as well have been 'shit'. "I did you a huge favor here, buddy! Bruce will be there to get you at eight-fifteen. If you want to clarify your demands with the restaurant, I'll email you their info. Speak to Clarence, he's the manager."

Great, I pissed her off. My life does not go well when Jane is pissed off. "I'm sorry, Jane. I'm just nervous. I really like this girl."

She pauses before answering. "Wow... you have definitely got it bad. I don't think I've ever seen you like this." She takes pity on me and my bizarre behavior. "Alright, I'll call them back. What's the girl's name by the way? These fancy places like to have all of their ducks in a row when you arrive."

I give Sydney's name to Jane and thank her profusely, telling her how great she is and how much I'm forever in her debt before I disconnect.

I have until I see Sydney Allen tomorrow night to figure out how to make her mine.

CHAPTER 5

After wiping the sweat out of my eyes with a towel, I take a long drink of water. I need to catch my breath for a minute before I can speak, so I hold up a finger to Damien Spader, my best friend and trainer, to let him know I need a break. It's already been a long day and it's only ten in the morning. I had to be up early to call in for an interview with *Entertainment Weekly*. I love talking about the movies I make, but they always try to pry into my personal life and it gets really tiresome.

"What's with you today, Forrester? Are you trying to kill me?" He's panting too. We're sparring at the gym Damien owns, the run down hole in the wall in Hell's Kitchen where Sydney came stumbling into my life.

I've been practicing Muay Thai and Ju Jitsu here for about eight years, ever since Damien was hired to get me in shape for a movie. He introduced me to both of the sports to prepare me to play a disgraced UFC fighter. We've been friends ever since.

Usually, we're pretty even when we spar, although I'm sure he could take me down every single time if he wanted to. He knows not to hurt me badly enough to do it. I sign contracts that require me to show up for filming in one piece, I can't turn up with a dislocated shoulder or a broken nose. It makes me feel like a pussy sometimes, that we can't just go at it, but I have to make a living and a lot of other people depend on those paychecks too. Damien hates it, but he understands. There are times when I think he really wants to kick my ass though.

"Sorry, D," I huff, throwing down the protective head gear and bending over to catch my breath. "I have a lot on my mind."

Actually, I was thinking about whoever made Sydney such a nervous wreck, and how I would pound the shit out of them if we ever met. I might have taken some of my hostility out on Damien. I may have also pictured that ass Adam Reynolds every time my fists and feet made contact.

"Whatever, dude. Just know that I could totally smash your pretty face into the mat," he says, but his expression tells me he's just kidding. I did hit him harder than usual, so maybe he's pissed and hiding it well.

Laughing, I point at myself. "Damien, this face makes millions of women drop their panties faster than you can blink. We can't destroy their dreams now, can we?"

I give him a shit eating grin and he smiles. He knows me well enough to know that I can't stand the attention from the fans, especially the female ones. When we go out, he gets downright infuriated at all of the interruptions from people coming up to me, bugging me for an autograph or a picture or a date. He sort of acts like my anti-wingman, keeping the adoring fans away so we can relax. Usually, I just wear my 'human-repelling' costume, as Sydney put it. It's easier when you're not spotted in the first place.

"Guess we can't. How could I sleep at night knowing that women all over the world are mourning the loss of your beauty? But it would be a hell of a lot easier going out for a few beers if you did fuck up your face." He punches my arm and we call it a day.

Normally, I just walk the six blocks back to my place in Chelsea, but I don't want to waste time getting stopped by fans today. I shaved this morning before I left, to keep the pads from irritating my face, so I actually look like Andrew Forrester today. Bruce is waiting for me out front with the car when I dart out the front door of the gym and hop in the back seat.

"Thanks, Bruce," I tell him as I shut the door. "Just straight home, please."

"No problem, Drew."

I've had Bruce driving me around New York for the past six years. I used to just call a car service whenever I needed to go somewhere, but it became annoying having all the different drivers want to have their pictures with me. Then, as I became more recognizable, the leaks to the gossip rags started to get out of control. I know the drivers were getting paid off to tell the vultures where I was and who I was with. Everywhere I went, the photographers just happened to turn up.

Bruce used to drive for a limo company that Jane had hired several times before and she quickly snatched him up when I mentioned getting my own driver. Personally, I think she likes him, which is fine by me. They're both a part of my family. It took me two whole years to get Bruce to stop calling me Mr. Forrester, but I finally wore him down.

I take out my phone and text Sydney about our date tonight while the car heads slowly down Columbus Avenue in the thick traffic.

Me <Pick you up at 8:30? Dress nice.>

I stare at my phone, willing it to answer me. Ten minutes later, Bruce pulls behind my brownstone and into the underground garage and I frown at my phone. I still haven't heard back from Sydney. Did she change her mind about going out with me? I feel sick to my stomach. She wouldn't do that, would she? She seemed to be just as into me last night. Fuck, I'm usually such a confident prick, I hate this feeling.

I tell Bruce to take the day off and be back here at 8:15 or so to get me for dinner. He doesn't think to hide his surprise that I'm going on an actual date, but fortunately he's too polite to say anything.

Angry, I slam the door from the garage and storm up the stairs to my bedroom as I rip off my sweaty clothes. I pace back and forth in front of the window, worried that she's blowing me off. *Shit!* I'm not used to chasing a woman. I have no idea if she's supposed to respond to my text right away. Maybe it's some chick thing to play hard to get or some crap like that. I hate not being able to control this situation.

A thought crosses my mind that halts me in my tracks. What if she's seeing someone else? I'd probably kill him if I met him. I. Don't. Share. What's. Mine. And I fully intend on making Sydney mine very soon.

This is ridiculous. I step into the shower and turn it to cold, letting the freezing water hit my skin. I need to get control of myself and my anger. Sydney doesn't strike me as the type to play games. If she were, she certainly wouldn't have freaked out so much in the café when she found out who Adam was.

This girl is making me absolutely fucking nuts. I haven't doubted myself in so long; I have no idea what to do with a real woman. One who doesn't fling her panties in my face five seconds after meeting me, which it turns out, is a real turn off.

Even the frigid water in the shower doesn't stop me from getting a hard on from thinking about Sydney. Jesus, I would think jerking off twice a day for the last week would have cured me of this obsession with her. It hasn't. Even now, under the cold water, my dick is getting hard.

Disgusted with myself, but unable to stop, I soap up my hands and reach down to run a hand up my length, squeezing as I reach the tip. My cock clearly doesn't care how cold the water is because it's rock hard and aching painfully. The thought of Sydney's full pink lips and tight ass make my dick throb and twitch in my hand.

Moaning, I drop my head and slap one hand up on the tiled wall to hold myself up as I stroke faster, letting the image of Sydney drive the pleasurable sensations through my body. My balls tighten up when I visualize tasting her wet pussy, her legs wrapped around my head as I dive my tongue in and out of her sweet cunt.

Every time I stroke up my cock, I run my thumb over the sensitive head and groan. What I wouldn't give to have her on her knees in front of me, wrapping those plump lips around my dick and swallowing it whole, sucking until she swallows everything I have inside. The thought is so erotic, that the stimulation quickly reaches a peak. I stroke faster and jerk harder until all of my frustration and desire sends hot sparks to the base of my spine and violently explodes out of me, forcing endless streams of come to jet out into the drain, wiping my mind clear for at least the next few minutes.

Appalled at my actions and my inability to what's turning out to be a sick obsession, I turn the dial to hot and catch my breath, leaning back against the wall until I catch my breath. I wash off quickly and hop out, grabbing a huge towel to wrap around my waist. Jerking-off did absolutely nothing to help me figure out what to do about my date. I throw on a pair of jeans and a T-shirt, grab my phone, and head downstairs to my office.

I don't really have anyone I can call to help talk me down from what I'm sure is an overreaction on my part. Damien? He'll just tell me to fuck her and move on. Jane? She was so shocked that I was going on a date that she couldn't speak. I can only think of one other person that I trust enough to call.

"Drew? What's up?" My sister Allie sounds surprised to hear from me. And she's right, it is unusual for me to bother her on a Friday morning.

"Hey Al, do you have a minute?" I feel so stupid calling my baby sister for girl advice, but really, if anyone knows what a young single woman is thinking, it's Allie.

"Sure, is everything okay?" I can hear her shuffling stuff and then walking somewhere. Probably so her coworkers don't hear her. She's a pharmacist at a hospital in Boston and she doesn't tell anyone that I'm her brother. She made that mistake in college and it became one big clusterfuck. My fucking job ruins everything sometimes.

"Yeah, I just need to ask you about … well …" I have no idea how to put this.

"Say it Drew, you're freaking me out!" Great, Allie's getting upset. She's probably thinking the worst right now.

"Okay, I met a girl."

"A girl? *You* are calling me about a girl?" She starts laughing uncontrollably. I can see her right now, hunched over, clutching her stomach while tears run down her face.

"Ha-ha, super funny, sis. I'm trying to open up to you here. Aren't women always saying that men are too emotionally unavailable? I need advice, so stop it!"

She calms down and attempts to be serious. "Okay, sorry. What kind of advice on women does the '*Sexiest Man Alive*' need from his little sister?" She starts giggling again.

"Allie! C'mon! You're making me feel like a wicked pussy here." Talking to my friends and family always brings back my Boston accent. I worked hard to ditch it, and it fires right back up whenever I speak to them. I explain the Sydney situation to her, keeping it short, and wait for a response.

"Al? What do you think?" I wait again. "Allie! What the hell?"

"Drew, I don't know what to say. If she really doesn't know who you are, then I'm amazed. Marry her, big brother. You'll never find another girl who has the potential to love you for just you. And I'm not saying that to make you feel shitty, but because I care."

"I know, Al. It's unbelievable that I found someone who has absolutely no interest in Andrew Forrester." We always refer to my public persona as a third person, because I am most definitely not him. He's not real. He's a product of excellent marketing. No one wants to buy tickets to see a movie starring Drew from Boston; the one who wears ugly old sentimental baseball hats and likes to have a beer with his friends.

That's fine by me because I don't want people to know me like that. I much prefer the two separate lives. But women only ever know the Andrew Forrester that they see on the screen and in the magazines; they don't have any interest in Drew. "She saw me in my Trevor Caldwell hat and still let me come back to her place."

"Wow. Just wow. Any girl that would hang out with you after seeing that disgusting piece of crap on your head is perfect for you. I wouldn't worry about the text, bro. She's probably getting a dress or getting her hair done. Or hey, ever think that she might be at work and can't check her phone? Some of us have jobs we have to go to every single day." God I love her sarcasm. She definitely keeps me grounded in reality.

"You're right. I'm just nervous, that's all. I gotta go Al, thanks for listening."

"Drew, if she's as great as you say she is, then she'll love you. You're an awesome guy."

"Love ya sis."

"Love ya too. Bye!" She hangs up and I stare at the phone for a second.

I really hope my sister is right about Sydney.

CHAPTER 6

Bruce is driving me the two blocks to Sydney's loft. She finally texted me back and told me that 8:30 was fine and that she would meet me downstairs, which made me feel like an idiot for freaking out earlier. She won't let me come up and get her like a real date, which is disappointing. I don't ever go on real dates and I was kind of looking forward to going all out.

At least this way, no one will see me get in and out of the car or walking through the lobby of her building. It's a Friday night and it's early, so there's sure to be more people out tonight than there were last night. We pull onto her street and I text her just like she asked.

Me <Waiting for you outside. Black Town Car. Can't wait to see you.>

As I'm thinking about tonight, Bruce jumps from the car and opens the back door for Sydney. I hear her acknowledge him kindly and she slides in gracefully next to me.

"My pleasure Sydney," Bruce responds as he gently closes the door.

Jesus, she's even more attractive than I remember. The sweet smell of her fills the car, making me hard already. "Sydney, you look stunning." She's wearing a short black dress and killer heels. Her hair is loose and wavy.

I think about grabbing her by the waist and pulling her onto my lap. The thought of having my way with her in the car makes me smile. I can't help myself, I have to touch her. Reaching up I put my hands on either side of her beautiful face and softly kiss the thick, full lips that I've been fantasizing about since that day in the gym. The crimson that flushes her cheeks and neck from our brief contact is so hot, it's making me even more uncomfortable in my pants.

"Drew, you clean up rather well yourself."

The way Sydney is looking at me makes my dick twitch again. *Shit*, I start running baseball stats through my head. Cold water doesn't work, so I doubt this will, but I have to try. I can't get out of the car at the restaurant with a hard-on. She'll think I'm a perverted asshole.

"Shoot. I forgot. You left your hat at my place." She breaks my concentration with her random thought.

I try not to laugh at her, doing a poor job of concealing my amusement. "My hat. Yes, I'll need to get that back. It's sort of my lucky charm." I know she hates that hat, most people do. Allie tells me she wants to throw up whenever she sees me wear it. They just can't appreciate how important that hat is. Without thinking, I put my hand on her bare knee and my dick swells again.

Shit, think baseball Forrester.

Sydney looks at my hand then up at my face, her piercing blue eyes filled with lust. "Lucky charm? Why is it lucky?"

Good, keep the conversation on baseball. "I was wearing it when I bumped into you at the coffee shop after I was convinced I'd never see you again."

What the hell? Why would I say that? Now I know for sure that my brain has detached from my body. My mouth and my dick are running the show here tonight. She freezes and swallows loudly at my words. Damn, if I don't get out of this car I'm going to take her right here on the back seat.

Thankfully, we pull into the parking lot and stop. "Sydney, we're here," I tell her.

I reluctantly get out and turn to help her out of the car. When she steps onto the pavement the length of her body presses into mine and I'm paralyzed by desire. I look down at her mouth. Would she be mad if I devoured her lips right here in the cold? Probably. "We better go in, it's cold out here." I step back and take her hand. She mumbles something as we walk, but I don't catch it.

"What is this place?" she asks.

I answer her as we keep walking, she's got to be freezing out here in that scrap of fabric she considers a dress. "This is Sunset House, on 76th street. We're using the back entrance. I've reserved us a private dining room."

I turn to hold the door for her and she speaks again. "Oh. Why a private dining room?" So many questions from someone who has given me absolutely no answers.

I tell her the truth, just not all of it. "So I can spend time with only you, of course. And you're too sexy for your own good. I don't like to share, Sydney. Every man in the restaurant would be watching you." And so you don't find out that I'm some super famous actor and inexplicably freak out and run away from me.

The host just inside the door greets us warmly.

Don't fuck this up for me dude.

"Mr. Forrester, Miss Allen, welcome to Sunset House. I'm Chase and I'll take care of you tonight. We have your room ready, please follow me." I notice Sydney stiffen a little when Chase addresses us. I hope like hell that she didn't recognize my last name.

I let Sydney go first and follow her up a flight of stairs. Chase opens the door to our room and allows us to pass. I owe Jane big, this is perfect. I watch Sydney's reaction to the room. She gently touches the wood buffet near the door and slowly walks toward the wall of windows that overlook the entire restaurant. I notice that she methodically checks out everything in the room, the chandelier, the table, the chairs. When she reaches the windows, she flinches slightly. She hates the windows, too exposed for her to be comfortable if I had to guess.

I move behind her to reassure her that she's safe. "Don't worry, the glass is one way. No one can see into the private rooms from the main restaurant."

Chase steps up, takes our coats from us, and leaves. I pull out a chair for Sydney and she accepts it graciously. I take the seat next to her. "I hope you like champagne, I ordered some for us." Well, Jane did anyway. She was miffed when I called her this afternoon and asked her to call the restaurant with more instructions. She must have felt bad for me and my rare case of nerves because she did it without arguing.

Chase breezes in with the champagne, and opens it, deftly pouring us each a glass before exiting the room again.

Sydney touches her glass as she looks at me with an odd expression on her face. "So, I'm impressed, Mr. Forrester. I guess I should find it odd that the host knew your last name and I didn't and we're on a date. Or should I be more creeped out that he knew mine?"

That's why she freaked out when Chase greeted us. She doesn't like that I know her last name. As secretive as she is, she probably thinks I did something illegal to get it or something. This girl is really damaged. Once again, I want to fucking kill whoever did this to her.

I attempt a smile, to keep her from seeing how angry I am. "Well, Miss Allen, if you must know, your doorman used your name last night. That's how I know it. I promise I didn't go through your mail to find out. And you never asked for my last name, so now you know it. There's no secret motive behind my actions, I just enjoy spending time with you and want to get to know you better."

Sydney looks relieved at my answer. Is someone threatening her? Did someone stalk her? Before I can ask, she holds up her flute. "A toast then, Mr. Forrester?"

"To getting to know each other better." I say confidently. I'm going to figure you out Miss Allen, even if it takes my entire lifetime. I hold my glass up to hers and look into her eyes.

"Yes. I'll toast that," she replies. But somehow, I don't think she means it.

Dinner with Sydney was perfect. She's charming and adorable and despite having to avoid such huge topics including almost everything about her and everything about my job we manage to have great conversation. She's very good at not asking questions that she doesn't want to answer about herself, so I was spared the awkwardness of lying about what I do for a living.

Now, we're in the car on the way back to her loft and I've been torturing myself by putting my hand on her bare thigh and rubbing my thumb back and forth. All of the flirting over dinner has turned me into a raging lunatic with yet another uncontrollable hard-on and it's getting difficult to hide it from Sydney.

Bruce stops the car in front of her building and waits. I have the glass divider up so he can't hear or see us. I can't bring myself to be a gentleman and say goodbye to Sydney here in the car, I have to see if she'll let us continue the date upstairs. Thinking about her all week has made me a wreck. I turn and put my hand on her cheek. When she licks her lips, looks at me seductively, and whispers my name, I know she'll say yes. "Can I come up?"

"Of course. I have to give you your hat," she responds wickedly.

I try to suppress a smile, she really hates that hat, but I don't think that's why she wants me to go upstairs. I lean in and kiss her, hesitant at first. I don't want to push her and ruin this, but when our mouths touch, Sydney unleashes an animal that I didn't know she had in her. She wraps herself around my body and tangles her hands in my hair, yanking my face down to hers in a mind blowing embrace. Sydney hitches one of her long legs over mine and winds her other arm around my neck, nearly climbing in my lap on the back seat.

She's so fucking hot. I have to stop her before I *can't* stop her. I gently push her away and groan as she licks her swollen lips. A small button on my door panel lowers the glass that divides the front seat from the back. "Bruce, you can go for the evening," I instruct my driver.

I step out of the car, quickly flipping up the collar of my long coat, and dash around the back to let Sydney out before anyone sees me. Her street has more foot traffic than mine so I don't want to take any chances by lingering on the sidewalk longer than necessary.

It's absolutely freezing out tonight, the wind having penetrated the thick layers I'm wearing from the five seconds I've been out of the warm car, so it won't seem strange that I'm hurrying her inside. I open her door and lean in to help her out. She looks bewildered by my hasty escape. "I don't want to take you in the back of the car, Sydney. And if we don't stop now, I won't be able to," I grin. She smiles and gratefully accepts my hand and we sprint into her building.

Once we're in the elevator alone, our eyes meet and the lust from the car slams back into me full force. Before she can protest, I move my body up against Sydney's and pin her to the wall. I know she can feel how turned on I am by the hard bulge pressing against her but I don't care. I can't hold back anymore, I *won't* hold back anymore. I've never wanted anyone or anything this much in my life. My hand skims down her side, my fingertips sliding until they reach the bottom of her dress where the soft skin of her thigh is exposed. I grip her leg, then brush my hand up her inner thigh, stopping just short of her panties. I want to touch her there so badly it hurts, but not here in the elevator. Splayed out and naked on her bed, that's how I want Sydney.

I stare into her eyes and see my desire mirrored back in the deep blue, her pupils almost fully dilated. Sydney's chest is heaving in and out with each breath, her soft breasts pressing against my torso. My gaze drops to her full mouth and I lean forward and tug on her lower lip with my teeth and suck on it, reveling in the taste. Sydney reacts the same as she did in the car, as if a switch were flipped.

She moans and her hands slide from my shoulders to my scalp as she grabs fistfuls of my hair, pulling me down to her open mouth. As I delve into her with my tongue, her hands release my hair and move to my ass. Sydney shoves me forward, forcing my hips into hers as she grinds shamelessly on my dick. I let out a deep, guttural groan as she rubs her body up and down the steel rod in my pants.

The elevator dings loudly and doors open on her floor. We reluctantly untangle, both of us panting heavily as we step onto her floor. I know she's as turned on as I am because I watch, amused, as it takes her several tries to get her key in the lock. Once inside, Sydney unceremoniously throws her purse and her coat on the floor and fixes her dark gaze on me. For a second, my breath catches and I freeze, completely absorbed by the look on her face, one of pure lust and determination. Without breaking eye contact, I slowly remove my coat and toss it on top of hers, my heart racing in my chest as I keep an outwardly stoic façade. Sydney holds out her hand and I take it, letting her lead me into her bedroom.

We should probably wait, get to know each other better and let the passion burn until there's more to this than physical attraction. But this electricity between us? It's too strong for either of us to resist. Maybe it's already more than just an attraction. It seems as if we've gone zero to sixty in the span of a week, making this moment feel right, more right than I've felt in a long time.

Sydney confidently strides across the dimly lit room and my eyes are glued to her swaying backside. She stops in front of a wall of floor to ceiling windows and I force myself to look at the rest of her to see what she's doing. I groan and clench my jaw, watching the way her dress clings to her flawless body makes me want to bend her over and fuck her against the glass.

Shit, I need to calm down or this will be over before it starts.

Still clenching my jaw, hoping to be able to control myself, I move behind her and gather up her long, silken hair, and place it over her shoulder to expose her slender neck. When I brush my lips across the exposed skin, she shivers and presses her tight ass back into my uncomfortably hard dick and a wave of her complex and intoxicating scent hits me. I have to have her … now.

"Sydney," I whisper in her ear as I push gently on her hips and turn her around to face me. Her chin up, eyes locked with mine, she reaches up and undoes my tie, seductively pulling it out and tossing it aside, never looking away from my face. I trace my hands up her body and stop, gently teasing her firm breasts through the silky fabric of her microscopic dress, working her nipples until they become tight then reach around and unzip the dress tantalizingly slow, letting it flutter to the ground at her feet.

Sydney is standing in the soft glow of the windows, the city behind her providing just enough light to see everything in the room clearly, bathing us in an ethereal haze. My gaze is glued to the impossibly stunning girl in front of me. She's wearing only a tiny black lace bra, little black lace shorts and mile high stiletto shoes. I didn't think my dick could get any harder, but it does. It's aching as it strains against the confinement of my clothes.

"Jesus, Sydney." I hurry to unbutton my shirt, itching to touch her. "You're so fucking beautiful." My head is spinning from looking at her, from being close to her.

She steps out of the small pile of black fabric and reaches out to help me get my shirt off. Her hands are shaking, just enough to let me know that the confidence she displays is a front, she's as nervous as me. I help her undo the buttons, not wanting to let uncertainty creep in.

Once my shirt undone and tossed aside, Sydney greedily slides her hands all over my chest and abs, mapping out every ridge. Thank god I've kept myself in good shape, anything else would pale in comparison to her tight, toned body. I groan and reach under her curved backside, lifting her hips to cradle my cock. She understands what I want and eagerly wraps her long legs around my waist and her arms around my neck, holding on tight. I kiss her like she's the only fucking woman on earth, and I think for me, she really is the only woman on earth. The only woman, period.

I gradually make my way over to the bed with Sydney clinging to me, grinding herself down on my straining cock, our mouths sealed together and our tongues probing. I turn and sit down on the edge of the bed, keeping her straddling me and continuing to kiss her deeply as she digs her sharp heels into my back. Fuck, I need to slow down or I'm going to come in my pants like a teenager.

"You're so perfect. Do you have any idea what you're doing to me?" I murmur against her lips as I pull back and hook my finger into the lace of her bra, yanking down one side to expose her swollen breast. Leaning down, I take the stiff peak into my mouth, circling it with my tongue and nipping at it with my teeth as she shifts on my lap and her breathing grows heavier, more urgent.

"Drew, I need you," she pants and writhes on me like she's going to lose it any second. I smile at her responsiveness, so fucking sexy. I move to the other breast, tugging the cup down with my teeth and sucking her tight pink bud until she begs. "Please."

She's got me too wound up. I can't deny myself any longer, not if she's going to beg. The decision made, I lift her up and set her on the bed, standing to remove the rest of my clothes. Sydney eagerly moves toward me and starts stroking my cock through my pants. Shit, I'll come if she does that.

"Jesus, Sydney, you're killing me."

She smiles wickedly and before I can protest, she jerks down my zipper and unleashes my painful erection, working her hand up and down the hard shaft. I throw my head back and suck in a sharp breath, all rational thought disintegrating from her touch. When I feel her tongue touch the end of my dick, I snap back to the present and drop my head to watch. It takes more self-control than I thought I had in me to put a hand out to stop her.

"No. I won't last if you do that. I want to be inside you."

Sydney reluctantly releases me and leans back on the bed, devouring me with her eyes as I do the same to her. I reach into my pocket and grab a condom, tossing it onto the sheets next to her, smirking at her surprised response. I'm always prepared, she'll learn that soon enough.

I put a knee on the bed and yank her toward me by her ankles, her body sliding easily across the sheets until her ass is on the edge of the bed. Slowly, I remove each sexy shoe and drop it to the floor, letting my hands linger on her soft skin. Then I kneel on the floor and lean in, pressing my face to her wet lace shorts, inhaling her sweet scent as I graze my mouth across her clit through the thin fabric.

"I don't think you need these either. Do you?" I ask as I grasp her tiny lace shorts at her hips and tug them down. Before she can say anything I tilt her hips to me and taste her like I've wanted to do since the minute I first saw her. Fuck, she's waxed bare and her pussy is the most addictive thing I've ever experienced.

Sydney bucks off the mattress as my tongue flicks and probes. She moans my name as I discover every trembling inch of flesh. God, she's fucking intoxicating. A quick glance up nearly does me in, she's watching me with heavy eyelids and parted lips, panting as I fuck her with my mouth.

I want to see her come completely undone, I *need* it. It's such an unbelievable turn on that she's so aroused and a very vocal lover. I thrust one finger into her tight heat, then add another, massaging the rough spot just inside. Sydney is thrashing around as I fuck her with my hand and gently swirl my tongue across her clit. She's so responsive, letting the moment consume her, that I have to pin her down with my other arm and press my fingers into her hips so she can't squirm out from under me. When she comes, she convulses around my fingers and makes some of the most erotic noises I've ever heard in my life.

When she finally collapses back on the bed, I remove my fingers and free her from my torture. She's without a doubt the most responsive lover I've ever had. Watching her shudder and scream as I bring her to climax has me as hard as steel, drops of pre-come dripping from my cock already.

I climb up on the bed next to her as she's catching her breath. "Sydney, that was the fucking hottest thing I've ever seen." She's so beautiful when she comes apart for me, I could lick her for hours just so I can watch her come again and again. She says nothing, instead, reaching up, she grabs my head and crushes her mouth to mine, plunging her tongue deep.

Sydney stops and pulls back, looking into my eyes, still trying to catch her breath. "That was the hottest thing I've ever felt."

She brazenly reaches across the bed for the condom, never breaking eye contact as she tears open the foil with her teeth and rolls it onto my throbbing cock. Having her hands on my dick unleashes a primitive growl from deep in my throat and I curl my hands into the sheets to keep from coming before we've begun. Once she has me ready and thankfully releases me from her tight grip, I grab her hands and pin them over her head, staring into her lustful gaze as I slowly sink into her warmth.

Incoherent noises escape from both of us and I moan. Again, I have to hold back from coming on the spot, squeezing my eyes shut and concentrating so I don't look like an asshole by only lasting two seconds. "Fuck, this is going to be quick babe, you feel too good," I admit to her. No amount of jerking off has prepared me for the blissful feeling of being deep in her wet tight sex, having her arms wrapped around me, and her body underneath mine.

Our eyes still locked, I catch the intensity of her blue eyes, feel the expanding passionate connection between us as I begin to move. "Wrap your legs around me," I demand, my voice hoarse from the effort it's taking to control my orgasm. Sydney lifts her legs to circle my waist as requested, hooking her ankles behind me, urging me on as I thrust faster and harder, driving us to our goal.

When she starts moaning and bucking beneath me, I know that she's close and I won't last much longer. Her convulsing pussy is gripping me harder with each stroke, the slick heat pulling at my cock until my balls become heavy and tight. I rotate my hips in a circle and she falls over the edge, crying out my name as she detonates around my cock.

I mutter an incoherent string of expletives as I finally let go and allow myself to join Sydney, exploding in a mind blowing orgasm that sends hot streaks of pleasure up and down my spine.

My head drops to her shoulder and my full weight rests on her trembling body, I'm so completely drained, I can't hold myself up an longer. After a minute, I remember to let go of her hands and prop up on my elbows so I can see her gorgeous face.

Sweaty and flushed, Sydney pulls me back down close and presses her soft, swollen lips to mine, locking me against her body with her arms and legs. I don't want the condom to spill out into her so I gently unwind from her grip and roll off of her to get rid of it. "I have to take care of this," I explain as I tie the used condom into a knot. I respect her way to much too accidentally knock her up. Not that I wouldn't give my left nut to fuck her bare, but that's beside the point.

After tossing the condom in the trash, I wash my hands and stare in the bathroom mirror. I'm surprised to see I look … happy.

Fucking thrilled, actually. Feelings I never expected to have are crammed into my head and start to overflow. I want to curl up in bed with Sydney and hold her close all night, protect her from the shit that keeps her from sleeping.

What the hell is happening to me? Usually after sex, the girl leaves my hotel room or trailer and I go back to work or pass out and sleep alone. This? This isn't a situation I'm familiar with or at all comfortable with, but I'm determined to see where it goes.

I run my hands through my hair and wonder if she'll let me stay over. *That's funny.* Isn't it always the guy trying to leave while the girl clings to him? That's something I avoid at all costs, now I've turned into such a pussy over this girl that I barely recognize myself. Shit, only one way to find out how she feels. I turn off the light and head back into the bedroom.

Sydney is lying back on the bed with the sheet pulled up, chewing thoughtfully on her bottom lip in the dark room. She seems preoccupied. Hopefully, it's not about how to get me the hell out of her house. She's not dressed and throwing my clothes at me, so I take that as a good sign. I climb under the covers and pull her to me, tucking her soft curves against my body. It's been so long since I've shared a bed with someone, I'm surprised at how perfectly she fits in my arms.

She seems distant, the sexy, confident woman from earlier is gone. *Crap.* I have to ask her. "Is it okay if I stay?" She doesn't say anything. Fuck, she wants me to leave. "I mean, I don't have to if …"

Sydney interrupts me and quietly speaks, her soft voice carrying in the quiet room. "I want you to stay, Drew."

My body, tense from anticipating rejection, relaxes instantly with her permission to stay.

"Good," is all I can think of to say. I sigh and gently kiss her neck until I feel her body unwind against me and her breathing slow into a deep, rhythmic pattern. Once I'm certain that she's asleep, I let myself drift off, holding her to me all night.

CHAPTER 7

It's early. Really early. I never have been one to sleep late. I would have thought that the extraordinary sex would have knocked me out for a good twelve hours, but here it is, 6am and I'm wide awake. Sydney is still asleep next to me, her hair a dark sheet across her pillow in the shadows of the early morning. Even with very little light, I can see her gorgeous face. Her perfect mouth, slightly parted as she gently breathes in and out. Her long lashes against her pale cheeks, occasionally fluttering in her dreams.

I resist the urge to touch her. I need to let her sleep. She didn't complain when I woke her up in the middle of the night and had my way with her again. It was slower, less frantic than our first time. I wanted to appreciate every touch, every stroke into her. If I wake her up again, she may not be as pleased.

I get up to look for my clothes and frown, forgetting that I only have my suit, which is currently balled up on the floor in a wrinkled heap. Sighing as I drag my hands over my face, I put on my boxer briefs, grab a blanket off of the end of the bed, and head out to the living area. It's cold out today, my bare feet are instantly turned to ice on the hardwood floor.

I need hot coffee, and a change of clothes. I also forgot she has no television so I should get a newspaper to read while she sleeps. But Jane's out of town so I can't call her like I usually would. I head back into the bedroom to fish my phone out of my pants pocket and dial up Bruce as I quietly walk back out and settle onto the couch with the blanket covering everything but my face. *Fuck, it's freezing!* Bruce answers after three rings, and from the sound of the shifting and scuffling noises, he was dead asleep.

"Sorry to bother you man, I need a favor. Can you get me two coffees from The Village Coffee Bar, a *New York Times*, and a change of clothes and bring them to Sydney's? Her concierge will bring them up. Tell him it's unit 8A."

"Certainly, I can be there in thirty minutes. Would that be okay?" he asks. I can hear the shuffling sound of him getting dressed.

Bruce is a godsend. "Yeah man, thanks so much." I hang up and smile. Now, when Sydney wakes up she'll have a cup of her favorite coffee and I'll have clothes so I won't be a block of ice on her couch. I feel moderately guilty for waking up Bruce, but the thought of making Sydney happy overrides the guilt about two seconds later.

Another shiver wracks my body, I bundle the blanket up tighter around me and decide to check my email while waiting for Bruce. Great, Chad is still nagging me about the *Mind of the Enemy* shoot that starts in a couple of weeks. We've only done five movies together and I've executive produced three more for him and he's flipping his shit over something as trivial as my flight?

Chad, or Thomas C. Sullivan, as the entertainment world knows him, was the director of the very first film I ever did. I've worked with him a lot since, and we've become very good friends. I know he's just pestering me to get under my skin, he loves to watch me lose my shit. I stab out a response to his whining.

To: Chad Sullivan <sullythetully@surgefilms.com>
From: Drew Forrester <bigdtrees@bigdtreesproductions.com>
What the hell dude? Do you have PMS or something? Jane is getting my flight today and sending you the info. You need a vacation before we start this shoot, because I'm not hanging out with you for six weeks if you're going to be on the rag the whole time. I'll be there, don't worry your little head over me. Just show up with your fancy cameras and shit and direct this thing. I want a shiny golden naked man statue to round out my bunch.
D

Interestingly, I get an almost immediate response to my email. It's what, 3am in L.A.? Why is he checking his email?

To: Drew Forrester <bigdtrees@bigdtreesproductions.com>
From: Chad Sullivan <sullythetully@surgefilms.com>
Unwind your panties, pretty boy! The studio head is breathing down my neck for your shit. I shouldn't have to hold your hand, this isn't your first rodeo. And I definitely think I can make you look good enough to get one of those little gold men, I mean, I already have 4 myself, so I guess it's your turn. And FYI, I'm currently on vacation at my perfect house on St. Bart's. It's my last day here so I'm living it up and don't want any more calls about you from the boss. Jealous of my vacay??
Chad

He included an attached picture of his view from a lounge chair on a hill overlooking a brilliant turquoise bay. Of course, you can see his mangy white feet at the end of the chair in front of a sparkling infinity pool. What a dick, I haven't been on a vacation in what feels like forever and he knows it. Suddenly inspired, I type out another email to Chad.

> To: Chad Sullivan <sullythetully@surgefilms.com>
> From: Drew Forrester <bigdtrees@bigdtreesproductions.com>
> Tell you what, big shot director. Let this poor exhausted working man use your house this coming weekend and I'll not only win myself an Oscar, but I'll make you look like the fucking genius that you always profess to be and get you another one too.
> D

The thought of Sydney with me on St. Bart's for a weekend, lounging by Chad's pool in a bikini is tempting. Several days of just me and her and no interruptions or time apart, she'd have to let me get to know something about her. My email alerts me to another response from Chad.

> To: Drew Forrester <bigdtrees@bigdtreesproductions.com>
> From: Chad Sullivan <sullythetully@surgefilms.com>
> Deal. You can even use my jet to get there and my boat. It's new so don't fuck it up, the boat not the jet. Just show up in LA in a good mood, and don't let

your pretty face get sunburned. The execs will lose their shit! Call me later and
we'll hammer out the details, right now I'm going to go sit in my hot tub.

  Chad

  Perfect, now I just have to convince Sydney go with me. A text alert lets me know that Bruce just dropped off my stuff and the concierge is probably on the way up. I step over to the foyer and crack the front door to keep him from knocking and waking up Syd. An older man steps off of the elevator a second later with two cups of coffee and a duffel bag from my house.

  He seems surprised when he sees me. Well, I'm sure he wasn't expecting Andrew Forrester to answer the door. Then I remember that I'm only wearing my underwear and that pretty much explains the strange look I'm getting. A famous movie star answering the door in his skivvies. This probably makes his top ten list of weirdest moments.

  I know Bruce tipped him well for me so I kindly ask him to forget about seeing me here. "You won't mention this to anyone, right?"

  The concierge looks affronted. "We are quite discreet here at The Greenwich Tower, I assure you, Mr. Forrester. Our residents and their guests enjoy complete privacy. In fact, this conversation didn't happen." He smiles and pushes the button to go back down to the lobby.

  Stunned, I close the door behind me with my foot so I won't spill the coffees. *Well, that was easy.* I hope complete privacy includes not telling Sydney that he spoke with the famous Andrew Forrester in the doorway of her loft. I bring one of the cups of coffee to the bedroom and place it on the nightstand for Sydney and take a few quick gulps of the other one, letting the hot drink warm me up enough to move around without the blanket.

The rest of the stuff I bring into the bathroom with me and take a scalding hot shower and brush my teeth. Bruce packed my toothbrush even though I didn't think to ask for it. I'm willing to bet that he called Jane to ask her what to put in my bag. If he did, I'm sure I'll hear about it from her later. Not only is it the middle of the night in L.A., but I haven't spent the night with a woman in all the years that Jane's known me, and she's sure to have a million questions.

As I leave the bedroom, I scoop up my discarded suit and shove it into the duffel bag, then make my way into the kitchen, grinning like an idiot. The coffee keeps me warm as I get out a plate for the croissants that Bruce so kindly included with our drinks, and put everything on the kitchen table and sit so I can read the paper. It's sometimes difficult, but I try to keep up with current events when I'm in town. When I'm on location or in L.A. it's just about impossible, early call times and late nights make reading anything but a script a luxury.

I pull the newspaper out of the bag and unfold it and realize that this is the *New York Post*, not the *Times*. Crap, well, Bruce isn't an assistant, and everything else was perfect so I can't blame him. I look at the clock. It's not quite seven. I can't wake Sydney yet. Great, I open the *Post* and start to read the sports section, but it's just a quick scan. The Pats are out of the playoffs so I'm not interested in football news. Baseball doesn't start for two more months and I can't stand basketball or hockey even though the Celtics and the Bruins are both great teams.

I finish both the News and the Metro sections and move on to the Entertainment section. Surprisingly, there's a small mention about my upcoming movie, *A Soldier's Burden*. Unfortunately, it's accompanied by the photo taken with the two girls I met in the street after leaving Sydney's loft the other night.

I scan the caption, *"Actor Andrew Forrester poses with fans in NYC's West Village"*.

Isn't that just wonderful? I scowl at the photo in disgust. You can't trust anyone to keep anything private.

I'm still stewing over the picture when Sydney walks into the kitchen, looking absolutely radiant. She makes the awkward, post-sex disheveled look seem easy to achieve, perfect skin, tousled hair, slight beard burn on her chin and swollen lips, my dick starts to take notice.

Shit, the photo of me is front and center on the table. I scoop up the newspaper, hastily folding it and tossing it far enough across the table that Sydney can't reach it. Standing, I pull her in for a kiss. "Good morning."

She looks around at everything spread out in her kitchen. "Well, you've been busy." Then her head tilts to the side in confusion, her brow furrowed as she studies the table. "How did you get out of my loft and back in without waking me for the key?"

Okay, now I feel stupid. Normal guys don't have newspapers and coffee and bags of clothes delivered to them, I should have thought of that. "Oh, I didn't. I had someone pick up the pastries and coffee and bring them to your lobby. Your concierge brought them up," I admit to her, somewhat embarrassed.

"Oh." *Oh?* What does that mean? "Well, thanks." Sydney picks up a croissant and takes a big bite. Her sharp gaze finds the wadded up *Post*. "Did they bring the paper as well?"

Crap. I have to distract her so she won't ask to see it. "Yes. Did you sleep well?" I look right into her deep blue eyes, willing her to talk to me.

"Except for when you woke me up in the middle of the night like a horny teenager, I slept like a rock. Which is actually unusual for me."

Holy shit, it worked! Although, she seems displeased to have spoken so openly. Me? I'm ecstatic to have been thrown a crumb of information, accident or not.

I try to continue the dialogue, hoping to learn more about her. "You have trouble sleeping?" I'm not surprised, given how many secrets she seems to harbor. Hiding all that shit and keeping it inside would give anyone a bad case of insomnia.

"Ummmm, well, yes …" she doesn't want to talk about it, that's obvious, her eyes shift around the room, not meeting mine directly. "I sometimes have bad dreams, but really, it's not a big deal." The casual shrug she throws in is stilted and stiff and not at all convincing.

Bullshit it's not a big deal. But she didn't have nightmares last night. Maybe I'll have to sleep with her every night to keep them away.

I tap my finger to my lips. "Hmmm. Maybe we've found a cure for your problem." I blatantly check her out in her tiny little robe, her pert nipples visible through the thin fabric, and think of everything I could do to help her sleep better.

Adorably, a deep crimson creeps up her neck. She's embarrassed by my flirting. I can't help but laugh, she's so endearing. I haven't met a woman who feels emotions like self-consciousness in a really long time. Usually, I'm surrounded by overly confident Barbie dolls that I want to ditch as quickly as humanly possible. She's such a refreshing change from all that phony crap. "Sydney, your reactions always surprise me." My eyes flick down to the table, where her arms are resting. "How's your arm? It looks good."

She immediately stiffens and tucks her arm under the table. "It's fine."

Okay... She doesn't want me to ask about that other scar again. The one that freaked her out when I mentioned it at the gym.

A glance at my phone shows that it's already later than I thought and I realize that I should go soon. I have to call Chad and arrange for next weekend, and I don't want to overstay my welcome. Sydney eyes me inquisitively as I stand and walk around the table so I can kneel down next to her chair and take her hand in mine. "I have to get going, when can I see you again?"

Sydney answers without her usual caution. "I have no projects lined up, and I'm just waiting for my current client to call to start work, so I'm fairly open in the next few weeks." Then she shrinks back, as if she caught herself telling me too much too soon.

"I'll call you later today, okay? I need to get home and check some things on my calendar." I lean in and brush my lips across her inviting pink mouth several times before I stand up, remembering to snatch the *Post* off of the table before I go. I retrieve my duffel bag from the floor and head toward the foyer, Sydney trailing behind.

As I shrug on my coat she stops me, holding up a hand to keep me in place. "Wait here," she says with a mischievous smirk. She ducks into the living room and comes back just as quickly. "A gift, I don't want to take a chance losing our luck." My Red Sox hat is balanced precariously on her outstretched palms, as if she's trying not to let it touch too much of her skin, which is probably exactly what she's doing.

Amused by her disgust for my favorite hat, I give her my biggest grin, take it from her hands, and shove it on my head, pulling it down low. Might as well get my costume ready now for when I hit the street.

"Me neither. Sydney, I'll call you later." I spin the brim around so I can lean in and get one more taste of her before I leave. As usual, she doesn't disappoint.

CHAPTER 8

"Chad, what's up? When did you get to the Caribbean? Last I heard you were still scouting sites with Lou for the shoot."

I have my calendar pulled up on my laptop, which took thirty minutes of Jane explaining over the phone to get me to the right place. So, I'm not a computer whiz, what does it matter? I usually do everything from my phone, but it's easier to see my work schedule on the larger laptop screen instead of the teeny-tiny one.

Chad is clearly in an open top car, the wind roaring around as I speak to him. "I got here six days ago! I pushed some stuff off onto Lou so I could visit this fabulous home I own but only get to use every two years or so!" Damn, he's yelling since he's having trouble hearing me. "Sorry, I'm on my way to the airport! Convertible, you know?" Yeah, I figured.

Lou Pierce is the EP, or executive producer for the *Mind of the Enemy*, the film we're shooting in California. Chad and Lou formed their production company, Surge Films, fifteen years ago when they couldn't find anyone willing to finance their first project, *Upsidedown*. Their unwanted film turned into the darling of the Sundance Film Festival that year and Surge Films is now worth an estimated $300 million.

"Lou must be thrilled," I say dryly. "Anyway, what's up with the house? You change your mind yet about letting me use it?"

"Why, you're not going to bring fifty of your closest friends and have a raging weekend-long kegger are you?" I hear the amusement in his voice. He knows me pretty well and is quite aware that not only would I *not* want to be around fifty people for more than a few hours, but that 'raging keggers' are not exactly my style.

"You got me, Chad. I guess I'd better change my plans," I laugh at him. "Actually, I'm bringing a girl. Just me and her, and I need a little help."

"Huh? You? You're bringing a girl on a weekend vacation?" He bursts out in hysterics. "No really, what are you doing this weekend?"

Nice, he doesn't believe me. So what if I'm not known for my long term relationships, he doesn't have to be an ass about it.

"Chad, I'm serious. I think I found the girl I'm going to marry." I'm not sure what possessed me to say that out loud, or even to think it. But somehow I know, I *have* found her. It's nothing specific about her that I can explain, it's just *her*. I just have to get Sydney to feel the same way. Go big or go home, right? That's what I've always said to myself and I'm not going to change now. That still doesn't explain why I'm telling this to Chad like we're two teenage girls gossiping at a sleepover.

"I'm speechless, Drew. If it's true, then I'm happy for you man. Really." I know he's being sincere. This isn't like me at all, so I'm well aware that it's probably blowing his mind.

"Thanks, there's just one thing." I enlighten to Chad on the Sydney situation and explain that I need him to clear his place of anything related to the film industry. After he finishes laughing his ass off at me, he agrees to call his caretaker and have him move all of his personal items to the locked office.

I hang up with Chad and put my head in my hands, praying that his guy doesn't miss anything at the house. I can't ruin this with Sydney. My plan is to make sure she falls for me before she finds out who I am and what I do. Not my best idea, but it's all I have until she's willing to tell me what her issues are with fame and magazines and televisions.

There's a ton of stuff that needs to get done, so I turn to my work laptop and click on the email icon. Three days without an assistant and my life is already a mess. I have no clue where to begin. Jane will be back later this afternoon, and I'm looking forward to having her taking care of all this shit for me.

How she does all this every day is beyond my comprehension. I have about a million emails in my work inbox, there's over ten voicemails on my work phone, and a huge stack of scripts that I have to go through is sitting on my desk.

Fuck this.

I stand up and head for my bedroom to change. I'm going to the gym to hit something.

After sparring with Damien for an hour and a half, my head is ringing and I'm drenched in sweat, but it's still better than slogging through hours of emails. The bastard hit me harder than he usually does, still pissed about the ass kicking I gave him yesterday.

"Forrester, drinks tomorrow night? I'll buy since you got your ass handed to you in the ring." He's just as sweaty as I am and sticks it to me like the poor winner he always is.

I sit on a bench and towel off my face. "Sure, why not?" Then I glare up at Damien to see him smirking at me. "By the way, you're a dick. If you'd have busted my nose, I'd get sued for breach of contract."

That motherfucker laughs. He thinks it's so goddamn funny that I make my living partially because of my looks. Not everyone can be like him and have their nose broken four times in the cage and receive a paycheck for it each time.

"Sorry, Drew. I couldn't help myself." Damien takes a long drink of his water and then dumps the rest on his closely cropped hair. He doesn't look or sound sorry at all. "You were out of it today. Where the fuck was your head at?"

"How about I tell you about it later? I need a shower. I can smell myself from here." I gather my stuff to leave.

"Okay dude, tomorrow at six at The Hub? Bobby wants to go out. The Packers play the Chargers." He puts his fist out and I bump it with mine then smack the back of his head before he can react.

"Hey!"

"That's for being an ass," I tell him, ducking out of the way of his tightly wound towel as he snaps it at me.

The Hub is a dumpy little sports bar near the piers that we frequent. They show all of the games and have about a hundred different beers on tap.

"Six, okay. See ya there. I'll be the asshole in the Red Sox hat and the ridiculous wig." Damien laughs so hard that he's still going at it as I leave the gym. Dick.

My phone beeps as I get into the car and I see that Sydney texted me. She initiated contact? That's a first.

Sydney <Hey, stuck in hell at Bergdorf's with Leah. Can't wait for tonight.>

I smile. She's so radically different from every other woman I've ever known. What girl doesn't live for a day of shopping at high end department stores? I type out a response and hit send.

Me <Only you would think Bergdorf's is hell. Bring your appetite tonight! The car will get you at six.>

Now to impress Miss Sydney Allen enough to get her to say yes to St. Bart's.

CHAPTER 9

I can't believe I'm nervous for a date. Incredibly nervous actually. As nervous as I was the first time I stood in front of a camera and the director yelled *"action"*. Everything is ready for Sydney to arrive, so now I'm stuck waiting around with nothing to do except freak the fuck out.

I still have about fifteen more minutes until Bruce drops her off so I use the time to do a quick double check of the house to be sure that I didn't miss any movie paraphernalia. Earlier, I gathered up all of my books, scripts, photos … everything and threw them all in a huge pile on the couch in the office. I'm finishing the final sweep when my phone buzzes from my pocket,

Bruce *<Pulling onto your street>*

Sydney is here. I hurry downstairs so she doesn't have to stand on my doorstep in the glacial cold and open the door just as she steps up to the front landing. Bruce gives me a nod and takes off for the night.

I drink in Sydney's beauty as though I haven't seen her in months instead of days. "Hey, you look gorgeous. Please come in." She's the first girl I've ever had in my home and it feels right having her here, as though all of the pieces in my life are finally falling into place.

Her bright blue eyes are wide as she surveys the entryway to my brownstone. "Thanks, this is beautiful, Drew."

Unable to wait any longer, I pull her against me and lower my mouth to hers, tasting her sweet lips. The smell of oranges and flowers and Sydney surrounds me, making me forget myself for a moment and I deepen the kiss. *Manners, Forrester.* It's not very chivalrous to attack her in the foyer while she's still wearing her coat.

"Sorry, I couldn't wait to do that. I've been thinking about kissing you all day." I help her out of her coat, hang it on a hook, and hold out my hand to lead her up the stairs. "Come, I have wine chilling. We can drink while I finish dinner." She follows me up to the first floor, which is comprised almost exclusively by the kitchen.

I head over to the food prep area and watch Sydney check out the room. She's behaving similarly to the night in the private dining room; viewing each individual piece of furniture, every cabinet, each framed piece of art with an analytical eye. When she's done, I pull out a barstool for her and she sits down willingly. I quickly fill two wine glasses and hand her one over the huge granite island. "I hope you like filet."

Sydney starts to get up to join me by the stove. "I love it. It smells wonderful in here. What can I do to help?"

No way is she cooking for a date at my house, I stop her by holding up a hand before she can move. "I've got everything. I want you to sit there and we can talk while I finish up." If she's trapped, and I'm busy, she'll have to do all of the talking. That's my pathetic plan anyway.

Surprisingly, it turns out that my plan isn't all that pathetic. She tells me about shopping with Leah at Bergdorf's. Now I understand why she said it was painful, Leah is pretty horrific to shop with if Sydney's description is even half as bad as it really was.

While I continue prepping our dinner, putting out plates and dishing up the salad, Sydney takes sips of her wine as she talks, loosening up even more. When she explains that she's the interior designer for the Warren nightclub remodel, everything comes together for me. The mention in *GQ* by Adam, her appreciation for the room at the Sunset House, the way she looked around my kitchen, all of it makes sense.

That fucking bastard Adam Reynolds trying to hustle an invite to the party with Sydney really pisses me off. My best acting performance to date is keeping the disgust off of my face as Sydney describes the nightclub while I'm fantasizing turning Reynolds' smug face into pulpy mess.

I take a seat next to Sydney at the island and tell her about shopping for the steaks at an awesome butcher shop at Chelsea Market that buys only local, grass fed meat. I'm careful not to mention the part where one of the patrons freaked out when she noticed me and caused a huge crowd to swarm around like locusts. It took me an hour to get the hell out of there. I'll let Jane continue to arrange my shopping from now on.

Sydney says she doesn't cook, which is fine by me because I've been doing it for a while. It's hard to keep yourself entertained when you're pretty much stuck in your house for fear of causing a riot every time you step outside. I keep sneaking glances at her as she eats her dinner, ridiculously pleased that she likes my cooking.

When we finish, I place the dirty dishes by the sink and hold out my hand. She takes it and I lead her up another flight of stairs to the main living room. Now that I know she's an interior designer, I expect her to evaluate everything in the room, but of course she surprises me again.

Sydney heads straight for the back wall of my brownstone which is made almost entirely of glass. It cost a fortune to have it specially tinted so no one can see in, but it's worth every penny. Even when it's dark out and the interior lights are on like they are now, it's impossible to see into the house.

"You have a view of the Empire State Building!" she squeals as she looks outside. Then just as quickly her voice gets softer. "I love looking out at the city. It relaxes me. I could sit in this room and look at this view all day."

I'm staring at the complex girl in my living room. She's gorgeous and shy, exuberant then disillusioned, fascinating but secretive, simple to please yet the most complicated person I've ever met. I think if I watch her carefully for long enough, I may eventually figure her out.

She says she loves the view out the window? I love the view in front of me. "Me too," I respond to her statement.

Sydney turns with a huge smile on her face. When she sees that I'm staring at her and not at the city, she flushes crimson and drops her eyes to the ground. Again, her reactions astonish me. What girl doesn't love a compliment? Most women fish around for them endlessly. Sydney? She gets embarrassed and changes the subject.

She walks over to the wall of books that I own, assessing each volume. She's trying to figure me out the same way I attempted to do at her loft, getting answers without having to ask the questions. Unlike her, I'll answer pretty much anything she asks me.

Sydney takes a step closer to the fireplace where I have several photographs displayed. Quietly, I move behind her and pull her back against my front, wrapping my arms around her small frame. I know she'll never ask me straight up, but she's probably dying to know, so I point at the first three photos and explain. "My sister, Allie, and my parents."

She nods, and takes a step to the left to see the last picture. I move with her, unwilling to go without the warmth and soft feel of her body as I explain the final photo. "Meeting Red Sox catcher Trevor Caldwell at Fenway Park. That was a great day." I leave out the part where I threw out the opening pitch at the game.

Her curiosity squelched for now, Sydney turns in my arms to face me and I can see a mischievous glint in her eyes. She takes my hand and guides me over to the huge sectional sofa that is in front of the fireplace and windows. Sydney places her glass of wine on the end table and lightly pushes on my chest, implying that I should sit down. I fight my natural instinct to take over and instead, I do what she wants, interested in seeing where she's going with this. When she climbs on top of my lap and threads her hands in my hair, I not only know what she has in mind, I'm instantly hard as a rock.

"Sydney," I groan as she gives my scalp a sharp tug and a fire begins to burn inside me. I wrap my hands around her waist and drag her hips back and forth across my lap, desperate for some kind of friction to relieve the pressure of my hard dick straining against my jeans.

Sydney takes in a sharp breath and frantically attempts to remove my shirt, the uninhibited girl that I saw after our date at the Sunset House is back and ready to be let out. I release her waist and reach back to grab the back of my collar, yanking it off in one fluid motion. Once the fabric barrier is gone, Sydney bows her head and glides her soft tongue across my chest and up my neck, murmuring my name, sending sparks shooting down my spine and into my groin.

The need to touch her skin overwhelms my thoughts as my cock throbs under her wanton movements. I push her away and rid her of her T-shirt and bra, not thinking rationally enough to do anything except get her naked as fast as possible.

"Christ. So fucking gorgeous, Syd. You drive me insane. I want to be inside you every minute of the day," I tell her, dragging my hands over her soft curves. I dive in to taste her aroused peaks, drawing one into my mouth and raking my teeth over it. Sydney writhes in my lap, making me even closer to the edge of losing control. Using intense concentration to hold myself steady, I move my mouth to the other tight bud and greedily circle it with my tongue.

"I want to pleasure you in every way, Sydney," I groan against her flushed skin. With my hand and mouth, I torture both of her sensitive nipples as she grinds against the denim of my jeans. Neither of us stops until Sydney comes loudly and uninhibited on top of me.

Fuck! She just wiped my mind clear of every other woman I've ever been with. So fucking responsive. After this, there will only ever be images of Sydney when I think of sex. To let her rest, I trail delicate kisses up to her collarbone and find her parted mouth, brushing my lips across hers as she catches her breath.

"That was incredible, and definitely a first for me," she pants.

Good, because the thought of anyone else touching her like that makes the edges of my vision haze over with streaks of red.

Wanting more than this intense physical connection, I lock eyes with her and tell her exactly how I feel, "I'd like to have a lot of firsts with you, Sydney."

My words cause her pupils to dilate and she lowers her lashes seductively, causing the fire in me to ignite hotter than a blowtorch. Heat floods every inch of my skin as my heart pumps faster with each brush of her fingers against me. I slide my hand behind her head and force her mouth to mine, claiming it aggressively as our teeth and tongues crash together. My only goal is getting both of us naked immediately. I grip her ass and lift her up, placing her back down on the sofa so I can stand and strip off my pants.

Before I can begin to undress, Sydney hooks her fingers into the belt loops of my jeans and roughly jerks my hips toward her. The wicked smile on her face causes every drop of blood in my body to drain into my cock, swelling even more painfully against the thick fabric.

"I want to taste you, Drew," she moans. She opens her gorgeous mouth and uses her teeth to stroke down the rigid bulge in the front of my jeans.

"Jesus." My head involuntarily arches back as electricity hums through my body, possessed by the inferno she's stoking. I don't notice that Sydney has unzipped my pants until her hot, wet mouth wraps around my dick.

My head snaps up to the incredible sight of her luscious lips wrapped around my cock, eagerly tasting every inch of me. "Fuck, Sydney." This girl is going to unman me, I can't watch this but I can't turn away either, I'm mesmerized, watching my dick disappear between those lips.

Sydney trails her hands around my backside to grip my ass and thrusts my hips forward and backward, forcing me deeper and deeper down her throat with each shove. God, she wants me to fuck her mouth, *holy shit!* When she pulls all the way out and swirls her tongue around the swollen head, I shudder from the strain of holding back.

"Shit, stop." Sydney complies, letting my disappointed cock fall out of her mouth and she pouts like I've snatched away her favorite toy.

The base need to fuck her is the only thing in my brain, controlling every thought, every movement. I tear off her remaining clothing and then discard my own, and her pout is replaced by a sultry grin. Hurriedly, I remove protection from my pocket and roll it on quickly. I pick a shocked Sydney up and sit in her place on the sofa, pulling her onto my lap facing me and roughly impaling her as I bring her down.

She groans in my ear and I can hardly speak with her wet heat wrapped around me. "Fuck, you're so tight. I love the way you feel."

Then she starts to move, kneeling on either side of my legs, she uses her thighs to raise her hips up and down over mine. With each downward stroke, I grip her waist and slam her down on my cock as far as she can go, dragging long, incoherent words from her parted lips.

Our pace quickly becomes frenzied, both of us already covered in a light sheen of sweat. When she shifts against me one last time, Sydney detonates around my shaft loudly, her orgasm seeming to last forever. I continue to thrust up into her a few more times and follow her in a mind blowing release as I yell out her name.

With the intense pleasure still vibrating through my body, I wrap my arms around her shoulders and pull her to my chest. She lays her head on my heart, breathless from exertion. I brush small kisses on the top of her head, secretly inhaling the intoxicating scent of hair. If I told her I loved her would she freak out and leave? Probably. I'll save that for another time.

Gently lifting her to separate us, I hold her tight and stand, carrying her up the stairs to my bed. Seeing Sydney Allen, naked on my sheets, is a vision that will be forever emblazoned on my memory. She must know that I'm studying every inch of her body, because the corner of her mouth twists up in a knowing smile and she wickedly drags a hand over her breast and down her stomach.

Grinning, I climb on the bed with her, and we make love slowly, pleasuring each other until exhaustion sets in.

CHAPTER 10

I wake up to Sydney burrowing her back into my chest, attempting to get even closer than she already is. Her heart is racing under my palm, which is tucked over her waist and up between her breasts. Is she scared? Dreaming? Does she want to get up and run out of here, thinking she made a mistake? For about the millionth time I wonder what the hell happened to her that made her such a nervous wreck.

Not knowing what else to do, I trail soft kisses across the back of her neck until I feel her physically relax, her body melting into mine. "Good morning," I whisper in her ear.

Sydney wiggles her backside against my hard cock and playfully answers, "Good morning yourself."

Even though she can't see it a broad smile crosses my face, her responses always surprise me but I'm more than happy to play. "Is that how it is?" I ask.

My hand trails down from her chest and I slide it between her legs, finding her wet and willing. "I think you want me again, Miss Allen." I tease her clit, circling it with the tip of my finger. She whimpers and pushes back against me again. I can't think about anything but sinking into her when she's this close to me, let alone naked and grinding her ass into my dick.

Sydney starts protesting as I lean away, reaching behind me to pull a condom from the nightstand. When she sees what I'm doing, she stops and petulantly waits for me to finish. I make quick work of getting it on and return my hand to continue exploring Sydney's slick folds. Impatient, she reaches behind her and grips my length tightly, positioning the head at her opening.

"Fuck!" She cries as I bury in her with one swift move. Continuing to massage her hard nub, I thrust in and out of her from behind, relishing each long stroke. Sydney twists the sheets in her hands and pushes back against each one, anxious for me to go faster. I swing a leg over hers, clamping down to keep her still so I can pound into her even harder, each thrust going as deep as possible and drawing out long, unfiltered moans from her.

At this point, I'm running on instinct and adrenaline, chasing that unbelievable high with Sydney. My brain is so focused on reaching that intense peak that words just start to fall out of my mouth randomly as I speed up my movements. "God, Sydney, I can't get enough of you," I growl as I roughly suckle on her earlobe, not letting up one bit on the relentless pace.

She falls over the edge and I can feel the heat rushing through her every inch of her skin as she clamps down around my needy cock. Blinded by unfamiliar emotions combined with the incredible sensation of being inside her as she comes, I mumble, "I think I love you," as I spill into her sweet depths and fall back onto the bed.

Once I've caught my breath, I toss away the used condom and gather a very limp Sydney in my arms and turn her to face me. Nuzzling her lips and neck I whisper in her ear, "Go away with me."

Her body becomes instantly rigid. *Shit, she's not ready for this.* If that's the case, I really hope she didn't hear my unedited declaration a minute ago.

"What?" Her eyes are wide with panic.

She doesn't trust me enough yet. Somehow, I need her to see that I'm safe for her, that I'd never hurt her, so I explain the situation calmly. "I have time before my next project, you have time before the nightclub needs you, let's go away. A friend of mine has a home in the Caribbean and offered it to us for this coming weekend."

Of course, I can't tell her who my friend is or what he does for a living. What a fucking hypocrite I am, begging her to trust me but omitting the truth at the same time. I feel like a selfish bastard all of a sudden, undeserving of her trust but wanting it more than anything.

I can see her running the options through her mind, her desire to go warring with her fear of… well, of whatever the fuck she's afraid of. My eyes are imploring her to choose me as I wait, practically bursting to scream out that she's going whether she likes it or not, which, most likely, is not the best way to get her to trust me.

She finally speaks, seemingly embarrassed to answer, "Okay. I'll go."

That beautiful but inexplicable blush creeps up her neck and stains her high cheekbones a rosy pink under that adorable smattering of freckles. She's so charming that I can't help but grin. Once again, her reactions astound me. Then, as if she's aware that she never does what I expect, she pokes out her tiny tongue and drags it across my cheek, swirling it in the dimple that marks one side. She must notice my amused expression because she laughs, "I've just been dying to do that."

Fuck, do it all day every day, whatever makes you happy.

"You can do that anytime, babe. Absolutely anytime."

We get up and I make coffee, handing Sydney a cup as she sits on the sofa, looking out at the Empire State Building. Today, the giant gray structure melds with the steel gray sky, becoming all but invisible along the skyline. I take a sip of my coffee and sit next to Sydney.

"So, I have most of the arrangements done for St. Bart's already." Sydney turns and lifts an eyebrow at me accusingly. "Okay, I wasn't overly confident, just hopeful that you would go with me." She smirks and sips from her cup. "We'll leave Thursday morning and come back Monday, does that work for you?"

"I'll have to double check everything on my calendar, but it should be fine," she says. She curls her feet underneath her and leans against my shoulder. I'm so happy that she initiated the contact that I smile, knowing that she can't see me from her spot tucked up next to me.

Syd's wearing one of my T-shirts and a pair of my sweats. She had to roll the waist up three times to keep them up and even now, I'm not certain that they won't fall off. Syd's sexier in my old clothes with no makeup on than most women are when they're all dressed up to go out.

Sitting on my sofa in the dull light of the morning, she looks radiant. Her reddish-brown hair is tangled up in a knot on the top of her head, her smooth, pale skin is flushed with this morning's activities in bed and again in the shower, and I can see the scattering of tiny freckles across the bridge of her pixie like nose. She's absolutely perfect.

"I have a few things to get done in the next few days as well, so just let me know if your schedule is clear and we'll talk later," I say as she snuggles back into my side and makes a contented noise. Yeah, I could do this every day for the rest of my life.

A mere hour later, I find out just how tenacious the seemingly docile Sydney Allen can be and, unfortunately, she gets a peek at just how overbearing I can be when I'm determined.

"Sydney, you're not walking home. I'm not letting you leave here in last night's clothes like some kind of prostitute!"

God, she's so fucking stubborn!

I refuse to kick her out on the street after a night of sex. It's disrespectful, plus I never know when a photographer will decide to stake out my front door. I can't have them approaching her and asking questions, or worse, following her home and staking out *her* front door.

"Drew, you're being ridiculous. Walking two blocks home is no big deal," she says to me calmly as she slides her feet into her shoes and stands in front of me and puts her hands on my hips.

No big deal my ass!

"No! You will most certainly not be doing the walk of shame out of here and onto a busy New York street. Bruce will drive you home. End of story."

I'm having a difficult time restraining my anger. I know I'm too bossy and controlling sometimes, hell, most of the time, but there's no way I'm giving up this fight. I protect what's important to me, I have no intention of making the same mistake that I did ten years ago by not watching out for my girl.

The corner of her mouth quirks up at my demand. "It's not a walk of shame if *I* don't feel shame." She folds her arms defiantly, thinking she's won.

Oh baby, don't play this game with me. You won't win. I step forward and pull her against me, murmuring into her soft hair, "*I'll* feel shame if you walk out of here like that, Sydney." I place a chaste kiss on the top of her head.

Her chest expands against mine right before I hear her sigh. "Fine Drew, you win. When can Bruce be here?"

I smile and bury my face into her neck, inhaling the addictive scent and committing it to memory. "Thank you, Sydney."

CHAPTER 11

The front door slams shut and I hear footsteps stomping up the stairs. Prepared for the worst, I spin around in my office chair and wait for my certain death, staring into the hallway until it appears from the stairway. Jane comes hurtling around the corner and toward me in a flurry of activity and instructions.

"Drew! When am I meeting the woman that completely changed your life in the four measly days that I've been gone?" she shrieks. Her chatter comes to an abrupt halt when she reaches her desk and looks around the room. "Holy cow! What happened in here?"

Her wide eyes scan over the piles of untouched mail, stacks of scripts, and oh yeah, the mess of photos, books and other movie related crap that I threw in here before Sydney came over.

Uh-oh. Disappointing Jane is something I avoid doing, mostly because she tends to make me feel like I'm a ten year-old kid again.

"Ummmm, well… I had to hide all of my industry stuff. And, uh, the mail overwhelmed me so I left it. Plus, I was kind of busy having a life crisis while you were gone." I scratch my head and look up at Jane, hoping to see some sympathy. *Crap, she's glaring at me.* Actually, she looks really pissed.

Jane huffs loudly. "While I'm very happy that you've found some sort of soul mate, Drew, you do realize that the business that is

Andrew Forrester must keep on rolling forward regardless of whether or not you are in love?" She's angrily stacking mail and scripts and shoving them into a bag as she chastises me. "I told you to let me send one of the junior assistants over here while I was gone. This is going to take a few days to sort out. I'll just bring it all home with me."

"Janey, you know I can't stand having anyone in my office except you." I give her my best Andrew Forrester smile. She doesn't fall for it, she never does. Damn, at least big puppy eyes still work on my mom, because Jane is immune to most of my charms.

"Drew, I'm warning you, next time you're bringing in help." She points at me and gives me her patented Jane Hardy, hairy-eyeball, death glare.

I shiver dramatically and hold up my hands in defeat. "Fine, you're right. It's a mess in here. Doesn't housekeeping come today? Maybe they could put all of my shit back where it belongs …"

Jane swoops in and smacks me on the head with a letter. "Stop swearing in front of me, Drew! And no, they don't come today! I'll add it to the list of things I have to do." She shoves aside a stack of books on the couch and sits, looking up at me with a twinkle in her eye. "Now, tell me about this girl."

CHAPTER 12

I make it to The Hub a little earlier than my friends and enjoy a quiet beer. It's always easier to be hidden in a booth and wait twenty minutes than it is to walk through a crowded bar after the game has already started. This way, there's less of a chance of anyone recognizing me and making our day miserable.

"Hey! Drew, what's up?" Damien says as he and Bobby slide into the semi-circular booth across from me and stare.

Bobby busts out laughing once he gets a good look and I know what's coming next. Naturally, he doesn't disappoint. "Nice hair! You look like a total douche." Bobby says this, Every. Single. Time.

"Thanks, asswipe, at least I have hair," I grunt. Bobby shaves his dark head every day. He says it makes him look like a scary fuck and he's right. "You remember the last time I went out and didn't wear it? No way, unless you want to miss the Packers game to pose for a thousand pictures and listen to repeated requests to speak to everyone's favorite uncle on the phone to prove that they really met me."

Bobby is another fighter from Damien's gym we I hang out with and I sometimes spar against. He's just starting in UFC and has done fairly well so far. He loves to mess with me over the stupid shaggy brown wig I wear under my Sox cap, but he always forgets that when I don't wear it, we can't watch the game or even hold a conversation. The steady stream of clingers-on and hopeful women prevents us from having a good time.

"Nah man, thanks for uglifying your pretty self so I can watch my Packers kick some ass." Bobby tugs on his Green Bay hat and smiles.

I laugh and take a swig of my beer. Damn, it's nice to go out and just be myself. Well, myself in a stupid wig and hat, but it's better than the usual house arrest or the boring Hollywood events I have to go to.

"This shit is itchy as hell, so you'd better appreciate it," I respond. Turning to Damien I nod with my chin, "What about you? What's up?"

"No way Drew, you're not getting out of this. I want to know why you let me beat the hell out of you yesterday. Usually, you're more focused. Do you need to go back down to remedial lessons on defending yourself against attacks?" Damien is staring me down with his hands folded on the table and his scar riddled eyebrows knitted together as he waits for my response.

"Hi, I'm Holly and I'll be your server tonight. Can I get you gentlemen something to drink?"

Saved from Damien's inquiry by the waitress.

Holly is clearly completely disgusted by me in my hat and wig. She can barely even glance my way. My 'human repelling' costume as Sydney would call it, is working perfectly. Holly bats her overly made-up eyes at Damien, waiting for his answer.

"Guinness," barks Bobby, without taking his eyes off of the big screen across from our booth where the teams are flipping the coin. "And a big plate of hot wings, sweetheart." He's so charming.

Holly flicks her gaze to Bobby for a split second, then back to Damien, smiling coyly when she makes eye contact with him. "And for you?" she purrs, stepping a little closer to Damien.

He looks at me and smirks, then turns to grin at Holly. "I'll have a Stella, draft please." She blatantly checks out Damien then spins on her heel and heads to get their drinks.

"Ha! Not so hot without your superpower of fame, are you Forrester?" Damien gloats, pointing his finger in my face before his attention is focused on the kickoff.

"Bro that is all you. I'm over it. Plus, I'm kind of seeing someone." I sit back in the booth and take another big sip of my draft, not really invested in this particular football game.

Bobby and Damien both stop watching the game and turn their eyes on me at the same time. "No way man," says Bobby. "You, dating someone? I don't believe you." He shakes his head back and forth on his thick neck. "I've known you three years and I've never heard you talk about a chick. Not once."

"It all makes sense now," says Damien, rubbing his stubbled chin thoughtfully. He sits back and folds his tattooed arms across his chest. "That's why you sucked in the ring yesterday. Your head is all full of that girl! Ha! Never thought I'd see it. You, pussy whipped by a woman!"

The two of them laugh their asses off and fist bump like it's some sort of joke that I'm dating someone. Okay, it is true that I don't date, but how is that funny?

"You guys are wicked fuckwads. Let's just watch the game, all right?" I sound pissed, but honestly, I'm too happy to be mad.

"Fuck, he went Boston on us," Bobby says seriously as he turns to smirk at Damien. "Better watch your ass next time you're in the cage with him, Damien. You know what happens when Forrester gets all Boston'd out," Bobby warns as his dark eyes wrinkle in amusement.

Every once in a while, I'll ham it up since my accent seems to amuse them. Damien is from New York and Bobby is from some little town between Milwaukee and Green Bay, so hearing me 'go Boston' always cracks them up.

"Fuck you ya chowdaheads. The Pats have the most wicked quartahback evah, so it doesn't mean that Denvah is bettah for winning the playoff game." They stare at me for a minute before we all bust out laughing and enjoy the rest of the game.

CHAPTER 13

Sydney is going to think I've lost my mind. She saw me in my dress-down, fan repelling clothes at the café and in my sparring shorts the first day we met. But the last two times I've seen her were in private, so I was able to dress like a normal person.

I texted her yesterday from The Hub before the game started to see if she wanted to get together today. She offered for me to join her on her run. That means going out in public, which in turn, means an ugly disguise. Since I can't wear my wig in front of her, I grab my oldest, baggiest gym clothes and throw them on, praying that no one will recognize me.

The doorman, Richard I think, apparently knew I was coming over because he opened the door as I approached and told me to head straight to the elevator bank. I'm once again thankful that her lobby staff are so discreet.

I knock on 8A and when Sydney opens the door and takes a look at me, her reaction is purely comical. Her hand flies up to her mouth and she lets out a little bark of laughter. Her blue eyes are shining with amusement.

"Interesting choice of clothing," she says, struggling not to laugh in my face.

Sydney looks delectable in her tight black Lycra pants and thermal running jacket, I'm unable to stop staring at her ass as she turns to let me inside.

I look like a complete bum and she called me on it, so I feel like I have to defend myself a little, even though she's completely right. "What? I think I look like a guy who wants to work out."

She eyes my tattered B.C. sweatshirt and Patriots skullcap and smiles, bumping me gently with her hip. "You look like you crawled out of a sewer and stole from the lost and found at a college student center."

God she's adorable. I wrap my arms around her tiny waist and drag her over to me, rubbing my two day old stubble all over her face and neck. "You love it!" I say as she squeals and struggles to free herself from my torture.

She's laughing uncontrollably now. "Stop! It tickles! Stop it!" I laugh with her and reluctantly let her go.

Her body in her super tight clothing is dangerous, not only can I not keep my hands off of her, but I start to get aroused, which makes me flirtatious. "Well, we can't all be as sexy as you when we exercise."

Her gaze darkens at my words and her voice gets husky, letting me know that my charms have worked on her. "Trust me, you are sexy. It's just hidden under all of that hideous clothing." She smiles, continuing, "You know this is New York don't you? Some might take offense at all of that Boston paraphernalia."

Once again, she says something completely unexpected and I love it. "Am I wearing my human-repelling costume again, Miss Allen?"

"Why I believe you are, Mr. Forrester. But once again, it's not going to keep me away. Now, let's hit the pavement."

Sydney leads me on what she says is her normal jogging route. She says she normally does anywhere from six to eight miles each time she runs. She's in phenomenal shape. I admit that I wasn't sure if she would actually run that far in this cold weather but she does.

We go all the way from the West Village to Battery Park and back up. It's easier than sparring with Bobby or Damien, but it's infinitely more difficult because I have Sydney's Lycra-clad ass inches from me and I can't do anything about it. More than once I think about yanking off her bright pink ear warmer, tying her hands together with it, and fucking her until she passes out. Not my finest moment, but I am glad I wore baggy sweats.

We walk the final half mile back to her building and enter her loft covered in sweat. The two of us stagger to the kitchen and Sydney hands me a cold bottle of water from her fridge, watching while I immediately down the entire liter. She's drinking hers when I turn to her and say one word, "Shower?" Maybe she was thinking about sex the entire run too, because she doesn't hesitate to hold out her hand and lead me to her room.

Sydney goes straight into the bathroom and starts the shower while I peel off my damp clothes and leave them in a heap on the floor. When I step into the en suite, she's already in the huge enclosure, her toned body partially obscured by the layer of steam that's formed on the glass. I stand there gaping for a minute, I don't know if I've ever been so aroused in my life.

"Mind if I join you?" I open the door and press against her, kissing her inviting mouth. She eagerly lets me in, wrapping her arms around my neck and rubbing against me, quickly driving me to the edge of my self-control.

I place my hands on her waist and yank her hips into me, fitting my cock so it slides between her legs, but not inside her. Sydney lets me push her back until she's flat against the tile wall, the hot water raining down on us as we devour each other, nipping and tasting each other's mouths while our tongues twist together in ecstasy. The entire time I keep sliding my wet cock back and forth against her slit, devouring every moan that she makes as the friction increases her pleasure.

Needing more contact, I reach down and grab behind each knee, pulling her legs up and holding her against the wall by cupping her tight ass. I continue grinding my dick between us, up and down her folds as she whimpers into my mouth. Before I can protest, her hand snakes down and guides me inside her. I gasp at the feel of her bare skin clenching around my cock. It's too much to take.

"Sydney, I can't last like this. Are you on birth control?" I ask, barely able to sound out the words as the thrilling surge of pleasure nearly blinds me.

"No, just pull out. I need you Drew," she moans and bucks against me again, nearly incapacitating my ability to think. *Fuck, she's going to kill me.* What if I can't pull out in time? The only thing that stops me is my overwhelming respect for Sydney. My head drops over her shoulder and I press my forehead into the wall so I can regain control of myself.

"Sydney, I can't do that to you." I slide out of her and reach over to turn off the water. "Keep your legs around me." I carry her out of the shower and put her on the counter next to the sink. "Wait here," I demand, staring at her until I'm sure she won't move. Sydney watches me with heavy lidded eyes as I hurry and pull a condom out of my discarded pants and rush back into the bathroom as I'm rolling it on.

"Hurry Drew," Sydney begs as she digs her nails into my ass and pulls me back between her legs only happy once I sink back inside her tight heat.

She's immediately groaning and writhing and it quickly spirals into something too intense for me to handle. The sensation of our wet skin slapping together as I fuck her, sends sparks flying across my field of vision. Any remaining shred of rational thought that I had left, leaves my body and once again my dick is now in complete control. I grip her hips hard enough to leave bruises thrust violently into her, pinning her against the counter.

Once I pick up the pace, Syd starts convulsing and screaming, pulling my hair fiercely as she comes apart. Shit, she must have wanted this as badly as I did because she is fucking gorgeous as she comes. Trying to hold her slippery body in place on top of the counter takes a lot of effort but it's worth it. I continue diving in and out of her tight pussy, the unbelievable rightness of it overwhelming me. Hot and wet and gripping, I can detect every movement she makes.

"Hold on to me Sydney!" I yell as I keep driving in and out, slamming in deeper each time. She tightens her arms around my neck and moans into my mouth when I lift her up and fuck her hard until I come forcefully into her, sparks of pleasure shoot down my spine and through my balls until I'm completely empty. Spent and panting, I lay my forehead on her shoulder, still holding her up against the sink.

Sydney loosens her tight grip on my neck and slowly lowers her feet to the floor. Still recovering, all I can do is stand there, leaning against her as I breath heavily into her wet, disheveled hair. She runs her mouth gently up and down my neck and shoulder until I finally have the energy to look up. Overcome with emotion, I kiss her gently and pull her close, wrapping my arms around her back.

"How about we shower again, using soap this time?" she asks, then she laughs and squirms out of my arms so she can turn the water back on.

Fuck, I'm totally in love with her.

CHAPTER 14

"Jane! Is my suitcase in here?" I yell from the walk in closet in my bedroom. "Janey!" Shit, she either can't hear me or is ignoring me. I leave the bedroom and walk down one flight of stairs to the office. "Jane, did you hear me?" She's sitting at her desk with her arms folded, shooting daggers at me.

"Yes, I did hear you. Why are you yelling at me? I already told you that I'd have your bags packed for you." She is clearly miffed at my attitude.

I sigh and yank on my hair in frustration. "I know, I'm sorry." I slump down on the couch. "I guess I'm just nervous." I glance up at Jane. Her body is turned toward me and her mouth is hanging open. "What?" I ask.

She smiles at me. "I just never would have thought. I'm gone one weekend and you've turned into a complete wreck over a girl." Jane claps her hands together in satisfaction.

"Why are you so happy that I'm a freaking mess?" I rub my hand down my face, exhausted from my freaking out.

"Because, Drew. It means you're in love. And that makes me happy for you." She moves from her desk chair to sit next to me on the couch and pats my knee with her hand. "I've known you a long time, and you've always been pretty much alone. Trapped by your fame, untrusting of others because of it. I'm glad you've found someone worthy of you. You're a great person, Drew." Jane reaches around me and gives me a hug. Besides Sydney, she's the only person who can leave me speechless.

"Now," she continues, "go finish looking over those scripts that I left on your desk. I'll take care of the rest. Your schedule for California will be emailed to you sometime while you're gone so be sure to check your inbox." She pats my knee one last time and gets up, leaving me alone.

Surprisingly, I'm able to focus for a few hours and read two scripts. One isn't for me, but I'd be more than willing to help produce it if we found the right lead. The other I find extremely intriguing. I put it in Jane's box with a post-it note that says 'this one' on it in my chicken scratch handwriting.

After finishing with the scripts, I return a few calls, one to my agent Quentin Adair, to finish up a few loose ends regarding the release of *A Soldier's Burden*. Then I call Rhys Porter, the head of my public relations team, to discuss the premieres and a few magazine interviews that I'll have to do for the movie. Thankfully, he can schedule them all while I'm in California shooting *Mind of the Enemy*, so I won't have to make a special trip out there for the photo shoots or worry about them once I'm back home.

Apparently the buzz for our little independent movie about an Army Special Forces soldier whose unit is torn apart by a friendly fire incident, is growing exponentially. He expects that after our limited release, it will hit over 1,000 theaters the following month. That's huge for a film with a budget as small as ours.

Finishing up my calls, I decide to text Sydney. Not seeing her today is just about killing me.

Me *<Hey babe. Missing you. Is your day going well?>*

I don't even have to wait a minute for a reply.

Sydney *<Better now. Miss u 2. Can't wait for tomorrow>*

Smiling, I make sure she knows not to try to haul her stuff downstairs by herself.

Me *<Me too. Be there at 6am. I'll come up to help with your bags>*

Yes, I know I'm bossy but I can't have her struggling while I'm sitting in the car like a spoiled baby.

Sydney *<OK. See you then>*

Good, she's not arguing with me about the suitcases like she did about the ride home from my place the other morning. She's catching on that I'm going to take care of her. I quickly type out my response.

Me *<Yes, yes you will. ☺>*

Tomorrow can't come soon enough for me.

"I'll be out in a few minutes, just wait here for us," I say to Bruce as I leave the car and hustle across the dark sidewalk into Sydney's building. It's so early that I have to buzz the concierge to get in, but she left my name with the front desk. I thank God again that they are as discreet here as they say they are. No one, not even

Sydney, has heard a single word about me from any of the employees.

Nerves plague my stomach as I take the elevator up to the 8th floor and I have to lean back on the wall and close my eyes to calm down. I'm starting to doubt my ability to pull this weekend off without Sydney finding out who I am. There are too many variables that I can't control. Not being in control of any situation that can harm a loved one is my second worst fear. Losing Sydney has become my worst. This trip has the potential to expose me to both.

"Get your shit together, Forrester," I mutter to myself as I step up to unit 8A and knock. The door flies open almost immediately, letting me know that I'm not the only one who's anxious this morning. Sydney stands in the foyer, slightly breathless either from exertion or lust. From the dark look she's giving me, I'd say lust is a good bet.

That look starts me fantasizing about tearing off her clothes and throwing her down on the hardwood floor of her loft which makes me smile, and unfortunately, instantly hard. "Hello, Sydney," I say as I stride across the threshold and pull her against me, playing with fire by touching her when we're both clearly thinking the same thing.

"Hello, Drew," Sydney groans against my mouth.

She makes me so hot that I can't help myself, I wrap my hands under her tight ass and pull her into the hard ridge in my jeans. God, she's making me harder just by saying my name. The now familiar feeling of rampant, overwhelming desire takes over, trying to crowd out all of my other thoughts. I attempt to step back and put some space between us, but Sydney isn't having it. She stands on her toes so she can take my lip in her mouth and begins sucking on it erotically.

Fuck! I literally won't be able to stop myself if she keeps doing shit like that.

"Sydney, as much as I want to throw you down and surround myself with you, we have to go." Frowning, I unhook her arms from behind my neck and run my hands through my hair in frustration. I try to ignore the disappointed look on her face by scooping up her bags. "Is this everything?"

Sydney puts on her coat and glances up at me, the same frustration I'm feeling is mirrored on her beautiful face. "Yes, it's everything. I'm ready."

As I turn for the door, I see her expression change in my peripheral vision. She's nervous. I can see it in her clear blue eyes as easily as if I'm reading the words from a script. I decide not to say anything about it, not wanting to start a discussion that may make her decide to stay behind. Instead, I take her bags over to the elevator and push the call button.

I'm waiting for the doors to open when I look back at Sydney, standing a few feet away from me in the hall. She is quite obviously checking me out, her eyes roaming up and down my body as she bites her lower lip.

Smiling, I can't resist teasing her. "Like what you see, Miss Allen?"

She surprises me yet again. Instead of blushing like I expect, Sydney walks up to me and sensuously drags her tongue over my dimple. I inhale sharply at the contact and flinch when the sensation hits my already frustrated dick.

Sydney steps back and runs her eyes in an exaggerated motion down to the bulge in my pants. "Why yes, Mr. Forrester, I definitely like what I see," She purrs as she licks her lips suggestively.

Oh baby, we're going to have a lot of fun this weekend.

"Me too, Miss Allen. Me too."

Out front on the sidewalk it's still dark out and I don't want to chance being recognized, so I drop Sydney's bags by the trunk for Bruce to load up and usher her into the back seat. After she gets in, I slide in next to her, wrapping my arm around her shoulders so I can bring her close. I hadn't noticed how good she smelled upstairs in her place. Now, in the car, the orange and floral body wash mixed with the scent I now know is unique to Sydney, surrounds me. It drives me crazy to sit next to her and not be able to have her.

Sydney stops my wandering thoughts when she speaks. "So, where to? JFK, Newark, La Guardia? Or is it a surprise?"

Hmmm, she's actually asking me a question? That's a first.

"No, not a surprise, Sydney. We're taking a flight out of Teterboro straight to the Gustave airport on St. Bart's. A car will take us to my friend's house about ten minutes away, and what we do next is up to us." I whisper the last part as I stare at her, eager to see her reaction. She doesn't disappoint, her lips part and her thighs tense up.

She's going to kill me if she keeps looking at me like that.

"So we're taking a private jet then?" Her blush is gone and apprehension takes its place.

Is there anything that doesn't freak this girl out? Now I'm worried she'll bolt if I answer wrong and I have no idea what the right answer is. "It's a private jet, yes. There's not really another way to get to the island without a bunch of flight changes. It's the easiest way... is that okay?"

Don't flip out and leave me.

"It's fine," Sydney fires back at me. I have no clue why she's acting pissed. Is it the jet? Then, just as sudden as her freak out started, she puts her small hand on my knee and her features soften. "Really, it's wonderful. Thank you for inviting me. I'm really excited."

Something's wrong. She's smiling but it isn't touching her eyes. In an attempt to make her feel better, I pull her close and press a kiss to her head.

The rest of the ride to the airport is silent. I'm afraid of saying something that will freak out Sydney and she's probably sitting there afraid of whatever the fuck it is that scares her. We stop in front of Chad's huge, white and gold, fourteen-passenger Gulfstream. I feel Sydney's body go rigid in my arms.

Shit, this was a bad idea. Bruce opens Sydney's door and helps her out of the car. I quickly jump out of my side and hurry around to guide her up the stairs of the plane. She's smiling at least, so I'm able to relax a little.

The flight attendant takes our coats and thankfully, doesn't do or say anything to make me uncomfortable. She's part of Chad's staff, so I'm sure she's seen plenty of celebrities before. Plus, I had Jane call and speak to all of Chad's employees about pretending I'm just a 'normal' guy. I didn't trust Chad to do it himself, it's too important to me and he kept laughing at my situation. "Please sit anywhere, we'll be departing in a few minutes," the attendant named Gail says, then heads for the cockpit.

We step into the cabin and I watch as Sydney takes in the plush interior. I'm used to the way she scrutinizes every space she enters, the designer in her taking everything in. I walk over to the couch on one side of the cabin and motion for Sydney to sit. No way am I letting her sit in a chair across from me for four hours. Unable to keep my hands off of her, I reach over her lap and grab her seatbelt as soon as she sits down. "Safety first, Miss Allen," I joke as I snap the belt together. Her eyes get heavy and she leans toward me. I'm about to claim her gorgeous mouth when Bruce comes pounding up the stairs with our luggage, ruining the moment.

My phone vibrates in my pocket. I told Jane I wasn't available for any calls this weekend. Everything should be done via email until I get back. Irritated, I yank it out and check it, scowling when I see it's a text from Damien.

Damien <Have fun pretty boy! Hope your chick doesn't own your balls by the time you get back!>

Nice. What an asshole. You'd think your friends would support you when you're trying to land the girl of your dreams. But I'll admit, I have been acting strange lately and they probably have no idea what to make of it. I type a quick response not wanting to be rude to Sydney but knowing if I don't answer he'll just keep texting me.

Me <If you knew more about this girl, you'd want her to have your balls...>

There. I shove the phone back into my pocket and lean back into the seat.

"Is everything alright?" Her bright blue eyes are wide with concern.

God she's so fucking sweet. "I'm with you, everything is perfect." I'm unable to stop from smiling like a total idiot. Damien's right, I'm totally whipped by this girl and I don't even care.

Gail brings us breakfast once we're in the air. I told them to keep it light since I wasn't sure if Sydney was prone to airsickness. She places egg-white omelets with fruit on our trays and then comes out with my surprise. It takes Sydney a moment to notice that Gail is bringing us coffee from her favorite shop, the one where I ran into her, or stalked her, depends on the definition. When her eyes bug out and her mouth drops open in shock, I feel kind of stupid. Maybe it's too much. It's fucking embarrassing.

"I had them stop by the café this morning so we could have it with our meal," I attempt to say casually. I don't want her to think it's some huge thing if she's freaked out by it.

"It's perfect Drew. You're the most thoughtful person I've ever met. It's a little over the top, but I can get used to over the top." I exhale the breath I was holding, glad that she doesn't think I'm an idiot. Then Sydney smiles at me like I fucking hung the moon and I freeze. She's so unbelievably beautiful. How is she not already taken?

"Mmmmmm."

My attention snaps up from my plate to her mouth. The sexy sound that comes out of her gets me instantly hard. Her perfect lips are pressed together and her eyes are closed as she swallows a sip of the coffee. I stare at those full, pink lips and imagine them wrapped around my cock again … *Shit!* I have to stop it. I can't take her back to the bedroom and fuck her senseless, can I?

I force my attention back up to her eyes and notice that she's gone completely still, staring at me as I stare at her. She wants it too, but she's way too good for a quick fuck in the back of a plane. That doesn't mean I can't play.

I reach over to take her cup from her, purposely brushing the side of my hand over one of the tight little nipples that I can see through her shirt, and I'm rewarded with a discreet gasp. Then I move my hand to cup her face and using as much control as I can possibly manage, I lean in and lightly trace her lips with my tongue, holding back from taking the deep, consuming kiss that I desire.

"I do tend to go big or go home, so you definitely need to get used to me acting over the top." I have to stop touching her to keep from ripping her clothes off right here on this couch. "I cannot wait to get you alone, Sydney. You are driving me insane. I need to be inside you, soon."

I sit back when Gail comes back into the cabin to clear our plates. Crap, I desperately need to adjust my hard on, but I don't want to be obvious about it. Instead, I turn sideways and flip open the armrest where Chad has his ridiculously expensive sound system control panel. I'm able to shift my junk while I scroll down and select a tropical playlist. When I turn back, I see a confused look on Sydney's face as the music comes over the speakers. Shrugging, I tell her, "I just wanted to prepare us properly for our vacation."

"Trust me, Drew. I'm more than ready to start the weekend, but the music is a nice touch, very smooth. So tell me…" Sydney says as she takes a deep breath and makes a weird face, like she might puke or pass out or both, "what kind of work do you do that allows you to take private jets to exclusive tropical islands?"

Holy shit! She's actually asking something personal about me? I thought it would take for-fucking-ever to get to this point with Miss Evasive. Unable to stop the smirk from appearing on my face, I decide to go the indirect route. Maybe I'll get more insight from her reaction instead of from my answer. "I have to admit, Sydney, I didn't really think you liked personal questions very much." I watch her face carefully for her response.

I feel like a dick as her adorable face falls, then pales. I hope I didn't just fuck this all up with my stupidity. "I don't," she says, "when they're directed at me. I'm a very private person… usually. But I'm finding myself in an odd situation."

She's actually talking to me, and unbelievably, she's opening up. I'm not going to waste this opportunity by simply answering her question… yet. Maybe I can get more out of her, like why she won't fucking tell me a single thing about herself. "What situation is that?" I ask, knowing I may be pushing her too hard, too soon.

Sydney squirms in her seat before answering. "I ummmm, well… I guess I just really want to know a little more about you. That's rare for me."

It worked!

A huge smile spreads across my face. I'm finally breaking through her giant fucking wall and getting to her! I can't help but tease her. "So what you're saying is, I'm special?"

I'm rewarded with an adorable eye roll and her heart-stopping laugh. "You make it sound so dorky, but yes, I guess you are. So…are you going to answer my question?"

I can't answer your question, gorgeous. Because then you might leave me, and I can't let you do that. Especially since I have no clue why you would run if I told you the truth. I try to form my words to be as honest as possible about movie making without scaring her away with my Hollywood shit.

"I freelance, so my work varies with each project I take on. I'm what you could call an … independent investor. I invest in projects, sometimes I direct them, sometimes I have a more hands-on role, and sometimes I just hand over money and wait for a return on my investment. The amount of input I have over each project varies. It's actually pretty damn complicated sometimes, but fun."

I watch her face crumple in confusion and disappointment.

Fuck, I'm such a dick.

"Huh. So you're an investor? Like in companies?"

She wants to know *me*, probably the only person she's ever let past that tough exterior, and I fucking lie to her. But I just can't risk losing her. It's too soon to tell her anything.

"Sort of," I explain. *How in the hell do I say this?* "I'll hear about a money making investment, usually through a contact or a previous client, then I research it to see if it's worth the time and money, and go from there. Sometimes it just needs funding to get whatever the client needs off of the ground, sometimes I work on every aspect including marketing. It's a wide range of possibilities." I conclude as I give her the most pathetic explanation ever for how a movie gets made.

She looks so lost, and sad. "That's…. interesting," is all she can manage to come up with to my whitewashed description of my job.

Now I have to drop a real bomb on her. "It's okay, Sydney. I know it sounds confusing, but that's the best way I know to explain it to you right now. The downside of my work is that I travel quite a bit. Some projects are in different states, some in different countries. That's actually why I wanted to go away with you this weekend. I leave for California at the end of next week, and have to be on site for five or six weeks." More disappointment appears on her face, which I fucking hate doing to her, but at least it means she doesn't want me to go and might miss me a little while I'm gone.

"Oh. I guess I never really thought about whether or not you traveled for your job. I mean, I don't usually worry about things like that. Crap, that's not what I mean. I'm sorry; I'm really new at this whole dating thing. I mean, we are dating, right?" She smacks her forehead in frustration, embarrassed by her rambling. "Okay, tell me if I just screwed this all up."

God she's so fucking cute. She's afraid to label us as dating because she doesn't want to freak *me* out. How would she react if she knew I would marry her right here and now?

I lean in and kiss her gorgeous mouth. "I'd like to think we're dating, if that's okay with you?"

And I'm pathetically and hopelessly in love with you.

I watch her reaction to make sure she's okay. "And you haven't screwed anything up, Sydney. I should have told you about my trip sooner. I just didn't want to scare you away. Plus I hope to be able to come back to New York several times during the six weeks, so with any luck you'll be willing to see me when I'm home."

Sydney gives me a small smile. "Well, you're not wearing your hat to bring you luck, but I'm sure you don't need it." She looks down at her hands. Her voice drops to a near whisper, "Of course I want to see you Drew. That's all I seem to think about these days."

I can't stand not touching her anymore. I don't give a shit about Gail, or my raging hard-on. I reach over and unbuckle her seatbelt and pull her onto my lap. Jesus, she feels so good and fits right on top of me. "Me too," I admit as I take her delicious mouth and spend the rest of the flight tasting it.

CHAPTER 15

We land on St. Bart's on a terrifyingly short runway with the bright turquoise ocean gleaming at the end. Gail opens the door and the salty smell of the sea surrounds us as we walk down onto the hot pavement. It's perfect here. Warm, ocean breeze, gorgeous girl on my arm... I couldn't be happier if I tried.

Chad's caretaker, Philippe, gets out of his Mini-Moke, a Jeep-like car I've heard about but never actually seen in person. Chad was supposed to tell this guy not to act weird around me or say anything about who I am, so he better not fuck this up.

Philippe introduces himself to Sydney then to me, shaking my hand just a little too long for me to be a normal person. The dude is super-cheerful, with short tufts of gray hair, and is way, way too tan. He grabs our stuff out of the plane and I help Sydney into the back seat of the open top Moke. I can't ride around in this thing without my disguise, so I get my Sox hat out of my bag and pull it down low.

When I climb in next to Syd she bursts out laughing at the sight of my hat. Nice, she thinks I'm an idiot with hideous fashion sense, which I find quite charming. I grin at her. "What? I know you said I don't need luck, but it can't hurt."

Philippe starts the Moke and takes us to Chad's villa. He describes a bunch of stuff about the island, but I could care less. I'm too busy watching Sydney take in the surroundings, her long auburn hair whipping around her face as we wind through the tropical greenery. When Philippe points out some wild peacocks, I think Sydney's going to fall out of her seat she's so excited. I chuckle at her reaction. She's so happy and carefree, as if the island has lifted a huge burden from her weighted down shoulders. Her outright joy is contagious.

I'm so fucking gone on this girl.

When we pull into the gravel driveway of Chad's house, the nervousness from this morning comes back full force. What if this Philippe guy left movie shit all over the house? If Sydney sees it, she'll freak out and he seems like a little bit of an idiot.

I hear a banging sound and see Philippe struggling, he's already opening the front door and bringing our bags into the house. It's like this guy is on speed or something he's so damn quick. I need to get him alone and make sure he took care of everything.

Sydney and I step into the huge open kitchen behind Philippe, who's nowhere in sight. While she's looking at everything I lean in and give her a quick kiss. "Wait here a minute, I'm going to chat with Philippe." She nods and I hurry after the caretaker and find him in the master bedroom, placing our bags on the bed.

"Hey, Philippe, can we talk for a minute?" I corner the really tan, really happy guy in the bedroom.

"Of course, Mr. Forrester, what can I do for you?" He stands there looking way too fucking delighted to listen to me bitch at him.

"I need to make sure all of Chad's movie stuff is out of sight. He said he explained to you the importance of getting rid of it all."

Philippe nods and starts to leave the bedroom. *Fuck dude!* I can't talk about this shit in front of Sydney. "Yes, I got all of it. No worries."

Like I'm not going to worry that the fate of my relationship with the woman I love is in this weirdo's hands. "You're sure you got all of it?" I ask, trailing after him down the hall.

"Yes, yes. All of it." Philippe responds as he continues to walk back toward the kitchen.

"And you put it all in the office, correct?"

"Yes." He stops to give me a funny look, clearly starting to think I'm either OCD or crazy as he hurries back to Sydney. I watch him pull a key out of his pocket and place it on the countertop. Then he quickly shows us a map of the area. "Here are some additional phone numbers you may need." Philippe points to a list on the refrigerator. "The fridge and pantry are stocked, let me know if you need anything, day or night. My number is on the list." He shakes Syd's hand then mine and leaves.

"Well, Philippe is…" Sydney says.

I want to say 'a twitchy fuck' but I stick to saying, "Interesting?" instead.

"That's one way of putting it, I suppose," she responds. We both crack up at Philippe's expense.

I hold out my hand and ask her if she wants to see the house. She takes it without hesitation, and threads her fingers through mine. I have to admit, Chad has great taste. The house is massive, with comfortable furniture. My favorite part is the huge deck. I start imagining all the things I can do with Sydney on one of the plush double lounge chairs.

Gently tugging on her hand, I lead Sydney across the hardwood deck. "This is even better than I imagined," I tell her as I yank her down with me onto one of those tempting chairs, making her squeak in surprise.

"You've never been here?" She asks, looking somewhat confused. Did I tell her I've been here before? I don't think I did, but she's acting like I have.

"No, I haven't. Why?"

"I'm not sure, I just assumed. You said the owner was a friend, I don't know why I thought that." Oh, she made her own assumptions because she never asked me any details about this house or the trip. Just like she never asks me any other questions. Or answers them.

"The owner is a friend, as well as a business partner in some of my investments. But I work a lot, and haven't had the opportunity to just take off and come here. I don't get to take a lot of vacations." I don't need to tell her that she's the first girl I've wanted to spend this much time with since I was a teenager. It would probably freak her the fuck out.

"Yet you're here with me, I assumed you brought all the girls you date here." She gives me a fake smile to hide her embarrassment.

Now this line of questioning makes sense. She wants to know if this is something I do a lot, seduce beautiful women and bring them here for a weekend of sex. "No, no other girls, Sydney. Just you. You make me want to take time off from work." I push her down on the poolside chair and roll her hot little body underneath mine. My tortured cock responds immediately.

"Miss Allen, I do believe we're wearing too many clothes for this tropical heat. What do you say we fix that?"

I can't wait any longer to have her. Sitting next to her for four hours on that plane nearly killed me. My fingers are literally itching to touch her skin. I lean my head down and bite along her slender neck, her scent, amplified by the hot sun is driving me mad with lust.

She moans and throws her head back so I can have better access to her throat. Her voice is raspy and needy, "Mr. Forrester, I couldn't agree more."

That's all I need to hear from her to ignite the throbbing that I've been trying to ignore since I walked through her front door and she gave me her fuck-me eyes. I pull off my coat and throw it on a nearby chair and quickly shuck my shoes and socks.

Sydney is lying on the lounge chair, watching me with her wide blue eyes like I'm the predator and she's waiting for me to pounce. She probably didn't think I'd want to do this right here, right now, outside in the open. I can see the hesitation written on her face. She's so easy to read sometimes, not good at schooling her features like I do so well. I also see desire, it's rolling off of her in waves. Her gorgeous lips are parted slightly, her nipples are hard and straining against her shirt, and she keeps shifting uncomfortably on the chair as I undress.

Fuck, she is so fucking sexy.

Done waiting, I grab the hem of her shirt and pull it off. She doesn't stop me or offer to help. Then I yank off my own shirt and toss it carelessly to the ground. Still standing next to her chair, I extend a hand to Sydney and she takes, letting me pull her to her feet. When I step close enough for our bodies to touch, she gazes up at me and the look she gives me makes me want to drop to my knees and worship every inch of her perfect body.

Instead, I unfasten her jeans and lower them to the ground, then do the same with mine. I groan at the sight of her, my dick actually hurts from it. It takes everything in me to not just throw her down and fuck her senseless on that inviting lounge chair. She's better than that though, because I wouldn't last long and she's looking up at me with trusting eyes. A trust I know she doesn't give away easily, a trust that makes me want to take care of her, protect her, satisfy her completely.

"Want to go for a swim?" I ask, staring down at her, my voice husky from desire.

"Yes."

That one little word gives me the go ahead to touch her, something I've been dying to do. The fire building inside of me urges me to step out of my tight boxer briefs to release my aching cock from its prison. I watch Sydney's gaze skim down my body and land right on it. Her eyes get dark and she licks her lips hungrily. I don't think she even knows that she's doing it.

Christ, I need to see her. I reach out and slowly pull down the little scrap of lace that she calls underwear and unhook her bra. God, she's fucking perfect. I want to bury myself in her and never come out.

I hold out my hand and she takes it, letting me lead her into the warm water. Once we're in the cool water, I push her against the edge of the pool, trapping her between my arms. She meets my gaze, but she's nervous, like something heavy is weighing down on her.

I know she won't tell me what it is, so I do the only thing my fuzzy, sex-addled brain can think of; I press the length of me against her soft body and kiss her like it's the last kiss I'll ever have. Our tongues tangle and I suck on hers gently. When she moans, it drives me crazy with desire. My dick is as hard as a fucking rock. I can't take her in the pool, without a condom, so I have to stop.

I'm barely strong enough to push away from her and swim to the other side of the pool.

"What's wrong?" She has a hurt look on her gorgeous face. Water is dripping from her hair, running in rivulets to her pink lips, swollen from our kisses.

Shit, she thinks she did something wrong.

"Nothing's wrong Sydney, I just want you so badly and I can't have you in the pool." My voice is strained. I rub my hand down my face in frustration.

She swims over and wraps her arms and long legs around me, every part of her making contact with every part of me.

"Then let's get out," she says. Mesmerized, I watch her tongue dart out and hold my breath as she leans in and licks from my neck up to my ear.

Shuddering, I grip her ass and walk up the stairs and over to a huge double lounge chair, collapsing on it with her beneath me. "You're amazing," I tell her as I reach down for my discarded pants and pull out a condom.

Driven by a singular goal, I rip the package open and roll the damn thing on as quickly as I can. Sydney, dripping water from the pool, moaning and writhing naked under me isn't helping my concentration so I fumble before getting it on right.

Once I'm ready, I reach down and run my hand over her slit. "God Sydney, you're so wet."

"I want you Drew," she whispers in her sexy fucking voice. Sydney hooks a leg over my hip and pushes down, encouraging me to hurry up. Christ, she's killing me. My resolve shatters and I can't wait any longer. Shifting my weight, I press into her slowly, wanting to feel every inch as it sinks into her hot tight depths.

"Jesus," I groan as I start to move on top of her. The slick water on our skin, the warm sun beating down on us, her scent magnified in the heat… I've never felt so alive during sex.

Fascinated, I watch as she bites her bottom lip and her eyes roll up in her head while each slow thrust pulls a husky moan from her throat. She can close her eyes this time, but next time I want her to watch as I fuck her. I lean in and taste her swollen mouth. I can't get enough of her, I don't think I ever will.

"Drew," she cries out as I thrust harder and nearly burst at the sound of my name on her lips. She starts to spasm around my cock and I know she's there. With Sydney pulling me with her, a jolt of white hot pleasure streaks down my spine and I join her in falling over the edge.

It takes us a minute to catch our breath, then I roll to the side, afraid that I'm crushing her. She's so tiny, I'm sure my weight isn't easy for her to bear.

"Hungry?" I ask.

"Famished," she responds with a brilliant smile, not seeming to give a damn about having been trapped underneath me.

After our very satisfying workout, we decide to make a grilled chicken salad for lunch. Sydney has already admitted that she can't cook, so I show her how to make the salad while I manage the grill. I can barely focus on the food as she struts around the kitchen in a barely there yellow bikini, miles of her creamy flesh exposed for my visual pleasure. I just had her twenty minutes ago and my dick is hard again already.

Shit! Stop thinking about sex, Forrester.

I'm taking the chicken off of the grill when I hear her speak to me from inside. "So your friend, where does he live? Is he in New York? I'd love to meet him and find out who decorated this place."

Cautiously balancing the plate of chicken, I walk through the open living area and bring the it into the kitchen.

"Chad lives in L.A," I answer as approach her.

When I lean against the large island next to her scattered bowls of salad ingredients, I realize that she hasn't listened to a word I've said. My focus flicks up to her face and I instantly recognize that look in her eyes. She's checking me out, her gaze roving up and down my body. In a hurry to make something to eat, I threw on just a loose pair of shorts and Sydney's greedy eyes are currently all over my chest and abs.

"What? Who's Chad?" She snaps out of her daydream with a confused look on her face.

It's too tempting to pass up. I smirk at Sydney and put the plate of chicken on the countertop, having decided to mess with her. I lean in close, so close that I can smell her flushed skin and the scent of sex from our tryst.

"Were you just eye-fucking me, Miss Allen?"

I lean back and watch amused, as she turns a million different shades of red before quickly turning her focus back to the lettuce that she's tearing apart and tossing onto plates. "Ummmm, I'm not sure what you mean," she sputters.

She was definitely eye-fucking me.

Certain that my presence has affected her, I slowly reach my arm in front of her and grab a piece of fruit out of a bowl on the other side of Sydney, making sure that my naked upper body brushes against her exposed skin. I toss it in my mouth I speak quietly, whispering into her ear and smiling when I see a small shiver escape.

"Okay, we can play it that way, Sydney," I drawl. Laughing, I start chopping the chicken, satisfied that I've wound her up as much as I always am when she's near. "Chad, the guy who owns this house, you asked me where he lives and I said Los Angeles."

"Oh. Where in L.A.?" she asks, her voice a little shaky from my teasing.

A quick splash of vinaigrette and I've finished up the salads. Sydney grabs them and spins on her heel, fleeing to the outdoor table to avoid her embarrassment. She's so fucking cute.

Chuckling, I follow her out with our drinks and put them down as I sit. "Brentwood," I mumble between bites, answering her previous question.

It's fascinating to watch her process the information. I can almost see the gears turning in her head as she eats For someone so secretive, she's very easy to read. Usually, the problem is that even though I might know the emotions she's feeling, the reason behind them is always a mystery to me.

"Is he involved in the project you have in California?"

"Yes, he's a principle investor as am I." God I hate bending the truth to her. "He'll be on site with me most days. That's probably why he let us use his villa. He plans on bugging the shit out of me for six weeks and is just trying to butter me up." This is actually true.

If she only knew what I told Chad about her. I sounded like a complete pussy asking if I could use his house to impress a girl.

Sydney laughs, "Not a bad plan if you ask me."

"I agree. He's a pretty smart guy."

Once we finish eating she picks up our dishes and brings them into the kitchen. We both need a breather, so I grab a couple of beers out of the fridge. "Let's just relax outside by the pool."

Sydney smiles and accepts one of the bottles from me. "Sounds great."

This place is perfect, serene and open, but very private. We walk back outside and watch the sun set over the Caribbean while relaxing on a lounge chair together. Syd tucks herself between my legs and leans back against my chest while we just enjoy each other's company.

I'm so comfortable with her physically, I just wish she would feel more comfortable with me mentally. She's so closed off, afraid of being hurt. I've been wracking my brain to figure out why she hates celebrity shit so much and all I can come up with is that she used to date someone who dumped her when he made it big.

He's a fucking douche if that's what happened, and it better not be that jackhole Reynolds!

My fists are aching to pound his worthless ass into the ground.

After she finishes her beer, Sydney gets up and sits by the edge of the pool, tucking her legs underneath her. Maybe if I tell her about myself, the non-acting stuff, she'll open up some for me. I'll take whatever she'll throw my way, any scrap of information about her would be like a drop of water to a thirsty man.

"So, when I was a kid in Boston, my sister was the biggest pain in my ass. She's four years younger than me so I started noticing girls when Allie was still a kid. There was this one girl in my class that I liked and Allie knew it. But she was pissed at me over some stupid thing I'd done, so she told the girl that I couldn't wear deodorant because I was allergic to it. God, it was awful for me at school after that."

The memories of the crap Allie and I used to do to each other makes me laugh, shaking my head at the ridiculousness of it.

"Stop, stop, there's no way your sister told a girl you liked that you were allergic to deodorant!" Sydney is laughing so hard that she's clutching her stomach.

"She did, believe me. She lied and told everyone that I couldn't wear any because it gave me armpit rashes. It was revenge for the time me and my friends hid a walkie-talkie under her bed and made monster noises. She cried every night for a week. We were really mean to her that time."

"We used to tear it up all over that city. Me and my two best friends, Mike and Matt, would get on our bikes and ride over to Kenmore and catch the Sox at Fenway. Sometimes we'd ditch school to get autographs from our favorite players and see batting practice."

I'm sure I'm rambling like a starry eyed kid. I tend to lose myself when I talk about the Sox and what they meant to me as a kid. It was all we ever talked about back then, we were all going to play for them one day, together. In Boston, the sun rises and sets over Fenway Park.

"That sounds like so much fun. I didn't do anything like that growing up. Do you still talk to your friends from home?" She stretches out her long, toned legs and dips them in the pool.

It takes me a minute, but I tear my gaze from Sydney and stare out at the sea, the waves glistening in the light of the moon. I hate talking about what happened to Matt, losing him is probably what started my tendency to be overprotective of my family, but I don't want to be closed off or she may never talk to me about herself.

"I still talk to Mike. Matt died of cancer when we were in high school. They were brothers." I try to make it sound like it's no big deal so she won't feel bad about asking.

The chair suddenly seems cold and impersonal, so I get up from and move next to her by the pool, wanting to be able to see her face as we talk, needing the intimacy.

"I'm sorry," she says kindly, placing her soft hand over mine in a comforting way.

"It was a long time ago." I shrug, tilting back my bottle to drink more beer. Then, Sydney shocks the hell out of me by telling me a story about her childhood.

"In the third grade, Denny Hirschler tried to kiss me by the swings at recess." Shocked, I look over at her, fascinated to be given a clue to her past. She's staring dreamily out at the ocean, her eyes not really focusing on anything in particular. "When he puckered up, I reached down and threw a handful of dirt in his face, then ran away." Her face lights up in a smile, then the corners of her mouth tug down at the memory.

Hmmm, even back then she was reluctant to reveal her feelings. I file that away for future reference.

"It's your fault for being so kissable." I lean in and kiss her gently.

Somehow, I know she grew up alone, I don't even have to ask, but I do anyway just to keep the conversation going. "You don't have any siblings, do you Sydney." I avoid looking at her, hoping that she'll be more willing to talk about herself if I'm not staring expectantly.

"No, I'm an only child."

God, she sounds so heartbreakingly sad. I turn back to her, upset by her tone of voice. It must freak her out, because she gets up and sits back in the chair, trying to put her walls back up between us.

Fuck that, I'm not letting her get away from me when she's being so open and agreeable. "You know you don't have to answer anything that makes you uncomfortable?" I stand up and climb behind her on the chair, pulling her back against my chest.

"I know. I'll let you know if I'm freaking out. I'm sorry I'm so difficult. I…I don't date much. Part of the whole not wanting to talk about myself hang up I have."

For about the millionth time I want to find out who fucked up this gorgeous, perfect girl and beat the ever-loving shit out of him. It takes all of my energy to keep my anger from showing. I don't want to scare Sydney with what my family calls my 'freakish over-protectiveness' before she's ready.

Instead of getting mad, I wrap my arms around her small frame and comfort her. "You're not difficult, Sydney. Everyone is affected by life's events differently. When and if you want to tell me what happened to you, I'll be here. In the meantime, I'm happy just to spend time with you."

And I am happy just to be with her. Would I love to know everything about her right now? Yes, but if she makes me wait forever I will.

"My parents are divorced. They haven't spoken in twelve years, and I haven't seen my dad since then either."

Holy shit! She just volunteered information about herself! Without me pestering or pulling it out of her. A divorce story isn't really what I was expecting to hear. Maybe her parents fought over her and dragged her into all of their bullshit. The thought stresses me out. I have to hold in all of the questions I have running through my head to keep her from shutting down.

"That must have been hard; how old were you then?" I decide to go with an easy question first.

"Twelve. Yes, it was very hard. It made me very untrusting, as I'm sure you can tell."

There she goes again, pointing out how fucked up she thinks she is.

"I think you're perfect," I say as I brush my lips across her shoulder.

Sydney turns to look at me, her pupils dilating when our eyes connect. "I don't think I feel like talking anymore." She slides her hand down my abs and over my growing dick. I don't know if she's trying to distract me or not, but right now I don't care.

This girl is going to kill me.

"Me either." Desire shoved every other thought out of my head the second her hand brushed across the front of my pants.

Determined, I scoop her up in my arms and stalk into the bedroom. I'm going to find out whether or not she likes one of the kinds of control that I enjoy. I lay her down on the giant bed and climb over her writhing body, not letting any part of our skin touch, drawing out the torture.

"Drew," she moans, and the raw sound of her voice turns my cock into steel.

Sydney tries as hard as she can to join her hips with mine, desperately wanting the friction it would provide. Smiling, I lean down and tease her with my mouth, licking and tasting every bit of her lips.

"Please, I need you." she groans into my mouth. Begging is so fucking sexy on her.

My teasing is working. If I get her worked up enough, she'll let me have my way with her. Frantic, Sydney clamps her long, athletic legs around my waist and attempts to pull me down to her. Fuck that if she thinks she's taking control of this situation. Instead of giving her what she wants, I run my lips up and down her neck, driving her wild with longing. I chuckle against her skin when she moans in frustration at my barely-there touches.

"Patience, Sydney. I want to savor you. I can't get enough of your skin, your smell, the feel of your body. Let's discover everything about each other." Plus, there's no way I'm giving in so easy when I've got her like this.

I hook a finger in one triangle of yellow fabric and yank it aside, revealing a perfect pink nipple. Shit, my dick is fucking killing me right now it's so hard. I lick and bite and tease her until she's panting and arching into me. Then I pull down the other side.

Fuck, she's so fucking gorgeous. It's taking everything I have to not just rip off her scrap of a bathing suit and sink into her right now.

I untie her top and throw it somewhere, I don't really care where it ends up at this point. "So beautiful," I whisper as I taste her swollen lips again. I can't take it, I have to see her completely naked.

I drop to the side of the bed, kneeling on the floor so I can remove the bottom of her bikini. Thank God it has ties on either side or I'd probably ruin it by tearing it off. I fling it aside and expose everything to my insatiable eyes.

Christ, her wet, pink pussy is calling out to me. "I need to taste you," I tell her as I shove her legs apart and slide my tongue over her addictive slit. "Jesus, Sydney." It's fucking addictive, and I know without a doubt as I taste her that she's the only woman I'll ever want.

I attack her clit and swirl my tongue around it until she's breathing hard and moaning non-stop, scrabbling to grab on to anything to ground herself, the sheets, my shoulders, my hair. When I know she's close I thrust two fingers into her tight passage and pump them in and out, finding that sensitive rough spot inside. The reaction I get from her is instant and volatile.

"Oh God, Drew!" She loses control as she screams and bucks up and down on the bed.

I can't tear my eyes from her, watching her come apart. It's the sexiest fucking thing I've ever seen. She gazes down and our eyes lock, sending her over the edge.

"Don't stop, I'm going to come!"

I continue torturing her as her pussy convulses around my fingers and I lick her sweetness until she practically passes out on the bed.

Now she's ready to see how I like to fuck. Hard and fast and demanding. I stand up at the foot of the bed and grab her calves, yanking her toward me so her ass is on the edge of the mattress.

"I'm not done exploring you yet, Miss Allen," I tell her as I roll on a condom. I see her eyes pop open at the gruff tone of my voice. Then her gaze drops down my body and finds my hard cock, she licks her lips and her thick lashes flutter wildly.

Fuck, she likes it when I'm bossy. This girl has no idea how bossy I can be when I'm given free rein. I take her ankles and put them up on my shoulders as I stand between her legs next to the bed.

My cock positioned at her opening, I stare down at her flushed and sweaty face. "Are you ready for me baby? I want to fuck you…hard."

I hear her gasp when I say that and my dick jumps. My control is just about shredded, she's getting it whether or not she answers me.

"Yes, take me Drew."

Jesus, those words sound so fucking hot coming out of her sweet mouth. I savor them for a moment, closing my eyes and running them through my head again. When I open my eyes I'm done. She's watching me with a carnal look on her face, practically begging me to fuck her.

You got it baby. I roughly grab on to her hips and thrust into her, harshly and without any warning.

"Ahhhh." A groan escapes her lips as I feel her slick warmth wrap around my cock. I almost come just from one fucking second inside her. Hard as a rock and threatening to lose it, I struggle with my control before I can focus on Sydney again. When I do, her eyes have rolled back into her head in ecstasy.

Oh sweetheart, we can't have that. "Look at me, Sydney. I want you to watch me as I fuck you." No way am I not going to see her eyes as I take what's mine.

Her lips part slightly and I hear a sharp intake of breath. She likes it when I take charge. She'll probably never admit it though, she's too stubborn.

Our eyes remain locked as I begin to move. The brutal, rhythmic actions of my hips bringing us closer to the peak that we both need. And I do need it from Sydney, as much as I need to breathe. It's not an option for me anymore, not a desire. Having her is a full-out fucking requirement for me to live.

She claws at the sheets, holding them tight to keep from sliding back every time I pound into her. Without looking away, I turn my head to where her leg is up on my shoulder and drag my teeth down her ankle and calf. The primal noises coming from her bring me right to the brink, a spasm of pleasure tears from my balls.

I reach down and thumb her clit once, then twice and she shatters around my cock, convulsing and screaming my name as she comes. Fuck if it doesn't send me right over the edge with her. "Jesus Sydney," I grunt and shove deep into her as her body grips my dick and pulls every fucking drop from me.

With my legs too shaky to stand, I pull out and collapse to my knees next to the bed, laying my chest down on her flat stomach, my head resting between her breasts. Sydney pushes my sweaty hair back from my forehead and runs her nails down my back.

"Mmmmmm, that feels good." I lift my head to look at her. She's stunning, flushed and content. A light sheen of sweat is on her chest. "You're amazing," I tell her honestly. And she is, this scarred, flighty, damaged girl trusts me enough to leave her protective bubble and take a chance.

"Thanks for letting me in enough to come here, Sydney," I tell her honestly, watching her blue eyes widen.

"I wouldn't want to be anywhere else right now," she murmurs.

Me either. Who would have thought? Andrew Forrester, the ultimate bachelor. The guy who never brings dates to any events, who won't settle down, who hasn't had a girlfriend in almost ten years. Totally pussy-whipped by a girl I just met.

And I couldn't be happier about it.

CHAPTER 16

I look out of the back wall of the villa, the glass doors are pushed open allowing the deck and the surrounding trees become part of the house. Sydney is sitting by the pool, cradling her morning coffee like it's a cup of liquid gold. I've noticed that about her, she can't really function without her morning fix. It's adorable.

Yep, fucking pussy-whipped, just like Damien said.

I put my lucky Red Sox hat on and head out across the deck to see her. She hates my hat, I'm not an idiot, but if we're going out today I have to have it on to keep people from recognizing me and ruining everything. Fuck if I know what she'd do if she found out about my job. I don't want to go there yet, not until I know how she feels about me.

Shit, thinking about feelings and crap. I'm such a fucking girl.

I take the seat next to her. "So, snorkeling, hiking, jet skiing, sailing, what would you like to do today, Sydney?"

She turns her head lazily in my direction, a dreamy look on her face as she puts her hand up to block the bright morning sun. "Those all sound wonderful. Anything would be great."

Chad said his crew is discreet and that his new sailboat is amazing, I guess it's time to test it out. "Well, how about we take out a sailboat, and if we want to, we can snorkel, otherwise we'll just relax onboard and enjoy the day?"

And hopefully everyone on the boat keeps their mouths shut and treats me like a normal guy.

I see her eyes flick up to my hat and her nose wrinkles a little at the sight of it but she doesn't say anything. Knowing that she finds it repulsive and is too polite to tell me makes me smile.

She starts to get up from her lounge chair. "Sounds great, I'll just go shower off so we can go."

Fuck, Sydney naked in the shower? Absolutely, but first I have to make sure the crew understands the rules.

Sydney walks past me and I grab her arm gently to stop her. "I just have to make a few calls to arrange the boat and I'll join you in a minute, don't finish too quickly." The intonation in my words is clear, and she doesn't miss it.

I watch her eyes widen a fraction before her lids drop and she smiles seductively. "Don't worry, I'll let you wash my back." She turns and disappears into the house, leaving me with a throbbing dick in my shorts.

Shit, I need to hurry.

Once I hear the water start in the outdoor shower, I pull out my phone and call Philippe. He answers on the first ring.

"Mr. Forrester, what can I do for you?"

"Philippe, we need the sailboat ready in an hour, is that possible?"

"Of course, I'll call the captain right away."

"Philippe, you need to make sure they understand very clearly, that they do not do or say anything to indicate that they know who I am."

"Certainly Mr. Forrester." His tone is joking, as if my request couldn't possibly be serious.

Fuck, this guy isn't getting it. Now I'm getting pissed. This weird, hyperactive, too-tan guy will not fuck up my shit with Sydney.

"I mean it, not a word Philippe," I snap rudely.

"They are very discreet, I promise." He's being more respectful now that he knows I'm dead serious.

"Yeah? They bettah be. I'll have anyone who fucks up fired. I don't want Sydney to see anything that insinuates that I'm anything othah than a regulah guy." I rant at him, knowing I'm being a dick but not giving a shit about his feelings.

"Are you serious? She doesn't know who you are?"

"Oh, I'm very serious. She bettah not heah or see a thing? Got it?" I bark at Chad's caretaker.

"Yes sir, one hour correct?" Philippe seems to finally understand me on this matter.

"Yes, an hour."

"Yes sir. I'll be up to get you in 45 minutes."

"Okay." I hang up and toss the phone on the outdoor table, dragging my hands down my face. This had better not be a bad idea, it seems as if disaster could sprout up from where I least expect it.

Done with that, I head into the master suite and quickly strip. Worries about the boat and crew are suddenly gone, replaced with visions of a naked Sydney rubbing soap all over her delectable body.

"Everything okay with the boat?" she asks as I step into the shower with her.

I freeze under the spray, forgetting how loud I can get when I'm pissed. I'm left to wonder how much of the phone call she overheard. She probably wouldn't tell me even if she heard everything, she's so fucking secretive.

If she's going to pretend she didn't hear everything then I'm going to act like she didn't hear everything. I slip my arms around her waist and press my hard, willing, cock against her wet body.

"Everything's great babe. Philippe will be here in less than an hour."

She looks at me and the corner of her mouth curls up. I see a wicked glint in her eyes. "Well then, let's hurry, shall we?" she says as she begins to stroke my aching shaft with her soapy hands.

Jesus. I throw my head back as she skillfully rubs my cock, a slow burn beginning to ignite in my groin. When she reaches down and lightly tugs on my balls I just about lose it right there and then.

My head snaps up and I grab her wrists, pinning them to the wall behind her. She gasps at my sudden movements and I dive in to taste her parted lips. I can feel her trying to wriggle out of my grasp but I hold on tight, plunging my tongue into her mouth roughly, taking not asking.

Deftly, I switch my hold so I have both of her wrists trapped in one of my hands leaving one free to run up her wet slit.

"Fuck, you're always so ready for me babe," I groan into her mouth, devouring her in another brutal kiss.

I reach under and lift her ass with one arm, still holding her wrists with the other. Somehow knowing what I want without needing words, Sydney wraps her legs around my waist so I can plunge deep into her willing heat.

Finally, I let go of her hands and she immediately snakes them around my neck and threads them into my hair. When she gives my scalp a sharp yank and her nails claw at my shoulder, it stokes the fire into a passionate explosion of intense need.

"Fuck," I moan as I grip her ass and pound into her over and over as she shrieks in ecstasy.

It only takes a few minutes for her to spiral into a searing climax, pulsating around my cock until I come to my senses and quickly pull out, my come jetting between us, coating our bellies before it's washed away by the shower.

Breathless, I pant out an apology to Sydney. I was so caught up I nearly forgot that we weren't using protection.

"What are you sorry for?" she asks as I lower her legs and she regains her footing on the wet, pebbled floor.

"I didn't think it through. There are no condoms in the shower." I give her a quick kiss before reaching past her to turn off the water.

"Oh."

That's all she says, *'oh'*. What the fuck does that mean? Doesn't she know I'd rather cut off my own arm than hurt her? I almost come inside her in the fucking shower!

Sydney wraps herself up in a towel and heads back inside the house, brushing by me without making eye contact.

Knowing her dislike for deep conversations, I figure now isn't the time to tell her about how my girl can expect to be treated. It'd probably make her run like hell in the opposite direction. But bareback fucking with no birth control and without her permission? Never gonna happen no matter how fucking incredible it feels.

I pull on my shorts and T-shirt while she gets ready in the bathroom and sit on the bed to think about her. She likes being bossed around in bed. I found that out last night. Would she be frightened by my protective nature? My sister Allie says I'm a control-freak or, when she's pissed at me, an overbearing asshole.

I can't help it. If someone threatens one of my family or friends, it's like a haze of red-hot rage surges through every molecule in my body, shutting down the logical side of my brain. After Matt died, then my girl was pretty much raped at a party when I wasn't watching, I felt a lot of guilt. I know I couldn't do anything about Matt, but my girl? That shit was my fault, I should have looked out for her, protected her from it.

Years later, my mom had to quit her job because of the psychotic women that kept breaking into her school to meet me. When I found out, I destroyed an entire kitchen's worth of glassware and spent three days straight in the gym pounding the crap out of anyone who would spar with me.

It pisses me off so badly when I can't protect my loved ones from shit. Especially shit caused by my job. Fucking fame, if people only knew what misery it can bring.

"Ready to go?"

Sydney's sweet voice pulls me from my dark thoughts and back to the present. I drop my scowl and force my Andrew Forrester smile onto my face, pulling her close. "I just have to get my hat."

She giggles, and my fake smile becomes real. I've forgotten everything I was thinking about and there's only her.

CHAPTER 17

Philippe stops the Mini-Moke right on the beach that runs along a large bay. Out in the gentle turquoise waves is a large, modern sailboat painted a deep blue with white trim. I was expecting a much smaller, less outrageous boat. It's eye-catching though, I'll admit Chad has great taste.

Chad is someone who really knows how to live, enjoy each moment and make it memorable. I need to take lessons from him. I never take vacations, and I have my brownstone and a few expensive cars but that's it. What would I do with all of this shit if I had it? I probably wouldn't have time to use it even if I bought it tomorrow.

"Here we are," Philippe says.

Sydney's eyes widen and her mouth drops open. "It's beautiful. Whose boat is it?"

"It's Chad's," I tell her. "He has a crew on call, so I had them prep the boat and they'll sail it for us since I know nothing about sailing and this boat is too big for one person anyway."

Sydney seems uncomfortable all of a sudden, using her hands to pat down her dress. Fucking Chad and his fucking ostentatious boat!

"You have a great friend to let us use all of his expensive toys. I hope I get to thank him in person someday," she murmurs.

Oh. She's uncomfortable because it feels like she's taking advantage of his generosity. As much as I'd love for Chad to meet her, that can't happen until she knows about me.

"Yes, hopefully," I agree. "Let's get aboard, ready Sydney?"

We trudge across the sand to a small inflatable with an outboard motor and a teenager at the helm. First test, don't screw this up for me, kid.

The pilot barely glances our way as I help Sydney get seated on the side of the dingy. I toss our stuff in and hop up on the other side. I scan the beach and pull my hat down low in the hopes that it will help when we meet the crew and face the caretaker. "Philippe, around 4pm?"

The good-natured man smiles and pretends to tip his hat. "I'll be here, Mr. Forrester. Miss Allen, enjoy your day."

Philippe pushes the inflatable out into the shallow surf and the kid starts the engine. He doesn't say a word, or make eye contact with either of us. I guess the dressing down I gave Philippe did the trick.

Nothing is better than when Sydney lets her guard down, so I spend the short trip watching her relaxed appearance. Normally so stressed out and reserved, her excited blue eyes are taking in everything around us and her beautiful mouth is pulled up into a huge grin. She's fucking stunning, her long auburn ponytail whipping back in the wind, the ocean spray shining on her face. I want to capture this moment and burn it on my brain.

The dingy pulls up to the sailboat, which looks even bigger from here than it did on shore. *Jesus, Chad.* Two men in white are waiting to greet us as our pilot tosses them a rope.

"Welcome to the *Magic Hour,*" the older man says as he extends a hand to Sydney.

"Thank you. I'm Drew, this is Sydney."

He shakes our hands and introduces himself and the younger man beside him. "I'm Frederick, your Captain, and this is Robert, one of the crew. I'll give you a quick tour and we'll head out. Winds are perfect today; the water isn't too choppy. It's going to be a great sail."

The captain shows us around the sailboat, and I'll admit it's impressive. "This is a 200ft Perini Navi sloop. She has five cabins and can sleep twelve. With her sails up she can reach 15.5 knots, which is about 20 miles per hour if you were wondering. She's two years old and has every modern amenity you could ask for."

Frederick walks us through the main cabin and tells us about the integrated satellite and sound system that is controlled by touch screens installed in each room. We go down two separate levels to see the bedrooms and the movie-screening room. Sydney tenses up when we see the built in theater that Chad has onboard and I have to clench my fists so I won't punch the wall.

It frustrates me to no end that I can't ask what the fuck happened to her.

Frederick finishes the tour up top on the deck where I bring Sydney to sit with me on the giant curved couch.

"So, sail around the island? Maybe a stop at a nearby reef for some swimming and snorkeling? What do you think, Sydney?"

The crew starts prepping to leave as we wait for her to approve of the plan.

She grins and reaches up, turning my cap backwards. "Sounds great," she says as she leans in to kiss me. "Let's go."

I smile broadly, how can I not when she looks at me like that? "You heard the lady, let's do it!" I tell the captain, who has been waiting patiently while we decided where to go.

Once he's gone I pull her to me and bury my nose in her neck, inhaling her addictive scent. The sound she makes when I touch her sends a jolt of desire straight through me.

Not now Forrester. I would never debase her by fucking her on this boat with a half-dozen crewmembers around. No way. She's too good to be treated like a whore, no matter how badly my cock is aching by the time today is over.

Sydney leans back against my chest as the sails go up and we begin to move. This boat is smooth, as it should be for the price. If I had to guess I'd say that Chad shelled out 100 million on this boat, maybe more. Not that he can't afford it, *shit,* not that I couldn't afford it. But a boat? Not where I'd spend my money but this sure is nice.

We manage to have a great time despite having to dance around such massive subjects as Sydney's past, my job, our future and pretty much anything else serious in nature. Even still, she's playful, sweet, and funny.

A young woman dressed in the same white polo shirt and shorts as the other crew members approaches us and asks if we'd like anything to eat or drink. Sydney asks for a water as do I. When the girl returns, she questions us on our lunch preferences.

"Syd? Anything you'd like for lunch?" I ask her.

The woman won't look either of us in the eye. Shit, maybe I went a little overboard with the directives when I spoke to Philippe.

She just shrugs. "I don't know, something light? So we can swim later."

"Okay, something light. Tropical or something," I tell the girl. She just nods and scurries off. Christ, she probably thinks I'm the world's biggest asshole. One of those dicks who doesn't want the lowly staff making eye contact or speaking to them.

The captain anchors the boat in a small cove near a tiny, rock covered island just off the coast of St. Bart's. Lunch is ready, so we make our way over to the shaded outdoor dining table and enjoy our meal of grilled snapper with coconut rice and mango salsa.

"This is delicious," Sydney says as she takes a bite.

Fascinated, I watch her face contort sensually at the pleasure she gets from the food. How am I supposed to eat if she's going to do that?

"Excuse me," Sydney says to the girl serving us. "Can I have a coconut rum and pineapple juice?"

The girl nods and waits for me to say something. Shit, I did go too far with my orders to the crew.

"I'll have one too," I say stupidly, too embarrassed by my earlier instructions that have made this young woman afraid to even look at us to think about what I just ordered to drink.

She comes back moments later and puts a fruity-ass looking concoction in front of me. It even has a fucking miniature umbrella in it.

"What is this?" I ask Sydney as I cringe away from the glass.

She can't answer me. She's too busy laughing hysterically, tears streaming down her face. Her joy is a sight to see, but I have no clue what's so fucking funny.

"What?"

"I can't believe *you* are drinking a panty ripper," she says between uneven breaths.

A panty ripper? Is that what this thing is called? Great.

I stare at her, an annoyed look on my face. "It's just pineapple juice and coconut rum, Syd. Besides, you're drinking one." I try to drink from the glass, but the little umbrella and the wedge of pineapple on the glass get in my way and smash against my nose.

That starts Sydney uncontrollably laughing all over again. I try to glare at her, but her attempts at stifling her laughter make me smile. I'll never admit it to her, but the fucking panty ripper was really good.

We finish eating and Syd asks if we can sunbathe for a while before swimming. Her, in a bikini, two feet from my face? *Hell yes.*

I pull a huge white bottle from my bag and turn to Sydney. "Can you sunscreen my back?" Chad and the other producers will have a fit if I show up for filming all sunburned. I'm not even supposed to get a tan, so I'm using SPF 8000 or something ridiculous like that.

There's a pause before Sydney answers me. "Sure." I hand her the bottle and quickly realize that maybe this wasn't such a good idea. Her soft hands are roaming all over my body, rubbing across every inch of muscle and skin. I'm going to sport a boner in front of the whole crew if she doesn't finish soon.

From next to me, I hear Sydney throw down the bottle of lotion and flop onto her chair dramatically and I realize that she's just as turned on as I am. I grin and lean over her. "Did you enjoy molesting me Miss Allen?"

"No, not at all," she says unconvincingly, her face buried in a towel.

I laugh and pull out my iPad, studying the scenes that I need to know by next weekend.

We read for a while, and relax in the sun. I spend way too much time staring at Sydney as she rests. Then we snorkel around the boat, watching the schools of fish and the massive green turtles that drift along the bottom of the sea.

Once we're back on the boat and in dry clothes, I see Sydney pulling out the sunscreen again.

"Hey, I think I've had enough sun for today. My face and shoulders are getting fried," I tell her. I see her glance at my face and scrunch up her nose. She knows I'm not burned yet. I'm not even tan, but I can't take a chance with filming starting in four days.

"Okay, let's go inside," she says agreeably, not questioning my contradictory statement.

We head into the main cabin for the sail back to St. Bart's. Sydney stretches out on top of me on the massive sectional couch and falls asleep almost instantly. The warmth of her body, the smell of her skin, the rocking of the sailboat… I fall asleep right after she does, thinking about how perfect today was and never having been as content as I am now.

CHAPTER 18

I wake up so early it's still dark outside. We've left the retractable walls open so the warm ocean breeze can blow into the master bedroom and I can hear the rustling of the trees outside.

Once my eyes adjust, I can see Sydney asleep next to me. She let it slip once that she has bad nightmares but I've never seen her have one. Maybe she's too exhausted from all the amazing sex we have. The thought makes me smile even though there's no one to see it.

I gently brush her hair away from her face. She's lying on her stomach, her pale skin glowing in the dark room. The sheets are tangled up in her legs leaving the rest of her body exposed, not a stitch of clothing in sight. I fight the urge to touch her, not wanting to be a douche and wake her up for sex, again.

I decide to get up, my mind too busy to sleep anymore. It's our last full day here and I have to leave for California in a few days. Will Sydney still want to see me when I get back? She's so fucking secretive I have no idea how she feels about us, about me.

Annoyed with myself, I grab my phone and head outside, sitting in one of the huge lounge chairs on the back deck. An uneasy feeling claws at my gut. I have no idea what to do. I'm so used to women using me for my name and me using them for sex. How the hell do regular people do this shit? How am *I* supposed to do this shit when neither will allow the other to know anything about them?

Frustrated beyond belief, I feel like punching something. *Control your shit Forrester*, I warn myself. Sydney most definitely wouldn't want to see me again if I woke her up by destroying some of Chad's crap or busting my hand on his wall.

Damien taught me a few techniques when I feel out of control. I breathe deeply for several minutes, distracting myself by checking emails and reading the schedule for the shoot. I pause to watch the sun rise over the Caribbean, the sky turning purple, then orange and finally a brilliant, cloudless blue.

Not paying attention because I'm busy responding to an email from Jane, I'm caught off guard when Sydney sinks down into the chair and curls her soft body up next to mine.

"Hey." I pull her closer to me.

"Hey, are you okay? You seem so sad sitting here. Did you sleep okay?" She gently rubs her hand over my arm.

Shit. So this is what it's come to? The chick is comforting *me*. I need to have my head examined when I get home. I'm supposed to be the strong one, looking out for Sydney, making sure she's protected.

Well, she asked a question, something she never, ever does, so I'm going to answer her.

"Yeah, I'm great. I've been checking emails, prepping for work. Just thinking about going back tomorrow and having to leave for California later in the week. About how little we really know about each other. About how much I'll miss you." I angle my head so

I can see her eyes, read her expressions since she never says anything with words.

I can see the conflict on her face. She doesn't want to reveal anything, but she desperately wants to give me what I want, to make me happy.

Then she says something I'm not expecting, "What do you want to know?" It's so quiet I can hardly hear her.

Holy shit! I sit up straighter, facing her fully so I can see all of her. She keeps her gaze lowered, refusing to look me in the eye. Once again, anger courses through me. An overwhelming desire to seriously maim whoever fucked her up like this.

Even though she doesn't like it, she's giving me my chance to ask her something, so I'm going to take it. Go big or go home, as usual. Hopefully, it doesn't backfire on me.

"Why don't you watch TV or read magazines or go to the movies?"

I watch as her mouth pops open in shock and she shrinks back, not enough to be obvious, but her body curls in on itself in a protective posture. She wasn't expecting that question. Now? Now I feel like a dick.

"I....it's just... I mean," she can barely speak.

Shit, I need her to believe me when I say I won't hurt her. I reach over and tug on her chin, puling it until she's looking at me. I can see the inexplicable fear behind her glistening blue eyes.

"Sydney, you can trust me. I care about you." I silently beg her to let me in.

Her words come out in a rush, stilted and forced. "It has to do with my parents, their divorce, it was ugly. It was public." She closes her eyes and takes a shaky breath. "That's really all I can give you right now, I'm sorry."

I pull her legs over my lap and take her face in my hands. She opens her eyes, just inches from mine. "Thank you, Sydney. For what it's worth, I'm happy that you trust me, even if it's only part of the story."

I can't help but wonder what the hell her parents' divorce has to do with hating TV. Was it turned into one of those shitty daytime movies or something? She has money, obviously. Maybe they're loaded and her dad's a big CEO or something. Maybe they dragged her through the courts and the newspapers and fucked her up. I don't know, it doesn't make sense.

I'll think about it more later. Right now, I want to taste her. I lean down and run my tongue over her soft lips, begging for access. She draws in a breath and opens her mouth to me, letting me taste and explore every inch of her depths with slow, lazy licks of my tongue. Our mouths slide together as we nip and tease and drink each other in.

Breathless, Sydney breaks the kiss and climbs on top of me, grinding her hot little pussy over my rock hard dick, a scrap of lace the only thing covering it. Not wanting to, but feeling the need to show her we're more than just sex, I stop her.

Sydney stills her writhing hips, but not without frowning in disappointment. *Shit*, as much as I want to spend all day fucking her I have to at least act like a gentleman and offer to take her somewhere today.

"So, what do you want to do on our last day here?"

She sulks, "I thought I was showing you what I want to do today." Sydney grabs my face and sucks my lip into her mouth, whimpering as she resumes shifting back and forth on my lap.

Unable to contain it, a groan escapes from my throat. She's so fucking sexy, I literally can't think with her sitting on my dick, just a few thin pieces of clothing between the two of us. When she reaches down and unzips my shorts, gripping my cock firmly and stroking it, I'm done fighting her.

"Sydney, what are you doing to me?" I whisper. She's destroying every notion I ever had about remaining single forever, convinced that every girl I met just wanted my money or my fame.

She doesn't answer me. Instead, she gets up and with a heated look in her eyes, she shoves me back on the chair and rips my shorts down to my ankles. Powerless to do anything but stare, I watch as she drops to her knees and starts licking the head of my dick seductively, moaning as her tongue swirls around and around.

"Fuck!" I groan, my hips thrusting up from the contact with her hot mouth.

Looking down at her, I catch the hint of a smirk on her face right before she takes all of me deep in her throat and swallows around my cock, momentarily causing my brain to shut down. Hissing through my teeth, I run my hands through her hair and coil it up in my fists. It feels so fucking amazing I swear I might pass out from pleasure. Sydney sucks slowly, almost painfully so, but perfect at the same time. I try to control the pace by thrusting my hips but she won't let me, continuing to go at her own speed not matter what I do.

I can't help but grunt in frustration, wanting so badly to take control, throw her down, and fuck her senseless for tormenting me, but I hold back and give her this. She continues her slow, deliberate torture, sucking hard and swirling her tongue around with each stroke until I can't take it anymore, her mouth is so fucking perfect. Unable to fight anymore, I lie back on the chair and let her have her way.

Once I give up on trying to control the situation, Sydney speeds up the pace, simultaneously giving me what I want and destroying my willpower to stop her. Panting, I groan as I reach the edge, my hips bucking up from the chair, her fingers grip my thighs almost painfully to hold me down which only heightens my pleasure. My reaction gives Sydney even more determination and she deep throats my entire cock and swallows as I come into her mouth. I think I almost black out from how long and powerful the orgasm is.

Stunned, I try to catch my breath, but it takes me a minute to slow down and sort through what just happened. I rake my hand through my hair, confused by my feelings. I don't like surrendering control, but that was un-fucking believable. Abruptly, I sit up and grab Sydney's face, kissing her deeply, turned on by the taste of myself on her tongue.

"That was without a doubt, the most intense orgasm of my entire life. You own me, Sydney."

She says nothing, smirking like she won the battle. *I don't think so sweetheart, you may have won the battle, but I won't stop until I've won the war.* I stand up and throw her over my shoulder, carrying her to the bedroom as she laughs. I toss her on the bed and make love to her until she has no choice but to feel the same way that I do about her.

My phone won't stop buzzing as we lie in bed and gently caress each other. I can't stop ogling her and I keep catching her sneaking sideways looks at me. She's so fucking cute.

"You can stare at me if you want to Sydney. I won't stop you."

A expected, her face turns bright red from my observation. How can she be embarrassed after everything she just let me do to her body? "I wasn't staring," she insists.

I laugh at her. "If you say so, but one of these days you're going to admit that you enjoy eye-fucking me."

She leans in close enough for her lips to brush against my ear and whispers, "I prefer just fucking you."

I sigh and pull her on top of me, crushing my mouth to hers, and get pissed when my phone buzzes for about the hundredth time since I got up this morning.

"You can check it if you have to," she murmurs against my lips.

I don't want to move, but I know if I don't answer the incoming emails, the phone will start ringing and I really don't want to deal with that.

"Sorry," I grumble as I get up and pull on a loose pair of shorts.

"Going commando?" Sydney jokes as she lies back on the bed, completely naked.

"Were you just checking me out again?" I say to her as I get my phone off the dresser.

"Not at all," she laughs.

Well, that's not an admission, but at least she's not dying of humiliation at my flirting.

I check the notifications. Fucking-A, there are tons of last minute schedule changes, possibly requiring me to leave for California a day early.

"Shit," I mutter under my breath.

"Is everything okay?"

I turn to find Sydney right behind me, unfortunately, with a towel wrapped around her insanely hot body.

"Yeah, I mean no. Not really." Sighing, I try to explain to her without freaking her out. "There have been some schedule changes for the project in California. I have to answer some of these emails."

I feel like a giant asshole for having to work on our weekend together.

"It's okay Drew. I'll go shopping downtown while you handle your emails. Philippe can take me, right?"

"Yes, he can. Are you sure you're okay with this?" It's been my experience that women will tell you one thing, but they really mean another and get pissed if you don't know how to read between the lines. I don't think Sydney is like that, but what the fuck do I know?

Her eyes soften. "Of course it's okay. I'll just shower and get ready. Can you call Philippe for me?"

I lean down and give her a quick kiss. "You're perfect, you know that don't you?"

She scoffs at my declaration. "Yeah, don't I wish," and heads off to the bathroom.

Baby, if you only knew how perfect I think you are.

I dial Philippe and he picks up immediately.

"Yes, Mr. Forrester?"

"Hey Philippe. Sydney wants to go shopping downtown. Can you come get her and take her around?"

"Of course, what time?"

"Be here in about thirty minutes."

"No problem, I'll be there."

"And Philippe, I don't want anyone fucking with her or anything happening to her. Are we clear?"

I know I'm being an ass, but if I can't be there to protect her, he damn well better do his best in my place. I couldn't go shopping downtown even if I wanted to. Someone would recognize me and the shit would hit the fan.

"Yes sir, very clear."

"Good. See you soon." I disconnect the call and finish getting dressed.

After Sydney leaves with Philippe, I grab a bowl of fruit for breakfast and head outside to sort through this scheduling crap. Irritated at the changes, I call Chad first, not really caring how early it is in L.A. He always was one of those annoying morning people so naturally, when I call, he's already awake.

"Drew! What's up? How's the villa?"

"Chad, it's great. That boat is fucking over the top though, dude."

"Isn't it?" The fucker actually laughs.

I guess he figures you can't take it with you.

"So, what the hell is going on with the shoot?"

"Done with the pleasantries already, I see," Chad responds in a sarcastic tone.

I exhale in frustration, my head fucking hurts already. "Listen, I only have three more days with Sydney. If this happens, I'll only have two."

Silence.

"Hello? Chad? Fuck! Are you there?"

"I'm here, Drew. I'm just speechless. You're so done," he says, laughing his damn ass off.

"Ha-ha fucker. Get your laughs in but I'm dead serious, I don't want to lose a single day with her. She's very... closed off. Once I'm gone I don't know what's going to happen."

"You mean with you or with her?"

Jesus, I'm fucking talking about chicks with Chad of all people, for the second time in a week.

"Her."

Silence again.

Then Chad starts laughing all over again. "Are you telling me that you like this girl, as in *really* like her, and you don't think she'll wait for you while you film in California? That's fucking rich!" He continues laughing at me.

"It's not funny, asshole!"

"It's not funny Drew, it's just so surreal. The *'Sexiest Man Alive'* can't get the one woman he wants to commit to him. C'mon dude, you gotta see how it sounds!"

"I know exactly how it sounds, Chad. It's still my fucking life you're laughing at, and you know I hate that *'Sexiest'* bullshit." But as mad as I am, he's right. I'm a total sucker for this girl and I have no clue if she even wants to see me again once we get home.

"I'm sorry Drew, really I am. Can't you just ask her?"

"I don't know Chad. She's very, very private. Someone fucked with her and now she acts like she has more to hide than the NSA."

"That's fucked up."

"I know. So what's with the changes?" I ask, wanting to direct the conversation away from my love life.

I hear him sigh. This isn't going to be good. "The studio had to change one of the locations last minute. The abandoned airstrip scene can't be filmed at John Wayne airport anymore. Apparently, whoever we got the permit from wasn't in a position to approve it and now Orange County won't allow it."

"Shit." I drag my hand through my hair and get up to pace in front of the pool.

"Right. So now we have to find another site last minute. There's a little airfield outside San Diego that said we could film there, but it'll take an extra day to get the props and crew back and forth. That's why we have to start a day sooner. The entire schedule is fucked up from this one change."

"Jesus, so I have no choice? That's what you're saying."

"None of us have a choice, Drew. The studio is already pissed at the extra expense. They're not going to be okay with you delaying filming to spend time with your new girlfriend."

"I know that Chad!" I hiss. Now I'm getting pissed off. I should know by now that I can't take this many days off from working out without the stress and the anger building up inside me.

"I'm not trying to make you mad. Shit, you've been in this business for ten years. You know how it is."

And I do. I know exactly how it is. Which is why I don't live in L.A. I got my fill of the whole backstabbing, everyone out for themselves experience my first year out there.

"Alright, I'll be there," I tell him reluctantly. He's right, I signed a contract and this is my job.

"Now," Chad continues, "Did you get the email about the last minute rewrites?"

Jesus Christ. It never ends.

Sydney came back from shopping and we spent the rest of the day by the pool, relaxing and just enjoying each other's company. I haven't told her that I have to leave a day early for California. I'm nervous about freaking her out. I guess I'm officially without balls. Damien will be so excited.

We're about to land in New York and Sydney is sound asleep, her head in my lap as I gently rub her back. Gail comes in and tells me that we need to get ready for the approach.

"Okay, I'll get her buckled in." I thread my fingers through Sydney's long hair. "Sydney, we're almost home. You need to put your seatbelt on, babe."

She opens her eyes and looks confused as she sits up. I reach over and buckle her belt for her, smiling as I snap it in place.

"Thanks." She smiles back at me.

"You're welcome." I lean over and kiss her sweet mouth.

"I can't believe I fell asleep. How long was I out?"

"I can believe it. We didn't exactly do a lot of sleeping these past few days. You've been out about an hour," I tell her.

Her mouth falls open at my suggestive statement. She tries to pretend that she's offended, but she's a terrible actress. I always know what she's thinking or at least how she's feeling, even if I don't know why.

I wink at her when she starts laughing and waggle my eyebrows.

"We'll be on the ground in fifteen minutes," Gail says as she breezes into the room and checks that everything is prepared for landing.

Without being obvious, I watch Sydney and notice that the closer we get to New York, the more anxious she becomes. I've seen panic on her face before, the first time I met her she looked just like this. It's like she wants to run away and never look back.

Shit, I hope she's not changing her mind about us. I told her I'd come back to the city several times during my six weeks in California and she made it sound as if she'd be happy to see me when I'm in town. *Now*, it seems as though she can't get far enough away from me.

Sydney almost looks sick to her stomach as the plane touches down at Teterboro and taxis to the hangar. She's trying to hide it from me but I can see that her hands are shaking and her face is pale and drawn. What the fuck is happening to the fun, playful girl I was just on vacation with?

Before I can ask her, Gail comes back into the cabin with our winter coats. "You're not in the Caribbean anymore. The captain says it's only forty degrees out."

"Thanks," I say to Gail as I watch Sydney button her coat up over her chin, clearly trying to hide her facial expressions from me.

Suddenly, there's a freezing blast of air at my back. I turn to see Bruce entering the cabin and grabbing our bags, heading quickly back down the stairs with them. I lead Sydney over to the door and a ball of barbed wire knots up my stomach from the sight in front of me.

It's easy to recognize the looks on the pilots' faces, the eager expression people get when they're excited to meet me. Well, not me, but Andrew Forrester, mega-A-list actor. These guys were told to specifically act as if they didn't know me and instead, they're acting like giddy schoolgirls. *Fuck!*

One of them speaks as we reach the doorway. "Mr. Forrester, it's a pleasure to meet you," he says, shaking my hand and acting like a complete asshole.

Out of the corner of my eye I catch Sydney's expression. She's completely perplexed as to why the pilots would be ass-kissing their passengers like this. I turn back to the over-eager pilots and give them a dark look that lets them know I'd be more than happy to rip their hearts out of their chests if they don't stop fangirling all over me.

Shocked at my anger, they immediately tone it down and politely shake Sydney's hand. "Miss."

She returns the gesture, dumbfounded as to what just happened, I'm sure.

This is one time I'm glad that she doesn't ask a lot of questions. We get in the car and sit in awkward silence all the way back to Sydney's loft in the Village. It's dark in the car, but I can tell that something's not right. Her posture is stiff and she won't look at me or touch me.

Is she dumping me now that we're back in New York? Did I do something to piss her off? I'm wracking my brain but I can't think of anything specific. She only started acting weird after I woke her up on the plane. The hairs on the back of my neck stand up and my stomach cramps when I think of Sydney breaking up with me.

Shit.

Bruce stops in front of her apartment and she leaps out of the car as if it's on fire. Great, she can't wait to get away from me, running again. I'm not giving up this time. She's going to fucking talk to me.

"I'll bring your bag up Sydney," I tell her as I smoothly lift it from the trunk, making sure my hat is down low and my coat collar is turned up so passersby don't recognize me.

She doesn't thank me for helping her up. Instead, she makes a face when I insist on accompanying her to her door. She knows me well enough by now to know I won't let her drag it upstairs alone. Plus, I'm not letting her off the hook. She's going to tell me what I did that made her act like this.

Sydney avoids eye contact the entire elevator ride up to the 8th floor. I stare at her, willing her look at me, but she's stubborn and determined. I don't even rate a glance. When the elevator doors open, she sprints down the hall to her door just to get away.

At least Sydney holds the door open for me and waits in the foyer instead of slamming it in my face. She's expecting me to drop her bags and leave immediately. *Fat fucking chance of that happening.* I carry her luggage to her room and set it next to the bed, taking a seat in one of the chairs by the windows to wait.

Having no choice, she follows me into her room and slowly sinks into the opposite chair. I can see her trembling from stress, her gorgeous face looks tired and worried, her eyes are wide and fearful.

"Sydney, are you upset with me?"

Don't tell me you're leaving me.

I rest my elbows on my knees to get closer to her, staring into her eyes and holding her gaze.

"No, Drew. I'm not upset with you. I've had the best weekend. Really, it was wonderful. I'm…I guess I'm just nervous about work tomorrow."

She's lying to me, I know it and I'm sure she knows that I don't believe her. What is she really worried about? Is it whoever hurt her before? I'll kill the bastard if that's what it is.

I lean back, frustrated that she's not going to elaborate. She said it's not me and I have no choice but to believe her, pushing her will only drive her further away. "One of these days Sydney, I'll get you to trust me. If you say it's not me, then I believe you. But I don't like leaving here knowing that you're upset and won't tell me why." I reach out and take her shaking hands in mine and kiss our intertwined fingers.

If she only knew that I'd happily take a bullet for her. All she has to do is tell me what she's afraid of, who she's afraid of, and I'll do my damnedest to fix it.

Syd's made her decision though, she isn't ready to let me in. I drop her hands and stand up, crushed by her unwillingness to confide in me. She jumps to her feet when I get up, her eyes glassy and wet with unshed tears.

Shit, don't fucking cry. It'll destroy me.

"Drew. I'm sorry I can't tell you. Please, be patient with me. I have…issues that I'm dealing with. And I *am* dealing with them. I don't want you to feel like any of it is your fault. You're perfect. This weekend was perfect."

She stretches up on her toes and kisses me, hesitantly. I have no idea how to respond, she's upset and I don't want to be a dick and take advantage, so I just stand there uselessly. When she runs her tongue over my mouth, I instinctually wrap my arms around her and kiss her back. The thought crosses my mind that if she freaks out and leaves me, this may be the last time I kiss her. I tighten my grip and greedily devour her mouth with mine. Forgoing breathing just to taste her a little longer.

When it ends, I lean my forehead down to hers and give a cryptic, but honest response. "Whatever it is Sydney, it can't be that bad. It won't change how I feel about you. And hopefully, if you ever find out something about me that is unexpected or surprising, you won't let it change your feelings for me. Call me tomorrow after you leave work."

Inside, I'm freaking out knowing there's a chance that she may not call me.

"Yes, I'll call you tomorrow."

I kiss her quickly one more time and leave before I do something stupid, like scream and punch a wall out of frustration. I hope I can wait until I get home to do that.

CHAPTER 19

White hot rage flows through my body, exploding out of my fists as I duck and punch my opponent in the side. *Shit!* He catches me on the chin and my head snaps back. Shaking it off, I land a diagonal kick to his ribs and he grunts in pain. Before he can retaliate, I cuff him with a left cross on his jaw.

"What the fuck!" Damien roars and loosens his gloves and head gear, throwing them on the floor.

I stand there, staring at the mat as sweat drips down my back. He's pissed and he should be. We're supposed to spar, not actually fight and I caught him twice in a row. Hard. Being a lefty gives me a huge advantage in the ring and I just used it against my best friend when he wasn't expecting it.

"What is your fucking problem today, Forrester? This is bullshit!" Damien stalks out of the cage and grabs his water, taking a long drink before turning his flashing eyes on me.

"Sorry man," I say lamely as I step down from the ring. "I have a lot of shit going on in my mind." I make a random hand gesture over my head.

"Don't fucking take your problems out on me," he hisses. "Get your shit together before you get in that ring, understand?" He snatches up a towel and wipes the blood from his nose.

"Damn Damien, I don't know what to say."

Jesus, I'm a fucking pathetic ass. What kind of man takes his girl troubles out on his best friend?

"Well fucking control yourself. I know that's a problem for you sometimes, but I'm not going in that cage with you until you can manage it!" He throws down the towel in disgust.

"Fine. You're still coming to California though, right?"

Damien's supposed to train me while I film *Mind of the Enemy* over the next six weeks. I play a CIA operative during the Cold War with Russia. I have to stay in shape, which means I need Damien.

"Are you going to stop being a prick?" he asks. I look over and see the corner of his mouth turn up.

"I can try. But you and I both know that prick and Drew Forrester are synonymous, so it may be a difficult transition."

"Yeah, I know." And he does know. After this many years of knowing me, he'd be blind not see what an asshole I am most of the time.

I unstrap my gloves and throw them in my bag, holding out a taped hand to my best friend. He doesn't hesitate before clasping it and shaking wholeheartedly.

"I'll see you later." I grab my gear and take off, pissed at myself.

Bruce is waiting out front, so I jump into the back seat of the Town Car and slam the door. "Home," I snap. He pulls out into traffic and I run my hands through my damp hair. I can't let this thing with Sydney affect every area of my life like this. All I can do is hope that she follows through on her word.

Once I get home, I shower and start packing for California. Keeping busy will stop me from obsessing over her.

The buzzing of my phone a few hours later pulls me from my misery. Sydney. *She called.*

"Hey babe," I say, trying to exude calm instead of relief.

"Hey."

"Are you headed home?"

"Yeah, stuck on Lexington. Traffic is pretty bad."

Something's not right. She sounds freaked out. Ten brief seconds on the phone with her and I've forgotten about my shit and am paying close attention.

"Sydney, you sound weird, are you ok?" *Do you need me to kick someone's ass for you?*

"Ummmm, I had a really shitty day at work, that's all."

Bullshit, something's going on.

"I don't like this. I need to see you. Can I come over?" I ask her. I'm silently thankful that she called, but my gut is twisting at the tone of her voice, at the thought of someone upsetting her.

"Yes please. I'd like to see you."

I close my eyes and thank god that she wants to see me. All that freaking out for nothing.

"I'm at home packing for California, so just have your driver swing by and get me and I'll ride over with you."

"Okay, I'll see you in thirty to forty-five minutes depending on traffic," she says. She sounds a little better than she did when she first called.

I grab a small bag and shove a change of clothes and my toothbrush in it and pull on the hat that Sydney gave me in St. Bart's. Hopefully, her driver won't look hard enough at me to see my face. Since it's already dark out, I don't think it will be a problem.

My phone buzzes from my pocket.

Sydney <Turning down your street>

I throw my bag over my shoulder and leave my brownstone the second her car pulls up to my curb. I can't be on the sidewalk any longer than necessary.

I open the back door and slide in next to Sydney. She looks gorgeous as usual, but stressed out, also as usual.

She smiles at my duffel bag and my Good Luck hat. "Wishful thinking, Mr. Forrester?"

I can't help but smile back at her playfulness. Maybe my Sydney is back. "A man can hope, Sydney." I kiss her lightly on the lips. "We can talk later, just relax babe."

She seems happy to accommodate my request, cuddling up under my arm for the quick drive over to her loft.

We ride the elevator in silence again, this time surrounded by a completely different atmosphere than yesterday. Sydney leans against me, letting me wrap my arms around her protectively. Her day must have been really shitty to allow me to comfort her like this. Yesterday she acted like she wanted to slam the door in my face and never see me again.

She lets us into the apartment and I drop my bag by the door, wanting to help bring her out of her bad mood. I gather her in my arms and hold her tight. "Are you hungry? I can order something."

"Actually, I really want to soak in the tub. Care to join me?"

The thought of being naked in the tub with Sydney sends a wakeup call straight to my dick. I lean down and whisper in her ear, "A guy would have to be crazy to turn down an invitation like that."

She smiles and heads to her room to start the bath. Instead of following, I turn toward the kitchen and grab two beers out of the fridge. I think we both need a little help relaxing tonight.

The water is running when I enter the bathroom and find Sydney standing in her work clothes with her hair all knotted up on her head, looking lost. I set the bottles on the edge of the tub and walk over to her.

"Let me undress you," I whisper. I remove her jacket and place it on the counter. She lets me lead as I pull her silky tank top off and toss it aside, her eyelids heavy with desire.

"Turn around." She doesn't even hesitate my terse command. I unzip her skirt and let it drop to the floor. Sydney kicks it away and waits for my next demand. Compliant Sydney is sexier than I could have imagined, which I did, a lot.

I hold out a hand and guide her to sit on the side of the tub. Running my hands down one long, toned leg, I reach her tiny foot. I carefully remove her high heel, my eyes never breaking contact with hers. I do her other leg, letting the shoe fall to the tile floor. I shift forward, nudging her thighs apart with my body so I can move closer to her. I take my hat off so I can press kisses up and down her flat stomach.

Turned on to a point where I may not be able to stop, I get up and undress quickly, throwing my clothes in pile. "Stand up, Sydney." My voice is laced with desire. She immediately gets up from the edge of the tub.

The sight of her makes my pulse race through my veins, she's so beautiful. I reach around and remove her bra, hardly able to believe that she's mine. Her body is pressed into my front, searing my skin with her heat. I run my fingers along the waistband of her panties, letting them fall to the floor before I kick them aside. *Shit*, all I want to do is lift her onto the counter and pound into her until she screams my name. My dick is so hard it feels as if it's going to explode if I don't do something about it.

A silent struggles ensues in my head, my mind fighting my body for control. I hold out a hand and help Sydney get into the steaming water. Sliding in behind her, I hand her one of the beers and take a giant swig of my own.

"Mmmmm, the water feels so good," she moans.

My dick is pressing into her back and if she's going to make noises like that I'm going to lose the ability to restrain myself. "You feel so good. Talk now or later?"

"Later," she sighs, melting back into my chest.

If she doesn't want to talk, then maybe I can help her relax. I place my beer down and put some of her body wash on my hands. I lather it up and slide my hands over her soft skin, down her arms, her chest, then to her breasts. When she whimpers and arches her back, I freeze in place. She's as turned on as I am. Does it make me an asshole to want her so badly when she called me to comfort her after a bad day?

Fuck it, I'm hard as steel. If she wants me to touch her, then that's what she'll get.

I move my hands over her breasts again, this time tugging on her nipples and rolling them into stiff peaks. I pour more soap into my hands and wash down the curve of her back and around her small waist. She presses her ass against my stiff cock and I can't think about anything but sinking into her.

As usual, when I'm around Sydney, my brain takes a back seat and my libido takes over. I reach down and slide a my hand down her abdomen and over her clit and she moans. She starts pushing her tight, round ass back against my dick again, driving me insane and increasing the aching in my balls. The hot water, the smell of her skin, the slick soap… my senses are consumed by need. After thinking for twenty-four hours that I might never be with her again, touching her naked body overrides all of my rational thoughts.

I don't notice her hand until it reaches back, grips my cock and places it at her entrance. I nearly come right there from the searing pleasure. She slides down onto it, letting me fill her up completely and I convulse from the sensation.

"Ahhhh, Sydney." She stills for a moment, then starts bouncing up and down on me, her pussy gripping tight as she slides back and forth. "Fuck, I can't believe how good you feel."

I can't restrain myself. Any shred of willpower has been demolished by the searing pressure of her tight heat. I'm overwhelmed by her responsiveness, by the hot electricity pulsing through my cock as she strokes it with her slick sex. It's never been this intense for me, both physically and emotionally. I lean forward and bite at her neck and shoulder, rasping my teeth over her skin as she writhes on my dick with reckless abandon.

"Yes Drew, oh God," she screams as she slams up and down, grinding her sweet ass wildly on top of me. I'm close to losing it, so I grab her waist and help to lift her up and pull her back down over and over as I thrust my hips to hit that sweet spot. The raw carnality of it engulfs me and spreads out from my throbbing cock to every nerve ending in my body.

I groan as my balls tighten and I come spectacularly at the same time that Sydney falls over the edge, throbbing endlessly as her pussy clamps down. Her willing body accepts every last drop that I release as it pulses around me.

Holy fuck! I've never felt anything like that before. I can die now and say that I've experienced the best sex a man could ever have.

Sydney collapses back onto me, her damp back to my chest, as we both catch our breath and come down from our climax. I'm so spent I can barely move, so I lay my head back on the cool tub and close my eyes. I feel her turn around in the water to face me. When she moves and I slip out of her, my brain switches back on and panic sets in.

What the fuck did I just do?

Holy shit, I just fucked her without protection! Even in the shower in St. Bart's I was able to stop in time to pull out before I lost my mind. I *never* lose control like this. Stunned, I still can't believe I just screwed her without a condom. I've never forgotten before, that's how much this girl gets under my skin.

Sydney is facing me, we're sitting chest to chest with her legs around my waist. Is she going to hate me? I fucking hate me right now. I wouldn't blame her for hating me. I'm supposed to be the one that protects her and right now, I feel like a failure.

I lift my head and find her inches from my nose. Cupping her face, I kiss her softly on her gorgeous, pink lips while I stroke her cheeks with my thumbs. Sydney snakes her arms around my neck and kisses me back affectionately. I don't think she realizes what just happened.

I have to tell her what I did. "Sydney, I didn't wear a condom."

I watch as her face falls. Adoration replaced by anxiety, contentment by confusion. I did that. I put that look on her face. What the fuck kind of man does that?

Disgusted with myself, I scoot her off my lap and get out of the tub, grabbing a towel and wrapping it around my waist. I shove my hands through my hair and snatch up my clothes. Stalking out of the bathroom to pull on my shirt and jeans and toss the towel aside, pissed as fuck.

I have no idea how to fix this.

I'm supposed to protect her, this sweet, vulnerable, damaged girl. And I just fucked it all up with my dick. I fantasized before about her riding me bare and now that I've done it, I feel like a piece of shit. Not just because it was wrong, but because it felt so fucking fantastic that I would give my left nut to do it again and that makes me a selfish bastard.

Sydney comes out of the bathroom and quietly ducks into her closet to get dressed. Well, I've worried about what she would think of me if she saw my fucked-up over-protective side. I think I'm about to find out.

She leaves the closet and walks calmly into the living room without saying a word. I follow her, unable to comprehend how she can be so composed after my massive screw up. When she gracefully sits down on the couch, I can't bring myself to join her. I'm too agitated. Instead, I pace back and forth in front of those goddamn bookshelves that hold the pictures that reveal nothing in the sterile apartment that gives me no hint of who the fuck Sydney really is.

Sydney is quiet, watching me with a wary expression on her beautiful, flushed face. Alright, if she's not going to speak then I will.

"I can't believe I was so careless! I've never done that, never!" I yell, continuing my pacing as I berate myself.

"Drew, calm down," she says evenly.

What? I snap my head up to look at her. "Calm? Sydney, I'm pissed at myself. I can't believe I did that to you. I'm so sorry. I just don't even know what to say."

Her clear blue eyes widen in shock. "Wait, I was just as caught up in the moment as you were, Drew. It's not your fault. You didn't do anything to me that I didn't want you to do."

Is she fucking kidding me? No way is she taking the blame for this.

I drop to my knees in front of her and lay my head in her lap. "I'm so sorry, Sydney. It's the first time I've ever forgotten to use protection. I'm supposed to take care of you and look out for you, not put you into more stressful situations."

"I'm sure it's fine. Look at me."

I can barely bring myself to do it, I'm so ashamed. She pulls her fingers through my wet hair as I meet her apprehensive gaze.

"It's okay, Drew. I run so much I don't even get regular periods, so I'm sure nothing will happen. You don't owe me an apology. I won't allow you to feel like this. It was consensual, and we're both adults, we'll deal with whatever happens."

I can see in her eyes as she tries to reassure me, that she's freaking out over the fact that she might get pregnant. I'll admit, as fucked up as it sounds, the thought of Sydney carrying my child, whether now or someday down the road, makes my heart explode with pride. It's stupid, I haven't known her very long, but I know she's the one I want, my forever. I've been completely numb for almost ten years and in the ten minutes I spent with her in my gym, I changed. She changed me.

Now, like everything else I try to discuss with her, she's shutting down and cutting me off. It's as obvious from the look on her face as if she held up a sign saying "conversation over". I have no choice but to go along with her decision. If I push her, she's likely to slam shut her protective doors and keep me out permanently. As much as I want to throw her down and force her to talk to me, I'm too afraid of her deciding that I'm not worth it.

"Alright, but I don't like this at all Syd." I sigh in frustration at her ability to cut me off from discussing anything involving *us*. She's not getting away without at least a warning. "But I trust you. If you say you're not upset, then I'll let it go, for now. Just understand that I won't let anything or anyone hurt you, not even me."

"Let's order some food," she says, changing the subject and letting me know that this conversation is without question, over.

Pissed and irritated by my strained capitulation, I order Thai food to be delivered and we eat in silence, the stress of my fuckup combined with her constant state of denial is hanging over the kitchen table like a dark cloud. I attempt some small talk, but it's forced and unnatural. It's only when I tell Sydney that I've known Chad for over ten years that she seems genuinely interested in the conversation.

"Drew, how old are you?" she asks, her complexion turning a deep scarlet.

I smile. She's asking me a personal question. "Twenty-nine, I'll be thirty on March 8th."

She suddenly looks sick. *What the fuck?* "What, am I too old for you or something?" Jesus, what if she thinks I am?

"No, that's not it. It just reminded me that I have something to ask you, related to my work." She stands up and puts her dish on the counter. "Are you done? Let's go into the living room."

Like a condemned man on his way to the gallows, I follow her to the living room, knowing that whatever she's going to say I'm not going to like. I've never felt this way before, downright fucking insecure around a girl. She brings out the best and worst in me.

Sydney motions for me to join her on the couch and sits quietly for a moment. This is not going to be good, I can tell by the look on her face. She's freaking out. What would that have to do with her job? I'm always so fucking confused around her. She fucks with my control so easily.

She inhales deeply before starting. "Okay, you know that I'm redesigning the new nightclub at the Warren. Well, when one of these clubs launches, they have a huge party. They invite people who will bring the most exposure to their business, like…you know…celebrities and what not."

I stiffen up at the mention of celebrities. Fuck, does she know about me? That can't be it. She wouldn't have wanted to see me tonight if it was. She most certainly wouldn't have fucked me in her bathtub.

"Ummmm, the bigwigs that run the Warren Hotel chain saw the interview in *GQ*."

That fucking prick piece of shit Reynolds?

I whip around to look at her. "The interview with Adam Reynolds?" I snap a little harsher than I should have. I can't help it, I despise that slimy bastard.

"Yes, that interview," she confirms. "He mentioned Verve and that he knew about it through me, and called the Warren to get an invite."

Yeah, how could I forget? He's such a pussy he tries asking her out in a fucking interview instead of face to face like a man.

I can't let her see how pissed off Reynolds makes me. I'm not going to explain it and I don't want her to ask. Not that she'd ever actually ask me anything remotely personal. I drop my Andrew Forrester mask into place and play it cool. "Okay. Is that why you were so unhappy when you left work? You already knew about the article."

Well, ummmm…" She stumbles on her words and turns bright red with embarrassment. *What the fuck is going on?* "So, the mention in the article set off a firestorm of A-listers calling to get on the invite list. Management at the Warren feel it's only right to repay Adam by granting his request to be at the party…and…ummmm, his request to be my date."

What. The. Fuck.

This girl, who hates celebrities so much that just looking at an article in *GQ* sent her into a full blown panic attack. Who won't even watch television. Who is *my* fucking girlfriend and I can't even tell her what I do for a living. Is going to a party with Adam Fucking Reynolds?

I can't hide my anger anymore, a red haze drops over my vision and my fists ball up tightly in front of me.

"And you said yes?" I ask through clenched teeth.

She avoids my furious glare. "No. Not at first."

"Not at first," I repeat. So she said yes.

"Drew, I said no! I told them I was seeing someone, and I wasn't going on a date with anyone but you."

Holy Fuck! She mentioned me to her bosses! Then she does knows who I am.

"You mentioned *me?*" I choke out. I think I'm having a heart attack.

A flash of anger crosses her face and she narrows her eyes at me. "Well, I told them I was seeing someone. I didn't mention you specifically. Why, do I embarrass you or something?"

She thinks she embarrasses me? Jesus, I would parade her around everywhere I went if I could just get past all the secretive shit she's hiding from me.

Now I'm even more pissed. "Of course you don't embarrass me Sydney!" I yell. "You're the one who doesn't want to talk about anything, or know anything! I'm just shocked as hell that you would even tell anyone that I exist!"

She exhales quickly, my words stung. "That's how you think I feel about you? That I want to pretend you don't exist?"

Great, now I'm an asshole.

"No, that's not what I meant, shit. I don't know Sydney, I'm still stuck on the whole date with Adam Reynolds bomb you dropped on me. I don't share," I grit out between clenched teeth.

I'm so angry and confused. I run my hands through my hair in frustration, ready to pull all of it out if it will help me deal with this unbelievably bizarre crap.

Sydney is suddenly on her feet in front of me, her cheeks red with anger. "It's not a date!" she shrieks. "I told them I would only go if I could bring you and that Adam understood that we," she motions back and forth between the two of us, "would hang out with him and talk to him but that's it!" Her chest is heaving in and out with rage.

Fuck this! If she's going somewhere with Adam Reynolds then I want answers. That prick fucked me over once, and he's not doing it again.

I stand up and face her, towering over her as she fearlessly meets my furious stare. "But you can't stand celebrities, Sydney! That's what you said! There will be cameras and famous people everywhere! I just don't get it!"

"I don't like any of that shit, Drew! I hate it! It fucking ruined my life, okay? I'm still screwed up from it. I don't want to go to the party at all, but when the boss of a multi-billion dollar hotel chain tells you to show up at his party, you have to show up! I have no choice!" Sydney huffs and sits down heavily on the couch, crossing her arms and sticking her lip out in an adorable pout.

Now I'm the bad guy here. Adam motherfucking Reynolds wants my girl and I have to fucking take it like a chump because it's for her job. I want to find him and punch the ever living shit out of his stupid fucking face.

I slump over, defeated. I can't win this argument. Not with only half of the information available to me, and Sydney's not about to tell me the other half. I drop onto the seat next to her and attempt to control my fury. I don't like to lose, especially to that fuckwad Reynolds. There's no way he's going to make a move on my girl and live. I take a deep breath, making a concerted effort to not sound like the raging lunatic that I'm hiding inside.

I can't believe I'm backing down. It goes against everything I feel, everything I am, but I know if I push this and tell her she can't go with that asshole because she belongs to me, I'll lose her.

"I'm sorry Sydney. I won't ask you about your past, since you aren't ready to tell me, but I won't know if I can go with you until I get to California and see how my schedule is and how the project is going. I understand that you have to be there, but I'm not going to pretend to like it. In fact, it makes me want to punch Adam Reynolds right in the head."

Or destroy his fucking arrogant British ass with my fists. Or my feet. Or both.

I see her jaw drop slightly, then she closes it tight before apologizing for her job. "I'm sorry. I'm sorry for dumping this on you. It's on your birthday and it's probably not your idea of a good time. If you can't make it, I get it."

Sydney sounds defeated too, like she really doesn't want to go. And honestly, I believe her. She doesn't want to do it but her asshole of a boss is making her. To keep Adam Reynolds happy. That fucker better hope I can't make it that night. He has no idea what he's started by forcing my hand by screwing with my girl. Again.

I lean in and touch my nose to hers. "I'll try my best to be there, if for no other reason than to keep him from hitting on my woman. Let's go to bed."

I have no clue what just happened or how tonight went so wrong but I know one thing, if I see Adam Reynolds again, I'll fucking kill him.

CHAPTER 20

Bruce drops me and Jane off in front of terminal 8 at JFK for our 5pm flight to LAX. I hate airports. If anything got infinitely worse for me after I became an actor, it's air travel. Unless I fly private, it's always a giant nightmare. At least it's winter, so I can get away with an unshaven face, a scarf around my mouth, and my hat pulled low.

"I'll be there tomorrow," Bruce says as he gets back in the car. We didn't bother changing his flight; the studio will send a car to pick us up at LAX.

'Yeah, see ya man," I call out as I duck my head and enter the busy airport.

"Okay," Jane sighs as she hoists her bag over her shoulder. "Let's do this."

I smile at Jane. This sucks almost as much for her as it does for me. She gets mobbed just like I do, but unlike me, people don't hesitate to physically push and shove her out of their way. It pisses me off so much that I've almost taken a swing at a few people who went too far with their man-handling of my assistant.

We get in the express line at the United Airlines check-in counter. I have to go through all the same shit as everyone else at the airport, my only saving grace is that I always get to use the fast lanes. If I had to stand in the security lines with hundreds of other people, I'd probably never fly.

"I.D.'s please," the middle-aged ticketing agent says to us as we step up to the counter.

Please don't make this a big deal lady. After arguing with Sydney last night and the bathtub incident, I can't take any added stress today.

We hand over our licenses and I hold my breath. She must scan Jane's boarding pass first because it takes her a minute to get that look on her face.

"Oh," she gasps as her eyes go wide. She glances up at us and her eyes study me for a moment. Probably trying to figure out how the scruffy guy with the hideous hat is actually the attractive man in the photo on my license.

I give her a small smile, nothing big enough to encourage a dramatic reaction from her, but enough to keep her happy. She smiles back and hands us our paperwork and I.D.'s. "Enjoy your flight," she chirps breathlessly.

"Well thank God for small miracles," Jane mutters as we head toward security.

I smirk from under my scarf, knowing full well that the problem at the airport isn't the ticketing desk, it's getting through security. I can't keep my hat, scarf, or any other item on to hide under, so I'm always recognized by someone.

We step over to the first class security line to wait for our turn. I stall until the last possible second to take off the scarf as I hand the TSA agent my I.D. and boarding pass. Doing my best to seem happy, I smile when the agent does a double take and her bulging eyes meet mine. I must have luck on my side today, because she thanks us without any extra conversation.

"Wow, this is going way too smoothly," Jane says as she removes her shoes and throws them into a bin.

"I know. I guess one of the agents will have to steal something of mine to even it out."

My comment about stealing is both humorous and pathetic, because it's true. At least half the time I fly, something of mine goes missing at security. There's always a sticky-fingered agent that wants an Andrew Forrester souvenir, knowing that I won't notice until much later that it's missing. Last time it was my sunglasses, the time before it was my watch. Once, someone even took a fucking pack of gum. *A pack of gum!*

After six years together, Jane and I have devised a plan of attack. She goes through the body scanner first, and then watches my stuff as it slides through the x-ray machine, not giving the agent an opportunity to snatch something. Still, every once in a while a tricky thief makes off with one of my belongings. It's irritating to say the least.

I reluctantly drop the scarf into a tub with my lucky hat. If that hat ever went missing, I'd throw such a fucking fit they'd wish they never heard of Andrew Forrester. Luckily, it's so gross looking, that no one has tried to lift it, yet.

"Excuse me." I cringe at the soft voice behind me.

"Yes." I respond without turning around.

"I love your movies," the woman says kindly.

I can't be rude to someone who's being so respectful, even if I'm annoyed. It's not her fault that she caught me in a bad mood.

"Thank you." I turn to give her one of Andrew Forrester's best fake smiles.

"You're welcome," the young woman says, smiling back.

And that's it. If only every fan could be like her; polite, to the point and not pushy or demanding. We manage to get through security without any more problems and head to our gate.

Unfortunately, our good luck doesn't last. Before we can get to the private club lounge, someone spots me, and this woman isn't nearly as quiet or polite as the one at security.

"Oh my Gawd!" she screeches in her brazen New York accent as she runs over to me.

I hold up my hands to ward her off before she can put her outstretched fingers on my arm. You can look lady, but don't fucking touch.

"Hi, sorry we're in a hurry to make a flight," Jane says dismissively to the woman without breaking her stride.

"I just gotta say hi," she rasps in her obvious smoker's voice. "I love your work."

She's not going to go away, hurrying to keep up with us, and her loudness is beginning to draw a crowd. I hear my name being murmured throughout the terminal. Spreading from us quickly like a virus out into the masses as people realize that I'm here.

"Hi, nice to meet you," I say as we try to rush past the growing horde of Andrew Forrester fans and gawkers.

"Can I get a picture with you?" the annoying New York smoker asks.

"Sorry, like she said, we're late," I tell her, my hurried steps not slowing down.

"Come on! Just one picture! My niece will never believe this!"

Fucking A, this woman is irritating!

I see the camera phones out and pointed at me. She's the one hassling me and I get to be the asshole caught on video. Well tough shit. It's too bad for her that I don't give a fuck what they say about me in the tabloids.

Good thing I have Jane. We have a routine for when fans get too pushy. Jane plays bad cop and I play the cop who doesn't give a shit.

"Listen lady, we told you several times. We. Are. Late. For. Our. Flight. So, if you'll excuse us, you will not be getting a picture, an autograph, or anything else today. Have a nice day." Jane says all of this with a polite smile on her face and the woman's determined expression is replaced by one of anger.

Of course she's an angry one and not an embarrassed one. I have yet to meet a New Yorker that gets embarrassed over anything. Well, except for Sydney, but she seems to be the exception to everything. Fuck if I know, she might not even be from New York.

The throng of bystanders follows us all the way to the club lounge where they thankfully, aren't allowed.

"Well, she sure was an aggressive one," Jane says in disgust as the heavy club door closes behind us.

"Yeah, once again it's a wonderful fuckin' day at the airport."

"Drew! Stop swearing so much!"

Shit, I always forget that she hates it when I curse, which I do in almost every sentence I speak.

"Sorry!"

Only Jane could get away with scolding me like that. And Sydney. I mean fuck, Sydney went toe to toe with me yesterday over Adam fucking Reynolds! I've never let a woman get the best of me like that, except maybe my mom.

"Let's go sit," Jane says, patting my arm.

"Great." I've never been so unhappy to be going to work as I am right now.

CHAPTER 21

"Forrester, we need you on the set!" Chad's voice crackles through the overhead system.

Crap, I was spacing out. Thinking about Sydney… again. I hustle from my dressing room to the soundstage. I've been hiding out ever since we started filming. Apparently, my reputation of hooking up on set has preceded me and the women on the crew have been relentless in trying to get my attention. I can't walk ten feet without a PA or a sound technician jumping in front of me and flirting. I've pretty much been a dick about it too, but all I can think about is Sydney and it's making me irritable.

I enter the massive soundstage and sigh at the bare green walls and floor and the partial helicopter constructed in the center.

My co-star, Zane McNamara, and I have been filming chroma key scenes for the last three days. It's brutal, mind-numbing work, pretending to see things and react to events that aren't there, but we can't actually film an anti-Communist movie in Red Square or fly over Moscow, so this is what we have to do. I despise it, and being away from Sydney is making this the most difficult shoot I've ever done.

At least my character is under a lot of stress, because *that* I can manage to portray.

"Zane." I nod at the bulky blonde man who will play another CIA operative with me.

"Andrew," he says seriously. Zane is the guy who stays in character all the time. It works for him, but it drives me up the fucking wall. At least he uses his real name on set. Those assholes who insist on being called by their character's name throughout a shoot really get under my skin.

Luckily, the rest of the day goes well and we're done by 7pm for the first time all week. I rush back to the Sunset Marquis so I can Skype Sydney and show her the plane ticket I have for tomorrow. I can't wait to see her face. She cut off my Skype sessions when I kept apologizing for the no-condom bathtub sex and I only just got her to agree to Skype me tonight after I promised not to discuss it anymore.

I rush through the tropical grounds and past the pool at the Marquis to my suite in the Presidential Villa. It's the same one I stay in every time I'm in California. I would just rent it permanently, but the thought of putting down any kind of roots in this city makes me nauseous.

I drop into the desk chair and open the app on my laptop. Skype rings a few times before it clicks on. Sydney's gorgeous face lights up my computer.

"Hey beautiful, I miss you," I tell her, leaning towards the screen as if she's actually right in front of me.

"I miss you too," she whispers in a soft voice.

Then I see it. She looks terrible. Her eyes are rimmed with red and there are dark circles under them. Her lips are trembling ever so slightly, as if she's overcome with anxiety. She looks thin, way too thin. How the fuck could she have lost so much weight in one week?

My protective instinct takes over and the hairs on the back of my neck stand up. "Sydney? What's wrong? Why are you so thin? Are you okay? Do I need to send over a doctor?"

She lowers her eyes for a moment, then looks back up. "Nothing's wrong, Drew. I'm just tired, that's all."

Jesus Christ! I ball up my fists under the table where she can't see them. I wrestle with my desire to scream at the fucking computer until she tells me what the hell is going on. I am so sick and tired of being kept at arm's length while she falls to pieces.

I exhale deeply before speaking, afraid my anger will overtake me. "One day, Sydney, you'll let me in so I can protect you from whatever it is that haunts you. Between the shit you're going through personally, the extra workload, and that ass Adam Reynolds trying to steal you from me… I should have just cancelled this project and stayed with you!"

I drag my hands through my hair in frustration. If she would just fucking trust me!

"I know, I'm sorry. And Adam Reynolds isn't trying to steal me, Drew." The way she brushes off my concern over that prick makes my blood boil. "Oh! I forgot, I have news."

Sydney's face lights up with whatever news she has for me. Me? I'm wary of whatever she thinks is so great. Her last bit of news was when she told me she's going to a party with that douchbag Reynolds.

She smiles brightly. "Not pregnant."

God, she looks so relieved. Me, I'm ridiculously disappointed. I had been fantasizing about Sydney and me raising a little mini-Sydney in my brownstone. Stupid, I know.

"That's great, Syd. Really great. The timing would have been awful."

She makes a weird face but it's gone before I can decipher it. "I know," she says. "It's a relief to have a little less to worry about."

Thank fuck for that. This girl is under more stress than anyone I've ever met, and I've met *two* sitting presidents.

"If you're less stressed, then it's great, Sydney. So, I also have news." I can't wait to see her reaction. I pick up my phone and pull up the confirmation number for my flight tomorrow and hold it up to the camera.

"You're coming home tomorrow?" she screams.

I grin, a real one. Watching her face, flushed with excitement, is worth all the shit we've been through this week.

"Yep. I got Chad to rearrange a few things with the schedule so I can see my girl!"

"I cannot wait to have you here, should I get you from the airport? I can use the hotel car service."

Sydney? Seeing me at the airport? With a pack of fans following me outside? Over my dead body!

"No!" I shout, cringing when I see her face fall. *Shit, asshole.* "I don't want you to have to go all the way to JFK, I have Bruce to drive me. I'll swing by my place to grab a few things then can I stay with you?"

"Of course I want you to stay with me, just call me when you land. You get in at 7pm, right?"

"Yes, and since I won't be bringing any luggage I can just go straight from the plane to the car. So I'll probably be over around 8 or 8:30, sound good?"

"Sounds amazing!"

CHAPTER 22

Thank God I didn't let Sydney come to the airport. It's a nightmare, especially without Jane. I'm going to have to start bringing my own bodyguards with me. The media is just so much more aggressive than they used to be.

"Move!" The airport security guard yells at the paparazzi that swarm around me like flies to a carcass.

I'm thankful for his willingness to help me, but he's not very effective. A horde of men with massive cameras who are trying to play twenty questions with me as they push and shove each other, aren't receptive to listening to random security guards.

"Andrew! How's filming going!"

"Any ladies Andrew? Or are you still single?"

"What's it like working with Zane McNamara?"

"We heard you were just in the Caribbean, is that true?"

"Who were you with on vacation, Andrew?"

Jesus Christ! How do they find this shit out?

I spot Bruce at the curb, holding open the back door to the Town Car and jump in. He took an earlier flight while I finished my scenes so he could get the car and meet me here.

"Hey Bruce." I jump in and he pulls away from the shouting paparazzi.

I fish out my cellphone and shoot Sydney a quick text.

Me <In the car. Headed home. Will be over after.>

I'm about to make a call when my phone beeps back.

Sydney <Can't wait! xo>

I grin like an idiot. Then I remember the call I need to make and scowl as I pull up the contact and push send.

"Drew! What's up?" Rhys, my PR director, says.

"Rhys, you know I don't pay attention to any of that bullshit in the tabloids." I cut right to the chase.

"Yes," he replies hesitantly, guessing correctly that he's not going to like this conversation.

"Has there been anything about my St. Bart's vacation anywhere?"

Silence.

If that's not a yes then I don't know what is.

"How did they find out?" I growl, pissed that there might be a picture of Sydney out there.

"I have no idea. Someone saw you on St. Bart's or someone at the airport leaked your flight plan."

"Did they call for a comment?"

"Yes."

"Fuck, Rhys! Stop with the short answers and give me the fucking story!" I snap.

"Alright. The day after you returned I got a call from a tabloid wanting to know if you had been on vacation on St. Bart's. There were no other specifics and the article I saw had no photos with it. It was just a bunch of speculation as to where you stayed and what you did. No first-hand accounts."

"No photos?" I ask in disbelief.

"None."

"Thank God," I murmur more to myself than to Rhys.

"Is there a reason you care about this specific article?" Damn. Rhys knows me too well.

"No," I lie. "Just curious."

"Okay, well if you need anything else just call. Don't forget that the premiere for *A Soldier's Burden* has been scheduled for March 24th in L.A."

"Got it. Talk to you later."

I lean back on the leather seat and rub my face with my hands. How am I going to explain another trip to L.A. to Sydney? Or better yet, how can I get her to get over her shit and go with me?

A laugh tears from my throat. Dozens of women have hounded me to take them to an event. Reporters question me about my solo appearance on each and every red carpet I walk. I've been dubbed the 'Ultimate Bachelor' multiple times and I've never wanted any of the shit that comes with dating someone publically.

I finally find a woman I want to bring with me to a premiere, to show off to everyone, to claim as mine, and she would rather jump off of a cliff than go with me.

Fuckin' irony.

Thirty minutes later and Sydney's front door flies open, her beautiful, but too skinny face smiling at me like she hasn't seen me in months. God, she's so gorgeous it hurts.

I step into her loft and throw down my bag, grabbing her by the waist and pulling her firmly against me. "I missed you," I murmur into her hair as she clutches me back just as tight. The iron band that had been wrapped around my chest for the last week and a half has finally been loosened and I can breathe again.

"Me too," she says, tipping her head up to see my face.

Having her pressed into me sends a welcome rush of pleasure through my body, flooding my mind with every lustful thought I've had over the last ten days. Uninhibited, I lower my mouth to hers and greedily capture her soft lips, sliding my tongue along the seam until she opens to me. When she does, it's as if a tiny spark within her ignites into a roaring blaze of passion. She fists my hair and moans, fitting her lithe body around mine sensually.

I reach around and lift her by her ass, positioning her right over my hard cock as she winds her legs around my waist and locks her ankles behind me. Our mouths stay connected as I carry her into the dark bedroom and deposit her on one of the chairs by the windows.

"Why are you stopping?" she complains as I pull away from her grasp.

"Because I need to be inside you, now," I rasp, beginning to shed my clothes as quickly as I can. "Strip."

I see her eyes widen a fraction, then darken with desire as my words sink in. Sydney gets up and stands in front of me as she begins hurriedly removing her clothes.

By the time we're both naked, my control is hanging by a thread, ready to snap at any second. I have to rein myself in, or this will be over before we've begun. I grab Sydney and push her against the wall of windows that spans the back of her room.

"Drew," she moans, her eyelids half closed, heavy with desire.

"Are you ready for me?" I ask, sliding a hand down between her legs and skimming a finger along her needy slit. "Fuck, you're so wet."

"Take me Drew," she pants as she runs her hands down my chest and curls one around my throbbing cock.

"God Syd, I missed you so much." I rip open a condom and quickly roll it down my length.

Eyes roaming up and down her naked body, I step forward, pressing her against the windows and lift one of her legs, hooking it around my waist. Not wasting a single second, I position myself at her damp entrance and stare into her eyes as I roughly push into her tight heat.

"Jesus," I whisper as her wet depths surround me and pull me in. Sydney lets out a soft sound that's half-sigh half-moan, her warm breath tickling my ear.

I scrabble to grab behind her other knee, desperately needing to be closer to her. Finally finding where I'm reaching for, I yank on it and lift her up, pressing her harder against the window as she clings to me. Sydney licks her lips and closes her eyes, waiting for me, her breath held in anticipation.

When I start to move, the outside world ceases to exist. Sydney's eyes fly open and meet mine, our gazes are locked together as I thrust up into her, hard. Each snap of my hips shoves her further and further up the glass, her skin squeaking against the window, drawing a low moan from the back of her throat.

Unable to go slow, our pace is frenzied, the pleasure building quickly from the intensity and from our time apart.

Bending my mouth to her ear, I speak to her, each word falling from my lips in rhythm with the movement of my hips. "I. Missed. You. So. Fucking. Much. You're mine Sydney. Only mine."

She closes her eyes and lets the sensation take over. Her swollen lips part and her pink tongue darts out to lick them again, driving me crazy, making me want to devour her mouth.

"Say it!" I demand. Her eyes fly open and lock with mine again. "Tell me you're mine."

"I'm yours Drew."

"Fuck yes you are. No one else Sydney."

I crush my lips to hers and savor the taste of her sweet mouth. I can feel the tightening of her pussy around my cock and know that she's close. Shoving my hand between us, I circle my thumb over her clit and she comes apart, screaming and convulsing as she shatters.

"That's right baby, come for me," I grunt as I slam into her a few more times before the overpowering pleasure rushes through my body and gathers at the base of my spine, begging me to release everything I have into her willing pussy.

I grit my teeth and force myself to pull out, watching Sydney's eyes widen as she begins to protest the loss. "Turn around," I growl, lowering her feet to the floor and spinning her quickly so her front is crushed against the glass.

Sydney slams her palms down on the window one at either side of her head and turns so her cheek is pressed against the glass. "God Drew, yes!" she cries when I forcefully enter her from behind.

"Jesus, I love fucking you," I snarl. She whimpers and pushes her ass out, arching her back sinfully in a silent invitation. The temptation to manhandle her proves to be too much for me to ignore, especially when she's all but asking for it. I reach up and wrap her long hair around one hand and tug so her head bows back until it rests on my chest. Her long, slender neck is exposed, the creamy skin calling like a beacon in the night. I lick and taste and bite at the sinuous flesh, never slowing the furious thrusts up into her tight pussy.

Sydney begins wailing, a primitive sound that I don't think she realizes she's making. Her entire body shudders, and she lets out a stream of incoherent words as she comes around my cock again.

The sounds, the scent of her arousal, her perfect response to my rough handling prove to be too much for me. The pleasure explodes from my aching balls, shooting up through my spine into an orgasm so strong that I can't stop thrusting into her, over and over until the blissful sensation subsides.

When I finally am able to stop, the only sound in the room is our heavy breathing. I release her hair and drop my head onto her shoulder, trailing small kisses back and forth over her sensitive skin, overwhelmed by how much I feel for this amazing girl. Gently, I pick her up and carry her over to the bed and lay her down, climbing in next to her and pulling the covers over us.

Sydney snuggles right into me, her back to my front. I wrap an arm around her small shoulders and hold her against me all night.

Without a doubt I fucking love this girl.

"Sydney," I whisper softly.

"Mmmmm."

Not much of an answer, but after spending most of last night in bed and only half of that time asleep, she's exhausted.

I chuckle. "I have to run home for an hour or two to do some work. I'll be back after?"

Her eyes open a fraction and I see a small smile on her lips. "Where are you going?" She shifts a little to push against me and frowns when she realizes I'm no longer in bed.

Clearly, she wasn't awake when I just told her where I was going. Sydney is so adorable all disheveled and half asleep, her long hair tangled around her. I grin, "I have to run to my place for an hour to do a little work. Plus I forgot a few things in my hurry to get here," I say, feeling shitty about lying to her. "Bruce is waiting for me babe, I gotta go. I'll be right back, you just sleep."

"Okay," she murmurs, already slipping back into deep sleep.

I brush my lips across her lightly freckled cheek and head out on an errand that may turn out to be a huge mistake. As I hustle across the busy sidewalk in front of Sydney's building and climb into the car, I realize that she's left me little choice in this matter. We can't continue like this, with these secrets between us, and I can't tell her about me until I know why she's so freaked out by fame. I don't want to make that leap of faith when it could cost me everything…it could cost me Sydney.

"We're here," Bruce says when he stops the car in front of the Village Coffee Bar.

"Great, you can go. I'll walk back to Sydney's."

Bruce's eyebrow quirks up in the rearview mirror. "Are you sure?" He puts and arm around the passenger seat and turns to face me, a questioning expression on his face.

It's a busy Friday morning in New York and the streets are packed. He's worried about me walking down the sidewalk alone.

"Yeah, it's fine." I get out and slam the door. I'll most likely need the cold air to clear my head before I see Sydney again, so it's better if I walk back even if it means getting accosted by overeager fans.

Not wanting to invite trouble, I tug my hat down, pull up my scarf, and head inside. I have a moment of déjà vu remembering the first time I came here. The day that changed my life. The scent of cinnamon and coffee fills the space and the warm air is inviting.

Almost immediately, I spot Leah wiping down a table and walk towards her. I have no idea what Sydney's best friend thinks of me. All I know is that she hasn't told Sydney anything about me and for that I'll be forever grateful to the perky little blonde. But she might consider me to be a huge douchebag for deceiving the friend that she thinks of as a sister.

"Leah."

"Shit!" she yelps, jerking upright and dropping her cloth rag. "You scared me." Her sharp eyes look me up and down as she clutches her chest in surprise. "Nice disguise," she says sarcastically, snatching the rag back up from the table and shoving it in her back pocket.

"Can we talk for a few minutes?"

I feel like an idiot. I'm standing in a busy coffee shop begging my girlfriend's best friend to have a heart to heart with me. My man card has almost certainly been revoked.

Her sharp eyes narrow at me, as if contemplating my offer. "It's about time," she says, catching me completely off guard. She must notice the shock on my face, because she smirks and rubs it in, "Yeah, I've been waiting for you to corner me."

Who is this chick?

"Let's go to the back, it's more private." She spins on her heel and goes through a door behind the counter. I follow her through a clean, quiet kitchen area and into a small office. Leah shuts the office door and sits in the chair behind a cluttered desk.

"Sit." She gestures to another chair. "What's with the look on your face?" she asks as I unwind the scarf from my neck. It's hot as hell in here.

"What look?" Not many people, especially women, can or will speak to me so bluntly. It's actually very refreshing to find out that Sydney's best friend is completely unimpressed by my fame.

She tilts her head to the side and smiles knowingly. "The look that says you're surprised that I expected you to eventually come to see me."

"You're right, I am surprised. So if you've been expecting me, let's not waste time. Why did you think I'd turn up here?"

Leah smirks again, loving the fact that she has the upper hand here. "Oh no, I don't think so. You want something from me, you spill first."

I smirk back in admiration. This girl has balls. I'm glad she's the one looking out for Sydney.

"Alright." I lean forward, my elbows on my knees, and rub my face with my hands. "I have no idea how much Sydney's told you about us but I'm guessing it isn't much."

I look up and see Leah nod. "You would be correct, but I know a little. Continue."

Damn, she's tough and it makes me smile. "You're not going to make this easy for me, are you?"

"Why should I?" she smiles back. "This is my best friend you're here to discuss, if you want easy then go find someone I don't give a shit about."

I can't help but grin. Leah's protectiveness of Sydney is right on par with mine even if we could possibly be on opposing sides. I admire it.

Lean shifts in her chair and pushes some papers aside so she can lean her elbows on the messy desk. "Oh, and your lady-killing looks won't help you here, so don't bother trying to flatter me with your movie-star smile."

"I'm not trying to flatter you, I'm impressed with you."

Now it's her turn to look surprised. *Good.*

"Not many people would defend their friend against me," I continue. "In fact, most people would toss their friend under a bus then climb over their dead body to get a piece of the spotlight. Trust me, friends like you are rare. I'm happy that Sydney has you."

Leah thinks about what I said for a moment. "Well, thanks. Now, cut the bullshit and start talking."

"Can I ask you something first?"

"Sure, but you may not get an answer."

"Fair enough. Why haven't you told Sydney who I am?"

Again, she carefully thinks through her response before speaking. "Because Sydney doesn't connect with a lot of people. Actually, she doesn't connect with anyone. Ever. But I could tell she did with you. In fact, you're her first relationship."

I'm shocked at this knowledge, but it also makes sense. Sydney doesn't get close to people easily. It would be a challenge for anyone to get through those thick walls she has around her.

"And how would Sydney knowing who I am change that?"

Leah glares at me. "I'm not going to give up her secrets, *Drew*, if that's why you're here." She says my name harshly, probably at the fact that I don't go by Andrew.

I take my hat off and run my hands through my hair in frustration, getting more and more upset as I formulate an argument that might get Leah to explain this shit to me.

"Listen, I don't know how else to say this. She won't let me in. I cahnt stahnd hiding this from her! I want her to know me, but will she leave me if I tell her?" *Fuck*, my accent is coming out.

"I don't think so," Leah says slowly. "She's incredibly damaged, Drew." She flicks her eyes up to mine. "If she hears it from anyone else or finds out some other way, she won't trust you and yes, she'll most likely freak out."

"If I could just know why…" I begin.

"I'm not telling you that!" Leah snaps.

I grit my teeth in annoyance. "I fuckin' love her Leah! I cahnt tell her and have her leave me! I refuse to lose her to something that I don't even fuckin' understahnd!" I yell. "Jesus." I stand up and pace the tiny office, yanking off my heavy winter coat and throwing it on the chair.

Leah stands and comes around the desk, stopping me with a hand on my arm. "Listen, I understand your position, I do. And I get that you love her," she says sympathetically. "If it makes you feel any better, I've been encouraging her to tell you about her past."

I look down at her warily, this tiny little female, one of the few people who has the balls to stand up to me, let alone get this close to me when I'm angry.

"I shouldn't be telling you this, but I think she loves you. Possibly even enough to stick around and face her demons, but I'm telling you that when she finds about your identity, it has to come from you."

"Just tell me this." I squeeze my hands into tight fists, "What's the deal with that asshat Reynolds? Is he after her?" I can barely contain my rage.

Leah flinches and takes a step back, finally having the sense to be afraid of the explosive temper that I'm capable of. "No Drew, I've never seen anything like that. Hell, I used to encourage her to…" Leah's rambling stops dead when she sees my face as she discusses pushing Sydney into Adam Reynolds' slimy arms.

She holds her hands up in a gesture meant to calm me down. "Drew, she was never interested in him. Let it go."

I exhale and attempt to shake off the rage and frustration I feel building up inside me. "I guess I should go." And I really need to fucking punch something so I don't need to be here right now.

"Hey, I'll drop by tomorrow with coffee," Leah offers lamely. She turns around and scribbles something down on a scrap of paper before handing it to me. "Here's my number, just in case you can't reach Sydney." She shrugs. "It's good to have a friend."

I can only manage a small smile. "Sure, and thanks."

I pocket her number and put my 'disguise' back on so I can head out into the crowd on Bleecker Street. My only options appear to tell Sydney and hope she doesn't flip out, or to wait for her to decide to explain her fucked up past to me and still hope she doesn't flip out when I tell her about myself.

Two pretty crappy options.

Except for trying to get Sydney to hook up with that asshole Adam Reynolds, Leah seems to be on my side. I'm grateful that she thinks I'm good enough for Sydney, otherwise I'd be fucked.

"Andrew!" I hear a woman yell.

I turn around instinctively at the sound. *Shit!*

"It is you. Oh my God! I thought so!" The woman and her friend are hyperventilating in front of me. I guess my disguise isn't as good as I thought.

"I'm not sure what you mean," I say cryptically as I try to get away.

"Holy shit!"

"That's Andrew Forrester!"

Within seconds, there's a good-sized crowd circling around me and I can't walk away without running into someone.

"Now's really not a great time," I try to explain.

"Just one picture for us! Please!"

"My sister is never gonna believe this!"

"You're way hotter in real life, except that hat. Ewwww!"

I clench my teeth and try to calm down. I can hear Quentin, my agent, lecturing me about situations like this. "These are the people who made you a star. They can take it away at any moment."

He's right of course, but that doesn't mean that people own every second of my life. Exhaling, I put on my Andrew Forrester mask and smile for the group of people that have gathered around me. I need a way to escape without pissing everyone off.

"Hi, I really am in a hurry, so I can't take individual pictures with all of you. I'd be happy to let you snap a few right now if you like." A compromise is always a good idea. People would rather get something than nothing.

There's a flurry of activity as people pull out their camera phones and aim them at me. I feel like a complete idiot smiling on the sidewalk in the West Village in my ratty Red Sox hat and winter scarf, but if it will get me back to Sydney then I'll do whatever it takes.

After a few dozen flashes go off I decide that they've gotten enough pictures. "Thanks for your support. I really appreciate it," I tell the crowd.

I shake a few of the hands that are closest to me and rush down to the curb to hail a cab. I'm only going a few blocks, but I don't want anyone following me on foot back to Sydney's and finding out where she lives. I've had crazy fuckers trail me home and camp outside my house before. There's no way I'm bringing that shit to Sydney's front door. So much for my walk to clear my head.

"Syd?" I call out when she doesn't answer the door.

Fuck, I should get a key. What if something happened? What if she fell in the shower or hurt herself? I pound louder on the door.

"Sydney!"

After an eternity she finally answers. She's wearing tight little pants and a sports bra, her ear buds thrown over the back of her neck.

"Sorry, I had music on. Were you out here long?" She's looking up at me with her big blue eyes and flushed cheeks.

"Jesus Syd, you scared the shit outta me," I tell her as I close the door behind me. "I thought you were hurt or passed out in the shower or something."

Her eyes grow wide. "I'm sorry Drew. I didn't mean to frighten you."

I force my body to unclench some, not wanting to scare her or worse, send her into a panic by my over the top reaction to keeping her safe.

"It's okay babe, I guess I overreacted." I grab her wrist and pull her into an my arms. "Hungry?"

"A little," she answers, looking up at me and smiling.

We spend the rest of the day holed up in her loft. I can't take her out anywhere and honestly, I'd rather be here alone, just me and her. We barely bother to put clothes on, spending most of our time in bed, wrapped around each other. The sex is great but really, it's just a diversion so we don't have to talk about the giant elephant in the room. The fact that we still hardly know anything about each other.

Leah stays true to her word and stops by the next morning with coffee and croissants. She's actually quite nice to me. I had convinced myself that she'd be mad I tried to get information about Sydney from her, but she seems to respect me more now that I've admitted my feelings for her best friend.

Sunday afternoon comes too quickly and I'm in a foul mood. I don't want to leave Sydney here. She's lost weight since I've been gone, clearly not taking care of herself, and emotionally she's a train wreck. She got pissed when I asked what the fuck was going on with her job that has her so stressed out, especially when I asked if it had anything to do with that jackhole Adam Reynolds.

"What are you doing?" Sydney asks as she comes into the bedroom.

"Packing," I snap harshly. *You're such a dick, Forrester.* "Sorry," I say to her as she sits on the bed and tucks her legs underneath her too-lean body.

I grab another pile of clothes and stuff them in my bag, not caring how wrinkled or messed up they get. I'll probably just end up buying more in California anyway. Whenever I send my clothes to the cleaners, stuff always goes missing. Just like at airport security. Fucking weirdoes.

"It's okay," Sydney says softly.

I watch her as I finish packing. She looks sad, withdrawn. Several times I start to give in and tell her who I am, but each time I think about how she might never want to see me again and I can't. Not when I'm headed back out of town for who knows how long. When I finally tell her, I want it to be when I can spend time with her, convince her that I'm the same guy she met at the gym. Not drop this giant bomb on her and then put three-thousand miles between us.

My phone chirps from my pocket. I don't need to look to know that it's Bruce telling me he's out front waiting.

"That's my ride," I tell her, sitting next to her on the bed and pulling her onto my lap.

"I know," she whispers.

"I'll find out when I can come back." I press several soft kisses on her lips.

"Okay."

"Please Sydney, take better care of yourself. It'll kill me to know you're here withering away."

"I will Drew," she responds automatically, telling me whatever it is that I want to hear.

I sigh, she's so fucking stubborn, but I can't let her go yet. I slant my mouth over hers and memorize the taste of her on my tongue, sweet and sinful at the same time. Sydney grips the back of my hair and threads her fingers through it, tugging gently and scratching my scalp.

"Shit," I pant, breaking off the kiss. "I have to stop or else I won't be able to stop. My control around you is crap."

Pouting, she slides off of my lap back onto the bed.

"I'll call you tomorrow. It'll be too late tonight when I land." She walks with me to the door.

"Alright," she says in a quiet voice.

"I'll miss you Syd, so much." I reach up and trace her cheek with my thumb.

"Me too."

I press one final kiss on her lips and leave.

As I take the elevator down to the lobby, a sense of dread overcomes me. I can't explain it, but I get the worst feeling that if I don't turn around and go back upstairs and tell her everything, I'll regret it for the rest of my life.

CHAPTER 23

"You've been a real bastard this past week," Chad says as we sit on the terrace of his enormous Brentwood mansion.

"Yeah," I reply as I take a huge swig of beer.

"Not even an argument from you? You are fucked up in the head my friend. This girl must be something else to have you all knotted up like this."

I ignore him and stare out at the trees that dot his property, not looking at anything in particular. I was supposed to fly home this weekend but there was some fuck up at the hotel and Sydney had to work. Fuck, I should be with her right now.

"Jesus, I hate to get all touchy feely with you man, but are you okay?"

I respond with a grunt. I really am a moody prick. Putting down my empty beer bottle I turn my head toward one of my oldest friends, the guy who gave me my first job in this town, and grab another beer.

"No, I'm not okay." I snatch up the bottle opener and flick off the cap, taking a big swig of beer. Pissed and needing to vent, I huff out a breath, then proceed to tell Chad about Adam Reynolds and the big party at Verve and how I want to rip Reynolds' arms off and beat the shit out of him with them. "She's so sweet and caring! She can't even see that he just wants to get in her fuckin' pants! And this job she's doing? Her boss is a total douche and he's working her so hard that she's falling apart."

"So I guess you don't want me to tell you that everyone I know is trying to get an invite to that party?"

Frowning, I feel the white-hot rage surging through my body. I clutch the bottle too tight and swallow half of my beer in order to stop it from manifesting into something ugly. "No," I snap. "I don't want to fucking hear that. And yes, in case you're wondering, I did see the newest *Rolling Stone*."

That fuckhead Reynolds was on the cover and once again talked up the fucking party at Verve as if it's being thrown just for him. His hard-on for Sydney is getting on my last nerve.

Chad sighs and swings his legs off of his lounge chair so he's facing me. "Tell you what, I'll talk to production and see if they can juggle some scenes so you can be there for that party."

I perk up at Chad's offer. "That would be so… you'd do that?"

He reaches up and pats my shoulder. "Of course I would. First, I've known you forever and you've never asked for a schedule change, ever. Second, in all the time I've known you, this is the first girl that's ever played hard to get. It's damn entertaining," he says jokingly.

I glare at him and open another beer. "I'm glad my problems are fuckin' hilarious Chad."

He grins.

Bruce drops me off at the Sunset Marquis a couple of hours and too many beers later. I'm not drunk, but sporting enough of a buzz to not be completely sober. All I want to do is talk to my girl. I've worked late all week and I haven't been able to catch her in several days.

I collapse into the desk chair and boot up my computer. "Fuck!" I slam my fist on the desk when I open Skype and see that Sydney isn't logged in.

I stand up and dig my phone out of my pocket, dialing Sydney's number as I pace the room. When it goes to voicemail, I lose my shit. All of the agitation that I've felt over the past two weeks comes exploding out of me at once.

"Motherfucker!" I rear back and throw my phone across the room. It hits the wall and shatters into pieces that scatter everywhere.

That didn't do nearly enough to satisfy my rage. I spin on my heel and strike out at the nearest object, which happens to be the massive armoire. The door cracks upon impact with my fist. I pound on it over and over until the door is shredded and so is my hand.

"Goddammit!"

I slide down the wall and land heavily on the ground, cradling my bleeding hand in my lap. This girl is going to be the death of me. Either that or I'm going slowly insane.

Or possibly both.

A quick knock on my dressing room door alerts me right before it opens and Jane walks in, carrying a bag from the Apple store.

"Here's your new phone," she says, glancing at my swollen, makeup-covered hand with a scowl on her face.

"Thanks Jane." Embarrassed, I avoid eye contact. Only Jane and my mom can make me feel about two feet tall when I do something stupid.

"Want to talk about it?" She sits on the couch next to me.

All I really want to do is try to reach Sydney again. Without a phone since last night, I haven't been able to think about anything else.

I shrug. I'm tired of the sympathetic looks that she gives me when she thinks I'm not looking. And I already got bitched out by Chad, Lou the executive producer, and the makeup artist today for the scrapes and the black and blue marks on my knuckles.

"Well, if you change your mind, I'll be around." She gets up and leaves the room, closing the door behind her.

I yank the phone out of the bag and see that it's already powered up and has my contacts in it. *God, I love my assistant.* I find the correct number and hit dial.

"Drew?" Sydney's sweet voice calms me down instantly.

"Sydney," I breathe. "Where have you been? I've tried reaching you but you never answer."

I'm fucking pathetic. Sitting around wondering why a girl isn't taking my calls.

"I'm so sorry. I've been working all the time and when I get home I crash. I'm exhausted."

The anger I had yesterday comes mushrooming back up from my gut, about to boil over. "Your boss is a fucking asshole," I hiss. "You're going to get sick, Sydney."

"I'll be fine," she says, trying her best to placate me, which just makes me angrier. She should be worrying about herself, not me.

"Christ Syd, can you please just do as I say and take better care of yourself?" I growl, wanting to jump through the phone and make her take me seriously.

"Yes, I will Drew. So, how's your project? Is everything going well?"

I feel like such a shit for lying to her about my job.

"It's going great babe. The hours are long but the faster I get this done, the sooner I can come home."

"Well, as long as *you* take care of yourself," she jokes.

I laugh, she has no idea how much working out I've been doing with Damien just to vent my frustration at this ridiculous situation and the stress of being not being able to do anything while she falls to pieces.

"I manage to keep up," I say sarcastically.

"That's good, oh, hold on." I hear someone talking to her about chairs or something. "I'm sorry Drew, I have to go. A shipment just arrived."

"Okay Syd, if I call you tomorrow will you answer?"

So I don't have to break another phone, or possibly my hand?

She giggles and the sound goes straight to my dick. Fuck, this is unbearable.

"Yes, I will. I promise."

"I'll call you tomorrow."

"Bye Drew."

"Bye."

The crackle of the speakerphone in my room startles me. "Forrester, we need you on set."

Fuck! Late again.

I get up and hurry down the hallway only to be immediately intercepted by Jackie from wardrobe.

Shit.

"Hey Andrew," she purrs.

"Jackie," I nod and attempt to keep walking.

Naturally, she steps in front of me and juts her giant fake breasts in my face. Sydney or no Sydney, this chick and me would never happen. She just can't get that through her damn bleached head. As if I haven't noticed her eye-fucking me at every costume fitting. I should have shut her down then, but I didn't think she'd be so damn persistent.

"So, I was thinking…" she begins.

"Jackie, I really don't have time for this." *Ever*, I want to add.

When she reaches out and puts her hands on my chest, she's crossed the line. I wrap my hands around her wrists and she smiles, thinking she's won. Then I slowly remove her hands from my body, put them down at her sides, and release them.

"Don't touch me like that again, or you won't have a job," I say in a low voice.

She pouts her lower lip out. In her mind, I'm sure she thinks it looks sexy. It doesn't.

"I heard you were more fun than this," she whines.

"Well, don't believe everything you hear," I say as I step around her and dash to the set.

I really wish Sydney were here.

CHAPTER 24

It's been three weeks since I've seen Sydney and I'm beginning to unravel. When we're able to Skype, Sydney looks even thinner and more exhausted than ever. I can't harass her about it either, because she threatens to cut off my Skype time if I do. She's completely castrated me right where it hurts the most, my need to protect what's mine and keep her healthy and safe.

She did tell me she had caught a bug, but was feeling a little better in the last few days, but I don't know if she's just lying to keep me from freaking out. Having no control over anything in our relationship is driving me slowly insane.

"Drew," Chad calls me over to the video village to watch the last scene. He's leaning over the control panel, focusing on one of the dozens of televisions laid out in front of him.

"Yeah, what's up? Did we not get it?" I ask as I put on a set of headphones and edge up next to him.

We watch the last take of one of the fight scenes between me, Zane, and some KGB agents.

"What do you think?" Chad asks.

I shrug. "I think it looks great." I've been doing this a long time and I know a great take when I see one.

"Me too," he says smiling. "That means we're done for today."

Thank Christ, I think as I put the headphones down. "So what do you need me for? I'm pretty sure you didn't call me over here because you miss my pretty face."

Chad grins and hands me a small stack of colored papers. "What's this?"

"The schedule changes. You'll be done by Saturday morning."

"So… I can go to New York Saturday and not worry about coming back?" *Is that even possible?*

"Yep."

"Shit, I owe you man. This is great." I feel happy, something I haven't felt since I left Sydney back home. "I'll talk to you later," I call out as I hurry back to my dressing room to call Sydney.

Shit, her phone goes to voice mail. It's the middle of the afternoon in New York. She's probably at the club. Just as I'm about to call Jane and have her book a flight for Saturday, my phone rings in my hand, scaring the shit out of me.

Sydney.

"Hey sexy girl, how are you? Feeling any better? Need me to call that Jeff guy and tell him what an ass he is?" I hope I sound happy. I'm excited to tell her that I can make it to the party.

"Yeah, still tired, but much better. My stomach seems to have finally calmed some. And no, please don't call Jeff; I need him pissed at me like I need a hole in my head." I can pretty much tell that she's rolling her eyes as she says her boss's name. He's such a douche. Her voice lowers as she whispers into the phone. "I miss you so much."

My chest clenches at her confession. "I miss you too baby. So, I finally got Chad to give me a definite for next Saturday." I wait to tell her, teasing her a little bit.

"And…" Sydney waits for my answer but I make her sweat it a little.

"Drew! Stop keeping me waiting."

God she's so fucking cute.

"And he managed to alter the schedule so I'll be finished out here by that morning. I have a flight that lands in New York at 5pm on the 8th and I won't have to come back out here the following week either."

I'm ready to be back home with her, but I'm also nervous. I'll have to tell her everything before I can walk into that party. She may not want to see me again after that.

"So that's great! Right? The party doesn't start until 9. The celebrities don't start arriving until 10 or so. You should be here in plenty of time to make it. I'm just sorry that you'll be on a plane on your birthday."

More concerned about me than about herself, as usual. Like I could give a shit about my birthday when I'm worried about her flipping out and leaving me when I tell her who I am.

"Actually, I'm hoping we could meet at your place and go together. I wanted to see you first."

"That's perfect. Just so you know, Leah made me promise that I wouldn't revoke her invite just because you're coming with me, so we'll see her there. She doesn't want to ride with us though; she'll feel too much like a third-wheel. Her words, not mine." Sydney's laughter filters through the phone, making me laugh along with her.

"Yes, that's fine. As long as we're alone before we go to the party."

So I can drop a mushroom cloud on you right before your big career-making design is revealed.

Sydney readily agrees to my request. "We will be, don't worry. I'm so excited, Drew. You being there is going to make this potentially shitty night so much better, so long as you don't actually throat punch Adam that is."

"I can't make any promises about that, Sydney. He needs to keep his hands to himself. I just hope you're glad that I'm there with you at the party." And I'll most likely punch him either way, I'm sure.

I hear someone call for Sydney. She never fucking rests. Not even five minutes for a phone call. My hand tightens around the phone.

"Drew, I'm sorry. I have to go. They're calling for me. Thank you so much for agreeing to go with me. Tell Chad thanks too."

"I will baby, you're welcome. I'll talk to you tomorrow. I have a late night of work today." I checked the new schedule, lots of late nights in order to wrap up in time.

"Okay, bye," she says, her voice much happier than it was at the beginning of the call.

Me? Now I'm the one freaking out over celebrities and nightclub parties, but probably not for the same reason as Sydney.

CHAPTER 25

"Drew!" Chad calls out from behind a television screen.

I hustle over and reach out to grab a set of headphones. Chad stops me before I can get a pair.

"You don't need those."

I must look surprised because the fucker laughs at me. "What?" I narrow my eyes at him suspiciously.

"You just filmed your last scene. Get going," he says, his hands on his hips and a giant grin on his face

Now he has my attention. "Really? You're not shitting me are you?"

"Nope, go. Have a good time in New York." I turn to leave but he stops me. "And Drew, happy birthday."

"The jury is still out on that," I say sarcastically. "I'll let you know tomorrow if it's happy or not."

I call Bruce while I'm getting out of my wardrobe so he can grab my luggage from the hotel and get to the studio as quickly as possible. By the time I get out of the shower and say bye to everyone, he's outside waiting for me.

It's only 8am and I'm already done with work. I don't know how Chad did it, but I owe him big. The crew was pretty pissed that we had to start so early this morning, but they showed up and rallied to get the job done so I could make my early flight.

I'm so ecstatic that I don't even care that a pack of paparazzi hound me as I make my way through LAX without Jane, who's flying back Monday. Even the clingy fan that follows me to my gate doesn't bother me today.

I collapse in my seat in the first class lounge, close my eyes, and put my earphones on to make myself unavailable to anyone passing by. It's not until an airline employee taps my shoulder that I realize what time it is. My flight should have boarded by now.

"Mr. Forrester, I'm sorry to bother you," she says kindly.

I look at her expectantly, waiting for her to finish her thought.

"Well," her face reddens a little and I feel bad, so I give an Andrew Forrester smile. That encourages her to tell me why she came over here. "I just saw that you had headphones on so you probably didn't hear the announcement that your flight has a two hour delay."

Crap.

I must make a pretty intimidating face because the woman flinches back from me.

I drag my hand across the back of my neck. "Sorry, I just really need to get back to New York. Long day ahead and all," I say so she won't think I'm a total asshole.

"No problem. I'll let you know if anything else comes up." She gives me a weak smile before turning and walking away.

I pull out my phone to call Sydney. I should still land by 7pm and have enough time to make it to her place before the party. Maybe I could tell her in the car?

Of course, her voicemail picks up and I have to leave a message.

You've reached Sydney, leave a message and I'll call you back.

"Hey babe, I'm still at the airport in LA, my flight is delayed. They think we'll be in around seven or so. Try to wait for me before you leave. I know you have to be there, but I really want to talk to you before we go. Miss you."

I shove my phone in my pocket and wait.

An eternity later, they finally board my flight. I hang back until everyone else is on before taking my seat. Naturally, there's someone next to me. Fuck, I should have had Jane come with me instead of leaving her behind to tie up loose ends.

The older man stands to let me into my window seat. I can feel every set of eyes in first class focused on me as I take my seat.

"Hello," my seatmate says.

"Hi," I answer, looking at the guy warily. This better not be one of those flights where I'm next to a Chatty Cathy for five hours.

He pulls out a thick, economic newspaper, folds it to an article, and starts to read.

Thank God for that.

After takeoff, I pull out my iPad and watch some of the dailies that Chad uploaded and check my email.

About an hour and a half into the flight my neighbor taps my arm and gestures for me to remove my headphones.

"Yes?" I ask.

"You probably couldn't hear what was going on in coach, but apparently there's been an issue with one of the other passengers."

"What do you mean an issue?" Me and my goddamn earphones!

"A medical issue. We're going to have to land in Denver so he or she can get off of the plane."

I sit up straight. "What!"

"Yep, probably a heart attack or something, I'm not sure. They haven't said, just that we're landing in Denver."

I groan and drop my head into my hands. This is fate, I'm not meant to tell Sydney. I'm not meant to be with her. Adam fucking Reynolds will make a move on her tonight and get her wasted so he can treat her like a whore.

"Whoa, calm down," the man next to me says.

I open my eyes and realize that I'm clenching my hands into fists and gritting my teeth together furiously.

"Sorry, I just really need to get home. No offense to the sick person back there," I explain.

"Don't we all," he chuckles.

No buddy, we don't. I think, directing my anger at the innocent man besides me. I might lose the only woman I've ever loved tonight if I don't get there in time. Aggravated, I push the button to call the flight attendant. I've never needed a drink this badly in my life.

"Can't you go faster?" I ask the cabbie as he speeds through the Midtown tunnel.

"Buddy, this ain't the movies like you're used to. There's other cars on the road," he says in his heavy New York accent.

"Fuck," I groan to myself. It's already after 11pm and Sydney hasn't answered her phone any of the dozens of times I've called since landing at JFK. She did leave a message telling me that she wouldn't have her phone on her at the party so I'm not surprised that she didn't pick up. I'm so late, I won't even have time to change. I guess I'm going to this big nightclub opening in the same jeans, wrinkled button down, and leather jacket I've been wearing all day.

The cab finally pulls up to the curb outside the Warren, I toss the driver two fifties and jump out into the sea of vicious sharks waiting by the entrance.

"Andrew, we didn't see your name on the VIP celebrity list, are you here for the party?"

"Are you here with a date?"

"Did you just come in a cab?"

"I thought you were in L.A. filming."

The paparazzi are still hanging out on the red carpet outside this thing, even though everyone has probably already arrived. I pointedly ignore them and hurry inside to find Sydney, flashbulbs snapping from every side.

"How the hell am I going to do this," I mutter to myself. I ask security to put me into a conference room and have them send an assistant up to the club to find Sydney. The girl assured me that she knew who Sydney was and could bring her down to me.

I pace the room and formulate a speech while I wait the agonizing minutes for Sydney to arrive.

"Mr. Forrester?" I turn at the sound of a timid little voice.

I whip around and see the girl alone. "Where's Sydney?" I ask the assistant, who's cowering in the doorway, clearly intimidated by me.

"Ummmm," she fidgets anxiously and can't or won't look at me, "apparently she left a little while ago."

"What! Where the fuck did she go?"

"I'm sorry, I really don't know," the girl says, pale and cringing from my hostile glare.

I storm over to the exit and stare down the poor hotel employee, "Leave," I growl.

I pull out my phone and dial Leah, thankful that she had the foresight to give me her number when I met with her the last time I was in town.

"Hello?"

"Leah, it's Drew. I'm in one of the conference rooms of the hotel. They're saying Sydney left, is that true?"

There's a moment of dead space before Leah answers. "Crap, why don't I come down and meet with you," she says in a voice that lets me know something is very wrong.

"No, I'm coming up there! Wait for me," I bark back.

Fuck! I shove my phone into my pocket and storm towards the elevators. A couple near the elevator bank visibly shrinks back as I approach. I stab the button and jump in when the doors slide open.

Am I that frightening? I catch sight of my reflection in the mirrored doors as they shut and see that yes, I look pissed and pretty fucking scary.

When the doors slide open, I run out of the elevator and make my way into the crowded nightclub.

"Andrew, great to see you!"

"Hey Andrew. I hadn't heard you'd be here."

I shove right past people I've known a long time and people I don't know at all, not stopping to talk to a single one of them. I see others flinch back when they see me coming. *Smart.*

"Drew?" I hear someone call my real name and spin around to see who it is.

Leah is pushing her way through the thick crowd on the dance floor, her face pinched with stress.

"Leah, where is Sydney?" I demand when she finally reaches me.

"Drew, not here." Her eyes are darting around at the bystanders who are clearly listening in on our conversation.

Like I could give a shit. "Leah, don't fucking start with me! I've had a long fucking day. Where the fuck is she?" I ask in as quiet of a voice as I can manage, which isn't much right now.

"She left."

"What? Why?"

Leah starts to step back, so I take a step toward her, keeping the distance between us at a minimum. "Tell me," I hiss.

Her face reddens and she won't meet my gaze. "So, she was showing Adam the club…"

Instantly, I feel the anger pulsing through my fists. "And?"

"And Kiera came over because she was jealous of Sydney. I wasn't there for that part, but Sydney ended up telling Kiera that you, Drew Forrester, were her date and Kiera laughed in her face."

The anger in me turns to a lead brick of fear and plummets into my suddenly queasy stomach.

"Sydney got mad and asked Kiera what was so funny and one thing led to another…"

"She told her, didn't she?" I croak, clutching my middle as if kicked in the gut.

"No, she *showed* her on her cell phone. Pictures of *you*, Andrew Forrester the movie star, on the red carpet."

I feel sick. Destroyed. As if my entire future just vanished from existence and left behind a gaping black hole.

"Where is she?"

"I don't know. She's not answering her phone," Leah says in a desperate voice.

"Where's Reynolds?" I snarl.

"Drew, don't. It's not worth it."

Leah tries to hold me back by grabbing my arm but gives up when she sees my face. It takes me only a few minutes to find that douchebag, talking with Kiera Radcliffe by the bar.

They both notice me at the same time, their heads turning toward me in sync. Adam looks surprised, Kiera looks equally stunned. "Reynolds!" I yell as I storm up to them, getting within an inch of his stupid face.

His shocked expression turns cynical in the time it takes for me to say his name. "Forrester," he says in a cold voice.

I turn to look at Kiera, half hiding behind Reynolds like the cowardly bitch that she is. I stab my finger at her accusingly. "You! What the fuck did you say to my girlfriend?"

Kiera is shocked at my tone. Did she really think I'd be okay with her being rude to Sydney?

"I didn't think she was actually your *girlfriend*, Andrew. I didn't *say* anything." Her lips curl up in a self-satisfied fucking smile. "Why would you date a boring little nobody like her anyway?"

"I don't give a fuck what you knew or what you didn't say! And she's not a nobody, so shut the fuck up!" I bellow at the bitchy blonde. She visibly pales and her smug smile vanishes. "And you," I turn to face Adam Reynolds. "You stay the fuck away from her, do you understand?"

That motherfucker Reynolds just stands there with his hands up in front of him as if he had nothing to do with pissing me off. My fists curl up at my sides so tightly that I can feel my knuckles straining from the pressure.

"I didn't do a thing to Sydney," he says in his stupid British accent. "We're mates, that's all. She never even mentioned she was seeing someone, let alone *you*."

Then he smirks at me and I snap. "I'm going to fucking finish you, Reynolds!" I move to pound his face in.

"Drew!" Sydney's best friend has managed to squeeze her tiny body in between me and Adam Reynolds, preventing me from ripping his head off.

"Get out of my way Leah!"

"Drew, we have to go find Sydney. Now!" I tear my eyes from that asshole's face and focus on the little blonde who is pushing furiously on my chest in a futile attempt to move me back.

"What?"

"We have to go. She left a while ago. We may not have time to get there before she takes off."

"Takes off?" I ask, confused.

"Yes, that's what she does when she's freaked out. She runs."

"Fuck, let's go." I grab her hand and tow her through the crowd, Adam Reynolds and Kiera Radcliff forgotten for now.

We get down to the lobby and I realize I have no way to get to Sydney's. "I don't have a car," I tell Leah in a panic, my fists gripping my hair to cope with the out of control fear I feel in my chest.

She rolls her eyes and steps off the curb in her skintight black dress and mile-high heels, one arm held high, and whistles so loudly that my ears hurt. A cab pulls over immediately.

"What?" she says when she sees my shocked face. "Not all of us have drivers to take us everywhere."

We hop out at Sydney's building and the concierge buzzes us in.

"I'm sorry, I can't let you up," he says from behind his desk in the lobby.

"What? You have got to be kidding me!" I shout.

"Miss Allen isn't answering her intercom. It's policy. I can't let anyone into the building who doesn't have the permission of a resident."

I pace back and forth in front of the concierge desk before slamming my fists down on it, causing everything on it to shake violently.

"You've seen me here consistently for the last three months!" I yell. "Now you're saying I can't go up? What kind of bullshit is this?"

"Drew," Leah whispers as she clutches my arm. "There are other people in the lobby."

"Like I give a fuck," I snarl, done with caring who sees me or what they say. I turn back to the concierge. "If something happens to her, it's on you!" I stab my finger at the desk jockey.

"I'm going to call the police if you can't calm down, sir."

"Call the fucking police!" I roar. "Get them the fuck in here! She could be dead up there for all I know!"

"Please," Leah says to the concierge. "Let us go up and make sure she's okay. You know me and you definitely know him." She sticks her thumb out in my direction. "We're not going to do anything but look."

The concierge sighs and unlocks a cabinet beneath the desk, removing a key. "Here, just bring it back when you leave."

Leah unlocks the door to Sydney's loft and pushes the door open, allowing me to race in first.

"Sydney?" I call out as I run through each dark room, flipping on lights as I go. "Syd!"

"She's not here," Leah says as she comes out of the bedroom. "But she was. I found this." She holds up a black and white dress. "It was in the garbage. She was wearing it tonight."

"Where would she go?" I ask, my voice cracking from stress.

"I don't know. Normally? To my place. But she's mad at me because she knows that I knew everything this entire time."

Leah looks just as lost as me. She's known Sydney for twelve years and knows all of her secrets and has no idea what to do. I've only known her for three months and I don't know shit about Sydney's past. I have no fucking clue where we go from here.

"I want to wait here," I say, sliding down the living room wall to the floor. "To see if she comes back."

"I'll wait with you," Leah says, tears building up in her eyes.

"Don't start crying." I choke on the words. "I can't."

Leah sits on the floor next to me and puts her hand in mine. "It will work out. It has to."

"Yeah, It's not looking so good for me right now."

We sit on the ground for hours and stare at the door, both of us holding back unshed tears. My back is aching and my ass is numb from the hardwood floor I've been sitting on.

"Drew, we have to leave."

Leah has been saying this for the last two hours. Since then, I've had four glasses of Sydney's scotch, maybe five and I'm too tired to move.

"Drew, I'm serious, get up!"

I open my eyes and see Leah about six inches from my face, scowling at me.

"We should stay here in case Syd comes home," I slur.

Leah grabs my arm and pulls me up into a half-sitting position. "No, we're going."

I sigh and stand up, wobbling a little from the booze. Clutching Leah's shoulders, I stare at down at her. "She's not going to come back, is she?"

"She'll come back, or at least call me. Now, let's go. I'll call you the second I hear from her, I promise."

I finally relent and allow the tiny blonde girl that I outweigh by almost ninety pounds to shove me out Sydney's door and possibly out of her life.

CHAPTER 26

The next five days are the worst in my life. I spend most of my time pounding my fists against the different punching bags at Damien's gym. The repetitive sound of my knuckles on leather reverberates through the huge space.

Whap! Whap! Whap! Whap! Whap! Whap! Whap! Whap!

"Forrester!"

I ignore Bobby as he strides around the cage and heads my way.

"Forrester!" he yells, just a few feet behind me.

My refusal to acknowledge him must piss Bobby off because he slides behind the heavy bag and shoves it, hard. The bag slams into my body and knocks me back.

"What the fuck!" I scream at him, my fists up and ready to strike.

"Hey! Calm the fuck down!" Bobby yells, holding his hands up defensively. "What the hell is wrong with you man?"

"Nothing," I mutter and start hitting the bag again, this time with my shins. Roundhouse after roundhouse, I kick the heavy bag.

Thunk! Thunk! Thunk! Thunk! Thunk! Thunk! Thunk!

I keep going until sweat is stinging my eyes and my muscles are fatigued. I unstrap the gloves and drop them on the ground.

"Are you ready to talk?" Bobby asks.

I turn to walk away and Bobby grabs my arm and spins me around forcefully. The testosterone from the workout, the endorphins pulsing through my body, the anger, the frustration, the heartbreak. I don't know which one makes me do it but I swing at Bobby and catch him fully on the jaw. His head snaps back brutally and I see the surprise in his eyes turn to fury.

Fatigue has dulled my reflexes because I don't see Bobby's fist coming at me until it connects with my face. My neck wrenches sideways and a blinding pain shoots through my left eye.

"Fuck!" I clutch my chin and spit a mouthful of blood, staring angrily at my friend.

He storms over to get in my face, his massive chest inches from mine. "What the fuck is wrong with you!" he bellows.

"Nothing, okay? So leave me the fuck alone!" I shout back, turning again to leave.

"Drew!"

Fuck! Can't they just leave me alone?

Damien is jogging over to where Bobby and I are standing, looking confused as hell.

"Leave me the fuck alone," I hiss at them both.

Damien moves in front of me, forcing me to look at him. The rage that has been churning inside me since Sydney disappeared finally explodes out in an alarming display. I lunge for Damien with a left cross. He feints and grabs my wrist, throwing me down and pinning me to the ground in a brutal hammerlock.

"Let me up," I growl.

"Are you going to calm the fuck down?"

I breathe in deep and exhale into the mat. "Yes."

"Fine." Damien gets up and releases me from his hold.

I lay on the ground for a minute before slowly returning to my feet.

"Come on," Damien says, motioning me toward his office. "You're going to tell us what the hell is going on."

I grab my bag and remove my water bottle, drinking half of it quickly. Defeated, I sling the straps over my shoulder and follow Damien and Bobby into the small room at the back of the gym.

"Sit," he says forcefully, pointing at the nearest chair.

I take his order without hesitation, something I rarely do. Bobby sits next to me and Damien takes a seat behind his battered metal desk.

"Now talk," Damien demands.

I rub my jaw and look at the ground, unable to face my friends.

I hear Damien open the fridge behind him and an ice pack lands in my lap. "Take this, so your pretty little face doesn't get all fucked up."

I can't help but smile at his facetious comment.

"Fuck you," I say back, my attitude more sarcastic than angry at this point.

"Dude, just spill," Bobby says. "We know it has to do with your chick. You were already all fucked up by her months ago. And," he says leaning toward me, "I saw the shit on the internet the other night."

My head snaps up at this information. "What shit?" My eyes flash from Bobby to Damien and I can see that they know something that I don't.

Damien types on his laptop and swings it around to face me.

Andrew Forrester Goes Toe-to-Toe with Adam Reynolds Over Mystery Girl

March 9th

Written by Kate M.

Superhot superstar Andrew Forrester almost came to blows with sexy Brit rocker Adam Reynolds last night at the NYC launch party for Verve, the swank new nightclub at the top of the Warren Hotel. A partygoer tells us that Reynolds and an unknown smokin' hot redhead were getting cozy when Reynolds' ex Kiera Radcliff confronted the other woman. The redhead immediately left the hotel after exchanging words with Radcliff.

Forrester arrived thirty minutes later, looking incredibly angry, and headed straight for Reynolds and Radcliff who were still arguing over the departure of Reynolds' mystery date. Forrester reportedly got in Reynolds' face and was yelling at him over the beautiful redhead. A female friend intervened and convinced Forrester to leave the nightclub before any punches were thrown.

Who's the redhead that has these two gorgeous hunks fighting over her?
What did Radcliff say to upset the unknown woman and cause Forrester
to come to her defense? Will it affect the chemistry between Forrester and
Radcliff in the movie they are supposed to start filming soon? We hope to
find this lucky girl soon and get some answers!

"Holy fuck," I whisper as I scroll down the page. As my shock wears off I get pissed. Red-tinged, beat the shit out of someone, irrational, crazy pissed. Adam Reynolds 'cozying' up with my motherfucking girl? Jesus, I want to fucking swing at something again. I don't fucking share. Ever. My body is vibrating from adrenaline.

"Calm the fuck down, dude." Bobby's deep voice pulls me from my enraged thoughts. "You're going to break the computer in half. Loosen your damn hands."

I look down and see that I'm gripping the laptop so hard that my cracked knuckles have split back open and are bleeding again. *Fuck!* I breathe as deep as I can and swallow down the acidic rage that wells up from my gut.

Wonderful, there's a photo. It's of me about ready to rip Reynolds' head off, Leah squeezed in between us trying to push me away. And there's that bitch Kiera standing in the background with a smug smile on her face.

"Yeah man, everyone knows," Bobby says. "So tell us what the hell is happening to you."

I rub my hand down my face and throw the ice pack on the desk. I tell them everything that happened at Verve. How Sydney is afraid of celebrities but I don't know why, about my delayed flight and how it took forever to get to New York, how Kiera Radcliff told her who I was before I could get there, and about Sydney leaving the club and not being heard from since.

Bobby and Damien are speechless. Nothing I'm not used to by now.

"Damn man, that's rough," Bobby finally says.

"Yeah buddy, I'm sorry." Damien looks worried for me.

"Well, the heart to heart has been great and all, but I have to go." Embarrassed, I stand up, open my bag, yank out a T-shirt, and pull it on.

"Don't give up man," Bobby says. "She'll come back." He stands up and pats my back as I leave.

Once I get home I turn the water up as hot as it will go and stand in the shower forever, letting it scald my aching muscles. I revel in the burning sting on my skin. It's a more tolerable pain than the one I've been in for the last five days.

I've called Leah twice a day since Sunday when we left Sydney's loft early in the morning. She hasn't heard a thing, and hasn't been able to reach her. We've both sent dozens of texts and left voicemails until her mailbox filled up. Nothing. I've ignored every call I've gotten that hasn't been from Leah.

I get out of the shower and throw on some clothes. Not sure what to do next, I grab my phone and tuck it in my pocket and as soon as I do it rings.

It's probably my sister Allie bugging me about the article. She knows about Sydney and probably assumed that the woman referenced in the gossip blogs was her. She knows I hate talking about that shit.

I answer it without even looking, probably not a smart move since I'm avoiding everyone. "Allie, I'm fine. You can stop…"

"Drew?"

My breath hitches and I bend over. I feel as though I've been kicked in the chest. "Sydney?" my voice cracks.

She sniffs as though she's been crying.

"Where are you?" I ask as calmly as I can manage.

"At my place, can you come over?"

She has no idea that I'm already shoving my feet into a pair of shoes and heading for the door.

This time, the concierge allows me upstairs without harassing me. It's a different guy, but still, I haven't gotten over that bastard trying to keep me from my girl.

Bang! Bang! Bang! Bang! Bang! Bang! Bang! Bang!

I slam my fist over and over on her door until she answers. The first thing I notice is how tired and swollen her face appears but I don't care what she looks like. I'm so fucking relieved to see her, that I rush in and grab her, holding her tightly to me. I kick the door shut with my foot so I won't have to let go.

"Jesus, Sydney. You scared the crap out of me. I didn't think I'd ever see you again." I bury my face in her hair and inhale her scent, letting it wash over me. Shit, I missed her.

She wraps her arms around me and clutches me just as hard, then starts crying into my chest. Her small shoulders are shaking in my arms.

"Shhhh, it's okay babe. It's okay." This is what I'm here for, to take care of her when she needs it. She's finally letting me in enough to do this for her. I pick her up and carry her down the hall to her bedroom, laying her on the bed. I toe out of my shoes and lie down next to her, holding her to me as she sobs, my heart breaking a little more with each tear she sheds.

When the tears finally stop, I look down and see that her eyes have closed. She looks as if she's barely slept in the last five days.

Who am I to talk? I haven't either.

I watch her beautiful face as she sleeps, her lips slightly parted and her thick lashes fanned against her hollow cheeks. Did she call me here to break up with me face to face? I don't think she'd let me comfort her if that were true, but if I've learned one thing about Sydney, it's that she's impossible to predict.

Her eyes flutter and open and gaze into mine without a single hint of regret that I'm here. "Drew," she whispers as she threads her hand up into my hair. "I'm not going anywhere."

My heart soars at her words. When she leans in and gently kisses me, my fear ebbs and I hungrily kiss her back. "God, Sydney," I groan as I hold her against me, allowing myself to revel in the feeling of her body next to mine.

She knows who I am and she's still here, wanting to be with me. I have to tell her how I feel now that I've been given another chance. "I love you, Sydney. I can't be without you."

Her hand grips my hair tighter. "I love you too, Drew. I'm sorry I ran. I won't do it again."

Fuck, she feels the same as I do. I roll us until she's beneath me on the bed and crush my lips to hers. Our tongues explore and rediscover what we almost lost and my head spins from the emotions that flood me.

"Sydney, I want you. I need to know that you're still mine," I moan against her lips then drag my mouth down her neck, breathing in her perfect fragrance.

She breathlessly nods and it's all the consent that I need. I grab her shirt and rip it off, throwing it aside. Then I yank my own shirt over my head and toss it. Her lacy blue bra covers nothing, her pink nipples prominent beneath the scrap of fabric. I nip at them with my teeth and groan when they harden from my mouth.

The lust, the desire, the love I feel overwhelms me. I have to have her, now.

"I can't wait," I tell her as I start to quickly remove the rest of my clothes.

Sydney sheds hers as well. She's as desperate as I am to heal the rift between us. I lay back down over her and skim my fingers down her arms, wrapping them around her wrists and pulling them up to hold over her head. She writhes beneath me, throwing her head back when I lick across her collarbone and trail hot kisses up her neck.

Sydney arches her back and shifts her hips, moaning when my cock slides over her wet pussy. The response I get from her is so sexy that I rut against her several times just to watch her squirm.

When it seems as though she's about to beg me to fuck her, I slide a hand down between her legs and part her slick folds.

"Jesus, I missed you," I sigh.

I take a condom out of my discarded pants and tear it open with my teeth, rolling it on one handed so I don't have to release her trapped wrists. I position my cock at her entrance, prolonging the pleasure by pushing in only a fraction.

Frustrated, Sydney wraps her long legs around my waist and squeezes, trying to force me into her. I lap at her mouth, our teeth clashing as we furiously attack each other. She whimpers when I break the kiss, but only so I can stare right into her irresistible blue eyes as I sink into her welcoming depths.

"You feel so fucking good, Syd." My voice is close to breaking from the overpowering emotion of this moment. She's mine, she loves me, she's back with me… safe.

I finally let go of Sydney's hands and begin to move inside her, sliding in and out slowly, tantalizingly, her lithe body pinned beneath mine. I let my hands roam her smooth skin, caressing her breasts and skimming down to grip her waist.

"I love you Sydney," I tell her, our eyes still locked together.

She lifts her hips off of the bed in perfect rhythm with my strokes. The heat begins to build inside me, spreading up from my balls as they get heavy, primed to explode. I increase the pace, snapping my hips forward, pounding harder and drawing long wails from Sydney as she struggles to hold off her climax.

"I love you so much," I whisper as I capture her mouth with mine. I continue my affirmations as I drag my teeth along her neck, "I can't live without you," and up to her ear, "we belong together."

"God, Drew, I love you so much," Sydney cries out right as she hits her peak.

"Fuck Sydney, don't ever leave me again," I groan as she comes, her pussy clamps down and milks my cock until I fall over the edge into ecstasy. Jolts of pleasure are forced out of my body until I've been completely drained.

Exhausted, I lay on top of her, placing soft kisses on her swollen lips as we catch our breath. When I slip out of her and pull her close, I'm asleep before my head lands on the pillow.

Hours later I wake up to an empty bed. Sydney is gone. Alarmed, I bolt upright in the bed, scared shitless that she left me again. The smell fresh coffee brewing in the other room lets me know that she's still in the apartment somewhere, and I'm clearly overreacting.

Fuck. Get your shit together, Forrester.

Once I calm my racing heart, I pull on a shirt and wander out of the bedroom to find Sydney. She's in the living room, sitting quietly on the couch with her usual steaming cup of coffee.

"Good morning gorgeous." I kiss the top of her head, unable to resist inhaling her addictive fragrance one more time. 'Is there more coffee?"

She attempts to get up and fetch me a cup. "Yes, there's a pot in the kitchen. I'll get it for you."

"No, sit. Relax, Sydney. I'll be right back."

As I pour some coffee my heart starts pounding against my ribcage. We're going to have to talk about this, about us, about who I am and how I lied to her. All of my cards are laid out on the table. Will she show me hers? Or will I be left floundering in the dark, never understanding this mysterious girl?

Steeling myself for the worst, I pick up my mug and walk back into the living room, taking the seat next to Sydney. Determined to figure her out, I pull her legs across my lap so she'll have to face me while we talk. No ducking her head or averting her eyes this time.

After a few minutes of awkward silence, I decide that I may as well start since she's not much of a talker.

"You scared me, Sydney. I didn't know what happened to you. I couldn't get here. The damn flights kept getting fucked up." I drag my free hand through my hair, clutching my mug tightly in the other. "Then I find out I'm too late. That … well, you know, Kiera, told you," I snarl. "I came here with Leah; you wouldn't answer your phone, or the door. I thought … I thought …" my voice hitches. "I don't understand why, Sydney."

Hesitantly, she reaches up and touches my cheek, letting her fingers caress my skin before dropping her hand into her lap. "I know babe, I know. I'm so sorry. I want to tell you everything. I was going to tell you before the party, as a kind of birthday present. I guess we both have secrets. Great birthday, huh?"

I lean in and press my forehead to hers, willing her to close the gap between us, to let me past her carefully constructed walls. "I don't give a shit about my birthday and it doesn't matter what you tell me, Sydney. I'll still love you."

She swallows nervously, her fingers carelessly pulling at a thread on her T-shirt. "My childhood was … different." *Holy shit she's actually telling me!* "My parents, they weren't exactly normal."

Rage begins to swirl in my gut at the thought of someone hurting her and I can feel my eyes narrow. "What did they do to you?"

"Drew, it's not like that." She pauses and takes a deep breath. "My parents are Evangeline Allen and Reid Tannen. I'm Sydney Tannen."

What? My mind starts spinning, trying to make sense of this information. The only Evangeline Allen and Reid Tannen I know of are actors.

"So you … your parents are Evangeline Allen and Reid Tannen, the actors," I repeat.

This doesn't make sense. I thought she had a traumatic childhood or something, not raised by two of the wealthiest people in Hollywood.

"Yes. My mom took me away from California when I was twelve. My parents didn't feel that I was … that I was … safe anymore. The photographers, the lies, the stalkers, the crazy people…" her voice trails off as she struggles to finish.

Holy fuck, I remember now! I was young, maybe a freshman in college when they divorced.

Each piece of the horrifying puzzle slowly drops into place and I become more and more agitated as I speak. "I remember…the accident with your dad, the photographer who caused it. It was in the papers and on TV. I had just started school at Boston College …" *Jesus, she was almost killed!* "You were seriously hurt, Sydney! Your dad was arrested!"

"Yes."

That's all she says about being one of the highest profile victims of the paparazzi's reckless pursuits. Her childhood was a fucking nightmare because of her parents' fame. That's why she hates everything that has to do with…me.

I look down and see her rubbing her right arm and pull it towards me, flipping it over. There it is, the long pink line I saw the first day I met her. It's faded over time but still quite visible. I gasp when I realize what it is, what I saw in my gym. A reminder of everything that was completely fucked up about her childhood.

The breath is knocked out of my lungs, the invisible punch so strong that I have to fight not to hunch over and writhe in pain. It's over. Sydney can't be with someone like me. I will completely obliterate everything that is left of this damaged girl. As much as it hurts, as much as my heart is shattering into a million pieces and leaving a hollow spot in my chest, I have to let her go.

"I understand," I whisper. "My world scares you. It destroyed you. I'm so selfish Sydney. I had no idea; you don't need this in your life. You don't need me." I close my eyes and push her legs off of my lap, needing to get out of here before she sees me break down.

"No Drew, I do need you," Sydney says in a panicked voice. "Whatever your life is, it's what I want as long as you're there with me." She scrambles to grab me and tries to pull me back to her.

I look at her warily, two seconds from losing my shit over this entire crappy situation.

"That's what I've been figuring out these past few days. I was at my mom's in Belize. She helped me realize that I can't keep hiding."

As much as my splintered heart is more than willing to be selfish and stay with her, my head is telling me to push her away. To prevent my world from tearing her apart until nothing is left.

"Can you really live like that Sydney? The paparazzi? The fans? That's all part of the Andrew Forrester package. It's even worse now than it was back then, the internet and cell phone cameras and tabloid shows … it never stops. I mean shit, Sydney, there was even a blog the day after the party with a picture and an article that described how I argued with Kiera Radcliff and Adam Reynolds at Verve, fighting over an 'unknown female'!" I shout, angry and hurt at this whole fucked up situation. "One of the guests must have used their camera phone. If they find out who you are? It will go worldwide in about a half a second! I'm no good for you. I can't protect you from that." My voice is frantic and emotional as I try to describe my life in a way that she'll understand.

I attempt to unwind her hands from my shirt so I can escape the torture of losing her, but Sydney determinedly climbs up onto my lap and wraps her arms around my neck, clinging for dear life.

"Drew, I lost a lot when I was a child. I lost my home, my friends, my father…" Tears slide down her cheeks as she looks into my eyes and describes her shitty childhood. "I refuse to let our child lose those things too, simply because I'm too afraid to stand up and live my life."

Child? Our child?

"What?" I rasp. In that moment, I swear, the tattered remains of my heart stop, and my entire world collapses into a tiny pinprick containing only the two of us sitting on this couch.

"Our child, Drew. I'm pregnant."

I can't think or move. My mind can't make sense of this. It's too much.

"Child? But you said the test was negative. Are you sure?"

I try to stay stoic for Sydney, to not break down in front of her. If she's pregnant, then nothing else matters. Fuck the bullshit, the fake Hollywood crap, Adam Reynolds and all of that. The only thing I care about is Sydney and the child she carries inside.

Sydney's cheeks redden with embarrassment. "I took the test a week too soon. I didn't know there was a time frame in which it wouldn't work. I've been sick for a few weeks, I can't eat much. I thought it was stress, but I realized that it all added up to one thing. Yes, I'm sure that I'm pregnant, Drew."

She looks up at me, unsure, and I know in that moment, that we'll have each other. I'll do my best to protect her and the baby from whatever shit life throws our way.

Ecstatic, I pull her to me and hug her tight, crushing my mouth over hers. "I love you so much Sydney," I tell her, laughing. "I guess I shouldn't be this happy, but I am."

I can't stop grinning, everything is perfect now. All of our secrets are out and we're going to be parents. I can hardly believe it. Sydney's expression mirrors mine, elated.

"I'm happy too, Drew. Scared shitless, but happy."

"We're actually going to do this?"

"Yes, we are. We'll figure it out together. I have a doctor's appointment tomorrow if you want to go."

"Of course I want to go." Then I remember that I can't just walk in the front door like a normal human being. "Do they have a back entrance?"

And so it begins. Sydney's about to find out just how hard it is to be with Andrew Forrester, movie star.

CHAPTER 27

It turns out the doctor's office doesn't have a back entrance, so we have to make a special after-hours appointment. It's so fucking frustrating sometimes. But now that I have Sydney back, and I know about her childhood, there's no way I'm taking the chance that a fan will take photos of us in the waiting room and freak her the fuck out.

"Drew, can I ask you something?"

Sydney is sitting next to me in the Town Car as Bruce drives us over to Mount Sinai.

I turn so I can watch her as we talk. "Of course, Sydney."

Are you kidding? After months of avoiding every single subject you could possibly think of, just the fact that she wants to ask me something has me thrilled.

"You'll tell me the truth, right?"

Okay, now I'm worried. I always tell her the truth. Except for when I was hiding my job from her.

"Yes, just ask me and I'll tell you." Now I'm worried and intrigued. What could she possibly want to know?

Sydney pauses for a moment, carefully choosing her words before speaking. "Ok, well, when we were in St. Bart's, I accidentally overheard you on the phone. You were upset and yelling at someone. I could tell you were mad because I notice that your accent comes back when you get emotional and you were totally Boston."

Damn, I know that sometimes I can sound like I grew up in Boston, but apparently my accent is more pronounced than I realize. I've worked damn hard to get rid of it too.

"What was that?" she asks.

"Oh," I reply, embarrassed to have been caught hiding shit from her. "I was making sure the crew on the boat didn't say anything if they recognized me. I didn't want any looks or weirdness that would freak you out." I study her face intently, reading her reaction. "You're not mad are you?"

Sydney laughs. "No, I'm not mad. It seems like so much trouble to go through just to date me though."

Is she fucking kidding me?

"First, there's nothing I wouldn't have done to date you Sydney. Not knowing who I was when we met, that was a first for me, and I loved it. I could date like a real person, no preconceived notions about Andrew Forrester the public figure already in your head. I could just be Drew, a guy from Boston. I regretted letting you leave the gym that day without a way to contact you, so when you sat with me in the café and told me how repellant I was, I knew I had to get to know you."

We laugh at the memory of her calling me repellant.

"Then you were so upset by that magazine, by a celebrity, I wanted to find out why, but I also didn't want you walking home alone after having been so shaken up."

Sydney reaches over and takes my hand, curling her delicate fingers in between mine.

"You do get a little caveman sometimes."

"I know, sometimes I go overboard, but I want to keep you from getting hurt, Sydney. You make me that way." I stare at our hands, afraid that maybe I'm telling her too much. I'm tired of the lies though, of holding back my feelings. I'd rather be honest and let the chips fall where they may. "I've never felt so protective of anyone else outside of my family. It's because I love you. I probably loved you from the moment you called me repellant."

I glance up at her and see her eyes glistening at my admission. Crap, I don't want to make her cry, even if they are the good kind of tears, but she's giving me this chance to get it all off of my chest so I'm taking it.

"And you think the sailboat thing was difficult?" I continue. "I had to hide so much stuff, and I hated having to do it Sydney. It made me feel so crappy, but I wanted you so desperately. I just didn't want you to leave me without knowing the real me."

"What else did you have to hide?"

Where to start?

I make a noise, somewhere between a laugh and a scoff. "A lot, I had to hide all of my awards and photos at my house, all of my scripts that are usually lying around, my assistant, Jane, couldn't be around when you were. I had given her a weekend off since I was between projects anyway. You and I couldn't do any dates in public. I was so glad that you were as happy staying in as I am. The pilots on the private jet almost blew it for me, I had to have Philippe clear out Chad's awards and photos out of the villa and lock them in the office, I couldn't shop with you in St. Bart's, I had to wear my hat everywhere even though I knew you hated it … it was exhausting."

I think of the fun we had on the island, specifically the naked fun and give her a suggestive look. "But totally worth it."

Sydney squirms on the seat next to me and I know that she's remembering the same moments as I am. Then, as quickly as she was turned on, she becomes distant, angling away from me and staring out the window.

"Why go through all of that when you could have just dated someone you could just be yourself around?"

Is she serious?

"Sydney, look at me." Now I'm pissed that she thinks I'm anything but myself when I'm with her. "I wanted to date you *because* I could be myself around you. Andrew Forrester isn't real. You know this. Your parents had to have done the same thing. Be one person for the public, and someone else in private."

Sydney nods as she thinks about what I'm saying, probably remembering how her parents acted around people they didn't know.

"I can't find anyone who doesn't already know Andrew Forrester, and therefore, they think they know me. *You* know me. They don't. They get the façade that I give them, and you get all of me. When Bruce brought you into my gym, bleeding and hurt…" I close my eyes at the memory of her shivering, cold and in pain that day, "I felt this overwhelming urge to protect you. When you didn't know who I was, I couldn't believe it. You have no idea how rare that is for me." I reach out and touch her, desperate for the contact.

"Then I let you leave without a way to find you, unless I wanted to stalk your building, which I considered doing." She looks at me warily. I shrug. "Bruce had your address from dropping you off. But when Bruce gave me the napkin that he took from you, it said Village Coffee Bar. You must go there a lot because you showed up the first day I went there to find you."

Her eyes widen in surprise at my confession, then a wide smile crosses her beautiful face, lighting up the entire car.

"Your smile is so beautiful. I hate when I can't put it there for you," I admit.

I push the button to lower the glass partition, "Bruce, we'll be back in about an hour." We hop out of the car and go inside.

"What floor?" I ask Sydney as we approach the row of elevators.

"Tenth."

"Excuse me, are you Andrew Forrester?"

Fuck! I knew I should have worn my hat! I don't want Sydney to see this, not yet. She only just accepted who I am and what I do, I don't want to ruin it by encountering over-enthusiastic fans our first day out.

"Yes. How are you?" I unconsciously morph into my Andrew Forrester persona for the excited woman.

"Oh, oh my. I love your movies! Especially *Time Around*, it was just so great," the woman says excitedly. She keeps talking, but I'm watching Sydney's reaction. I can tell that she's beginning to freak out. Her face is drawn and the sound of the elevator arriving makes her jump in fear.

I turn to the woman and quickly dismiss her, "I'm sorry; we have to go, it's nice to meet you."

I follow Sydney into the elevator and watch as she smacks the button for our floor and retreats to the corner, looking pale and anxious.

"Syd, are you okay? You don't look well."

"I'm fine, I'll be okay. It's just weird. I remember that with my parents." She waves her hand in my direction. "I just can't reconcile you with this huge star that everyone knows. It's a little bizarre, that's all."

She's taking deep breaths, probably to calm herself down. Fuck, I'm such an asshole. I should have remembered the damn hat.

The second the doors open, Sydney scampers out of the elevator and down the hall. I'm mad at myself for making her feel this way. This isn't good for her, for her stress levels. Especially now that she's pregnant.

I enter the doctor's office and find Sydney already quietly talking to the girl at the front desk. When the girl's eyes meet mine, they grow two sizes larger and her face turns bright red.

Great. Another one.

Afraid to another fan experience will shake Sydney's confidence, I take a seat as far away from the desk as I can in the hopes that she won't notice the girl's reaction. When she comes to sit next to me, clipboard in hand, the scowl on her face lets me know that yes, she noticed.

Syd fills out the paperwork in silence, tension building between us.

"Sydney?" the doctor calls out.

It's our turn. Now *I'm* the one that's anxious, the unwelcome feeling making my stomach roil with nerves that I can only deal with by shutting them down. Numb, I follow behind Syd and the doctor, too zoned out to even care that the receptionist is still blatantly gawking.

"Okay Sydney, take off your clothes from the waist down and put this on." The doctor hands her a folded up piece of cloth and directs us into a room. "Then get up on the table. I'll be right back."

Before I can blink, Sydney strips and hops up on the exam table and the doctor is back. How did that happen so fast? It feels as though my mind is working in slow motion.

"Alright, let's see what's going on, shall we?" The doctor flicks on a machine and a grainy black and white screen comes on. She ducks her hand under Sydney's gown and watches the screen intently.

"There, see this tiny shaded area? That's the baby."

Huh? I don't see a thing. Just a fuzzy gray mess.

"The black hole?" Sydney asks.

"The black area is the gestational sac around the fetus. The baby is the very small spot on the edge of the sac." She rapidly types something and an arrow appears on the screen with the word 'baby' pointing at the hole.

"Wow."

I stare at Sydney after she says this, hoping she can help me see what is apparently supposed to be obvious. Her nose is scrunched up and her brows are pulled tightly together. She doesn't have any more of a clue what we're looking at than I do. I move closer to the little screen, still not able to figure out what exactly is the baby. Then the spot inside the black hole flutters and I flinch.

What the hell? "It moved, is that normal?"

"Perfectly normal," the doctor chuckles. "It's the baby's heartbeat. I'd guess you're about eight weeks pregnant with conception about six weeks ago?" Sydney nods. The doctor pushes a button and rips a piece of paper off of the machine. "Here, take this picture with you."

Holy shit. A heartbeat. A baby. Inside Sydney. My baby. Our baby.

Another rush of unfamiliar emotions flood my brain like a tsunami, crashing in and sweeping everything else out with the tide. Fear, love, apprehension, excitement, and mostly an overwhelming need to protect what's mine. My family.

How am I going to keep them safe?

"Thanks," Sydney says as she takes the picture.

"You can get dressed and we'll talk in my office when you're ready."

I vaguely register that the doctor has left the room and Sydney is dressed. I have no idea how I got to the doctor's personal office or how I ended up in the big chair across from her desk, but here I am. Freaking the fuck out, probably gaping like an idiot.

I'm so confused. I'm so fucking happy, but I'm so fucking scared. For Sydney, for the baby. I don't want to travel unless she's with me either. Having her away from me would drive me fucking crazy with worry.

Even with all that shit to worry about, the paparazzi, the fans, the tabloids that are going to go nuts when Sydney shows up swollen and pregnant with my child... I can't fucking wait to meet our kid.

I snap out of it and realize that the doctor is standing, waiting for me to shake her hand. "Thanks doctor. We appreciate your time." I let Sydney leave the office first and follow dutifully behind her.

Once again, I'm lost in my thoughts until Sydney grabs my hand and yanks me out of my stupor, pulling me down the hall towards the elevators.

"Hey, are you okay with all of this?" she asks, peering up at me with her huge blue eyes.

I stare back down at her, this fragile yet strong woman that I love so much. "I can't believe that my child is actually inside you," I whisper.

"Yes, it is."

Everything else is forgotten for the moment except us, our future. I grab her and hold her tightly against my chest. "I guess it just didn't seem real until now. I'm so happy, thank you for giving this to me."

"I thought you were in there freaking out, you know, trying to find a way out of this situation," Sydney says once we're in the elevator.

She still doesn't think that I want her, all of her, forever.

I tug on her hand and the length of her warm body presses up against mine. "No way would I ever want out, Sydney." I lean down and capture her mouth with mine, sliding a hand up to cup the back of her head. She responds immediately, wrapping her arms around my neck, nipping at my lips like she can't get enough.

Naughty Sydney, making my dick hard in the elevator.

Unexpectedly, the elevator doors open and Sydney jumps away from me, embarrassed. Me? I could care less who sees me kissing her. A young man enters the elevator, so engrossed in his phone that he steps right on my foot.

"I'm so sorry. I didn't expect anyone…" He backs away and glances up and I watch as his eyes widen significantly. *Shit, he knows me.* "I, I'm s-s-sorry," he stammers, turning bright red and spinning to face the front of the elevator.

Sydney looks at me and it's just about impossible not to crack up.

CHAPTER 28

"No! No fuckin' way Sydney!"

"Drew, I'm doing this," she says calmly.

Jesus Christ! She can be so fucking stubborn sometimes.

"No, I don't like it. It's not a good idea." The uneasiness makes it impossible to stand still. The instinctive urge to strike out and hit something is winning the war against my very small rational side. My hands itch so badly that I have to curl them up and stuff them in my pockets. "It's bullshit!" I yell.

"Stop being so dramatic, Drew. I promised my mother I would do this for her. After everything she did for me, I want to be there."

She gets up from the couch and walks over to where I'm pacing in front of the bookshelves in her loft and grips the front of my shirt in her hands. "Drew." I keep my chin up, unable to look at her. I don't want her to see the blinding fury in my eyes. "Drew."

"What!" I snap, still refusing to meet her gaze.

"Look at me," she begs.

Grudgingly, I force my eyes down and find hers wide and shimmering with tears. *Fuck!*

"My mom is going to be back in the spotlight, there's nothing we can do about it. Once that happens, they're going to dig and dig until they find me. It's easier this way. To do it on my terms, without someone popping out of the bushes with a giant camera."

My whole body tenses at the thought of Sydney exposing herself to the world, inviting that shit back into her life after the damage it caused. I need to get to the gym, to punch the shit out of something, to regain some control over a situation I have no control over.

"I hate this, Sydney. This is how it starts, the frenzy. I can't protect you and the baby from all that shit." I'm able to calm myself enough to speak without shouting, barely.

"I don't need you to protect me, Drew."

I give her a look of incredulity. *Is she fucking joking?*

"Of course I'm going to protect you Sydney. That's my job. It's something I have to do." She starts to argue with me and I cut her off, unwilling to compromise on this. "No, Syd. Don't bother trying to change my mind about it. This is how I am and it's not going to change."

"Alright," she says, looking up at me with those fucking puppy dog eyes. They kill me. Every single time. "I know you aren't comfortable with me appearing on *Late Night Report*. Just understand where I'm coming from, please."

I grind my teeth together in aggravation. Obviously, she's going to do this no matter what I say. As much as I want to, I can't lock her up and keep her here forever.

"Fine," I relent. "But know that I hate it, and I'm going with you."

Her arms wrap around my waist and she puts her cheek against my chest. Too tempting to pass up, I lower my head, burying my nose in her hair to take a hit of my favorite drug. Shit. This interview is going to kill me.

If I have to watch her pace this room one more time, I'm going to lose my shit. We shouldn't even be here. This idea is so awful there aren't even words to explain how awful it is.

"Sydney, please stop. You're going to be a sweaty mess if you keep running around like that." Sydney's mom is as calm as a cucumber. Of course she is, she's Evangeline Allen. She's been making movies since before Sydney was born. She's as calm as I would be if it weren't the woman I love about to expose herself to the entire world.

This is too stressful to let continue, I can't take it. I get up and stop Sydney from pacing. I have to try to make her feel better, no matter how shitty of an idea I think this is, it's my job to support her in this. "Syd, it's going to be okay. I'll be right off to the side where you can see me the entire time. They'll love you, but you can still back out if you want to."

I couldn't help but give her the chance to change her mind. But she's so fucking stubborn. There's no way she'll back out now.

"Miss Allen, Ms. Allen, it's time." The PA comes in to get them for their interview.

I watch Sydney take a deep breath and pretend that she's not on the verge of losing her shit. "Actually, it's Miss Tannen now, not Allen." She smiles at her mom.

She's so not ready for this. "Are you ready?" I ask, staring into her eyes to make sure she's not going to fall apart.

"Like ripping off a Band-Aid, right?" Her attempt at a joke lets me read her like a book. She looks pale and scared, and she's shaking.

Shit! I just want to grab her and run the fuck out of here.

"Let's go," she says to me, sliding her clammy hand into mine for support.

The closer we get to the stage, the harder she grips me with her trembling fingers. For some asinine fucking reason, Sydney thinks that making this appearance and explaining where she and her mom have been the past twelve years will close the book on this chapter of her life and satisfy everyone's curiosity.

Bullshit.

I know the tabloids these days. They. Will. Not. Stop. No way. This story is too fucking huge, so huge even I remember it happening. Young Sydney Tannen is stalked, attacked, run off the road by paparazzi and almost killed, her mega star dad arrested, then she and her Oscar-winning mom disappear for twelve years? It's too big to ignore or brush off with one simple interview.

Then, we're walking the red carpet next week at my premiere, which is looking more and more like a terrible idea each day. After that, the shit's going to hit the fan. It's the mother-lode of stories for these pricks. I thought about going to my premiere alone, leaving her out of it, but I'm selfish. I want here there. I've never wanted anyone with me before and now that I have her, I can't imagine walking it without her by my side.

I hear Brandon finish up his opening bit. *Shit, it's time.* I hug Syd to me and touch her still-flat stomach, rubbing my thumbs in circles. A gentle caress for the baby inside. "I love you Sydney, no matter what."

She looks up at me with frightened cobalt eyes, "I love you too, always."

And then she's gone. Walking out on that stage to have her hard won privacy ripped to shreds. She's already changed her name back to Sydney Tannen, she doesn't do anything halfway. When she has her mind set on something, there's no going back.

I don't hear or see anything but Sydney as I focus on her from my spot backstage. I make sure to stand where she can find me, in case she needs moral support. Even though I loathe this entire idea and don't want her out there, I'll be here for her.

Sydney takes the seat farthest from Brandon Eastlake, the host of the very popular *Late Night Report*. I've met him several times before, having done his show for every single movie release I've had. He's charming and funny onstage which gets him huge ratings, but he can be a slimy prick with the women he meets.

Syd's shaking like a leaf. It's subtle, but I can see that she's sitting on her hands to hide it from the cameras and the audience.

"So Sydney, how did it feel when you found out that your parents planned their split to get you away from L.A. and all of the trauma that you suffered?" Brandon asks after speaking with Evangeline for a few minutes.

Sydney's sweet face crumples and she looks like she's about to cry.

Mother fucker! I could literally punch him for putting that look on her face. I have to breathe deep and clench my fists to control the overwhelming need I feel to protect her.

"Well Brandon," she begins, her small voice breaking on the words. "It gave me closure. All of the pain I had felt about leaving L.A. and losing my dad, it made sense. It was a huge sacrifice that both of my parents made for me, and I love them for it."

I can tell she's struggling to keep the tears back. Her mom takes her hand and squeezes it, putting a small smile on my girl's face. Shit, that should be me out there comforting her. I feel castrated, standing on the sidelines like a useless asshole while she relives all of the shit she's been through.

"I heard a rumor that you don't own a TV? Is that true?" Brandon asks her.

A gorgeous pink blush stains Sydney's cheeks and she lowers her lashes in embarrassment. "Yes, it's true."

"So, have you ever seen my show?" Brandon leans over his desk so he can see her better. Fucker.

"I'm afraid I haven't, Brandon. I actually had no idea who you were until the other day when we were booked on your show,"

Syd admits with a shrug. The audience laughs at Brandon's dumbfounded face.

Ha! Egotistical prick! She didn't know who I was either, so don't take it personally.

"Sydney, you've hurt my feelings," Brandon jokes.

"Well Brandon, I guess I'll have to get a TV just so I can watch you," Syd says with a giggle.

The audience eats that shit up. Me, I'm seeing fucking red. That ass Eastlake flirting with my girl in front of millions of people.

The interview wraps up and I hurry to meet Syd in the green room, unsure if she'll still be a shaking mess.

I storm into the room and find her standing near the couch with a bottle of water in her hand. Needing the contact with her, I wrap my arms around her waist and pull her close, kissing the top of her head and burying my face in her hair.

"You did great babe," I whisper.

The door opens again and Brandon Eastlake's voice grates on me like nails on a chalkboard. He's talking to Eva while I have my back to him, so I can't see his face.

"Sydney! You did great!" Brandon walks over to us and stops dead in his tracks when he sees me glaring at him, his phony smile wiped off of his face. "Forrester? What are you doing here?"

Well, what I really want to do is punch the shit out of you for making my girl feel uncomfortable and for flirting with her.

I turn and put my arm around Sydney's waist and pull her to me. Territorial asshole, I know, but I recognize the look in Eastlake's eyes and I know his reputation.

"I'm here with my girlfriend, of course," I say smoothly. I don't miss the shock, then the disappointment in the prick's eyes the exact second he figures out that he has no chance adding Sydney to his list of conquests.

"Wow, well… uh… how come you didn't want to do the interview with her?" he asks, still clearly annoyed by my cockblocking existence.

"Today was about Sydney and Eva, not me."

"I just didn't want the media to go crazy, you know. I wanted to keep it focused," Syd says, trying to lower the tension between Eastlake and me by changing the subject.

I tense up. She's still in complete denial over how much of a shitstorm this interview is going to cause. She thinks it's going to be a one and done thing. She's so wrong.

Brandon attempts some small talk with me about football, but I'm still too pissed off at him and this entire situation to do more than snap back responses as Sydney sneaks away to talk to her mom.

Today, the fucking nightmare begins.

"I just need to get a few things from my place, Drew. It won't take long."

"Syd, we can't go to your place, it's going to be a clusterfuck of paparazzi. I've told you this." She is still in denial. Thirty million people watched the Eastlake show last night, a new record for late night talk shows. I know she's not naïve enough to think her life will be the same as before, but her idea of how this is going to play out is not anywhere close to reality, not even the same universe.

"Stop being so negative," she snaps at me.

I frown and lower the partition. "Bruce, we need to swing by Sydney's loft first." I turn to her, "Happy?"

She smiles and curls into my side, "Very."

Fifteen minutes after leaving Teterboro, Bruce attempts to pull onto Sydney's street. And can't. Because there are no fewer than ten white news vans with satellite dishes sticking up off of them parked all along the road and sidewalks. I can see her building halfway down the block and the massive crowd of people clogging the walkway out front.

Clenching my teeth, I lower the partition again, "Bruce, home. Now!"

"What? Why?" Sydney sits up straight and looks outside. Her hand flies up to her mouth and every bit of color drains from her skin. "Oh."

I pull her back in a desperate attempt to shield her from the terrifying sight. "It's okay Syd. You'll stay with me. They don't know about us and won't know to look there. Either way, I want you with me so I know you're okay." I can feel her small frame shaking against my chest. *Fuck!* This is exactly why I didn't want her to do that interview. Her life will never be the same and this stress can't be good for the baby.

Who the fuck am I kidding though? Next week, after she walks that premiere with me, it's going to be the same shit as this. Either way, we have to get used to the new normal for her, and for us. My days of only finding a random photo of myself buying fruit in the tabloids are almost over.

"We'll send Bruce and Leah to get your stuff, Syd." I squeeze her knee in support.

She doesn't answer me, her new reality is finally starting to sink in. She's scared as hell and there's nothing I can do to make it better. I really hate that.

I should have insisted that she not do that fucking interview.

We drag our stuff into the brownstone and Sydney immediately disappears upstairs. "Bruce, you can go, but be here tomorrow at ten, I'll need a favor."

"Sure thing Drew, see you then."

I head to the bedroom and find Sydney staring out the windows, her forehead pressed to the glass. Quietly, I cross the room and stand behind her, leaving just an inch of space between us. I'm not sure if she wants my comfort or if she wants to be alone.

"I…I guess I had no idea…"

The hitch in her voice stabs me right in the heart. I close the gap between us and pull her back to my chest, running my nose up her soft neck and curl my arm around her belly protectively.

"It will be okay... eventually, Syd. They can't stay there forever."

Shit, I can't even convince myself.

"Look at me, Sydney." Reluctantly, she turns towards me, her hands hanging limply at her sides. Defeated. I tilt my head and put my forehead to hers, holding her face in my hands. "We. Will. Be. Fine. I won't allow you to live in fear. This... this crap? We'll just have to find a way to adjust, okay?"

I carefully watch her, the way her eyes shimmer with unshed tears, her pouty lips pulled into a frown. She brings her arms up to my chest and slides them around my neck, "Okay, Drew. For you, for us, I'll be stronger."

Her words suck the breath out of my lungs. "Baby, you're the strongest person I know."

While Syd takes a shower, I pull out my laptop and check my emails and other work commitments. My parents and sister got the conformation for the airline tickets I purchased and will meet us at the hotel before the premiere. They're beyond excited to meet Sydney, I've never introduced a girl to them before, so this is huge.

Jane has been keeping up with work stuff, so there's not a whole lot to do. I've already sent her to L.A. to have every major designer send a dress for Sydney to choose from. I want her to feel beautiful standing beside me on the red carpet.

Bored, I do something I hardly ever do. I pull up Google and do a search.

Sydney Tannen Interview

Enter

Holy shit, the amount of information is staggering. I click on Brandon Eastlake's homepage and see a few photos and a video of the interview. I've already seen that so I go back and skim through the list of trashy blogs and real news sites and read their headlines.

Evangeline Allen and Sydney Tannen Reemerge After 12 Years in Seclusion

nbcnews.com- After shunning Hollywood over a decade ago, Oscar winning actress Evangeline Allen and Sydney Tannen, her daughter with recently crowned Oscar winning actor Reid Tannen, came out of hiding…(12 hours ago)

Sydney Tannen Breaks Down Over Broken Childhood

celebcast.com- Shaken and teary, the daughter of Hollywood royalty Sydney Tannen breaks down during her interview on Late Night Report. Reminiscing about the near-fatal car crash….(6 hours ago)

Sydney Tannen the Perfect Combination of Reid and Eva?

gossiphound.com- We all knew that any child of gorgeous stars such as Evangeline Allen and Reid Tannen would be beautiful. But who could have dreamed up a vision like Sydney Tannen?

She appeared on Late Night Report last night, watched by an estimated record-breaking 30 million viewers, and stunned everyone by being a complete knockout. Wearing a form-fitting, navy Burberry dress with strappy stilettos, the beautiful redhead won over the hearts of the audience, and the fantasies of the men who watched.

We're wondering how this hot, sexy girl managed to stay hidden for so long. You would think with a face like that, a body for sin, and those lips! Well, we just don't equate hidden away from what we've seen!

What. The. Fuck!

I admit, I imagined all kind of fucked up shit happening after Syd did that interview, but other men ogling her and lusting after her wasn't something that ever crossed my mind. In hindsight, I'm an idiotic asshole. Of course men are going to want her, she's fucking gorgeous, but seeing it in print, in such a crude manner? Rage isn't the word for it.

And because I'm a stupid bastard who loves to torture himself, I click on the comments section of the last article.

Bigdaddy12- Fuck yeah! She's hot enough to fuck without a bag on her head or on my dick!

Roman27- I'd even let her spend the night and make me breakfast after fucking her!

JessiePrinceSpider- No clothes, leave on the spike heels. I'll even be nice and pull your hair for you baby!

CelesteThornton00- You guys are pigs! Nasty pieces of shit. Leave her alone.

Ronniebigman- All I got to say is those lips, my cock. Nice.

I can't read anymore, my vision has gone red, pure undiluted rage coursing through my veins and burning me from the inside. Every muscle in my body is twitching to pound the fuck out of something or someone for that vile shit. Clenching my fists isn't going to work this time, neither is breathing deep.

Fuck. Me.

Standing up, I grab the laptop and crack it over my knee until it splits in half. Holding the two broken pieces, I throw them as hard as I can against the wall, watching the halves bounce off and scatter across the room. I still don't feel any better, the urge to throttle someone for disrespecting my girl running hot and raw at full speed.

"Drew? What are you doing?"

Startled, I look up from where I'm stomping on the shattered remains of the computer and see Sydney, dripping wet, wrapped in a towel, and looking scared to death. Of me. The fury drains from me when I see the expression on her face.

Damn.

Kicking the remnants of my laptop aside, I walk over to Sydney. She takes a step back, her eyes wide, shifting from me to the broken computer.

It kills me that she's afraid of me.

"Babe, I'm fine. I'm sorry. I just…" I bring my hands up to fist my hair and drop my head back to stare at the ceiling. "Shit."

"What happened?" she whispers, still keeping her distance.

I can't look at her, I'm too ashamed her having seen that behavior. Especially the fact that I'd do it all over again every fucking time.

With a sigh, I lower my hands and look at the floor. "I read an article about you. About the interview." I pause, eyeing her reaction. "Specifically, about how you looked… physically."

"Okay…" she sounds confused.

"There were comments… from men." I inhale deeply and look up at her. She sees my face and her eyes get even wider. I must still look pissed. I *am* still pissed. "Let's just say that they need to have my foot put in their disgusting asses and leave it at that."

Sydney's eyes narrow, then she takes a step toward me and smiles. *What?*

"You're so sweet, getting all caveman and protective of me." She reaches up and runs her hand down my cheek. "Maybe no more computer for a while, what do you think?"

Unable to help myself, I smile back at her and tug her hips against mine. "What do I get in exchange for agreeing to that?" Still smiling, I lean down and skim my mouth down her neck and nip at her shoulder.

"I can think of something," she says as she lets her towel fall.

CHAPTER 29

"Wait here, I'll jump out and get you all checked in." I watch as my manager, Quentin, hops out of the car and darts into the Sunset Marquis.

"I don't understand why we can't just check ourselves in," Sydney pouts on the seat next to me.

She's so funny, and still in complete and total denial. Laughing, I answer her. "Syd, you and I cannot just waltz into a hotel in Hollywood and stand around the lobby. Unless you want a riot to start."

Her eyebrows pull together, twisting her face into an adorable grimace and she grunts at me. She's so fucking cute when she's in a bad mood, and my excitement is starting to get on her nerves. I'm so fucking thrilled to have her here with me, going to my premiere tomorrow to let the world know that she belongs to me, that I'm riding an incredible high.

I can't keep my hands off of her, even though I know it's starting to piss her off. It appears that, it pays to be persistent, because I slide my hand up her shirt for about the millionth time today, and this time, she's too annoyed to swat at me. Before she can change her mind, I take advantage of her weak moment and yank down one side of her bra and run my hand over one perfect breast.

Sydney takes in a sharp breath and my already uncomfortable erection turns to steel at the mewing sound she makes. I pull up her shirt and tilt my head down so I can lave on her tight bud until she starts to pant and squirm on the seat.

"Drew, Quentin will be back soon," she moans.

A twinge of red flickers past my vision. "Don't think about him while I'm trying to seduce you, Sydney. I don't like it." Like I need his fucking name coming from her lips while I'm sucking on her. As punishment, I jerk down the other side of her bra and release her other breast. Switching to that side, I nip at her, hard. A deep hum escapes from her throat and my dick actually fucking hurts.

Out of the corner of my eye, I catch a glimpse of Quentin's brightly colored shirt and sit up, straightening her clothes before she even notices the car door opening.

"Here's your info and your keys. You're in the Presidential Villa, so you'll have a little bit of a walk. Drew, you know the way, right?" Quentin flops down into the front seat and reaches his hand back for me to grab the envelope.

"Yes, thank you for doing this. Sydney wanted to just walk right on in the front door," I smirk at her as I tell Quentin her brilliant plan.

Oops, now she's pissed. Damn, she's even cuter when she's pissed then when she's just in a bad mood. Syd makes a face and smacks my chest with her knuckles. "Don't be an ass, Drew."

Quentin bursts out laughing. "Man, I love to see someone who doesn't kiss your butt, pretty boy."

"Yeah, you would," I tell him as I grab Sydney's hand and drag her out of the car. My cock is straining in my jeans as I quickly lead her across the property towards our villa. I need to touch her, to be inside her, now. So much so that we're practically sprinting through the maze-like walkways.

I unlock the door and let Sydney walk in before following and kicking the door shut behind me. She spins around at the loud noise and her eyes widen when she sees me staring at her, undressing her with my eyes. Stalking her like a predator in search of my prey.

Stepping towards her, I yank off my shirt and toss it to the ground, not breaking eye contact with my goal on the other side of the room.

Then, as usual, Sydney surprises the hell out of me. She fucking takes a step back! Away from me! A challenge? She has no idea what she just unleashed. I thought my dick hurt before, now it's about to fucking rip through my jeans.

"Is that how it is, Sydney? Are you going to make me chase you?" I watch her sweet mouth fall open, just enough to make me think about all of the dirty things I want to do to it. Her eyes fall to my naked chest, and they dilate with lust.

She's turned on, it's as obvious on her face as everything else she's ever thinking. But what does she do? She takes another fucking step back, her hands clenched at her sides as if preparing to run. This? This is going to be very, very satisfying.

I casually open my belt and pants as I speak, the buckle rattling against the zipper. "I see." Stalking toward her I kick off my shoes, relishing the thought of what I'll do when I get her. "I will catch you, and then I'm going to make you scream for teasing me."

I can hardly hear her low, raspy voice I'm so fucking turned on. "I'm not teasing you," she insists. Watching closely, I see her thighs press together and I know she wants me, enjoys this game we're playing. I take another step, stripping off my pants and socks, my eyes never leaving hers.

Again, she steps back and now my cock is as hard as it's ever been. Sydney notices it too, because her greedy eyes are fixed on my tented black briefs.

I want to smile at her, but I'm too fucking wound up and my balls are heavy and they ache with need. "Eye fucking me again, Sydney?" I move closer to her, knowing she's just about out of room to go backwards.

Sydney can barely speak, her chest heaving with desire. "No." She takes her final step back and is pressed against the wall of the suite.

Fuck, it takes everything I have to not rip off her clothes and sink into her right now. Instead, I take the last step to close the gap between us and put either hand on the wall next to her head.

"Why are you trying to get away from me?" I drag my mouth up her neck and whisper in her ear. "Don't you want me, Sydney?"

She doesn't answer, so I unfasten the top of her jeans and slide my hand down her pants. Shit, she's so fucking ready. "Always so wet. I think you do want me, you just like to drive me crazy." I rub my finger over her clit, listening to her moan in pleasure, her rapid breaths blowing across my sensitive skin. Satisfied that she's as worked up as I am, I remove my damp finger from her panties and slowly circle it over one breast.

Sydney thumps her head back on the wall and murmurs my name, raking her nails down my chest and abs. My cock jumps at the feel of her hands on my skin and I almost come right then. She stops at the edge of my briefs, my dick just millimeters from her fingers and I hiss at the close contact. Jesus, she tests all of my limits, every fucking time.

Without warning, Sydney is peeling off her shirt, her breasts still jutting out of her bra from my earlier teasing. "God you're so fucking hot. You have no idea what you do to me, to my self-control."

I unclasp her bra and toss it and I'm done with this game. I can't stop anymore. I don't have it in me to hold back. I close my eyes and try my best to rein in my overwhelming desire to fuck her, hard and demanding, right here against the wall. When I look at her again, and see the unbridled lust on her face, I know without a doubt, that she *will* get fucked against the wall.

Before I can move to take her, she strips off her pants and tugs on my briefs, slamming my hard cock against her soft body. Jesus, she feels so fucking good.

Then she completely shatters my control. "I want you," Syd murmurs as she tilts her head and drags her tongue across my neck, sending a blazing hot spike of electricity down my spine and into my cock.

That's it. I shove her back and free myself from the tight restraint of my briefs. Too focused on getting inside her to think of anything else, I grab the thin scrap of lace that she calls underwear and rip them in half, throwing the pieces somewhere over my shoulder. I pin her up against the wall, reach under her ass so she can hook her legs around me, and sink my cock home.

"Fuck, you feel so good." I should feel guilty for pounding into her so hard and fast, but my brain has taken a back seat to the almost incapacitating desire racing through my veins, lust reining over logic. Sydney must feel the same way because she uses her legs and arms to hang on tight, her voice stolen by the heavy breaths which are coming in short, mewling gasps as she gets close.

I need her to come, soon. The pleasure is so intense that I can't stop my own crest from building. "Don't hold back Sydney!" I demand. It only takes one more hard snap of my hips for her pussy to clamp down on me as she wails. Her orgasm drags me right over the edge with her and it's so fucking powerful that I bite down on her shoulder to stay on my feet and keep from collapsing on the floor.

The villa is quiet except for the heavy panting coming from us as we recover. Nothing in my life can compare to being inside Sydney and nothing ever will. I never want it to end. I gently lave and kiss the red mark that my teeth left behind as I carry her into the bedroom, still buried deep inside her as I lay her down on the bed.

"I love you so much, Drew."

"I love you too, Syd." Exhausted, I pull out of her and tuck her up against my chest, wrapping my arms around her and our future that she carries within.

CHAPTER 30

"That one." I can't take my eyes off of Sydney as she assesses herself in the full length mirror that's been set up in the living room of the villa. She's wearing a long red dress that hugs every single one of her luscious curves as a stylist flits around her ankles.

She turns and gives me a shy smile, stealing the air from my lungs. The tiny seamstress comes in and whips off the dress when Sydney agrees with my choice then darts back out of the room with a pile of red fabric over her arm.

I get a good look at Sydney standing in her lacy black strapless bra and thong and a pair of tall gold stilettos before she shrugs into a robe. Great, now I have a hard-on.

The stylist takes the rack of rejected dresses and leaves the suite as Sydney sits on the couch to remove the shoes. I drop onto the seat next to her and tuck my hand into the neckline of her robe, needing to feel her soft skin more than I need my next breath.

She swats my hand away playfully, "Drew, stop it."

God she's so fucking adorable, I can't help but laugh. Her smile fades into a frown. She doesn't think I've noticed that something's up with her today, but I have.

"How are you feeling?" I tilt my head to wait for her answer.

"Fine," she replies, too quickly to be genuine.

I give her a look that lets her know that I'm well aware that she's full of shit. She's probably nervous about the premiere and won't admit it. Fuck, *I'm* nervous and I've done this dozens of times. I'm not stupid, this is going to be a fucking nightmare, but selfishly, I still want her with me. I want the world to know that she's mine.

She was perfect this morning with my family, and they lover her, just like I knew they would. Shit, my mom is fucking ecstatic that I've finally met someone. Syd could probably have a second head and she'd be happy.

"I'm going to go check on my parents next door, I'll be right back okay?" I press a small kiss to her wrist, inhaling her sweet floral scent before standing up and leaving. She nods, looking tired. If I stay here with her, I'll end up trying to coax her into sex and she won't get any rest. The premiere is going to be exhausting enough, especially since she's pregnant.

I pass the elderly seamstress, busy at work and duck out of our suite and around the corner. "Drew, come on in," my dad says when he opens the door to their villa.

"Thanks Dad, I just needed a distraction while they get Sydney's dress ready." I step inside and head straight for the bar, grabbing a beer out of the fridge and twisting off the cap.

My dad chuckles, as I flop down on the sofa. "Women, they sure do take forever to get done up."

I hand him a beer and he joins me in front of the television.

"I heard that Andy!" my mom calls out from the back bedroom.

Dad just rolls his eyes and takes a long drink from his bottle. He mouths 'high maintenance' to me and laughs. I can't help but laugh with him. Shit, I needed this. All of the stress with Syd's interview and going public today, plus the pregnancy and the fact that she isn't feeling well… it's nice to just relax and hang out with my family.

Thirty minutes later, my sister breezes through the room in a gorgeous blue dress. "Daddy, Drew, I'm going next door to get my makeup and hair done. See you in a little while." Her heels click across the floor and the door shuts behind her.

"See, son? High maintenance."

We laugh and watch random sports highlights until it's almost time to go.

"I'd better get back and see if Syd is ready yet."

"Alright Drew. We'll see you inside the theater." My dad stands up with me and puts his hands on my shoulders. "I'm proud of you son. This film, I know it means a lot to you, and Sydney… well, let's just say I've never seen you happier so don't screw it up, okay?"

It takes me a minute to find my voice. Having heart to hearts, giving me advice, it's not exactly normal behavior for my dad. "Thanks, Dad. She does make me happy. She's everything."

He nods his approval and smiles. "You're going to shock the hell out of them today with her on your arm, son. Good luck."

"Yeah, see you there Dad."

Well, that was one hell of a strange Hallmark-fucking moment for the Forrester men.

Time to go let the vultures pick my carcass clean. At least this time, I'll have someone I love by my side.

If Rhys doesn't shut the fuck up soon, I'm going to throttle him. His freaking out over me bringing an actual date on the red carpet is sending Sydney over the edge. I can see it on her face.

She is losing her shit. Half of the time that I glance over at her, she looks like she might throw up. Whether it's nerves or the pregnancy, or maybe both, I'm not sure. All I know is that Rhys needs to stop worrying out loud about the paparazzi's potential reaction to Sydney.

Jane and Quentin shoot me sympathetic looks across the back of the limo. Even they can see that Sydney is silently freaking the fuck out. Clueless fucking Rhys, as usual.

Finally, he ends his irritating phone call. I'm about to ream his ass out when he starts flinging directives at me.

"So, we're the last to arrive. Drew, you get out first, and help Sydney from the limo." I give him a sharp look. *Dumbass!* Like I'd leave Sydney behind or some shit. "Then Quentin and I will walk behind you, to make sure you have space and no one gets too close. Jane will walk in front of you to help you get to each reporter that we promised an interview to."

Then he turns to Sydney, who is probably just about on the verge of passing out she's so pale. "Sydney, you can join Drew for some or all of the television interviews, it's your choice …" her eyes widen in horror as he speaks.

Now I've had enough.

"She's staying with me the entire time." I turn to Sydney to reassure her that I won't leave her alone. "I don't want you leaving my side. Not for one second. It's going to be an absolute shitstorm out there with us together. No way will you be where I can't see you."

Rhys starts yammering again, "Drew, it's up to Sydney …"

Motherfucking Rhys!

"Rhys, it's not up for fuckin' discussion! That's it."

Sydney takes my hand. Hers is already slick with sweat and we're still in the car. "I'll stay with Drew, it's fine. That's what I want anyway. I'm too nervous to not be with him."

Quentin leans in and pats her knee. *Don't fucking touch my girl, ass!* Are the two of them deliberately trying to piss me off today?

"You'll do fine, Sydney. I mean heck, you were literally born to do this!" he says, ignoring the angry glare that I shoot his way.

Before I can yell at either of these dumbasses, the limo glides to a stop in front of the theater. I hear Syd take a deep breath and see her wince out of the corner of my eye. Something isn't right.

"Are you okay?" I ask her.

She gives me the biggest fake smile I've ever seen. "Of course, your fans are waiting babe."

Shit! I knew something wasn't right. She isn't feeling well. I don't know anything about pregnancy, maybe this is normal. I have no fucking idea. I'm about to tell them to screw the premiere and drive off when someone opens the limo door. It's too late now, I just have to hope that she'll tell me if she gets sick.

With one last look at Sydney, I step out of the limo and the huge crowd goes insane. There's more press here than I thought there'd be. I guess little independent films get the full media treatment when my name is attached to it, along with the great reviews it's gotten so far. I wave and let my eyes adjust to the bright flashbulbs before turning to help Sydney out of the car.

She swings out and stands up, all long legs and gorgeous body and freezes like a deer in headlights next to me. The pop of the flashes hit her and she visibly flinches back from the onslaught. *Fuck!*

Pulling her close, I take her hand and squeeze it to reassure her that I'm here with her and won't let go. "I love you baby, let's do this."

I hear Sydney's name being murmured throughout the crowd of paparazzi and realize that our bubble of privacy has officially been busted. So many people are screaming for us to pose for them that all I can do is wrap my arm around her waist and put on my fake Andrew Forrester smile.

We're pulled in so many different directions at once, I know that Sydney must be overwhelmed. The paparazzi aren't making it any easier with their questions, which I specifically refuse to acknowledge.

"Andrew! Does this mean you're not single anymore?"

"Sydney, are you the redhead from Verve?"

"Did you dump Adam Reynolds for Andrew, Sydney?"

"When's the wedding?"

Christ, the fucking parasites never stop! Sydney cringes into my side as we approach a group of female fans who are shrieking so loudly, that I fear my ears may start bleeding at any moment. As much as I hate it, I have to let go of Sydney to sign autographs and pose with the fans along the red carpet. They're all contest winners or something like that.

I return to her side as quickly as I can and grasp her hand. Leaning down so she can hear me, I make sure she's not falling to pieces. "You doing okay, Syd?"

She doesn't answer, but smiles and nods in response. Knowing her, I'm sure she doesn't want anyone to overhear whatever she has to say.

Jane magically reappears at my side and guides us over to our first interview. Shit, it's with Vicky Lester. I can't stand speaking to her. She's a vapid idiot and her questions are about as deep as the layer of makeup on her face.

"Hi Andrew, Sydney. So nice to see you here." Vicky flicks her blonde hair with a too long fingernail and sticks her microphone up under our noses. I wrap my hand tighter around Sydney's and pull her closer, trying to alleviate some of her discomfort.

"Great to see you, Vicky." I give her my Andrew Forrester smile and wait for the bullshit parade to begin.

Vicky doesn't disappoint, immediately turning to Sydney and asking her questions about her dress, how we met, and that fucker

Adam Reynolds. With me standing right fucking here next to her! I don't realize that I'm squeezing Sydney's hand too tight until she looks up at me and wriggles her fingers.

Jane rescues us and directs us to continue up the carpet. Syd's a trooper as we stop to do several more interviews and pose for so many photos that we'll both probably see flashbulbs every time we close our eyes for a week.

I told Sydney right before we left that I was going to kiss her on the red carpet. She didn't ask for my reasons why, but I'm sure she knows. I want, no I *need* everyone to know that she's mine. No speculation, no rumors, no guessing. Mine. That douchbag Reynolds and the gossip about her being with him may have something to do with my intentions, but ultimately, I would have wanted to claim her publically with or without Reynolds in the picture.

At the end of the carpet, I turn and tug her soft body into mine, using a finger to lift her chin up. I don't need to be Andrew Forrester for her, just Drew, so I drop the mask. Tuning out everything else, I only see Sydney. Her gorgeous blue eyes glittering under the bright lights, her sweet mouth slightly parted, waiting for me to take it. I tilt down and press my lips to hers, gentle and soft. Until I can get a ring on her finger, I'll claim her this way, letting everyone know that Sydney Tannen belongs to me.

"Well, well big brother. Nice show."

I excuse us from our conversation with some of the film crew as Allie and my parents cross the crowded lobby to where I'm standing with Sydney.

"What do you mean?" I ask.

Allie jerks her thumb back to the televisions hanging on the walls around the lobby. "They have the news on, they're broadcasting the premiere live. Nice lip lock. You're such a possessive Neanderthal, Drew."

I bristle at her very accurate description of me.

Sydney's soft voice surprises me. "It's okay, Allie. We planned it ahead of time. It's easier than explaining our relationship to everyone."

I swivel my head down to look at Sydney, my mouth gaping at her words. Surely Sydney didn't want to kiss me in public. She's too private for that. I know she only agreed to make me happy, so for her to justify it to Allie is downright shocking.

The lobby lights blink before Allie can think of a smartass comeback.

"That's our cue. Mom, Dad, Allie… we'll see you after."

"Good luck son," my dad says as he claps me on the back.

"We'll meet you out here Drew," my mom says as I lean down to give her a kiss on her cheek.

"Yep, see you guys later," Allie chirps. "Sydney, get excited for your first Andrew Forrester movie! You'll end up joining the ranks of his screaming fangirls soon enough!" She spins on her heel and flounces away before I can manage a sharp retort.

Such a pain in my ass!

"Ready Syd?" I kiss her hand and lead her to our seats.

Sydney wanted to sit in the back of the theater, in case she had to use the bathroom during the movie. It's just as well, since I hate watching my own films. Being in the back means that people can't gauge my reaction. I plan on staring at Sydney the entire time anyway. I'm nervous that she'll freak out during the movie since it's her first time watching one since she was a kid.

Sydney seems to enjoy herself. In fact, she seems awestruck. Is that possible? For her to see me like that, up on the massive screen, and still love me despite her past? I was tormenting myself with the thought that she may see me for what I am, remind her of everything that was awful about her childhood, and lose her shit when it finally hit her. Now, her face lets me know that if anything, she loves me even more.

The credits roll and the crowd gets to their feet and cheers. Ron Gravitt, my director, makes his way to the front of the theater to speak. I turn to say something to Sydney and see that she's still sitting, sweat beading on her forehead. *What the fuck?*

I sit back down and lean in close. "Drew, I need to use the ladies' room. I'll meet you in the lobby."

She moves to stand up and I grab her wrist. Like hell she's going there by herself looking like this. "I'll come with you."

Stubborn as she always is, Syd tries to pull her hand from my grasp. "No, you have to speak next. Five minutes, I'll see you out front."

Shit. She's right, I can't leave now. Jesus, maybe she just needs to go to the bathroom, but something tells me she's going to be sick. I should be there with her, to hold her hair back or something.

Frowning, I release her arm and nod. She's leaving me no choice. I have to speak and she's clearly in no position to wait for me. Syd gives me a quick kiss on the cheek and hurries out of the theater.

"…And now I'd like to introduce the man who made this film possible. He believed in Joe's story, fought to get financing, and gave up most of his salary to make it happen, Andrew Forrester!"

Sighing, I get up and join Ron at the front of the room, taking the mike from him and shaking his hand. I see my parents and they're positively beaming. Allie too. I can tell they're proud of me, of this movie. They know how hard it was to get this film made.

"I'd like to thank everyone for coming today," I begin. "Especially Joe Thurgood, the man behind Roger Hillston. The true hero, who fought for this country and went through hell and back to be here today and tell his story." I nod to Joe, who's sitting in the third row with his wife.

The theater doors swing open and I glance up to see if Sydney is back from the bathroom. It's a security guard, with several theater employees surrounding him. They file down the aisle and the man in front whispers something to the studio's PR chief, Katherine Galloway. Her hand flies to her mouth and her eyes meet mine.

My stomach drops into my feet. *Sydney*. It has to be about Sydney. When I see Kate stand up and start to make her way towards me, panic floods through my body. I throw the mike to the ground, ignoring the screeching feedback, and dart up the aisle. Kate tries to grab me as I run past, but I shove her aside and keep going.

"Andrew!" I hear her panicked voice as I sprint toward the doors. I feel sick, as if I might throw up or pass out, but the adrenaline rush from the crippling fear keeps me upright and moving.

A guard tries to stop me, but he must see the crazy look in my eyes because he doesn't lay a hand on me and steps out of my way. It's a good thing, because there's no doubt in my mind that I'd lay him out flat.

I shove through the doors and into the lobby and I swear, my life ends at the sight in front of me. Sydney, lying on the floor in a massive pool of blood, her head being cradled by a hysterical girl in a theater uniform as bare-chested male employee presses his blood soaked shirt to her side.

"Drew!" I vaguely register Allie calling out behind me as I reach the spot where my future is slipping away… my life, my love, spilling out onto the hideous patterned carpet of a theater in West Hollywood.

I collapse to my knees and take her from the crying girl, pulling Sydney's head onto my lap. It rolls to the side, lifeless, her lips white and her eyes half rolled into her head.

"Do something!" I shout. Turning to the girl next to me, I start yelling. "What happened? Who did this to her? What the fuck is going on?"

The girl just keeps sobbing, unable to control her emotions. The shirtless man at Sydney's side answers for me as he presses the now completely red shirt to her side. "I saw a man, an old man. She came out of the bathroom and he spoke to her. The next thing I knew, she was on the ground with him. I… I didn't really understand what was going on. Until," he swallows, "Until I saw the blood."

Holy fuck. Someone attacked her?

The man continues, "Then I saw Greg, our head usher, grab the man and throw him to the ground… and I knew what had happened."

"Where?" I croak out, and somehow, the guy knows what I'm asking.

Since his hands are still holding his shirt up to Sydney's wound, he uses his chin to point across the lobby. That's when the pieces come together. I see a huge guy wearing a theater blazer kneeling on a thin, disheveled old man, holding his hands behind his back. Rage begins to overtake the terror that I feel. I start to get up, my anger laser focused on the man who is trying to destroy everything I love.

"Drew, no." Allie's hand pushes my shoulder down. Her voice hitches in a sob and I only now realize that she's been kneeling next to me this entire time. "Stay with Sydney, she needs you."

I tear my eyes from the old man and look over at my sister. Tears are streaming freely down her face. My parents are behind her, my mom crying and clutching onto my dad. *This can't be happening.* I nod at Allie and turn back to Sydney. I can't fucking lose her. I won't leave her side again.

"Allie, I can't..." Words fail me. There's nothing I can say, nothing I can do to fix this. It's my fucking fault. I knew she was sick, I should have gone with her. I should have let her stay home, safe in bed, away from me and all my shit.

A flurry of activity fills the lobby as the police and paramedics arrive. The medics rush over to Sydney and take over for the guy with the bloody shirt, asking him to repeat what he saw.

I tune most of it out until the end. "...then they found a knife next to her."

My head snaps up at this information, a new wave of fury and despair washing over me. "Knife? He fucking stabbed her?" I don't know why I'm surprised, the blood had to come from somewhere, but hearing it makes it real.

"Sir, we need you to move aside so we can treat her," the medic says to me.

"Fuck that, I'm not moving," I growl.

"Sir..." he continues.

"Drew, please." Helpless, I see my mom crouching down next to me. She takes my hand and tugs on it, urging me to my feet. "Let them help her honey."

"Mom?"

I'm broken. I feel like a kid again, looking to my mother to make the pain go away.

"I know sweetie. You can ride with her, just let them do this."

Reluctantly, I carefully lay Sydney's head on the ground and gasp when it lists to the side. I stand up and pull my mom into my arms, or maybe she pulls me into her arms, and silently lose my shit.

The ride to the hospital is terrifying, worse than anything I could have imagined. The two paramedics circle around Sydney continuously, hooking up IV's, oxygen, electronic monitors, and speak to the hospital through a headset that they each wear.

Every time the ambulance turns or hits a bump, Syd's head flops to the side, reminding me that the life is literally draining out of her. I want to be pissed when they cut the designer gown and undergarments off and expose her naked body, but I'm not. I don't give a fuck what they see or do as long as they save her.

In my panic-induced stupor, I'm only able to catch a few words here and there, but it's enough.

"Stab wound, right upper quadrant…"

"Massive blood loss…"

"Hypovolemic shock…"

"Low O2 sats…"

"Possible miscarriage…"

Miscarriage? Our baby? I can't take anymore, I'm losing it… here, in the back of a fucking ambulance as the girl I love slips from my grasp. I put my head in my hands and sob.

The hospital is a nightmare. They rushed Sydney away immediately and won't let me see her, no matter how much I yell and threaten the staff. I'm stuck pacing in the staff break room while my parents and Allie watch me freak the fuck out. They threw us back here after the fucking media vultures showed up at the emergency room. The bastards even had the nerve to try and come inside. When I tried to physically attack someone in the waiting room who was filming me with a cellphone, the charge nurse offered the break room to get us, specifically me, out of their hair.

"Drew, your phone."

I look up from my pacing to see my mom holding my phone out to me, waiting for me to take it.

"I can't, Mom." Speaking about this, to anyone, will fucking break me.

"Drew, it's someone named Leah. She said she won't take no for an answer. Son, she's very upset."

Leah. I'm so fucking selfish, I didn't think about calling anyone else.

I take the phone and hold it up to my ear. "Leah?"

"Drew! What's going on? I'm at the airport with Sydney's mom. Jane called us and told us Sydney's been attacked! I saw the news. What the fuck is happening?"

Shit! Her mom! Thank God for Jane. It didn't even occur to me to call Eva. Her own fucking daughter attacked and she finds out from my assistant.

"Leah," my voice cracks and I have to swallow down the lump that forms when my throat constricts. "I don't know anything. They took her back, they won't let me see her." I pause to take in a shaky breath. "I have no idea what's going on. I heard something about surgery, maybe."

"We're on our way," she says firmly. "Jane added us to your villa. We're going to stay with you at the Marquis. You call us the second they tell you something, promise me." Leah is trying to be strong, but I can hear it in her voice. Her armor is cracking just like mine.

"I will, I promise." I end the call and turn the phone to silent. I can't take any more calls. Rhys, Quentin, and Jane are somewhere here in the hospital. Probably outside dealing with the media.

The door to the break room opens and I stop dead in my tracks. I didn't think anything could shock me at this point, but watching a wide-eyed nurse usher in a visibly shaken Reid Tannen, his eyes red and face drawn, shocks the hell out of me.

Me, my sister, my parents, we all gape at the newest addition to the room. No one thinks to speak to him.

Reid gathers himself together first. "I hate to meet you under these circumstances, but you must be Andrew." He strides over to me and holds out a trembling hand.

"No, I mean yes. Call me Drew, please." I shake his hand and he shocks me again, pulling me into a hug as he slaps my back.

"I'm Reid. God, I'm glad she has you here with her," he says gratefully as he releases me. "What's going on? They wouldn't tell me anything."

Well damn. If they won't tell her father anything, they certainly won't tell me jack shit. It doesn't matter, because I can't seem to do anything but stand there, like an idiot, my mouth hanging open as I'm stunned into silence by his presence.

"We don't know anything," my dad says, saving the moment from becoming even more awkward. "Andy Forrester, nice to meet you. This is my wife, Caroline, and my daughter, Allie."

God, I'm such a useless fuck up. I didn't even introduce my family. I'm still frozen in place like an incompetent asshole.

"I wish I could say it's nice to meet you," Reid says, "but this…" he inhales deeply, struggling to control his emotions. "…this is not the best of situations."

The door to the break room opens again and a middle-aged man in scrubs steps in, closing the door behind him. His eyes widen for a moment as he takes in Sydney's father, me, and the three other people in the room, and he composes himself to speak.

"I'm Doctor Sampson, I wanted to give you an update on Miss Tannen's condition."

My sister takes my hand in hers and squeezes it and I almost start crying. *I'm* supposed to be the strong one. Instead, I'm falling to pieces and letting my little sister comfort me.

"Doctor, can I speak to you for a moment? Privately?" I draw odd looks from my family and from Sydney's dad. I face them to explain, "Just one second, I promise."

They all nod and I step out into the quiet hallway with the doctor.

"Doctor Sampson, my family, they don't know about the… the pregnancy. Can you keep that part out of it for now? Tell me later in private?"

The doctor's curious expression smooths out as he comprehends what I'm asking.

"Of course. That's not a problem. Now, let's not keep them waiting."

We go back into the tiny room and I wait to hear what he has to say.

"So, as I was saying, Miss Tannen suffered a stab wound to her right side. The blade hit her liver and a fairly large vessel in it, which is what caused the massive hemorrhaging. She's currently in surgery to repair that vein. The knife missed her diaphragm and any other major organ. She was given several units of blood and should be out of surgery in a few hours."

"So, she'll be okay?" I ask.

The doctor looks at me strangely. "Yes, she should be fine once the surgeon repairs the blood vessel."

Reid questions the doctor. "Where is she? Can we wait there?"

"Of course, I'll find someone to take you up to the waiting room." The doctor gives us a weak smile and leaves the room.

CHAPTER 31

After Sydney came out of surgery and the doctors assured us that she'll make a full recovery, I was able to convince my family to go back to Boston. Leah and Eva just arrived at the hospital, and I don't want Sydney to have to face my family when she wakes up. She only just met them and as much as they love her already, it's going to be too much for her to handle.

Sydney's parents are quietly speaking on one end of the small, private waiting room, heads together, hands held in silent prayer for their daughter. Reid Tannen is obviously a much smarter man than I am. He brought his own security with him and stationed one at the door to the post-op recovery room, one at every door that leads to the floor, and one at the entrance to our waiting room. If only I had thought to bring a bodyguard with us to the theater.

Fuck, I almost break down again thinking about it.

Too fidgety to sit any longer, I walk over to where Sydney's best friend is sitting, flicking through her cell phone to keep her mind from wandering.

"Leah." Her head jerks up in surprise. I see her lip start to tremble and her eyes fill with tears. "Hey, I'm going to find out if they'll let me see her. Will you come with me?" I hold out my hand. She takes it and we slip out of the room.

"What's going on?" she asks.

I shrug. "I wanted to give them some privacy. Plus, I need to see her with my own eyes… I need to…" I can't finish.

Leah grips my hand tightly in both of hers. "I know Drew. Let's go find her."

We stop at the nurses station and they page the surgeon for us. He must have been nearby because he shows up in less than ten minutes.

"Can we see her now? We've been waiting… We just… She's been out of surgery for a while and I…" I let my sentence drift off, unable to form a cohesive thought.

A smile ghosts across his face. "Come on. I'll take you back. But you can only stay for a minute. They'll be moving her to our private floor soon and you'll get more time with her there."

We follow the doctor as he swipes his badge and opens a large white door that says STAFF ONLY. The room is quiet, only true emergencies require surgery in the middle of the night. He stops at the foot of one of only two occupied beds. "She's not awake right now, but you can visit for a minute. I'll have the nurse stop by to talk to you about which room she'll go to from here." The doctor leaves, allowing us a moment alone with Sydney.

She looks so small in the hospital bed, surrounded by tubes and machines. Leah bursts into tears and quickly moves to Sydney's side and grabs her hand. Me? I'm torn. Half of me wants to run to her and pull her into my arms, the other half wants to run the fuck out of here and beat the life out of the guy who did this.

My legs move on their own, choosing to carry me to her side. There are no chairs here, and it's just as well because I fall to my knees and drop my forehead onto the bed. I grab her free hand and hold on tight.

"Hi, I'm Kelly."

The kind voice gets my attention. I slowly lift my head from Sydney's bedside and focus my blurry eyes. The nurse's smile falters when I meet her friendly gaze. I'm sure I look like shit, probably not what she was expecting to see.

"Like I said, I'm Kelly… and I'm Miss Tannen's post-op nurse. Dr. Rutherford said you wanted to know what happens from here?"

Exhausted, I struggle to my feet as Leah stumbles around the bed to join me.

"Yes, anything you could tell us," I answer.

"Alright. We'll be going to the 8th floor, that's the locked VIP unit with exclusively private suites, as soon as we get transport down here."

"Doesn't she have to wake up first?" asks Leah.

"She has woken up," Kelly says.

"What? Why weren't we told!" I yell. Now I'm pissed off all over again. These fluctuating emotions are draining my mind of functionality.

Kelly makes a great effort to keep her face neutral and pleasant. "She wakes up, but she won't remember any of it. It's more like halfway between asleep and awake. It's just enough to speak or mumble and move a little, but not really be aware of what you're doing," the nurse explains.

"Oh," Leah says despondently. "When will she wake up for good?"

I nod at Leah and focus back on the nurse. This is what I want to know.

"Sometime in the next few hours. The pain medication is keeping her pretty sedated right now. You can go get something to eat or clean up if you like, and meet her up on the 8th floor."

I immediately blow off her suggestion. "I'm not fucking going anywhere."

"Drew!" Leah shoots me an annoyed look. I don't give a damn if I'm being an asshole. These people aren't going to keep me from Sydney.

"Leah, you can go to the Marquis if you want. I'm not leaving."

Nurse Kelly's face reddens, whether from discomfort at witnessing my douchbaggery, or embarrassment because I insulted her, I don't know and I don't care.

"I need to check her now, so you can go back to the waiting room," she says, eyeing me suspiciously.

"Fine." I go back to Sydney's side and lean over the bed. Cupping her face, I bend over and whisper in her ear. "I'll be right here, love. I'm so sorry." I press a kiss to her forehead and storm out of the unit.

"Drew! Wait up."

"Leah, I'm not really in the mood for you to chastise me for being an ass. I don't give a shit what they think of me," I snap as she catches up to me just outside the waiting room.

"Hey, that's not what I was going to say." Leah seems lost, her usual confidence gone.

I slump forward, my shoulders dropping from fatigue. "What is it then?"

"I was going to tell you that I'm going back to the hotel. Call me when Sydney wakes up. It's seven in the morning in New York, I'm exhausted and as much as I want to stay, I think I should go sleep while Sydney is still out. I'll want to be here later when she's awake."

"Alright. Do you want to see if Eva wants to go with you?"

"We can, but she's her mother. I doubt she'll leave."

"Thanks for going in there with me."

Leah smiles sadly. "Yeah, thanks for asking me to go. I doubt they'd let me back there by myself. You get to break all the rules," she jokes.

I look down at Leah, her face drawn and fatigued, her hair frizzing all over the place. "I get whatever I want all the time, Leah, except her. Fat fucking good fame does if it puts everyone you love in danger, right?"

Leah's eyes widen. "You blame yourself?"

I scoff at her. "Of course I blame myself. She was at that fucking premiere because I was selfish, because I wanted her there!"

The desire to hit something streaks through me again but I'm too tired to even curl my hands into fists. Too weak. Too broken.

"I can unequivocally tell you that this is not your fault," Leah insists, meeting my harsh gaze with a stern look. "Let's go see what Eva has to say." Leah turns and goes into the waiting room.

Not surprisingly, Eva declines going back to the hotel with Leah. Opting instead to head down to the cafeteria. Reid, clearly being more experienced than me with this sort of thing, insists that one of his security accompany her.

So here I am, sitting in a hospital waiting room with Reid Tannen, feeling awkward as shit.

"You know," he says as he takes a seat across from me, "this is like reliving the crap from her childhood all over again." My eyes flick down to his hands, which are tapping anxiously on his legs.

"In what way, exactly?" I can guess what he means, but I want to know more about Sydney and her dad is probably a pretty good source of information.

He absently checks his watch, a nervous habit I'd guess, and I notice his hand is shaking. God, he's just like her. Or she's just like him. Fuck, I'm confused.

Reid barks out a laugh, and not a humorous one. "This bullshit! I couldn't keep her safe back then. Nothing has changed! Not one fucking thing. All those years apart wasted, for what?" He jerks up out of his chair and paces the room, his hands clenched into fists at his sides.

Shit, now he reminds me of— me.

"I'm sorry my shit found her," I croak. "I let her down, let you down… I, I don't know what to say."

Jesus, I can't fucking break down in front of Sydney's father. He's supposed to be able to trust me with her safety, which, clearly, he can't because we're here.

Reid steps over to me and puts his hand on my shoulder. "Drew, this isn't your fault."

I fly out of my seat to stand facing him. "Of course it's my fucking fault! She was with me! I insisted on it!" I shouldn't be yelling at Sydney's dad, but I can't control myself. I'm exhausted, emotional, and fucking over this crap.

"Both of you need to stop."

We both swivel our heads in Eva's direction at the same time. Neither of us noticed her slip back into the room.

"Sorry, I didn't mean to startle you. The food looked… well, let's just say I'm not that hungry."

"I didn't mean for you to hear me like that." I sag back down in my seat.

"I know, but I did hear. And you both need to accept that you're not responsible for the actions of a crazy person. It's neither of your faults," Eva says stubbornly. Now I can see where Syd gets her hard head.

"But it is, Eva," Reid begins.

She cuts him off sharply, "No. Just stop. Bad stuff happens to random people all the time. It does. Has a lot more happened to

Sydney than most people? Yes, but that doesn't make it anyone's fault. It just is what it is!"

She breaks down and collapses into a chair, sobbing. Reid hurries to her side and holds her, trying to calm her down.

"I'll be right back," I tell them as I leave the tiny waiting room. I turn the corner and almost knock down nurse Kelly.

"Oh! I was just coming to get you. Sydney is in room 806. You can go up when you're ready."

"Is she awake?" I ask, hopeful to be able to talk to Sydney.

The nurse's expression falls, "No. I'm sorry, not yet."

"Thanks," I tell her as I hustle to the elevator and smack the button to go up. I'll tell her parents after I get a chance to see her and speak to a doctor privately first.

When I get to the 8th floor I'm stopped by hospital security. "This floor requires special access, sir."

Mother of all that is holy! It's like Syd's concierge all over again.

"Listen, you are not going to keep me from going in there." I point at the sealed double doors behind him. "I don't give a shit what I have to do, but…"

"Mr. Forrester?" I spin toward the voice coming from behind the nearby desk.

"What?" I growl.

"I have your pass right here. Kelly called up to get you access. This will open the door to the floor, the family break room, and your family member's private room only." A tiny woman in pink scrubs holds up a blue keycard.

I take it from her gratefully. "Thanks." Flashing it at the guard I shove past him and use it to open the sealed doors. My first instinct is to go directly to Sydney's room and wait for her to wake up. Instead, I force myself to walk over to the nurses' station where several employees, also in pink scrubs, are busy working.

"Excuse me," I say to the closest one.

"Yes... oh!" Her mouth drops open at the sight of me. "Yes, Mr. Forrester? What can I do for you?"

"Can you page the obstetrician that saw Sydney Tannen, room 806 please?" I have to know what happened with the baby. The paramedics mentioned possible miscarriage and all I know so far is that Sydney was stabbed. I'm praying that they were mistaken about the source of the blood.

"Of course. She'll meet you in the room." The nurse picks up a phone as I head towards Sydney's suite.

I scan my card and enter the room. It's dark and quiet except for the soft beeping of Sydney's heart monitor. I turn the corner and see her on the bed, asleep, in a plush suite that looks more like it belongs in the Plaza Hotel instead of a hospital.

There's a small couch right next to the bed. I fall onto it in a disheveled heap. Too tired to call, I pull out my phone and text Jane instead.

Me <Rm 806>

A few minutes later, I meet Jane at the guarded entrance to the unit and she hands me a bag of my stuff, clothes, toothbrush, all of that shit. I'm still in my formal wear, stained with Sydney's dried blood on the cuffs of my shirt and the knees of my pants. No wonder everyone is giving me weird looks, I'm a fucking mess. I quickly shower and change my clothes, sitting back on the couch to wait after stuffing the ruined suit into a hazardous waste container.

The door opens and I sit up to see a doctor in a lab coat and scrubs come into the suite, toting an iPad under her arm.

"Hi," she says softly, "I'm Doctor Bauer, the gynecologic surgeon who treated Miss Tannen."

I stand up to speak but she stops me, holding up a hand. "I know who you are Mr. Forrester. Why don't we sit." She gestures towards the couch.

"No, I'm more comfortable standing, thank you." I'm shaking all over, ready to go to sleep and wake up to find that the entire past 24 hours is only a terrible dream. "I guess since you saw her you know that she's pregnant."

As I say it, I know. I can see it in the doctor's eyes, the way her mouth pulls down in the corners.

"Mr. Forrester, I'm sorry. Miss Tannen was in the process of losing the pregnancy when she was brought in. I was called into the operating room to perform a D&C after they repaired her stab wound."

"So there's...?"

She shakes her head, "The baby is gone."

I stumble back and fall heavily onto the couch again, putting my head in my hands. How am I going to tell Sydney?

"Let me assure you, that this had nothing to do with the trauma she suffered today."

I lift my head. "What do you mean?"

"What I mean is that the pregnancy was already in the process of ending before the attack. Most likely, there was a defect with the fetus, we won't ever know, but the placenta was detaching and an indirect stab wound wouldn't cause that."

"You're sure?"

"Quite sure. The baby would be gone either way. Again, I'm sorry." She pats my hand and leaves the room.

I send a quick text to Eva, letting her know the room number then curl up in a ball on the couch and lose it until I pass out to blissful nothingness.

CHAPTER 32

I wake to the sound of moaning. Confused, I sit up. It's still dark out. I hear the beeping of the hospital monitors and the nightmare comes flooding back.

More moaning, this time, accompanied by an increase in the beeps on the monitor. I jump to my feet and see Sydney thrashing all over the bed, the glow from the machines lighting her face a ghastly green color.

"Shhhh, Sydney, you have to stop moving honey." I gently hold her shoulders down. She needs to stay still. I push the nurse call button.

The sounds coming from her get louder until she's panting. "My side hurts. Can't breathe."

Her face is coated in sweat. I push back her hair and kiss her forehead. "I know it does sweetie, relax. I'm getting the nurse."

The door opens and a pink scrub-wearing woman heads directly for the array of machines on the far side of the bed. She begins pushing buttons and reading numbers.

"You're awake. I'll check you real quick and let the doctor know." The nurse lifts the bandage over her stab wound and Sydney makes a noise so pitiful that I freak the fuck out.

"She's in pain, give her something!" I can't contain my anger.

"It's right here, Mr. Forrester," she plucks a needle out of her pocket and injects it into Sydney's IV line. "There, you should feel better already. I'll just go get the doctor sweetie."

My nerves frayed, I angrily watch the nurse leave the room. By the time I turn back to Sydney, she's out again. I drop onto the couch and am asleep before my head hits the armrest.

"What the…?"

I jerk awake to the sound of hysterical sobbing.

Sydney.

Jumping up from the couch, I see her helplessly clawing at the blankets as she wails. Her IV's have been pulled out, and her heart monitor is beeping rapidly.

"Syd, what are you doing? You're scaring me."

I'm afraid to touch her, afraid to hurt her. Her cries are becoming more desperate. *Fuck! What the fuck do I do?* I put my hands on my head and fist my hair in frustration.

She sobs again and I see tears flowing down her hollow cheeks.

"Stop it, Sydney! You're hurting yourself."

I can't watch this. It's as if that bastard's knife is slicing into me and carving my heart out, leaving behind a shell of a man. I gently grasp her wrists and pull her to my chest.

"The baby?" she whimpers.

Whatever is left of my empty heart shatters into a million pieces. I wrap my arms around her frail body and cry with her, mourning the loss of our future.

"Why am I sitting here again?" I ask Leah. She dragged me out of Sydney's room down to the cafeteria to eat something. The food isn't bad, especially considering it's hospital food.

"Because you're losing it, Drew."

I glare at Leah from across the table.

"What? You are. You haven't slept more than a few hours in almost two days. You need to go back to the hotel and rest." She pushes her plate away and sighs.

"Not hungry?"

I purposely ignore her comment about leaving Sydney's side. She's lucky she got me down here, using the excuse that Sydney and her mom needed to be left alone for a while. Reid left while she was still unconscious, after making sure Sydney would be okay. He almost lost it when he gave her a kiss on her cheek before taking off.

It sucks that Syd was sleeping and didn't get to see her dad, but he said he didn't want to add any more stress to her overflowing plate and I see his point. This isn't the time or place for an emotional family reunion.

"No, not really. I'm going to go back to the hotel for a while. You'll let me know if anything happens, right?" Leah asks.

"Yeah, I will." I see movement out of the corner of my eye behind her chair. Leah must see my eyes harden because she turns to follow my stare and gasps.

"Drew, don't do it," she whispers.

Too late. I'm out of my seat and charging at the guy with the camera before I can think.

I see the guy's eyes widen in surprise right before my hand makes contact with his chest. Shoving hard, the asshole goes flying backwards as I snatch the phone out of his hand.

"Drew!" I tune out Leah and stand over the guy, my foot on his neck, pinning him down on the institutional tile floor.

Rage flows like acid through my veins, scalding every inch of my body. It takes everything in me not to push down and snap his fucking neck.

When his face turns purple, I move my foot and bend over to hold him down with my hands. "What gives you the right to be here? To exploit my fucking pain? Sydney's pain? It's your fucking fault that she's here!"

He stutters, unable to speak as he scrabbles to loosen my hands which are wrapped around his scrawny neck.

"Drew!" Leah tugs on my arms, trying to break the hold I have on this pathetic motherfucker. She leans in and calmly whispers in my ear. "People are watching, security is on its way to escort him out. Let. Go."

Loosening my grip, I lick my lips and glance around the cafeteria. A hundred sets of eyes are fixed on us.

"We'll take it from here." I spin my head around and face two huge hospital security guards. They have their hands up in a non-threatening manner meant to calm me down.

I. *Am. Fucking. Losing. It.*

Swallowing hard, I release the terrified man and stand up. One of the guards jerks him to his feet and leads him out of the cafeteria.

"Drew, give me his phone," Leah whispers as the other guard approaches. I palm it to her before he can see what we're doing.

"Let's go somewhere more private," I say to the guard.

"Alright, after you," he says, extending an arm toward the door but keeping a safe distance between us.

Leah goes first and I follow her. Once in the hall the guard brings us to a nearby office and shuts the door.

"Look," he says, his face full of pity, "I know you've been through a lot. I understand completely why you did what you just did. Just... don't attack anyone else, okay? The hospital can't be a part of a lawsuit."

I bristle at his words and the hairs at the back of my neck stand up. I don't want his fucking pity and I could give a shit less about a lawsuit. All that matters to me is Sydney.

"Well, keep those fuckers away from me and my family and we won't have a problem," I snarl.

Leah speaks before the guard can respond. "Sir, we understand your point, but you have to see this from our side. We don't want to be filmed. I'm certain your hospital doesn't want to be caught on tape breaking patient confidentiality. I know that your administrators rely on very big donations from Hollywood's elite to run this place, and I'm sure that would change in a heartbeat if they knew that paparazzi could get pictures of them or their family members inside the hospital."

I watch as the guard's face blanches from Leah's little speech. Damn. She's good.

"Here's his phone. I hope you don't mind, but I've erased the videos he took. He had quite a few on there. You may want to let the administrators know what's going on around here, because if we see any videos like this on the internet or TV? Well, let's just say it won't be good for the hospital or its social standing in the community." She drops the phone onto his desk, grabs my hand, and storms out of the office.

I don't speak until we get to a quiet spot in a deserted hallway by a pathology lab. I stop walking, her grip on my hand pulling her to a stop.

"Leah," I begin.

"Yeah?" she looks up at me, anger still evident on her small face.

I can't help but smile. "Thanks." This isn't the first time this tiny blonde powerhouse has helped me out.

"You're welcome. No more outbursts like that. Deal?" She crosses her arms and glares at me.

"I don't know if I can agree to that," I admit.

She smirks, "I didn't think you would. I'm headed to the hotel. I'll be back later and then you're going to go punch shit or workout or whatever it is you do to de-stress, because this has got to stop." She spins on her heel and stalks away.

Fuck, that hundred-pound girl is ten times stronger than me right now.

CHAPTER 33

I run my hand through my hair in frustration as I listen to the head of the theater chain that held the premiere for *A Soldier's Burden* explain the lack of security at the event.

"I don't give a fuck what you're going to do! It's what you didn't do that pisses me off! If that sick bastard could get inside and attack Sydney, what else could have happened? You know psychos try to get close to actors all the time, especially at these types of events! There's no fucking excuse for it!"

I end the call before he can respond and resist the urge to throw the phone at the wall, instead clutching it so hard that my fingers hurt. I welcome the pain. It distracts me from my reality, the broken girl in the next room, the hollow place in my chest, the anger vibrating through my body.

Leah's right, I need to fight. Strike out. Feel physical pain. Feel something besides this nauseating ache that's pressing down on me.

When she gets back I'll go to the gym that I used when I filmed *Mind of the Enemy* last month. It's only a few minutes from here and I'm sure I can find someone to spar with.

"Syd?" I open the door from the suite's attached bedroom and step into her fancy hospital room. She's spacing out again, staring out the window with unfocused eyes. "Syd," I step closer to the bed.

She slowly turns to face me, her eyes are glassy and her lips are pale and cracked. "Yes?"

God, I wish I could take her pain from her. I'd suffer ten times over just to make her smile again.

"I was going to take a quick shower. Unless you need something."

She shakes her head. "No, go ahead," then turns back to the window and resumes staring at nothing.

Frowning, I go back into the bedroom and turn on the shower in the attached bath. Cranking it up as hot as it will go, I quickly strip and get under the spray, letting the water scald my skin. I revel in the harsh sting of the water, allowing myself to feel each blistering drop as it hits my weary body.

I have no idea how long I stand there before I quickly clean up and dry off. Wrapping a towel around my waist, I walk over to the mirror and wipe off the condensation with my hand. Shocked, I take a good look at my reflection, hardly recognizing the man I see there. He's gaunt, wild-eyed, angry.

I grab my bag and fumble through it, pulling out my razor and a can of shaving cream. Carelessly, I smear it on my face and start scraping at my skin with the blade. If I can look normal, I can feel normal, right? I shave faster, dragging the razor over again and again until I'm done. I splash some water on my face and dry off.

I stare in the mirror again, this time, I see myself reflected back. Only, it doesn't feel like me. The man I see is still broken, fucked up by a situation that I couldn't prevent, couldn't stop. I couldn't protect what's mine and now it's gone.

Two days of frustration and blame have taken their toll, I rear back my fist and slam it into the mirror, watching it splinter from the force. I hit it again and smile at the sharp burn in my hand as shards crumble and land in the sink.

"Drew?"

Sydney's soft voice snaps me out of my trance. Shit! I can't let her worry about me.

"Sorry babe, I dropped something. Don't worry," I call out.

Fuck! I toss the pieces of glass into the trashcan and rinse off my bloody hand, letting the red water swirl down the drain. Once it's clean, I'm surprised to see there's only a few cuts on my knuckles. They're already in the process of clotting up.

I get dressed and go back into Sydney's room, the monster inside me under control for now.

"What happened?" she asks.

I notice an untouched tray of food in front of her.

"Nothing happened. Do you want me to order you something else to eat? I can have something delivered." I point to her tray.

She grimaces, her eyes flicking to my hand and back up to my face. "No, I'm not hungry."

Sighing, I move her tray aside and kick off my shoes. "Can I lay with you?"

A small twitch, an almost smile, touches the corners of her mouth and just as quickly is gone. "Sure."

I pull the covers back and Sydney rolls onto her good side, giving me room to lay beside her. I climb onto the bed and tuck her up against my body, careful not to touch her injury.

I bury my face in her hair and inhale, her scent bringing back so many memories. "I'm sorry Sydney," I rasp, overcome with emotion.

"Me too," she whispers back. Where do we go from here?

A sharp rap on the door is followed immediately by a deep voice. "Miss Tannen? Is it okay if I come in and ask you about the assault?"

Fuck no! I jump up from the couch and block the man entering the suite. She's not even physically healed and they want to do this shit?

"Do we have to do this now?" I snap at the detective as he flinches back, holding up his hands to keep me calm.

"Drew, let the man in," I hear Sydney sigh from behind me.

I don't bother turning around to face her, this isn't happening right now. Instead, I keep the detective from being able to get around me and to Syd. I couldn't protect her the other night, I'll be damned if I don't protect her now.

"Sydney…" I warn.

"Please? I just want to get past this," she says weakly. I turn my head just enough to see that her eyes are glassy and her lips are trembling. "Please?"

She's going to break me, I know it. I have to give her what she wants, even though it goes against every instinct I have.

"Fine." I turn back to the detective, my jaw clenched. "Come in then," I bark in his face.

He gracefully moves around me and into the large hospital suite. "I'll leave my partner outside if that will make you more comfortable. I'm Detective Henry Keating, my partner Detective Paul Black is out in the hall." He nods towards the door. "We've been assigned to your case." Detective Keating grabs a chair and pulls it over to Sydney's bedside, sitting down so he's at her eye level.

A hissing sound comes from Sydney and I watch as she struggles to sit up straight, grimacing from the pain.

"Jesus, Sydney. Just stay still. You don't have to move around to talk." I help her get settled, so frustrated by this entire situation that I want to scream.

"Thanks," she says without further comment, then returns her attention to Detective Keating.

He removes a leather bound book from his pocket and flips it open, relaxing back into the stiff chair, one ankle crossed over his knee casually. "So, the man who attacked you is Peter Stubbins. He's the same man who broke into your bedroom twelve years ago and was arrested, then tried to break in again the following week."

"*What?*" I yell, grabbing the bedrail to keep my hands occupied and my body grounded so I don't fly off the handle. "The same man from twelve years ago?"

The detective's attention flicks to me briefly and he continues speaking calmly, as if he didn't just mind fuck me here.

"Yes, the same man." He returns his focus to Sydney. "Like I said, his name is Peter Stubbins. He's evidently been obsessed with you for a very long time Miss Tannen. He has a wall in his apartment full of cutouts and photos of you from magazines, some new and some very old. It appears that he personally took a lot of photos of you as a child."

Sydney's eyes fill up with tears and her lower lip trembles. She's about to cry again, motherfucker! Like she hasn't been through the emotional wringer enough already. This is why I didn't want to do this yet.

I interrupt before Keating can continue, "He was able to get close enough to her to take photographs of her, broke into her bedroom and assaulted her and was still out on the streets? He nearly killed her!" I roar at the detective who doesn't show one iota of emotion on his stupid, blank face.

"Mr. Forrester, you need to stay calm. Yelling won't help, and it seems as though you're frightening Miss Tannen."

What the…? Frightened is better than her shedding any more tears over this shit. This was a complete and total failure by law enforcement to keep a violent stalker off the streets and it almost cost me Sydney's life.

"Calm? You want me to be calm? I'm feeling the exact fuckin' opposite of calm right now! In fact, why don't we go outside …"

"Drew," Sydney's hoarse word stops me cold. Her small hand grabs mine and clenches it tight. "You have to let the man talk," she whispers. I drop my gaze from the detective to meet her tired, glistening eyes. "Please, baby. I know this is hard. It wasn't your fault."

The fight rushes out of me as if I'd been sucker punched in the gut. I can't refuse her request, not when she's sitting injured in a hospital bed begging me to get this part over with. She wants to do this interview now, so I have to give it to her, but I don't have to like it.

"Alright, Sydney." I sit on the couch next to her bed and scowl at the detective. "Don't upset her," I growl.

Keating continues reading from his notebook, as if he were threatened by angry movie stars every day. "There were no photos of you from after you left Los Angeles. He lost track of you when you disappeared. The only recent pictures he has are from magazines printed in the last week since the interview on *Late Night Report* aired."

The detective looks back down at his notes, "Stubbins lives near the theater where the attack occurred. It's our belief that he saw the live reports either on the news or internet that you were there, and immediately drove over to find you. There are no cameras in the theater, we're still interviewing witnesses to piece together the rest."

He flips the notebook shut and tucks it back in his jacket pocket. Keating leans forward, elbows on his knees, and clasps his hands together. "So, Miss Tannen, what happened in the theater? In your words."

The room is silent while Sydney gathers her thoughts. The urge to jump up and shield her is so strong that I have to physically fight myself to stay still. Detective Keating waits patiently, watching Sydney carefully, but managing to look kind and open while studying her.

"I ... I went to the bathroom. I wasn't feeling good." Her worn out voice strains to make the words loud enough to hear. "W- when I came out ... he was in front of me. He ... he told me he loves me."

Tears begin to run freely down her face as she describes the horror she went through. This is my first time hearing it. I didn't want to upset her by asking her to relive it for me. My body goes rigid. *That sick piece of shit told her he loved her?*

"He said what?" I whisper. I want to kill him. I've never wanted anything more in my life. Angry isn't the word for how I feel. Murderous. That's more accurate.

The detective must see me losing it. He subtly hints that I need to focus on Sydney, on letting the police catch this guy. "Mr. Forrester, please. Let her speak."

I clench my hands at the powerlessness I feel. The lack of control over anything, including my own emotions. I stand and turn away from the bed to pace the room, my hands on top of my head so I won't strike out with my fists as Sydney keeps talking.

"He grabbed me and slid the knife in. It was cold. He … he held me to him as I fell. That's all I remember."

I feel the blood rush from my head, leaving me dizzy. *Jesus*, she went through hell while I sat in a theater fifty feet away.

"Babe." Sydney calls out as I make another lap of the tiny room. I spin to face her. "Can you get me a Sprite or something?"

Anything to make her feel better. I school my features and put on my Andrew Forrester mask, giving her a smile that probably looks more like a grimace. "Sure Sydney. I'll be right back."

I stalk down the hall in a cloud of anger to the family break room where I know there's a fridge full of drinks. I scan my card and bang open the door to find the room empty. Snatching a Sprite from a row of cans, I slam the fridge shut and all of the rage I've been holding back comes flooding back at once.

Swinging my leg out, I use my heavy boot to kick the refrigerator over and over. The harder I hit it, the better I feel. All of my failures to keep people I care about safe inundate me; my girlfriend possibly raped at a party in L.A., my mom inundated by crazy women looking to be her daughter-in-law, my dad having random fans show up on his doorstep, my sister not trusting anyone after people lied to her in order to get to me, Sydney attacked by the psycho from her past- all of them are at the forefront of my mind as I strike out at the poor appliance.

I allow the frustration to spill out of me and into each kick, which brings me a satisfaction that I should find disturbing but don't. When I finally calm down enough to stop, I see that the door to the fridge is mangled and dented and won't close properly anymore and that makes me smile.

You're a disturbed bastard, Forrester.

A nurse comes into the family break room just then, probably because of the noise I was making, and sees the damaged refrigerator.

"Ummmm…" she looks from the mangled fridge to me, standing there, sweaty, my chest heaving, with a soda in my hand, and doesn't know what to say.

"Here," I pull out my wallet and slap three-grand onto the table. "I had a little difficulty with your refrigerator."

She stands there with her mouth hanging open as I slip out of the room, grinning.

I'm officially a fucked up mess if kicking the shit out of a refrigerator is the only thing that can make me smile.

I go back to the room and hand Sydney her Sprite. When Detective Keating asks me to step into the spare bedroom, he follows me in and softly shuts the door behind us.

"I thought we should do this in private so as not to upset Miss Tannen," he says.

The relief I felt from the fridge incident melts away in an instant.

"You don't think I've been doing everything I can to keep her from getting upset? You being here is what's upsetting her!" I yell, pointing my finger in his face.

"I understand your point of view, Mr. Forrester, but we have to get both of your statements in order to prosecute this guy." He sits on the edge of the bed and pulls out a pencil and that damn notebook again. "So, can you tell me what you saw?"

"Jesus." I sit down heavily on the bed next to him and run my hand down my face. "I ran out of the theater and saw her lying in a pool of blood. I thought she was dead. The girl holding her head was crying, and the guy... the one who took his shirt off, his shirt was soaked through with blood."

I can't sit. I shoot up off the bed and pace the room.

"Anything else?" he asks as he scrawls in his pad.

"Yeah. That fuckin' psycho was on the other side of the lobby underneath some big guy. His eyes, they looked crazy... I wanted to kill him," I admit.

"Is that it?"

"What the fuck do you want me to say?" I shout. "That it was the scariest fuckin' moment of my life? That I found out I would actually kill someone with my bare fuckin' hands? What do you want from me?"

The detective remains cool and impassive. "I'm just making sure you don't miss anything. Even small details can be important." He stands up and hands me something from his pocket. "Here's my card. Call me if you think of anything else."

"Yeah, sure thing." I stuff it in my pocket and storm out of the room after he leaves. Sydney is asleep. *Thank fuck for that.*

A couple of hours later, Leah comes in and drops on the couch next to me. "Hey, how's she been?"

"Crappy. The police came by to take our statements. Let's just say it didn't go well."

Leah narrows her eyes. "For you or for her?"

She knows me pretty well already. "Both."

Leah nods at my answer and turns back to watch Sydney sleep. "Has she been out long?"

"Not real long, a few hours, maybe. She was pretty upset so I'm not surprised she passed out."

"Speaking of sleep, are you getting any?" Leah asks, patting my knee compassionately.

"I get enough."

"Yeah, it shows. You're just the glowing picture of health," she replies.

"Don't start," I warn. "My moods haven't exactly been even lately."

"Oh, I know. That's why you need to go get some sleep. It will help you feel better and less edgy."

"Leah, the only thing that will make me feel less edgy is beating the shit out of the fucker who did this," I snap.

"Drew? Leah?"

We both turn to see Sydney watching us from her bed.

Leah slaps a giant fake smile on her face and jumps to the bedside, "Hey! You're awake. Good, because watching you sleep is getting so old."

Sydney smiles. It's barely noticeable, but it's there. Seeing it makes me feel better. Not much, but it's a start. It gives me hope that maybe we can both be whole again someday.

"Babe, Leah's right. You need to go back to the hotel and get some sleep," Sydney says, her sharp stare penetrating through my rough exterior.

"I'll sleep later," I tell her.

"No. You've been an angry beast. Go. If not to sleep, then to work out or spar or whatever. You're going to explode if you don't get out of this hospital for a few hours."

Shit. I want to go, but I want to stay. I wasn't there for her and she was attacked.

"Drew," Leah says, "go. I'm here, the guard is outside, and Syd's mom will be here soon. We're fine without you for a little while. Take care of yourself before you snap out and do something stupid. Bruce is waiting out front."

I need this.

"Alright, if you're sure." I fix my gaze on Sydney's and realize that she wants me to go. Her face is so easy to read. She wants what's best for me and she knows if I don't let out my anger, it will get a thousand times uglier than it already has. She probably needs a break from my constant state of fury, it can't be good for her either.

"I'm sure. Like Leah said, my mom will be here in a little while," she says, her big blue eyes pleading with me to take care of myself.

I lean in and kiss her gently. "I'll be back soon," I whisper. "Call me if anything happens," I insist, looking at Leah as I say it.

Leah pushes me towards the door, "Go! We'll be fine."

I grab my hat and sunglasses and duck out of the room. My mind elsewhere, I go directly down to the lobby and out the front doors where Leah said Bruce is waiting with the car. When I step outside, I'm instantly pissed at Sydney's best friend. Leah could have warned me that there was a gigantic mob of paparazzi in front the hospital.

I exit the building right into the shitstorm, alone and completely unprepared. The cameras click relentlessly and bursts of light hit me in the face.

"Andrew! How's Sydney?"

"Is she going to be released soon?"

"Did Reid Tannen offer to donate a kidney to her?"

"Is it true a priest give her last rites?"

"Are you suing the theater chain where the attack happened?"

Fuck! They crowd around me, and I can't move. This is not the day for them to do this. My hands have literally been itching to beat the shit out of someone or something. Having these parasites in my personal space, shoving and yelling… they're asking for it, practically begging for me to hit them.

I clench my fists and pull one back, planting my feet shoulder width apart on the sidewalk.

A loud voice addresses the reporters. "Move out of the way!" Then a hand clamps down on my shoulder, "Don't do it. C'mon. Let's get you out of here," he says to me.

I turn and see an LAPD officer has joined me in the crowd and he's pushing his way through the swarm of paparazzi as their flashes blind us. The urge to strike out at one of the locusts is overwhelming, so when we reach the car and I jump in, I'm beyond irritated and my level of agitation is at an all-time high.

"Hotel, now!" I bark out at Bruce. I need to change and get to the gym, ASAP.

I pull out my phone and dial Damien. He answers immediately, having called me several times since the incident. I haven't returned anyone's calls, including his. "Drew? How is everything going?"

Before he can ask about Sydney, I interrupt. "D, I need you to call Brian at the gym we use in Santa Monica and let him know I'm on my way and I want someone ready to spar with me."

"Okay, but can you…"

"Not now, Damien!" He knows me well enough to know that I'm not going to talk about the shit that went down at the theater.

"Okay, okay. I'm calling him. Just, well…we're all thinking about you and Sydney. That's all."

I let out a sigh, running my hand through my hair. "Thanks man. I can't…" Fuck, I start choking up. "I gotta go. Call Brian at North Hollywood. Tell him I'll be there in thirty."

I disconnect and shove the phone in my pocket, curling my hand into a fist.

Thirty minutes, you can make it until then.

I'm not sure that I will.

Thwack! Thwack! Thwack! Thwack! Thwack! Thwack!

Kicking the heavy bag isn't releasing the giant knot of stress that's sitting heavily on my shoulders. I glance at the clock on the wall of the fancy Santa Monica gym. My sparring partner should be here any minute. Turning back to the bag, I switch to combination punch/kicks.

Thud. Thud. Smack! Thud. Thud. Smack!

By the time I hear someone coming up behind me, sweat is dripping off of me and onto the floor. Not as private as Damien's gym, this is a place to see and be seen in L.A. They do hard core training, even have a few MMA champs, but it's a much higher profile place than I would prefer.

"I think you're waiting for me."

I stop kicking and turn to see a guy in blue fighting shorts and gloves. He's smaller than me, but looks like he could be lethal.

Scar on eyebrow? Check. Tattoos on torso? Check. Crooked nose? Check. Lean, ripped muscles? Check.

Good, he knows his way around the cage, because today I don't want anyone babying me or treating me different. I want to fight.

"Yeah, I am. Do you need to warm up?" I ask him.

"Just give me ten and I'll be ready. I'm Keith, by the way."

"Drew." I nod since I'm already gloved up I can't shake hands. "I'll meet you in the cage."

Keith nods and goes to warm up. I can feel dozens of sets of eyes on me as I grab my water and chug it down, glancing around the huge space. North Hollywood MMA and Fitness isn't remotely the same as being in Damien's dark gym in New York. This place is well lit, popular, and full of gawkers and winning professional fighters. The big names draw lots of attention, sometimes even paparazzi out front. Thankfully, not today.

Right now, I don't give a shit what everyone looks at. Brian, the owner, promised me that no one would take photos or videos, so that's better than nothing.

I wipe off and head over to the cage where Brian is helping one of his fighters perfect his body lock takedown. My skin is crawling to jump in with them as I watch them fall to the mat again and again. Frustration and anger is pouring off of me in uncontrollable waves.

I shouldn't fight like this, unrestrained and emotional. But nothing and no one is going to keep me out of the cage today.

"Ready?" Keith grabs his sparring pads and makes his way towards me.

"No pads," I tell him. He cocks his head and stares at me in disbelief. Scowling, I climb up into an empty ring adjacent and face Keith. "I want a real fight. Are you in?"

"Do we need a ref?" he asks, lifting one scarred eyebrow.

"Nah, I just don't want the fucking pads. We can keep it clean. So let's do this."

Keith shakes his head but hops up into the cage. "Alright, man. I have to say, I'm surprised you want to fight without gear, but I'm game."

I put my mouthpiece in and we tap gloves.

Keith doesn't do much at first but watch me. He's unsure of my ability, probably thinking I'm full of shit, not a real fighter. Some spoiled celebrity who doesn't know his ass from his elbow in the ring.

I dart forward and strike him with a jab from my right hand, then a quick punch with my left, catching his jaw. Following with a solid roundhouse kick to his waist. Keith stumbles back and narrows his eyes at me, then smiles.

That's right fucker, this is a real fight. Not a Hollywood bullshit session.

Keith throws a cross/hook combo and I'm able to block both punches. He doesn't know that I'm a southpaw yet. That always fucks them up.

We go at it for a while. He lands a few good ones, including one on my ribs that hurts like a bitch. The pain makes me happy. At least I'm feeling something besides the oppressive mental anguish of the last few days.

We're both drenched with sweat and slowing down when he lowers his guard and I get him solidly behind his right ear. *Fuck!* He goes down, hard.

A nearby trainer sees Keith hit the ground and jumps up into the cage with us. Keith comes to before either of us can get to him.

"You okay?" the trainer asks.

Keith sits up, stunned for a moment. "Yeah. Damn, nice strike. You fucking knocked me out."

I help him to his feet. "I guess I did."

"Great fight, man. Thanks for the opportunity. I thought you'd be easy. Shit, was I wrong. How long you been doing this?" Keith asks, rubbing his head with his hand.

"I know you thought I'd be easy. I could read it on your face." I watch his eyes widen at my assessment. "And I've been practicing for eight years. Can't ever get anyone to actually go at it with me, so thanks. You know, for treating me like a normal guy."

"Fuckin' lefty, huh?" Keith laughs.

I smile for the first time in days. "It always takes people by surprise." I throw my gear in my bag and pull on a shirt. "Thanks for the fight."

"Anytime."

Bruce is waiting out front and I slide into the back seat. "Hotel, please."

"What happened to you?" Bruce has turned around in his seat, his eyes wide and his mouth hanging open.

"What do you mean?"

"Your face? You're...you're all banged up."

"Oh. Nothing. Just sparring. I need to get back to Syd, can we go?" I feel like a dick for dismissing his concern, but I'm not answering to anyone.

When the car pulls up in front of the Sunset Marquis I tell Bruce to wait and leap out. I yank my hat down and walk as fast as I can to my villa, avoiding anyone and everyone that might see me. Once inside the suite, I head straight for the bathroom and take a quick shower, wincing when I wash my left side where Keith kicked me repeatedly.

In a hurry to get back to Sydney, I wrap a towel around my waist and grab my clothes, struggling to pull my jeans on before I'm completely dry.

Based on Bruce's reaction in the car, I decide to check myself in the mirror before I leave for the hospital. The sight in front of me is shocking. I have a swollen, split lip, a large bruise on my left jawline, and my right ear is red and inflamed. My entire left side, from chest level to the end of my ribcage, is black and blue.

My reaction? I laugh. I can't stop laughing. My fucked up, mangled face and body is so funny to me that the ridiculous laughter keeps coming until I can't laugh anymore.

I always have to worry about how I look, be extra careful not to get sunburned or damaged physically in any way, so to not give a shit and let someone beat on my face… it's feels fucking incredible. Sydney's going to be pissed when she sees me, but it was worth it. For the first time in a long time, I feel normal. No hiding shit, no protecting my precious face or image…it's unbelievably freeing.

Now, back to my shitty reality and my broken girl.

CHAPTER 34

The last thing I expect to see when I walk into Sydney's room is Brandon Eastlake, sitting next to her bed, chatting like they're old friends.

That fucker is so lucky that I just punched the shit out of someone for the last hour, or he'd be dead.

"Eastlake, what are you doing here?" I breeze past him and over to Sydney, placing a kiss on her lips as I glare at him. Her eyes bug out when she sees my face, but I know she won't say anything in front of an outsider.

Yeah, she's still mine asshole.

I can tell that he's embarrassed I caught him here, but has the common sense not to say anything. He knows my reputation for being somewhat volatile and he knows that I'm well aware of his reputation for being a man-whore. Plus, I'm sure I look intimidating as hell with my fucked up face.

"I felt bad about what happened to Sydney. It feels like it was my fault for having her on the show." He shrugs, an automatic response to hide his nervousness. "I wanted to make sure she was okay."

Wait… he thinks the attack was his fault?

"Why would it be your fault? You weren't even there?" I ask, dumfounded by his rationale.

Sydney interrupts before Eastlake can speak. "I told Brandon he had nothing to do with it. Once my mom went back to acting in a few months, that media and that crazy man were going to find me." She turns and looks at the shocked TV host. "Whether it was your show or some other show, an obsession like that wasn't going to go away and I was tired of hiding."

"What happened to you?" Eastlake asks, staring at me incredulously.

"Nothing." I blow him off easily. "When did all of these flowers get here?" I ask Sydney, tired of Brandon Eastlake already.

Sydney's pale cheeks flush bright crimson. God, it's good to see her with some color in her face. "Ummmm, the nurses brought them all in a little while ago. They said they've got a bunch more, but these are the ones from people we know. I guess Leah went through the cards earlier." She shifts on the bed, self-conscious with receiving so much attention.

She's so used to being invisible that she doesn't know how to handle having people other than her mom and Leah care about her.

"Well, I better get going," Eastlake says awkwardly. "We film in a couple of hours." He stands up and pats Sydney's hand. If he had tried to kiss her cheek I would have had to take him out in the hall and punch his face in. Then we'd have matching bruises.

"See you later?" he asks me, putting out a hand for me to shake.

"Yeah, I'm sure you will," I respond, reluctantly shaking his hand so I don't look like a dick in front of Syd and stress her out.

Plus, if I fuck up my relationship with Eastlake and his show, Quentin will have a fit. I give him Andrew Forrester's best smile.

"Bye Sydney, get well." He turns and leaves the suite.

It only takes two seconds for her to start.

"What happened to you?"

"I told you I was going to the gym. You wanted me to punch something, so I did."

"I didn't tell you to get punched back. You look like shit." She folds her arms across her chest and scowls.

I can't help the laugh that escapes from me, she's almost back to herself. Leaning in, I trace her cheekbone with my finger. "What? Am I not sexy anymore?"

She grunts and waves a hand at me as if I'm ridiculous, "No, you are. Of course you are…" she pauses, biting her lip. "Actually, it makes you more sexy, if that's even possible."

I smile and give her a quick kiss. "You're not mad?"

Sydney relaxes into her pillows. "No, I'm not mad. I know you needed it. I'm just glad you didn't break any bones."

That went better than expected.

I don't notice the phone lying on her lap until it's shrill ring scares the shit out of both of us.

"I thought you had it off?" She said she didn't want to talk to anyone, not that very many people have her number. But I would guess it's pretty easy for unscrupulous people to get their hands on it.

"I did. I only turned it on today." She picks up the phone and answers it. "Adam?"

The peace and happiness I felt from this morning's workout takes a sharp nosedive at the thought of that prick calling my girl on her phone. Where the fuck does he get off?

"Hold on…." Sydney covers her phone with her hand and looks at me, flicking her gaze from my face to my hands which are balled up tightly in front of me. "Drew? Are you okay?"

I can't stand here and listen to half of a conversation with him, and I can't take her phone and break it in half. Instead, I spin on my heel and storm into the other bedroom, slamming the door behind me. Asshole move, but I fucking can't believe that jerkoff has the nerve to call Sydney.

I crash on the bed and check my email. I haven't looked at it since before the premiere. My voicemail is full too. Rhys keeps pestering me for a statement. I know I have to release one, I just have no desire to think about that shit.

Knowing I can't avoid him any longer, I dial Rhys' number.

"Drew? How's Sydney?" I haven't seen him since the attack, letting Jane do all of the communicating for me so I could focus on Syd. Besides my family, Jane's the only person I've spoken to.

"Better. I wanted to get the statement out of the way." I pull my feet up onto the bed and lean against the headboard.

"Okay, what did you want to say?"

Damn! "I was kind of hoping you had something put together already," I admit.

"Drew, I have no idea what the hell is going on except for what Jane told me, which isn't much. The media has been relentless trying to get any bit of information from me that they can. I was briefly interviewed by the police, but since I didn't see anything, they wouldn't tell me a thing."

"Shit," I mutter, dragging my hand down my face then wincing when it runs over my bruised cheek.

"Why don't you tell me what the doctors' said about the wounds and her recovery? Let's start there." Great, Rhys is going to try and hold my hand? I don't think so.

"Here's what I want you to say. Just put it in better words. Sydney was attacked by a fucking psycho who stalked her as a kid."

"What?" Rhys yells.

"Don't fucking interrupt, Rhys. This shit isn't easy for me," I bark at him.

"Okay, sorry Drew. I just didn't know," he admits.

"So put that in there about the crazy fuck," I continue. "He stabbed her and hit her liver, which was repaired surgically. He missed her diaphragm and lung. Ummmm, they said we could go home tomorrow if nothing goes wrong, but tell them it'll be a few days to throw them off. And the asshole was arrested. I guess that's it." Sighing, I close my eyes and wait for Rhys to respond.

"Alright, I got it. I'll polish it up and release it to the media. Are you going back to New York?"

"Yes. I already have it all set up. We're going back with Leah in Eva's jet."

"Eva?" Rhys asks.

"Sydney's mom."

"Oh yeah. I forgot. Sorry Drew, this is just…" he stops, too choked up to continue.

"Yeah, I know. Hey, I gotta go." I have to get off the phone before I go back to being a fucked up mess.

"Okay. Bye."

I hang up and decide that Adam has had long enough with my girl. Walking back into the room, I see that Sydney is already off of the phone and she's speaking to the doctor.

"What's going on?" I ask, pissed that they would discuss her care without me.

"I was just telling Miss Tannen that she can go home. Today if you like," he says with a giant smile on his face.

"Today?" I look down at Sydney. "You want to get out of here?" I can't help but grin.

She smiles back, a genuine smile. She wants to leave this fucking place as much as I do. "Yes."

"Done."

CHAPTER 35

"Just get down here and clear out the sidewalk. It's unbelievable out there. Cars can't even get through." I stare out the living room windows of Sydney's loft at the huge crowd of paparazzi and media outlet vans lining the street in front of her building as I bark out orders into the phone.

"We're sending someone now, sir," the police dispatcher responds.

"Good. Thanks." Ending the call, I take a deep breath. Sydney and I have been back in New York for a week and a half. She's getting better, physically and mentally, but I can tell that she's scared to death to leave the building. Hell, *I'm* scared for her to leave the building. How do you know who the next psycho is? How am I supposed to keep her safe from someone who may or may not exist?

I pull myself from my dark thoughts and decide it's time to discuss my work commitments with Sydney. I've been getting a lot of pressure from Quentin and Rhys and this can't be put off any longer. Worn-out, I shove the phone in my pocket, walk into the bedroom and freeze. She's not in bed.

Where the fuck is she?

I scan the room and find her in one of the chairs near the wall of windows.

"Sydney, you shouldn't be out of bed." I take the seat across from her and sink back into the comfortable cushions.

"I'm fine, Drew. I can't be in bed anymore. I need to get out of here. I'm going crazy." I watch her carefully, studying her face to make sure she knows what she's asking for.

It's now or never.

I sigh and drag my hand through my too-long hair. "I have to be at three more premieres for *A Soldier's Burden* this week and on the set in two weeks to start production on *Downtrodden Masses* in Vancouver." I lean forward and put my elbows on my knees. "One of the premieres is here in New York, but one is in Chicago and the other is in Miami. I've pushed them back as far as I can. It's in my contract, Syd. I have to be there. It's a limited release independent film, not a huge blockbuster. I can't leave the people who financed it hanging."

I feel like such a dick for having to abandon her. Thank God I had Jane hire Steve to be here while I'm gone. I wouldn't even think of leaving without someone here to watch over her and keep her safe.

Sydney reaches across the gap between us and takes my hand. "I know you have to be there. I'll have Leah stay with me while you go to Miami and Chicago." *Wait, she wants me to go?* "Go Drew, walk the carpet, answer the questions. We have to be normal again."

Is she fucking kidding me? Normal? What does that even look like?

After seeing the sour face I'm making, she continues. "Okay, as normal as we can be. Then when you have to start filming in

Vancouver, I'll go with you. Maybe getting out of here would be good for us."

I'm so confused. I thought she'd be done with that, would want to be as far away from the Hollywood bullshit as she could get.

"You'll come with me? I didn't think you'd want to go. I thought you'd be done with that part of my life after what happened at the premiere."

Her face softens and she clasps my hands tighter. "I want to be with you, Drew. I love every part of you, even your work. Your film was beautiful, you have to continue to act and I have to be with you. What happened was not because of your job. It was because of a crazy man who was obsessed with me. He knew me long before I met you, Drew."

Sydney runs her lips across my knuckles. "Besides, I don't think time apart would be great for us right now. I need you to get through this, and you're too nervous about me being alone. So, can I come with you to Vancouver?"

God she's so fucking strong. I love her so much. All the shit she's been through and she still wants to be with me. I untangle our hands and open my arms for her. She quickly climbs up into my lap so I can hold her tight. I missed the feel of her, being close like this. Burying my nose in her hair, I inhale her sweet fragrance.

"Please come with me babe, I'd go crazy with you thousands of miles away. I need to know that we're okay." I kiss her head and pull her closer. I can't be apart from her, ever.

"We're definitely okay," Sydney says as I tilt her chin up and kiss her gorgeous mouth. "I haven't been to Vancouver in a long time; I wonder what I should pack?"

Her statement is so unexpected that I can't help but smile at her. She grins back.

Who would have thought? Me, Andrew Forrester. Hollywood's ultimate bachelor, head over heels in love with a girl.

Loving Sydney makes me irrational, emotional, and confused as fuck… and I am thankful for every single feeling she inspires, good and bad. It means I'm finally fucking living. With her. Always with her.

Plus, with all of the downtime in Vancouver, I'll be able to work on controlling my temper.

Acknowledgements

First, I have to say how much I appreciate the fans of the Famous series. The people who love Drew and Sydney just as much as I do. It's going to be so hard to let them go, after writing four books about them. They're like family to me.

Next, as always, I have to thank my husband, Brian. He stood by me as I took the leap on this crazy road, not once thinking it was strange that a pharmacist decided she wanted to write romance novels.

Of course, I need to thank my awesome Betas again, Heather DeLuca, Amy Woods, and Krystal Wiles-Austin. Thanks ladies for laying it down truthfully and keeping it real.

To Deborah at Tugboat Design, thanks for giving my books the face that they deserve. Your covers are brilliant and you always seem to know exactly what I want.

I have to give my bloggers their shout outs! Thanks to Erin at MeReadALot, DK at A Book Lovin' Junkie, the girls at After Dark Book Lovers, Shannon at Cocktails and Books, Jennifer and Natalie at Love Between the Sheets, Toni at Promiscuous Book Blog, Chantale at Canadian Book Addict, and especially everyone at The Rock Stars of Romance who started this whole thing for me. Whew, if I missed you, I'm so sorry! I love you all!

Lastly, I want to thank my girls at the Georgia Romance Writers. Thanks for being my proofreaders, my pals, and for helping me navigate the crazy world of writing.

H.C. Leigh

About the Author

After growing up in New England, Heather C. Leigh lives just outside of Atlanta, GA with her husband and two children. Her favorite things include traveling, chocolate and of course, the Boston Red Sox.

Links

Follow us on social media for contests and release dates

https://www.facebook.com/relativelyfamous

https://www.heatherleighauthor.com

https://www.goodreads.com/goodreadscomHeather_Leigh

https://www.tsu.co/HeatherLeighAuthor

https://twitter.com/HeatherLeigh_8

http://instagram.com/heatherleighauthor/

The Famous Series

Relatively Famous

Absolutely Famous

Extremely Famous

Already Famous (Drew's POV)

Suddenly Famous (a novella)

Reluctantly Famous (a novella)

Sphere of Irony Series

Incite- Adam Reynolds

Strike- Dax Davies

Ricochet (a serial novel)

Locked & Loaded

Friendly Fire

Extraction Point

Made in the USA
Las Vegas, NV
07 April 2025

20630071R00213